THE NAVIGATOR

THE NAVIGATOR

ERIN MICHELLE SKY
& STEVEN BROWN

TRASH DOGS MEDIA, LLC

This book is a work of fiction. All events and dialog contained herein are purely fictitious. All characters, with the exception of certain well-known historical and public figures, are products of the authors' imagination and are not to be construed as real. Where real-life historical and public figures appear, the situations, events, and dialogs concerning those persons are fictitious. The inclusion of certain historical facts is not intended to change the fictitious nature of the book.

Library of Congress Control Number: 2019944292
(hardcover edition)

ISBN: 978-1946137043

Printed in the United States of America

Cover art by Benjamin P. Roque
Layout & design by Jordan D. Gum
Edited by Lourdes Venard

Trash Dogs Media, LLC
1109 South Park St, Ste 504-327
Carrollton, GA 30117
trashdogs.com

10 9 8 7 6 5 4 3 2 1

For everyone
who has ever forged ahead
against all odds

CHAPTER 1

Every good story begins with trouble.

This is the one kind thing that might be said for trouble, as it is a nuisance in every other regard and best avoided. But Wendy Darling is already in a good bit of trouble, whether she realizes it or not, and things are about to get much worse.

Trouble number one: Wendy is exceedingly pleased to have made her way aboard *The Dragon*, but Captain Hook does not appreciate her presence. He is itching for an excuse to place her or any of her friends in irons. This includes John, Michael, poor Reginald, Thomas (the Royal Society fellow), and even Nana, the monstrous Newfoundland dog.

Don't think Hook is above placing a dog in irons, because he is not.

Trouble number two: Wendy is being treated as the navigator by the first mate, who happens to be her dear friend, Charlie. No one else in Hook's crew wants her to hold such an important position.

There is a good bit of grumbling about this belowdeck, where you might not hear about it, but where it has the ability to fester.

Unfortunately for the crew, Wendy is the only one who *can* be the navigator because the magical compass only works for *her.* But if you have ever tried to argue logically with an angry mob, you'll know that it isn't helpful.

Trouble number three—

Well, let's watch together as Wendy discovers it for herself.

She is standing on deck next to Charlie, who has the helm. She is wearing a pair of men's breeches—dark brown—tucked into her tall, black boots, with a white linen shirt and a cream-colored waistcoat. This is a bold choice for a seventeen-year-old woman in the year 1790, but Wendy is a sailor now and prefers to dress the part. She wears her sword at her left hip, with a brown leather pistol holster strapped to each thigh. She has a larger holster strapped to her back, so her musket would peek over her left shoulder if it were present. Sadly, it is not. All three of her guns are locked away in the ship's armory. Hook is the only one who carries a gun aboard *The Dragon* unless the ship comes under attack.

(If you had ever seen the crew drinking and carrying on—which does not happen every night, but often enough—you would understand this policy.)

Wendy holds the compass in her left hand as she stares out to sea. The rest of her platoon is scrubbing the deck under John's direction. They are not regular members of Hook's crew, and this is the only shipboard task they are qualified to perform. Besides which, it amuses Hook to watch them perform it.

Wendy feels like she should be scrubbing the deck too, out of solidarity. But she also remembers the cruel taunts of Mortimer Black and the strange song that has haunted her ever since that eventful day some seven years ago.

If women ever sail the sea,
They'll scrub the decks for men like me!
They'll marry none but Davy Jones,
And for their children, only bones!

As you can imagine, she would prefer not to scrub the deck if she can help it, no matter how guilty she might feel over having managed to avoid it.

As for Nana, she is sitting calmly by Wendy's side, not at all bothered by the fact that she has been excused from the scrubbing detail. And Thomas is hovering just behind Wendy's left shoulder, his hair appearing even more wild at sea than it did in London. He stares at the compass in fascination every time she opens it, as though each instance of its operation is a brand new miracle.

"Astounding!" he says. Or, "Marvelous!"

So now we're all caught up, and this is how things stood when Wendy opened the compass yet again, reassuring herself for the hundredth time that their course had not altered. Only this time, Thomas said nothing at all.

Startled, Wendy glanced over her shoulder, only to find him staring up at the crow's nest, high over their heads. She followed his gaze to see the lookout holding a spyglass to his right eye, staring intently off to starboard (which is how Wendy, having been trained in nautical terminology, thought of the right side of the ship.)

"A sail!" the lookout shouted. "A sail!"

Immediately, Smee—the bo'sun (who hated Wendy perhaps more than anyone)—whistled several sharp tones through the silver instrument that hung around his neck.

"Alert," Charlie said. Wendy nodded, holding her breath.

Suddenly, the lookout whipped a blood-red flag straight to the top of the mast, and the ship exploded into life.

The bo'sun's whistle sounded again, and sailors shouted to each other, sprinting across the deck.

"What?" Thomas exclaimed.

"French," Charlie said between clenched teeth. "They've seen us. It's the call to man the cannons."

Wendy's hands fell uselessly upon her empty holsters. "My pistols!" she exclaimed.

Charlie nodded. "Go now. While you can. I won't have you unarmed if we're boarded. Find Nicholas. He'll make sure you get them." He said nothing more, but the look he gave her as their eyes locked sent shivers of fear down her spine.

For the first time since she had left London, Olaudah Equiano's warning came back to her—as clearly as though he were speaking it now, directly into her mind: "There are worse ways to live, Miss Darling. There is a price to changing one's destiny."

Wendy narrowed her eyes and her lips tightened into a line of steel, the hidden kiss in the far corner disappearing altogether. She clasped Charlie's shoulder and held his gaze just a moment longer. Then she sprinted off to join the throng of sailors making their way belowdeck, with Nana racing faithfully behind.

CHAPTER 2

Wendy found Nicholas in the captain's quarters, but Hook was already giving the boy orders of his own, having nothing to do with Wendy's pistols.

"She's going to run. Signal *The Cerberus* and *The Tiger* to chase her down. We'll catch up once they engage. I want that ship!"

"But ..." Wendy said quietly, and then she trailed off, not really having meant to say it out loud.

Nicholas paused and glanced her way, but Hook raised his eyebrows and thrust his chin at the door.

"Aye, sir," Nicholas barked, and he scampered out.

"But what, Miss Darling?" Hook leaned back against the captain's table and crossed his arms over his chest.

Wendy squared her shoulders and met his gaze, but she said nothing.

"But chasing French ships isn't our mission?" he prompted her.

"Well, it isn't," Wendy agreed. That was exactly what she had been about to say.

"On the contrary. Chasing French ships is *always* our mission. I do not keep my commission by standing around in a London office staring at maps on the wall. I capture French ships and send them home."

"I see." Wendy placed her hands on her hips and then dropped them to her holsters, tapping her fingers meaningfully on each one. "Well, Captain, if we are to engage the French in a sea battle, I would prefer not to be unarmed. Charlie sent me to get Nicholas, to escort me to the armory."

"Oh he did, did he?"

"He thought I might need some assistance, or at least a proper introduction. After the way I was treated by the quartermaster in London," Wendy reminded him sharply, "I thought it a reasonable suggestion."

"You won't need the assistance because you won't need the arms," Hook countered. "*The Tiger* and *The Cerberus* are both faster than *The Dragon*. They'll make short work of that ship before we even get there. And in any event, I'm not letting you out of my sight."

"You're ... what?"

"Like it or not, Miss Darling, you are a target. Englishwomen fetch a fine price in certain parts of the world, and I won't let that happen on my watch." He paused, offering up a slow, wry grin. "Not even to you."

"I can take care of myself." Wendy's left eyebrow drew itself up to its full height, daring him to say otherwise.

"Hmm. Be that as it may, I am *ordering* you to remain by my side until further notice. Do I make myself clear?"

Wendy ground her jaw back and forth and locked eyes with him for a long moment before responding.

"Aye, Captain," she finally said. He was the captain, after all. It was the only thing she *could* say in response to a direct order.

"Excellent." He smiled, but the light of it never reached his eyes. "Follow me, Miss Darling. It promises to be a fine show, and we shall have the best seats in the house. I do enjoy a good tragedy."

They made their way through the ship and emerged, blinking, beneath the midday sun. Only a few white, puffy clouds in the distance marred the perfect expanse of bright blue sky above the endless sea. Hook raised his spyglass to his left eye and turned it toward the hunt, but Wendy didn't need a contraption to see what was obvious. The French ship was under full sail, doing its best to flee, but *The Cerberus* and *The Tiger* were gaining on it.

The Cerberus was a Portland-class ship of three full-rigged masts, with square sails just like *The Dragon* and fifty guns to her name. She was smaller than *The Dragon*, but faster—roughly the same size as the vessel she was trying to chase down. *The Tiger* was smaller yet. She was a survey ship of only ten guns, with a mere hundred crewmen. Designed for speed, she was already ahead of *The Cerberus*, but she was staying carefully out of range of her quarry. She wasn't about to take on the larger ship until *The Cerberus* could join the fight.

They watched in silence as the scene played out, the two British ships slowly closing in on the third. Just as *The Cerberus* was coming into range, Nicholas rejoined them, weaving his way through the crewmen who stood by on deck. *The Tiger* was already in position on the starboard side of her prey, just out of range of the cannons, and *The Cerberus* moved in on the side opposite, flanking the French vessel.

When *The Cerberus* finally opened fire, Wendy gasped.

"No!" she cried, her voice almost lost amidst the raucous shouts of the crew.

"Perhaps now you see why the fairer sex has no place on a fighting ship, Miss Darling," Hook commented.

"What? Oh for heaven's sake, look *up*!"

Hook was still looking through the spyglass, focused on the details of the battle, so he hadn't seen what was obvious to everyone else.

Frowning, he removed the glass from his eye and then uttered a half-strangled yelp. A ship was hovering above *The Cerberus,* just below the distant clouds—a three-masted, full-rigged fighting ship, almost as large as *The Dragon* herself. A *flying* ship. And a line of everlost stood shoulder to shoulder along the rail, firing their muskets onto the helpless crew below.

Hook stood impossibly still. "It flies," he whispered.

"I told you it did," Wendy reminded him.

"It *flies,*" he repeated.

"I *told* you it did," Wendy said again.

"IT FLIES!" he shouted. He exploded into motion, his coat sleeves snapping as he pointed this way and that, roaring out commands. "All men to arms! Man the cannons! Get us into range!"

His arms dropped to his sides, and his forget-me-not eyes locked onto the flying ship in the distance.

"Captain," Wendy prompted him, but he didn't respond.

"Captain?" she tried again.

He turned his head toward her and grunted incoherently, but his eyes never left the everlost.

"My guns, Captain?"

Hook nodded, once, obviously still distracted, but that was enough for Wendy. "Nicholas?"

The boy tore his own eyes away from the spectacle and glanced at her.

"I need you to take me to the armory. To make sure I am properly armed for whatever comes. Do you understand?"

Slowly, his gaze came into focus. He blinked several times and then nodded. "Aye, ma'am. I'll take you."

He headed toward the ladder that led belowdeck, with Wendy and Nana following. But every few steps he looked back over his shoulder, until he could no longer see the sky.

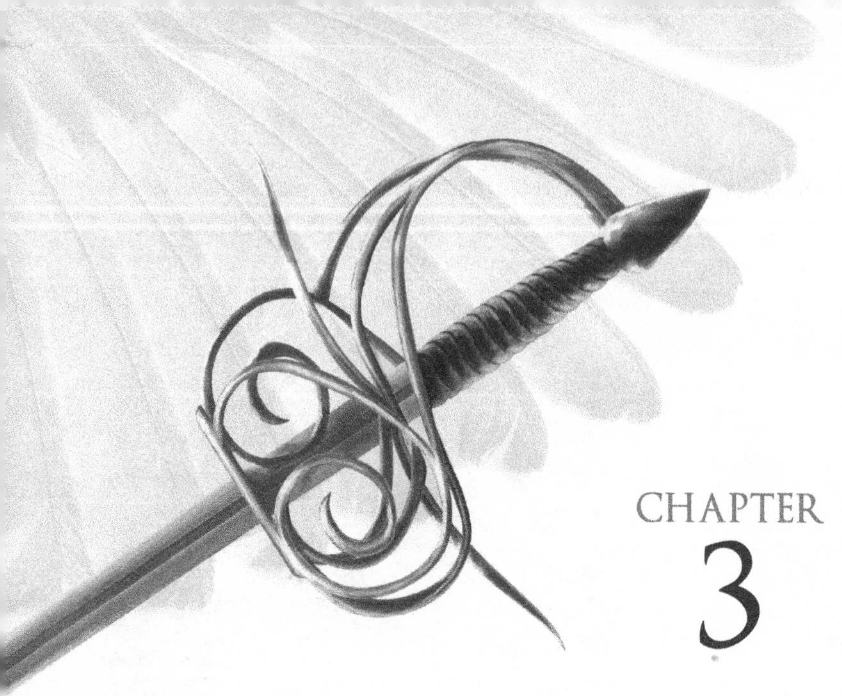

CHAPTER 3

The entire ship was in an uproar.

"A ship that flies!"

"The everlost are helping the French!"

"She *flies*!"

The flying bit was no surprise to Wendy, but why was Peter protecting the French vessel? Had the everlost and the French been allies all along?

Her mind raced with the implications.

Peter had given her the compass. He had told her to give it to Hook—and to use it to come find him. Then they had encountered a French ship, located directly along their course. They had chased it, and Peter had been waiting, ready to ambush them.

He had been using her. Ever since he had learned she was at Hook's estate. He had been using her to get to Hook all along.

She didn't want to believe it, but what other explanation was there?

By the time they reached the armory, Wendy was fuming. The

quartermaster took one look at the raw fury in her eyes and handed over her weapons and ammunition without comment.

Wendy and Nicholas emerged back on deck just in time to see the flying ship tilt wildly and open fire with her cannons on *The Cerberus*. The everlost took to the air like a swarm of hornets dislodged from their nest, but they soon reorganized themselves, lining up to balance on the far edge of the ship's airborne hull while the battery tore into the ship below.

Wendy tried to find Peter in the mayhem, but she was too far away to make out any face in particular. And soon enough her gaze was torn from the distant figures by the sickening crack of *The Cerberus* losing her mainmast. She watched in horror as it parted near the bottom, tilted slowly, and began to fall. The men below scrambled to avoid the timbers that slammed into the deck, and then a second crack signaled the end of the foremast.

The barrage of cannon fire finally ended, but the damage was done. The everlost surged over the side of the flying ship, firing their muskets from midair. Wendy watched as one after another pitched backward through the sky. At first she thought *The Cerberus* was firing back, but then she realized it was just the recoil of the everlost's own weapons. The men of *The Cerberus* were being slaughtered.

With only one mast left and the entire deck in chaos, *The Cerberus* wasn't going anywhere. Which meant that *The Dragon* was finally catching up. Fast.

Hook started barking orders.

"Pay attention to her height! Get in range of that hull! Blast her out of the sky!"

Wendy couldn't help but wonder whether damaging the hull would do any good. Could you even sink a flying ship? But of course, they had to try.

Peter must have recognized that Hook was gaining on them because his ship turned broadside toward *The Dragon*.

They're going to fire on us! Wendy realized.

Peter had given her the compass, and it would only work for her. He had to know she would be on *The Dragon*. Somehow, even in the middle of a sea battle, Wendy had still expected him not to fire on *her.*

That was the last straw.

Wendy reached over her shoulder and snatched her musket from the holster strapped across her back. She didn't know what good she could do with it. She had seen Peter both shot and stabbed to no real effect. But she wasn't about to give up. Not without a fight. She loaded the weapon and waited for them to come into range, but she never got the chance to fire a single shot.

The cannons on Peter's ship spat out another barrage of destruction.

"Take cover!" Hook shouted.

"Get down!" Nicholas echoed, and he all but pushed Wendy back through the hatch. There wasn't time for both of them to get through, and she watched in horror as Nicholas threw himself flat onto the deck.

Michael! John! Charlie! Wendy had no idea where any of her friends were—only Nana was there with her, by her feet as always and barking like mad into the confusion. But the cannonballs screamed harmlessly overhead. The everlost weren't aiming for the hull. They were aiming for the masts, just like they had with *The Cerberus.*

Disabling the ships, not sinking them, Wendy suddenly realized. Maybe Peter was trying to protect her after all.

Another barrage soared through the sky, and this time both the mainmast and the mizzenmast split in two. There was no slow-motion teetering, no chance to dodge the falling timbers. The masts just exploded in the middle, the top half of each crashing down sideways onto the deck below.

And just like that, it was over. *The Dragon* fired a parting volley, a multitude of explosions so loud that Wendy felt them in her entire body, but the cannon fire didn't come anywhere close to hitting the flying ship. It had risen high into the sky as soon as *The Dragon* was disabled. Wendy could only watch as it hovered above the fleeing French vessel, escorting it away.

Of the British fleet, only *The Tiger* remained undamaged. It circled back toward *The Dragon,* prepared to render whatever assistance it could.

A furious, inarticulate roar proved that Hook had survived the onslaught. Moments later, he stomped across the deck, vaulting over the debris and trampling the fallen sails beneath his feet.

"Nicholas!" he barked as soon as he saw the boy. "Find Mr. Hawke. I want to see him in my cabin immediately."

"Aye, Captain!"

Wendy was about to go look for her platoon when Hook's next growl stopped her in her tracks.

"What do you know about this?"

"Me?" Wendy's eyebrow jumped in surprise and then crouched dangerously low, followed immediately by the other. "Captain, I would never! We might not always see eye to eye, but I am no traitor!"

Hook regarded her for a long moment in silence.

"We shall see," he said finally and then turned back to Nicholas. "Find Mr. Hawke, then escort Miss Darling to her quarters. Keep her there until I send word otherwise."

"Aye, Captain," he repeated, refusing to meet Wendy's gaze.

"And fetch Smee while you're at it."

"Aye, Captain." He waited to see if there was anything else, but Hook waved him off. The captain tapped his foot impatiently, waiting for Wendy to clear the hatch. Then he glowered at her ominously and disappeared below.

Despite the slight rocking of the waves, Wendy stalked back and forth in her tiny room. The compartment could only hold three angry steps in any direction, which made her pacing seem all the more agitated by comparison.

Nicholas stood by the door, looking apologetic.

"I'm very sorry, miss," he said for at least the fifth time in as many minutes. (Had he been much older than his twelve years, he would have stood outside, as a matter of propriety. But he hadn't felt right about standing out in the passageway as though she were a prisoner.)

Wendy was about to reply when there was a knock on the door.

"Finally," she muttered.

Nicholas opened it to find Charlie on the other side.

"Is he locking me in irons?" she demanded, having gotten herself well worked up while pacing back and forth. How dare Hook accuse her of conspiring to ambush the king's ships! As if she would ever! "Or maybe I'll be walking the plank for doing absolutely nothing wrong! I wish him luck finding the everlost without me."

"Neither of those," Charlie said with a grin, "although the day isn't over yet."

"Well, what's it to be then?" Wendy placed both hands on her hips and glared at him defiantly.

Charlie raised his hands in front of him. "Don't shoot me. I'm just the messenger. But it's nothing like that, I promise."

Wendy realized she was still wearing her pistols, and her hands were now dangerously close to their grips. She pursed her lips in chagrin and crossed her arms across her chest instead, but Charlie's eyes were twinkling.

"We're reorganizing. *The Dragon* and *The Cerberus* are too damaged to continue, but the captain doesn't want to turn back. He's sending them home for repairs, and we're transferring to *The Tiger*. To be honest, we were only slowing her down anyway. *The Tiger* is by far the best ship of the three for a scouting mission. *The Dragon* might be better in a sea battle, but I don't know what *any* ship could do against an attack from above."

"I suppose he's sending the rest of the Fourteenth back home as well." Wendy glared at him, but Charlie shook his head.

"No, they're coming. *The Tiger* only takes one hundred for a full crew, but Hook made room for the whole platoon."

Wendy raised an eyebrow.

"It surprised me too, but there it is." Charlie shrugged. "I'd tell you more, but it's not like he gave me his reasons."

Wendy sighed. "Of course not." She glanced at her trunk, secured to the outer bulkhead. "At least packing isn't an issue. When do we leave?"

"You can make the transfer as soon as you're ready. But ..." He trailed off, obviously not sure whether he should continue.

"Go on," Wendy prompted him. "But what?"

Charlie watched her for a long moment and then finally asked the question she had known was coming. "Did you know the ship could fly?"

Despite their year apart, he still knew her better than anyone in the world. She hadn't mentioned anything about the flying ship when she had told him about her adventures. She had been afraid even Charlie wouldn't believe her about that. But it was one thing to skip over something while they were catching up with each other. It was another thing altogether to lie to her closest friend.

"Yes," she admitted.

"Hmm. I had a feeling."

They regarded each other in silence.

"Did you know Pan was working with the French?" Charlie finally asked.

"Of course not!" she exclaimed.

"All right," Charlie said, and he held up his hands in protest. "I believe you. But maybe you should tell me the whole story again. Without leaving anything out this time."

Wendy sucked gently on her lower lip and then sighed again.

"Fine," she agreed. "But let's board *The Tiger* first. There will be plenty of time for stories once we're back underway."

CHAPTER 4

Boarding *The Tiger* was not a simple affair.

The decks of *The Dragon* and *The Cerberus* were in a shambles after losing two masts each. *The Tiger* was the only ship that could still maneuver properly, and there were three full crews to be redistributed. But the first complication Wendy encountered had nothing to do with any of that.

She made quick work of untying her trunk from the bulkhead and was about to lift it when Nicholas stopped her.

"Oh no, miss. You mustn't."

"And why not?" Wendy snapped. "I'm a sailor, Nicholas. The same as everyone else. I'm perfectly capable of carrying my own things."

She liked the boy, but enough was enough. She was already annoyed that Hook had left her so long in her quarters. It hurt her to think even Nicholas might start treating her as though she were incompetent.

She bent to grasp the trunk by the handles, without waiting for

a reply, but Nicholas dashed over and sat on it before she could lift it. (He hadn't wanted to grab her, and sitting on the trunk was the only other thing that occurred to him.)

"A sailor, yes, miss. But not the same as everyone else. You're an *officer.* You can't carry your own trunk in front of the men. It wouldn't be right. Hook would have my hide if I let that happen."

"I ... what?" Wendy straightened back up and stared at the boy suspiciously, but his eyes were wide open, his eyebrows slightly knitted, betraying a clear mix of sincerity and mild panic.

"You *are* the navigator, aren't you?" Nicholas asked. "Mr. Hawke has you setting the course. And he calls you 'Navigator Darling' in front of the crew."

"Well ... I suppose that's true," Wendy agreed.

"Then you're an officer," he pronounced. "And officers don't carry their own trunks. Just wait here, and I'll fetch someone for you. Please, miss. Promise me you won't land me in trouble."

After a long moment of hesitation, she finally relented. "Yes, all right," she said. "I promise."

Nicholas stood up slowly, keeping one hand on the trunk and watching her all the while, as though he wasn't sure he should trust her. When she made no move to pick it up, he finally let go, but he continued to watch her as he crossed the compartment and opened the door. He hovered at the threshold, narrowing his eyes, at which point Wendy couldn't help but reassure him.

"You have my word, Nicholas. As an officer."

The boy sighed in relief. "Thank you, miss," he said. "Don't worry, I'll be quick." He finally turned and left, shutting the door behind him.

Wendy stared at the door a moment longer, then raised both eyebrows at once, uttered a tiny mew of surprise in the back of her throat, and sat down on the very trunk she had only moments ago been about to lift.

"Well, what do you think of that, Nana? Me! An officer!"

Nana barked, once, and sat by Wendy's feet to stare at the door too. She wasn't sure what they were expecting, but she sensed from Wendy's demeanor that something extraordinary was happening and she wanted to be prepared.

Fortunately, Nicholas returned very soon indeed, followed by a thin, older gentleman with a gray beard and a prominent nose that suffered a distinct list to starboard. Despite his age (and his nose), he stood ramrod straight and walked with a sprightly gait, reminding Wendy of Monsieur Dumas. She stood, of course, for a more proper introduction.

"This is Mr. Starkey," Nicholas told her. "Or Gentleman Starkey, as we like to call him. On account of his manners."

"How do you do, miss?" he said, and he bowed with a flourish. "Master Nicholas tells me you have a trunk in need of transportation."

Wendy couldn't help but smile. "How do you do, Mr. Starkey?" she replied politely. "I appreciate your assistance. Though I must admit I'm not accustomed to the idea that I can't carry my own things."

"Oh, don't you worry, miss. This is the right way to do it," Starkey assured her. "Officers got better things to do than haul trunks from ship to ship. I'm no officer, that's for certain. I've seen more years at sea than most, but even if I could afford a commission, I wouldn't spend the money. No, thank you. Leave the deciding to wiser men than me, that's what I always say. Just let me do the lifting."

As though to demonstrate his position on the subject, he stepped forward and lifted the trunk easily.

"Navigator Darling will be joining the crew of *The Tiger*," Nicholas told Starkey. "I can show you to her new quarters."

"Aye, sir," the old sailor replied easily. "Just lead the way."

They emerged beneath the bright blue sky to a racket of hammers and axes and heaving grunts as the men labored to clear the deck of debris. The sails of the fallen masts had already been untied and rolled for storage, and men swarmed over the remaining wreckage, salvaging whatever they could.

One mast would be enough to get them home, but the destruction still brought a tear to Wendy's eye. She loved all ships, and most especially *this* ship. Her *first* ship. She hated to see it so badly treated.

But she swiped the tear away quickly. She was an officer, after all. She had to set a good example.

They crossed the deck in a line—first Nicholas, then Wendy, then Starkey, then Nana—making their way toward *The Tiger*, which had been lashed to the port side. Wendy searched the men for any familiar faces and finally found John, who was overseeing the repairs to one of the ship's railings.

"John!" she called to him in relief, and his face lit up at the sight of her. He came to meet her in long, glad strides.

"Wendy! Thank heaven you're all right!" He started to reach for her hand but thought better of it while standing on deck, in front of Hook's crew.

"And you! But where are the others? Was anyone hurt?" She was thinking particularly of Michael, but she didn't want to give John the wrong impression. (If she had seen Michael first, she would have asked him the same question, thinking particularly of John.)

"Everyone's fine. Nothing worse than a few bruises in the Fourteenth, I'm pleased to report."

"And you're all transferring to *The Tiger*?" It wasn't that she didn't believe Charlie. She just wanted to hear it again.

"We are. I've been given the order." He glanced over his shoulder as he said it, and Wendy followed his gaze. Hook stood by the center mast, well out of hearing, watching the surrounding work crews with a vigilant eye. He had a scowl on his face, as you might imagine, given the circumstances. He wasn't taking any risks with the one mast they had left.

Just then, the watch at the top of the mast hollered out a warning and pointed toward the distant clouds. All hands turned to see a single everlost speeding toward them through the sky.

The men still had their arms close at hand, and they raised them now toward the enemy, but Hook stepped forward, shouting at the top of his lungs.

"Hold your fire!"

Smee echoed the command from his own position farther to stern, the distinct tones of his whistle carrying easily across the ship even though Wendy couldn't see where he stood.

Everyone paused to watch as the everlost flew closer. He bore no white flag, but he held no weapon in his hands either. As for Hook, he stood tall and proud, his scowl intensifying as it found a target for its fury. His hair was tied back against the wind, but his long, blue coat flapped gently in the breeze.

It was the only thing on the ship that moved.

As the everlost approached, he slowed his descent, raising his wings behind him to catch the air. He landed gracefully on the edge of the ship's railing, his legs apart, his hands on his hips, surveying them all with a look of disdain.

His build and his posture reminded Wendy very much of Peter, but his wings were ragged and unkempt, and there was a cruelty in his features that Wendy had never once seen in any of

Peter's men. He leaned forward and addressed Hook, shouting loudly enough for them all to hear.

"I come on behalf of the great Captain Blackheart! Surrender your ships, or else!"

Or else what, they would never know. Hook's reply was simple but effective: He drew his pistol in the blink of an eye and shot the everlost square in the chest.

Wendy expected the winged man to laugh, but instead, he looked down at the wound in surprise. His face had just enough time to register pain, and then shock, and then fear, before he toppled backward into the sea.

CHAPTER 5

A cheer erupted from Hook's crew, but Wendy was so startled that all she could do was stare at the empty railing where the everlost had been. She kept expecting him to burst out of the water at any moment. To laugh and fly away. But nothing happened.

Finally, she couldn't stand it any longer, and she sprinted to the railing. She leaned out as far as she could, and sure enough, there was the everlost man, lying in the water on his back, his eyes open and empty, staring at nothing.

His wings had held him afloat for a moment, but now their edges curled around him as he sank into the sea. In his final moment of surprise, his face had lost its cruelty, and Wendy couldn't help but be reminded of Peter.

This was exactly how she had imagined him on that terrible morning in Dover, when she thought Hook had killed him.

She watched as the everlost sank beneath the surface. His hair fanned out around his face. The water closed in over his eyes. Over his mouth. Over his nose. And then he faded away.

Literally.

Wendy blinked. The everlost hadn't sunk until his body disappeared beneath the waves. He had just disappeared. Period. There one moment, shimmering ethereally just below the surface, and then gone. Vanished as though he had never existed at all.

And then a voice pulled her attention back to the ship. The crew had quieted, and Hook's calm pronouncement carried easily through the stillness.

"From now on, officers and other designated defense personnel will carry muskets and pistols with them at all times. Not just on *The Tiger*, but on the ships returning to England as well. Mr. Smee, see to it."

Wendy spun toward him.

"Aye, sir!" Smee responded. He had obviously moved toward the commotion while Wendy had been looking over the railing because he stood next to the captain now.

"How did you do that?" she blurted out. "All you did was shoot him!"

Hook stared at her coldly. "As I told you in London, Miss Darling, I do not tell you everything." Then he turned his eyes to the distant clouds.

"Smee," he continued, "I shall be in my quarters. At the first sign of trouble, I am to be alerted at once. Make sure the officers are armed immediately. Assign defenses for each ship. Set up watches. You know what to do."

"Aye, sir," Smee repeated. He offered Wendy a smug leer before turning away to bark orders of his own.

Hook left the deck through the nearest hatch, never once looking back. Apparently, he thought that was the end of it.

But, of course, it wasn't.

Wendy knocked on Hook's door, quickly but firmly.

She had known the everlost could die. Hook had told her so, and she had believed him. But knowing it and seeing it were two different things. She had imagined the secret to be some elaborate ritual. An incantation beneath the stars, perhaps, chanted in seven voices while drawing ancient, mystical symbols in the ashes of a fire.

It had never occurred to her that the key might be shooting them. Especially not when she had seen it tried so many times, with such a complete lack of results.

"Enter!" Hook barked.

Wendy opened the door to find him writing in his journal at his captain's desk. Chronicling the day's events, she realized. It was an important duty, and she almost felt sorry for interrupting him.

Almost.

Hook glanced up to see who it was. When he had his answer, his face darkened considerably. He glowered at her for a long moment and then turned his attention back to his journal, starting to write again even while addressing her.

"Yes, Miss Darling. What is it now?"

It occurred to Wendy that demanding information was not likely to get her very far, so she decided to begin politely and see how things progressed. (It is much more effective, after all, to sound rude later, after first being polite, than it is to sound polite after first being rude.)

"Please, Captain," she said, "I would like very much to know how you did it."

"I'm sure you would," he replied, but he said nothing more,

continuing to write in his journal without so much as glancing in her direction.

"I would like to be able to protect myself, if the need arises."

"The need will not arise, Miss Darling. My men are more than capable of protecting you, as they are every other unarmed member of my crew. Why should you be any different?" He stopped writing and looked up, watching her closely.

But Wendy said nothing. She tilted her head and narrowed her eyes, gazing back at him. Thinking. There was something about the way he was watching her. He was up to something. But what?

Hook returned to his journal, acting as though he had forgotten all about her. But, of course, he had already given himself away. There had to be a trap in it somewhere.

And suddenly, Wendy knew what it was.

He wanted her to say that she needed to be treated differently because she was a woman. To lay the argument between them to rest, once and for all, by her own words—thereby setting the precedent for any number of "special treatments" he might see fit to place upon her in the future.

Wendy smiled. As any well-trained logician knows, traps can work in either direction: once laid, they don't care who they catch.

"I'm so glad to hear you say that, Captain," she said. "As it happens, that is exactly the point I was about to make. Why should I be treated any differently? As you yourself have just implied, I should not."

Hook looked up to watch her again, this time with obvious suspicion.

"The officers are to be armed. To protect the crew," Wendy continued.

"That was the order," Hook agreed slowly.

"And the navigator is an officer."

Now Hook laughed.

It was a short but relieved sort of chuckle—the kind of laugh that implies one had believed oneself to be in trouble, only to have that trouble turn out to be nothing at all. Which should tell you that Hook still didn't know Wendy Darling nearly as well as he thought he did.

"So that's your game," he said. "Unfortunately for your argument, you are not an officer, and therefore you do not need to be armed. Although I admire the attempt. You are to return your weapons to the quartermaster, for safekeeping."

"Permission to speak freely, Captain," Wendy replied.

"Traditionally, Miss Darling, one makes such requests at the *beginning* of a conversation," Hook observed. Wendy decided to take this as an answer in the affirmative.

"What are the primary mechanisms by which every captain maintains his authority at sea," she asked, "to protect himself and his ship against the ever-present threat of mutiny?"

At the word "mutiny," Hook rose to his feet. His voice lowered to a snarl, and he placed both his hook and his good left hand before him on the desk, crouching over it as though he might leap across it at any moment.

"Be very careful what you say next. Men have walked the plank for such provocations."

"Discipline," Wendy replied calmly, answering her own question, "and the diligent separation of officers from seamen. Officers must maintain the respect of the crew at all times. If I hold the position of navigator, which I think we can agree has been firmly established, then how will it look if I am treated differently from the other officers? Will it not undermine the regard in which the crew holds me? Will it not, in fact, even place me in some danger?"

Hook continued to watch her, saying nothing, but his jaw shifted from side to side as he worked through her logic. She

wasn't wrong. If the men saw her as an officer, his refusal to arm her would undermine their respect for her perceived rank. And a ship's officer who held no respect among the crew was a dangerous precedent to set.

On the other hand, the one thing she hadn't said—the one thing they both knew to be true—was that the crew held her in low regard already, precisely because of her gender. Which meant he was damned either way. If he treated a woman as a full officer, he risked losing the respect of his crew. If he did *not* treat her as an officer, he would be undermining the strict discipline of his own ranks.

Impossible. The woman was *impossible*!

The only thing protecting them both was the ambiguity of her position. An ambiguity he had to maintain at any cost.

"Miss Darling," he finally said, speaking softly but clearly, "you are hereby assigned to the defense personnel of *The Tiger*. You will be armed, as will every other member of the watch, officer or otherwise, but you will *not*, under any circumstances, wear an officer's coat. You are only *attached* to this regiment. You are not *of* this regiment. Nonetheless, you are still under my command, and you will address me with the respect I am due as your commanding officer and as the captain of this ship. At all times. *Especially* in front of my men. Or I shall be forced to make an example of you—to maintain the very *discipline* for which you are so concerned. Is that clear?"

"Of course, Captain," she agreed. "Perfectly clear. But as a member of the ship's defense ..." Wendy paused for just the briefest of moments. "Well, forgive me, Captain, but surely the ship's defense personnel need to know how to kill the enemy?"

Hook inhaled deeply through his nose and then exhaled slowly. Their eyes remained locked together for what felt to Wendy like an eternity, but then he finally reached into the ammunition

pouch that hung from his belt and retrieved from it a single musket ball, which he placed on the desk before him.

She walked toward it slowly, watching him for any sudden movement. But he remained perfectly still as she reached for it. If she had expected a glow, or some telltale warmth of magic, she found nothing of the kind. It was a perfectly ordinary musket ball, like any other, with one single, obvious exception.

It was made entirely out of silver.

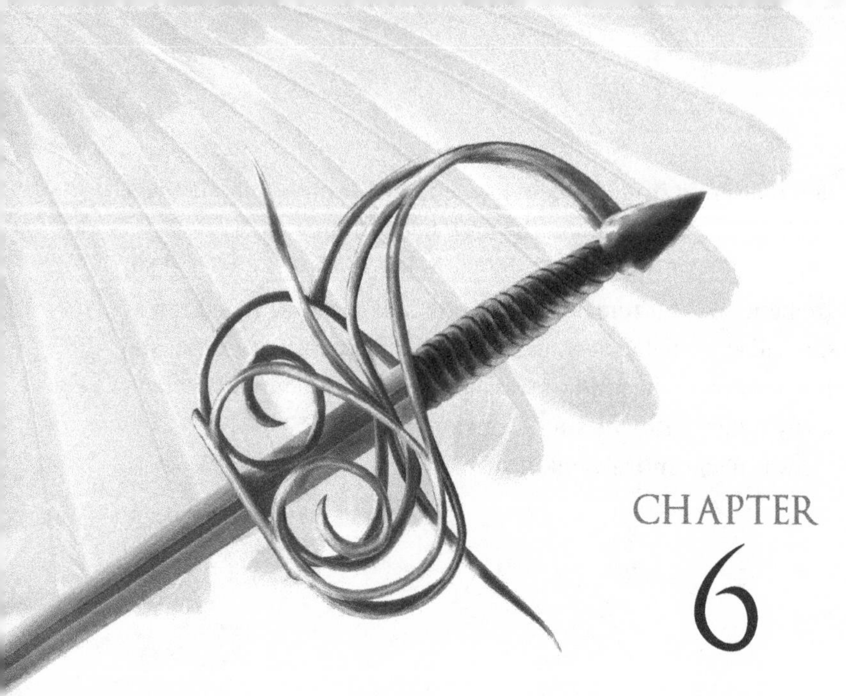

CHAPTER 6

At that exact moment, just as Wendy took the silver musket ball into her hand, and right there in that very same ocean, a little fish snorted in disgust. Or, at least, it tried to. A fish isn't designed to snort or even to grumble properly, but this one clenched its jaw and expelled the sea through its gills in an angry sort of way nonetheless.

This might not seem like a momentous event. There were a great many fish in the ocean at the time, and while very few of them were trying to snort, the attempt would hardly be worth mentioning if not for the fact that this particular fish had a personal history with Wendy.

It was tiny. It was as red as dragon fire. And its name was Tinker Bell.

As you might recall, Peter Pan's ship can only fly because of a magical trinket in the shape of a thimble. Tinker Bell made it and gave it to Peter, telling him it was a kiss. It was the most precious

gift she could think of, so you can imagine how angry she was when she found out the Wendy had stolen it.

And how *furious* she was when Peter refused to be angry at all.

Tinker Bell insisted it was part of an insidious plot and the Wendy was coming back to kill them. Peter insisted it was an accident. Or some kind of game. Or maybe the Wendy just didn't want them to leave without her.

It was almost as though he *wanted* her to have it!

Now, it's true that the trinket belonged to Peter, so he could do with it as he pleased. And perhaps the innisfay was overreacting. But in Tinker Bell's defense, when you give someone a gift, you don't expect them to go around giving it away to other people. (This is especially true of kisses.)

So, when Peter eventually retrieved the thimble, crowing proudly that he had been right all along—that the Wendy had defied Hook himself to come rescue them—and when, in return, Peter had given Wendy the magical compass to lead the British to Neverland, well, it had all been more than poor Tinker Bell could take. She had flown off in a huff, fully expecting Peter to follow her and soothe her ruffled feelings with kind words and bold promises and maybe even a song or two.

Unfortunately for everyone, he had not.

As a result, Tinker Bell was exceedingly bitter. She had followed Hook's ship all the way from London, first as a bile-green fish, reflecting her mood; then as a pearlescent silver fish, while she contemplated what to do; and finally as an angry red fish, because she couldn't come up with any way to stop them.

Then, when Blackheart showed up, Tink thought for a moment that luck might have finally turned her way. She was no friend of Blackheart's, but war makes strange bedfellows. If that good-for-nothing proved useful enough to drown the Wendy and Hook and a few hundred British sailors with them, she might even make him another thimble with her own hands.

But, of course, that isn't how things played out.

So now she was swimming in the sea behind *The Dragon*, snorting in disgust. If it seems like a coincidence that she should snort in the exact moment Hook showed Wendy the silver musket ball, it isn't really. Tink had been attempting to snort as a fish ever since that coward Blackheart had flown away. In fact, she had become so caught up in the experiment that she had almost forgotten about the Wendy and Peter and that vile Captain Hook.

Almost, but not quite.

Every so often she would rise to the surface, shift into her natural state, and fly up to glare through the very bottom corner of Hook's window. She wasn't trying to spy on him as much as she was just giving him the evil eye, but this time he wasn't alone. Tink caught the glint of silver as the Wendy lifted the musket ball to stare at it in wonder, and that gave her an idea.

It was a brilliant idea. A *perfect* idea. She ducked out of view, trembling with excitement, and for the first time in days, her hair shimmered back into gold.

Wendy strode through the passageways of *The Dragon* with an air of determination. She clutched in her hand a wax-sealed order, written by Hook himself, granting her the right to silver ammunition rations for her arms. But when she arrived at the armory, she found it in an uproar.

The quartermaster was a lean but exceedingly tall man with

dark, thinning hair and a perpetually somber expression. He stood just inside the door, issuing quiet but urgent orders to at least a dozen sailors who were taking items from various shelves and placing them into crates.

"No, not that one. That goes back to England. I said the *fifth* shelf goes to *The Tiger*. Yes, that one. Good." He nodded to Wendy as she stepped through the doorway, then turned his attention back to the men, speaking to her without looking in her direction. "Yes, Miss Darling, how can I help you? All right, Mr. Deighton, that's enough in that one. Close it up. But don't take it yet. Just start on the next row."

"I apologize for the timing, Mr. Quinton," Wendy said. "I can see you're very busy." Unlike the quartermaster in London, Mr. Quinton had never shown her any sign of disrespect. She certainly didn't want to upset him now.

"It is what it is, I'm afraid. *The Tiger* is a much smaller ship and will have a much smaller crew. There's a lot to go through to make sure we have the best possible provisions for the journey. But we will persevere."

"I'm sure we will, Mr. Quinton. I'm sure you will do a wonderful job."

He paused for a moment to glance at her, then nodded again. "Thank you, Miss Darling. Did you have a requisition?"

"I did. Or, rather, I do, yes."

Wendy handed him the orders. He didn't even bat an eye when he saw the wax seal, nor did he show any outward reaction when he read its contents. A boy who appeared to be just a bit older than Nicholas was working farther into the storeroom, and he scrambled to his feet when he saw Quinton with the paper. Wendy realized he must be the quartermaster's apprentice.

"Do you need me to fetch something, sir?" he asked quickly.

"No, no. I'll fill this one myself."

"Aye, sir." The boy settled back down to his knees beside the crate he had been packing.

"Wait here, please, Miss Darling." The quartermaster fished a key from a pocket hidden beneath his waistcoat and used it to unlock a door in the bulkhead behind his desk. "I won't be long."

This, Tinker Bell thought to herself, was taking forever.

She hovered at the side of the ship, peeking over the edge of the rail, waiting for all the elements of her brilliant plan to come together. And, of course, the Wendy was late—trying to ruin *everything*, as usual.

There were *so* many men chopping at the timbers scattered across the deck and hauling the pieces about. *Too* many for them all to pay proper attention. There was a scrub bucket right *there.* And a man walking toward it with a load of debris piled high in his arms. It would have been easy to dart in and make him trip over it. Oh, how Tinker Bell wanted to see him go sprawling across the deck! He might even drop the heavy timbers on his own foot! Imagine how he would hop about!

If she got the timing just right, he would blame the man next to him for moving the bucket. That would surely start a fight. And then they would *all* start fighting! Just *think* how much fun that would be!

But, no, Tinker Bell had a very specific plan, and it depended on the Wendy, who was clearly taking her time.

Tinker Bell's entire body wriggled with anticipation. It was all she could do not to abandon the whole scheme and wreak as much havoc as she could right then and there. But she watched. And she waited.

She was very proud of herself.

She had even decided who she would target to set the plan in motion. He was louder than all the rest—a surly man with dark hair and dark eyes, a barrel chest and a small button nose, and an unusually wide mouth. He liked to yell at all the others. He wore a whistle around his neck and a gun at his hip.

And when the Wendy finally did step onto the deck, followed by that wretched dog, he was in exactly the right spot. Tinker Bell flew over the rail and bolted straight for him. The other men shouted and pointed. The dog barked like mad. Tinker Bell tugged at the surly man's shirt front. He swatted at her, but he was a big, clumsy human and she was a tiny innisfay. She raced around him and tugged on the back of his shirt, making him spin. Some of the men started laughing.

"Don't just stand there!" he shouted. "Get it!" But they laughed even harder.

She flew above him and tousled his hair. He slapped at her, but he only managed to smack himself in the head. She flitted down and tweaked his nose. The men roared.

Tinker Bell darted out of reach, shouting taunts at him in delicate jingle bell chimes. He pulled out his pistol. She danced a jig in the air, taunting him while he loaded the weapon. He lined up his aim.

"No! Hold your fire!" Only John and Michael had seen what was about to happen. Tinker Bell was in a direct line between Smee and Wendy. They shouted at him to stop, but the men were laughing too loudly.

Smee sighted down the pistol and fired.

CHAPTER 7

In every life, there are moments—terrible, heartbreaking moments—that we wish we could undo. They move by in a flash, from the future to the present to the past in the blink of an eye, and by the time we realize what is happening it has already happened. The damage has been done, written in history, where it cannot be changed. For Wendy, this would forever be one of those moments.

She never even saw it coming.

She stepped onto the deck and heard the men roaring with laughter. She heard Nana barking. She caught a hint of the taste of pickles within the brine of the sea air, and then she saw Tinker Bell. She had just enough time to think, *Why it's Tink—*

And then two things happened at once, long before Wendy realized there was any danger at all. One, Smee fired his pistol. And two, Nicholas, who had stepped onto the deck right behind Wendy, saw what was about to happen and shoved her as hard as he could.

Wendy was taken completely by surprise. She staggered to the right, barely managing to keep her feet as chaos exploded around her. The shot rang in her ears. A dozen men's voices called out at once. And then suddenly, silence. All eyes turned to Nicholas, who stood perfectly still. He stared at Smee for a long moment, and then he glanced at Wendy.

"Good," he said. "You're all right." He even smiled.

Then he blinked twice, and a small crinkle formed above his nose, as though he were trying to solve a puzzle. He looked down at his own left side, where a stain of fresh blood was spreading across his shirt, and his eyebrows rose in quiet wonder. "Well, look at that," he said. "I think I've been shot." Then his knees buckled under him and he fell to the deck, passed out cold.

When Wendy finally understood what had happened, she couldn't even move. It was as though time itself had stopped, and she wished with all her might that she could turn it backward. Not for a day. Not for an hour. Not even for a minute. But just for one crucial moment. Surely that wouldn't be asking too much. One tiny moment to take back the worst thing that had ever happened in her life. So she would see it coming. So she would notice the gun. So she would stand her ground when Nicholas tried to push her.

She wished and wished, as hard as she could, and for one agonizing moment she thought it might be working—that she had held off the flow of time itself, stopping it between one breath and the next. No one spoke. No one moved. Even Tinker Bell froze like a hummingbird in midair. But it was just an illusion, and time marched inevitably forward.

Smee lowered his gun, his face rigid with fear. Wendy fell to her knees at the boy's side and pressed her hands desperately across his wound, trying to stop the bleeding. The red stain on his shirt continued to spread, and suddenly Wendy remembered

poor Reginald, the night his leg was severed clean through and his blood had pooled on the lawn of Dover Castle.

The night he had died, and then come back again.

Still leaning over Nicholas, Wendy turned to Tinker Bell and shouted, "Get Peter!" And then she started to cry. "Please! He needs help! Please, get Peter!"

"What's this? What's happened?" Hook's dark baritone startled her. He had come running when he heard the shot, and now he emerged through the hatch to find Nicholas lying on the deck, obviously wounded.

"Dear God in heaven," he murmured. Hook turned to Jukes, the barrel-chested man with tattoos up and down his arms, who happened to be standing nearby. "Find Mr. Pettigrew," he ordered. "Hurry!"

"Aye, sir," Jukes barked, and he disappeared down the hatch in a flash, sliding down the rails without even touching the steps.

Then Hook knelt by Nicholas' side. He brushed Wendy's hands away and took hold of the boy's shirt where the bullet had punctured it. Thrusting his fingers through the hole in the fabric, he tore at it, ripping the front of the bloody shirt in two. Then he shrugged off his blue captain's jacket and tugged his own shirt off over his head. He balled it into a wad and thrust it at Wendy.

"Use this," he told her. "Keep pressure on it."

"Aye, sir," Wendy mumbled. She reached for the crumpled shirt without even looking at him, feeling too guilty to meet his gaze.

Hook stood and turned his attention back to the crew.

"Who did this?" he shouted.

He didn't bother to retrieve his jacket. He stood bare-chested under the sun, ramrod straight, his dark locks tied back at the nape of his neck, and he glared at each man in turn, one after another. Most of them looked down at their feet, but Cecco, the handsome

Italian, stretched out a perfectly sculpted arm and pointed accusingly at Smee.

"It wasn't my fault!" Smee blurted out. "It was her!" He looked around for Tinker Bell, but the tiny innisfay had already flown away. Unfortunately, that left only one female to whom Smee might be referring, which was exactly the conclusion Hook reached.

"If Miss Darling shot the boy, then why did Mr. Cecco point to you, Mr. Smee?" Hook's voice was a quiet growl, rough and menacing.

"She didn't shoot him," Smee admitted. "She was in the way." He squared his shoulders and thrust his jaw forward. "I was shooting at the enemy, sir."

"I was not in the way," Wendy finally snapped, the streaks of her tears still glistening across her face. "I was in your line of fire, which is not the same thing! You were shooting at a tiny fairy, without even looking to see who might be standing behind her! Nicholas took that bullet to save my life!"

Her voice caught in her throat, and she turned back to the boy, sobbing quietly as she pressed Hook's shirt to his side.

Just then, Thomas appeared in the hatch. He stepped forward and knelt next to Wendy. "Let me see it," he said. Wendy moved Hook's shirt aside, and Thomas sucked in his breath.

"Can you help him?" Hook asked.

"I don't know," Thomas replied, "but I can try. Help me get him to the infirmary."

"Wait!" Wendy said, and she placed a protective hand on the boy's chest.

"Why? What is it?" Hook demanded.

Only then did Wendy stop to consider what she had been about to say—that Nicholas should remain on deck, in case Peter came to save him. But, of course, that was impossible. If Peter showed up at all, Hook's crew would kill him long before he could help the boy. Her hands trembled at the thought of it. She could only hope that her foolish outburst wouldn't end in another tragedy.

"Nothing," she said quietly. "Just ... be careful with him." She pulled her hands into her lap and said nothing more.

Hook thrust his chin at Cecco, who moved in immediately to pick the boy up and ease his way through the hatch, with Thomas hard on his heels.

Then Hook turned to glare for a long moment at Wendy, and she waited for him to say what she was thinking herself. That if she hadn't been on the ship, Nicholas wouldn't have had to save her. That if she had been paying attention, she could have spared them both. That this was all her fault.

But Hook didn't say anything at all. He just turned on his heel and stalked toward Smee in quick, terrible strides, snatching the pistol from his hand.

"As for you, Mr. Smee," he snarled, "you shall no longer carry arms until I declare otherwise. Your recklessness is inexcusable. That you would even consider firing your weapon toward any member of this crew ..."

Whatever Hook had been about to say, he trailed off into silence. But you can imagine for yourself what he was thinking.

And, of course, so could Smee.

As for what Smee was thinking, well, he had no way of knowing how much he now had in common with that horrible little fairy, but they agreed with each other on several points, nonetheless.

One. They both hated the Wendy.

Two. They both blamed her for everything that had just happened.

And three. They had both decided, once and for all, that the world would be a better place without her.

CHAPTER 8

When Hook went below, Wendy followed. He snapped up his captain's jacket without a word and dropped through the hatch, thrusting his bare arms through the sleeves as he charged along the passageway toward the infirmary. Wendy couldn't help but notice the forceful set of his shoulders. The angry clench of his jaw. He hadn't invited her to come along, but at least he didn't try to stop her—a fact for which she felt humbly grateful under the circumstances.

They arrived to find Nicholas lying on a bunk, still out cold. Thomas hovered over him, holding Hook's bloody shirt tightly to the boy's side with one hand, while Cecco stood before a tall wooden cabinet with row upon row of cubbyholes and drawers, all individually latched against the fickle moods of the sea.

"My ligature kit," Thomas was saying. "It's in the blue tin. Third row, second drawer from the left. Yes, that one. Good. Now find me some fresh egg yolks."

"Egg yolks?" Cecco asked.

"That's right. At least two. Preferably three."

"But ... just the yolks?"

Hook interrupted before Thomas could launch into an explanation. "Go to the chicken coop and find us three eggs, Mr. Cecco," he ordered. "I don't care if you have to lay them yourself."

"Aye, Captain!" the Italian barked. He ducked through the door and took off running.

Hook glanced at Nicholas and then turned to Thomas. "How bad is it?"

"Well, it could be worse." Thomas ran his free hand through his unruly hair and then abandoned the gesture halfway through, as though he had forgotten all about it. His palm rested on his head as he spoke, his fingers still entwined in his own locks, his elbow jutting out at an awkward angle. "The bullet passed through him, far enough to the side that it hit muscle. No vital organs. He lost a piece of a rib, but he can live without it. I'm more concerned about the loss of blood and the possibility of gangrene."

Hook nodded soberly. "What else do you need?"

"I should have the rest here in my medical supplies," Thomas replied. "Rose oil. Turpentine. I'll pack the wound and stop the bleeding. Bandage it against miasmas, but there are no guarantees. And he'll be in terrible pain when he wakes up."

"He'll have my rum for that, at least," Hook promised.

Thomas nodded and finally let his hand fall to his side.

"I'd like to help," Wendy said quietly.

The two men turned to look at her. Hook's forget-me-not eyes pierced her very soul with unspoken accusation, the muscles of his jaw clenching in protest, but Thomas nodded distractedly.

"A surgeon's mate would be most welcome," he said. "I could use an extra pair of hands."

Hook darted a suspicious glance in his direction, but the young man's face remained as guileless as ever. After a long moment,

Hook relented. "So be it. Miss Darling shall assist you for the duration. And the quartermaster shall have standing orders to give you anything you need. I'll see to it myself."

Just then, Cecco returned with the eggs, gently cradled in his hands.

"Excellent," Thomas proclaimed.

"You want only the yolks, correct?" Wendy asked.

"Yes, that's right," Thomas agreed. "Just the yolks."

"I can separate them. Do you have any cups? Or small bowls?"

"Top row, far left," Thomas said, thrusting his chin toward the cabinet.

Hook dismissed the Italian and was about to leave as well when he turned back toward Wendy from the doorway.

"Save him, Miss Darling," he told her. And as he closed the door behind him, she heard him add, muttering under his breath, "It's the least you can do."

For Wendy, time passed in a blur of fear and exhaustion.

It took three days to complete the transfer of men and supplies to *The Tiger*. The ship was lovely. Fast and proud. Her decks gleamed in the sunlight, so shapely and new one might almost have called her elegant. But Wendy barely noticed. She cared only that it was small, making it easier for her to memorize the route from her tiny quarters, where she slept, to the infirmary where Nicholas fought for his life.

He had developed a fever, so Wendy fetched fresh buckets of seawater to cool him every day, ignoring the hard glances and dark mutterings of the crew.

"Shouldn't be here."

"No place for a woman."

"Only leads to trouble."

But whenever she tried to face them directly, they turned away, dissolving into a facade of innocence. Just men minding their own business, swabbing the deck or playing games of chance. Wendy couldn't help but feel as if a terrible storm was brewing in the belly of the ship itself—a hurricane that had awoken and now held its breath, waiting to see what would happen to Nicholas.

But the most terrifying moment repeated itself three times a day, at dawn, noon, and dusk, when she bent over the boy's side to sniff at his wound, praying she wouldn't smell the hint of rot that would signal the beginning of the end. She learned everything she could from Thomas, who had studied anatomy and medicine under the great John Hunter himself, but all she really knew was that gangrene led to death.

And that there was nothing they could do to stop it once it started.

Nicholas was so brave it almost broke Wendy's heart. He smiled at her weakly every morning when she arrived, and he bid her good-night every evening when she left. In between, he did his best to hide his pain, and when she knelt by his bunk to sniff at his side, the only sign of his own fear was the thin line of his lips, pressed together tightly, and the slight dimple of worry between his eyebrows. He would watch her closely, and when she looked back at him and smiled, his head would fall back to the pillow and his eyes would stare up at the ceiling, with just the smallest tear of relief.

And then, to distract him, Wendy would tell him a story.

She told him about the orphanage where she and Charlie had grown up, and about her mentor, Olaudah Equiano. She told him about Bartholomew Fair, with its exotic animals and impossible acrobats. She told him about King Arthur and Robin Hood, about Hercules and Odysseus, about Ali Baba and Aladdin and Sinbad the Sailor.

And every night she would return to her quarters, with its tiny bunk and its tiny desk and its simple hanging lamp, so much like her quarters on *The Dragon*, but even smaller. (With the addition of a tiny porthole, through which she could see the stars.) She would press her eyelids tightly together, trying not to cry, and she would pray for Nicholas to recover—begging God and all the heavens, over and over until she fell asleep.

Three weeks passed in this new rhythm—this narrow, worried existence that left room for nothing else—and they were both the shortest and longest weeks of her life. The shortest, because they all ran together, one day into the next, until she had no idea how much time had passed or hadn't. The longest, because nothing makes time drag its feet like the terrible combination of fear and helplessness.

It was then, after twenty-one days of fear and exhaustion, that they sailed into the fog.

CHAPTER 9

It hadn't been there in the morning.

Wendy had consulted with Charlie just after first light, as she always did, checking her compass and assuring him they were still on course. The sky was blue. The horizon was bare. And although the compass had given them a new heading twice in the first few days of sailing, the needle hadn't moved since.

"Truly?" Charlie muttered. "Another week and we'll be running aground in South America."

"Nothing's changed, I'm afraid," Wendy replied quietly. "Nothing at all."

Charlie lowered his head and met her worried gaze. "Nicholas?" he asked.

"The wound isn't healing as fast as it should," she admitted.

Charlie's eyes fell, and he nodded. They both knew what that could mean, but neither of them wanted to say it. Charlie reached out to hold her hand for just a moment and then let go. It was a

small gesture. A quick and simple comfort between friends. But it did not go unnoticed.

A pair of dark eyes, hovering above a button nose and an unusually wide mouth, stared at them cruelly. Ever since Nicholas had been shot (which, of course, was how Smee thought of it—*since Nicholas had been shot*, as though the act had been committed by no one in particular, or better yet, *since Nicholas had gotten himself shot*, implying it was the boy's own fault), Smee had been watching Wendy like a hawk, hoping she would slip up in some way that might redeem him.

If only he could catch her in some despicable act, he would gladly report her to the captain and expose her true colors, proving she was unfit to sail the seas among men, and certainly unfit for the crew of the great Captain Hook. But in all that time, she had done nothing wrong whatsoever.

She had performed her duties as the navigator without fail, and she had tended to the wounded boy with unflagging dedication, hardly even sleeping, as far as Smee could tell. This moment of holding Charlie's hand was the worst thing she had done, and even Smee could see that Charlie had initiated it.

Besides, the rest of the crew might not hold hands very often, at least not as far as Smee knew, but it wasn't expressly forbidden.

So he still had nothing to show for all his hours of stalking Wendy through the passageways and eavesdropping on her conversations whenever he could, but Smee wasn't one to give up. He would keep watching. He would keep listening. And eventually, when she finally made a mistake, he would be waiting.

Wendy spent the rest of the morning with Nicholas, but things were looking grim. The boy seemed restless, shifting about in the bunk in fits and starts. The smell of death was not yet upon him, but the skin around his injury was showing new signs of redness, and it was warm to the touch.

She tried to tell him stories to distract him, as she usually did, but he kept shutting his eyes and drifting off. So she just sat nearby and let him sleep. It was all she could do for him. She was unwilling to leave his side, not even to eat, so Thomas brought her a bowl of thin stew at midday. Nicholas ate a few meager bites but then pushed it away feebly and fell back asleep. After that, Wendy and Thomas finished their meal together in silence.

Until they felt the ship begin to turn.

Wendy looked up at Thomas, who raised his eyebrows and shrugged, as if to say, "How should I know why we're turning?"

"Go," is what he said out loud. "I'll take care of our patient."

But Wendy still hesitated.

"I won't leave him," he promised, holding her gaze as he said it.

Wendy finally nodded, and she headed topside, with Nana in tow.

When she reached the deck, she could hardly believe her eyes. Where the morning horizon had been crystal clear, now a wide barrier of smoke-thick fog lay ahead of them, dark and heavy. They were turning to go around it.

When you think of dangers at sea, there are others that might sound more frightening: hurricanes and tidal waves, sirens and krakens. But fog can be just as dangerous as these. Fog near land can ground a ship, or dash it against the rocks of an unseen shore. And a fog as thick as the one ahead, even on the open ocean, could hide an entire flying ship, full of everlost, ready to fire on you from above.

So Hook and his crew would sail around the fog, just to be safe, returning to their course on the other side.

Only ... they couldn't.

As they turned to port, Wendy opened her compass, watching the outline of the island glow as the needle moved. She had expected this: The needle would turn to give them their new direction, pointing always toward the isle of Neverland.

But it turned more than it should have. And the farther they sailed around the fog, the more it turned, until it became perfectly obvious that the needle was pointing into the heart of the fog itself.

"Neverland," Wendy breathed.

"What?" Hook's head snapped toward her. "What about it?"

"It's in there," Wendy said, her voice still quiet. She looked across the starboard rail, gazing at the fog bank in wonder. "No matter how far we sail around it, the needle still points into it."

"Let me see that," he demanded, and he snatched the compass from her with his good left hand, but the moment it left her grasp, it fell dark, as it always did. He scowled and thrust it back at her, coming instead to stand where he could look at it over her shoulder.

It was, of course, just as she had told him. The compass pointed straight into the fog.

"We've found it," Wendy said, looking in her excitement at Charlie, who couldn't help but grin in return. "We've actually found it!"

"We haven't found anything yet, Miss Darling," Hook growled, and Charlie wiped the smile from his face before the captain could see it. "We have no idea what's waiting for us in there. And whatever it is, we won't see it until we're right on top of it. Or right below it, for that matter."

Wendy frowned. Hook was right. Even if it wasn't a trap—even if what waited for them was the isle of Neverland itself—the

flying ship that had fired on them was still out there somewhere. And who knew what magical creatures might guard the island itself? Naturally, she thought of sirens. And krakens.

“Mr. Smee!” Hook called out.

“Aye, Captain!”

Wendy almost jumped out of her shoes when Smee barked his reply from just behind her other shoulder. Where had he even come from? She could have sworn he was nowhere near the helm.

Even Hook looked a bit startled, but only for a moment.

“Prepare the ship,” he ordered. “All hands silent. Slow and steady. We’re going in.”

CHAPTER 10

They furled all the sails but one, lashing the rest down tight, but Hook stationed men throughout the rigging, ready to set every sail again at a moment's notice. The order of "all hands silent" was carried to every corner of the ship, both above deck and below, and a hush fell over the world. On a nod from Hook, Charlie turned the ship into the fog.

As *The Tiger* prowled into the swirling dark, it seemed to Wendy that all her senses came alive. The heat of the southern climate closed in around her, stifling her as it never had before. She heard every creak of wood, every gentle lap of the sea against the hull. She felt the tension in the men around her, coiling in their bodies, preparing to fight.

And when the fog finally reached her, she sensed that, too. She felt its cool caress against her cheek. She tasted the salt of it. And she smelled just the slightest hint of green. Nana growled quietly, but Wendy shushed her. This was not the scent of Peter

Pan or the everlost. It had no form. No direction. It was simply all around them. It was the scent of the fog itself.

And the fog *enveloped* them.

From where she stood, next to Charlie at the helm, the front third of the ship had disappeared. She could barely see the foremast, let alone the lookout standing at the bow. Without Peter's compass, they would not have been able to navigate at all. She held it open where Charlie could see it, and he kept them moving forward through the dark, swirling shroud, which seemed to Wendy more like a thundercloud than a fog.

She reached out her free hand and moved it slowly through the air, letting thin tendrils drift between her fingers, while Peter's voice spoke in her memory: "I bet you've never touched a cloud!" She shuddered, just a little, and let her hand fall back to her side.

Their eyes were all but useless, so they strained their ears instead, listening for any sign that they were not alone. The creak of another hull. The snap of another sail. The metallic click of pistols being made ready, or the muffled sound of muskets being loaded. But they heard none of these. Only the thin wail of a seagull, crying somewhere ahead, in the dark.

A seagull! Wendy thought to herself. *Neverland!*

Hook, of course, had the same thought. (Or, at least, the land bit. The presence of seagulls indicated land up ahead, but the nature of that land remained to be seen.)

"Sounding line, Mr. Smee," Hook ordered in a whisper.

"Aye aye," Smee answered, just as softly. He scuttled away toward the bow until he disappeared from view. It wasn't long before they heard the distinct sound of a chain being lowered into the water. Then silence. Then a quiet rattling as the chain was retrieved. Another silence. And then the chain being lowered once more.

But measuring the depth of the seabed does little good when you don't know the shoreline. Rock outcroppings hidden beneath the waves can dash a ship to pieces without any warning. And with no visibility, a ship can sail straight into the plunging cliffs of land while still in deep waters. So they crept forward slowly. Carefully. As the fog stretched on and on.

Until finally, after what felt like an eternity, the bow reappeared in a soft halo of golden light. The ship brightened. The fog cleared. And suddenly, they were through.

The gray veil now hung behind them, and before them lay the sun-bright shores of Neverland, its emerald green foliage and pearl white beaches stretched out upon a turquoise sea.

"Neverland," Wendy breathed.

"Back into the fog, Mr. Hawke," Hook ordered at once.

"Aye, sir," Charlie replied, without hesitation.

Wendy held her tongue, but her left eyebrow was already hoping for explanations.

"Circumnavigate the island," Hook continued, speaking to Charlie, his voice pitched soft and low. "Keep to the outer edge of the fog. We'll use it to our advantage. Get the full lay of the land before we come out into the open."

"Aye, sir," Charlie said again.

Wendy stared wistfully at the shore, but she knew it was a reasonable plan. More than reasonable, given the everlost attack that had crippled *The Dragon* and *The Cerberus.* Still, that didn't mean she had to like it.

One more day, she reminded herself. *Perhaps two, at the most. We've found it. We'll be ashore soon enough. And there's still a patient to attend.*

The very thought of Nicholas sobered her. She had forgotten all about his condition for a moment, but now the guilt came flooding back and her excitement fell away. Neverland had cost them so much already. What greater price would they pay before it was over?

With one last, pensive glance at the island, she turned and headed below.

Unfortunately, Nicholas wasn't any better. If anything, he seemed worse. His fever had risen, and the redness had spread. Wendy took her evening meal in the infirmary, doing what she could for him. Cooling him with seawater. Bringing him fresh water to drink when he was aware enough to swallow it. Moistening his lips when he wasn't.

Thomas promised to stay the night with him, and Wendy finally returned to her quarters with Nana pacing faithfully behind, the dog's head hanging low in silent commiseration.

"We must *do* something, Nana," Wendy said quietly, once they had settled in. She sat near the head of her small bunk with Nana's monstrous form lying next to her, taking up most of it.

As for Nana, she had no idea what to do for Nicholas, but she was more than willing to try anything Wendy suggested. She placed a paw on Wendy's leg in solidarity.

"Thank you, Nana," Wendy said, sighing a little, and she stroked the dog's head, looking down at her fondly. "But I'm afraid I don't know what to do either. I've looked through every medical book on the ship, but there's nothing useful in any of them. The only thing I know that could help Nicholas now is Peter. And even if we could find him, we could hardly bring him here, now could we?"

Nana raised her head. She didn't know anything about bringing Peter or not bringing Peter, but Wendy had sounded hopeful for just a moment, and Nana wanted to be supportive.

"What, Nana?" Wendy asked her. "What is it?"

Nana looked back at Wendy with complete and utter confidence. Her mistress would think of something. She always did. And sometimes, that's all a good idea needs to be born into this world: for someone else to look back at it with complete and utter confidence.

Suddenly, Wendy felt it coming. Her back straightened, and her eyes darted about the room—up and to the left, then sideways to the right, ready to pounce on the idea as soon as it landed. She must have caught it on the desk, because that's where she was staring when she said what she said next.

"Nana, that's it! We don't have to bring Peter here. We only need his blood!"

Nana cocked her head to one side, listening intently.

"No, don't worry," Wendy assured her. "We won't hurt him. Remember how he saved poor Reginald? Just two drops of blood. His thumb healed right up again, and it saved poor Reginald's life. I'm sure Peter would do it if we asked him!"

Nana's tail thumped against the foot of the bunk. She didn't fully understand the plan, but Wendy seemed happy, which was all that mattered.

"We'll need something to carry it in," Wendy continued. "I'm sure we can find something in the infirmary. We'll look tomorrow while Thomas is at the mess. Then we'll borrow a rowboat and sneak off to the island tomorrow night. We'll follow our noses to Peter. But we can't tell anyone, Nana. *Especially* not the captain. He'd never let us go, and we can't get any of our friends in trouble."

When Wendy said the word "captain," Nana growled a little in the back of her throat.

"Now, now, Nana. It's not his fault. Captain Hook would only keep us here to protect us. He would never hurt Nicholas on purpose. But we know what Nicholas needs, don't we. So we'll just have to take care of it ourselves."

Nana fell silent and dropped her head back onto the bunk. But she hadn't been growling at what Wendy said. She had been growling at the faint shuffle she heard outside the door, and at the scent of a certain man with dark eyes, a button nose, and an unusually wide mouth.

A man Nana did not like at all.

CHAPTER 11

Meanwhile, Hook sat at his desk, writing in his journal as best he could. The penmanship of his left hand had become easier, over time, but it still felt awkward. Cumbersome. It reminded him of what he had lost. As a result, this was not a duty he enjoyed. It was important, so he did it. But it tended to put him in a bad mood.

Still, at least for tonight, there were happier thoughts on his mind.

Neverland! he wrote.

After all this time, is it possible we have arrived? Have we, at long last, discovered the island homeland of our enemy? Our hopes are high, but nothing is certain, nor shall it be until we have seen the truth of it with our own eyes. We must proceed with caution. Even if our suspicions are correct, the ship lies in dangerous waters. We shall remain—

Here, he paused. *We shall remain what?* he wondered. He had almost written *cautious*, but he had used *caution* already. *Alert?* Perhaps, but it didn't carry the proper weight. He was considering

vigilant when he was interrupted by a sudden rapping at the door, and now we shall never know what it was they were going to remain. (Although we might reasonably assume they were going to remain all three.)

"Yes, what is it?" he barked. His hair hung loose, as was his habit in the evenings, even aboard ship. He set down his quill pen and ran his good left hand through it, ink stains and all, then looked up from his journal. He scowled when he saw who it was.

Mr. Smee closed the door behind himself and stood with his head slightly bowed. He held a rag in his hands, fidgeting at it with his fingers.

"Begging your pardon, Captain," he said, "but I have a report."

"From Mr. Hawke?" Hook shifted his weight as though he were about to rise. "Have we found something?"

"No, sir," Smee blurted out. "I'm sorry, sir. It's nothing like that. It's just ... I've *overheard* something. Something I thought you should know."

Hook sighed and sat back in his chair. For that one brief moment he had appeared energetic. Alert. (Or, perhaps, vigilant.) But now it disappeared from his countenance, and he stared at Smee coldly.

"Well, what is it?" he demanded.

"It's ... it's about Miss Darling, sir."

Hook's jaw thrust forward, and his eyes narrowed dangerously, but he said nothing. After a long moment, Smee gulped and forged ahead.

"I overheard her plotting to steal a rowboat, sir. Tomorrow night. She intends to row to the island to find Pan. I believe she's in league with the enemy. Sir."

"Plotting with whom?" Hook snapped.

"I'm sorry, sir?" Smee asked.

"With *whom*, Smee—plotting with whom? Surely Miss Dar-

ling doesn't intend to row *herself* to the island. I doubt she's ever rowed any sort of vessel in her life. I doubt she would even know how."

"With ..." Smee's fingers moved more quickly over the rag. "I believe she was speaking to her dog, sir."

If Smee had expected outrage, that wasn't what he got. The captain sat up straight and furrowed his brow. Then he rested his hook on the right arm of his chair, planted his left forearm on the table before him, and leaned forward with a look of such confusion that even Smee began to doubt his own report.

"She was *plotting* ..." Hook said, pausing for effect, "with her *dog*."

"Well, I don't know, sir," Smee mumbled. "There might have been someone else with her, I suppose. Now that you mention it, I'm sure there was."

"Did you *hear* anyone else, Mr. Smee?"

"No, sir. No, I didn't. But I wasn't there for very long."

"You weren't *where*, exactly?"

"Outside her quarters, sir. I was just passing by. And I heard her speaking. She said they would steal the rowboat, whoever they are. And then she said, 'We'll follow our noses to Peter.'"

"We'll follow our noses to Peter," Hook repeated quietly.

"Yes, sir," Smee affirmed.

But Hook was no longer listening. Instead, he was entertaining two ideas, one immediately following the other. The first was that there were only two noses on the entire ship capable of smelling magic, so Wendy Darling had, in fact, been talking to her dog. There really was no end to the strangeness of that woman.

The second idea was this: *She could follow her nose to Peter. And Peter would never suspect her.*

"Mr. Smee, you will say nothing of this."

"Sir?"

"You heard me. Absolutely nothing. And you will do nothing to stop her."

"Aye, sir," Smee replied, looking disappointed.

"Tell Mr. Abbot and Mr. Bennet to report to my quarters at once."

"Aye, sir!" he agreed, sounding a little more hopeful.

"And, Mr. Smee."

"Aye, sir?"

"I find it terribly convenient that you happened to be passing by Miss Darling's quarters in the exact moment that she made this confession."

"Very convenient. Aye, sir," Smee agreed.

"No, Mr. Smee. You misunderstand me, so let me be clear. In the future, you shall not hover outside Miss Darling's door. That's an order."

"Aye, sir," Smee grumbled.

"Then you are dismissed."

Miss Darling was still an Englishwoman under his protection. An odd one, to be sure, but a woman nonetheless. He didn't want his men getting any ideas. And besides, this would all be over soon enough.

He was about to set the perfect trap for Peter Pan.

CHAPTER 12

Everything was ready.

Or, at least, Wendy *believed* everything was ready. One can never be certain, which is the very nature of planning. At some point, one must simply forge ahead. Still, Wendy had prepared as best she could, which is essential to every worthwhile venture, even those that don't proceed as we intended.

She had commandeered the necessary specimen vials from the drawers in the infirmary. She had strapped her sword to her hip, as she always did. She had tucked Peter's compass safely into her bag, and she had filled two leather-covered bottles with fresh water, just in case.

She had also squirreled away a healthy supply of silver bullets for her musket and pistols, with plenty of lead ammunition besides, along with the necessary powder. She hoped not to need any sort of bullets, silver or otherwise, but it seemed wise to have them along. Who knew what dangers lay ahead, on the shores of Neverland?

Satisfied with her packing, she sat next to Nana and waited for the last rays of sunlight to fade from the sky.

And waited ... and waited.

The aching slowness of the planet as it turned within the heavens gave her plenty of time to think. *Too* much, in fact. Unoccupied time is the richest of soils—the slumbering earth in which our dreams and our fears grow best—and as Wendy sat on the little bunk in her stateroom, an insidious vine of doubt crept up her spine to brush the back of her neck, taunting her with its gentle persistence.

She had noticed, for example, during the long night before, that she had seen no lights on the island. Not even one. But this was *Neverland.* She had expected the phosphorescent dance of the innisfay. The haunting song of the sirens. Ethereal midnight pageantry beneath the stars. She had expected a dazzlement of fairy lights skating just beneath the waves, or perhaps trailing up the slopes of the stony peak that loomed above the jungle in the distance.

Instead, she had seen nothing.

At the very *least,* she had expected to see a hint of gas lamps, sparkling through the greenery. Or fires. *Any* kind of light to mark the presence of thinking, rational minds. Instead, there was only the dark, lumbering suggestion of the island itself, blocking out the stars on the horizon—a lonely sentry in the midst of the vast ocean—and only the moon reflecting upon the sea.

Needless to say, this was troubling.

"Perhaps they are very deep within the jungle," she said quietly to Nana, stroking the dog's neck for reassurance. "Or perhaps they can see well enough by the moonlight. That would explain it."

Nana wuffed softly, but not at Wendy. The dog lifted her head and whined, and then Wendy heard a knock at the door.

She scrambled to hide her pack, stuffing it into the sea chest and securing the latch. Then she stood, smoothed down her vest, and walked the two short steps to the door. No matter who it was, even if it was Hook himself, anything would be better than sitting still and worrying for even one moment longer.

But then it occurred to her that it might be Thomas, or John, or Michael, come to tell her that Nicholas had taken a turn for the worse. Or, what if he ... she couldn't even *think* it. And all before she had had the chance to find Peter and make it right.

She took a deep breath and opened the door to find John and Michael standing there together, looking distinctly uncomfortable. A surge of fear tightened in the small of her belly, and her hands began to tremble.

Michael glanced at John as if to say, "*You're* the ranking officer. *You* tell her," and a tear formed in Wendy's left eye.

"Nicholas?" she barely managed to whisper.

"Sorry?" John had been about to say something else, but now he closed his mouth, furrowed his brow, and tilted his head slightly to the right, clearly puzzled. He had planned out his speech very carefully, but it didn't involve Nicholas in any way, leaving him no idea how to proceed.

Michael, however, understood immediately.

"No!" he blurted out. He leaned forward and shook his head, holding Wendy's gaze. "Nothing like that. The boy's condition hasn't changed, as far as I—" He glanced back at John. "I mean, as far as *we* know."

"Ah," John said. "No, nothing like that."

Wendy exhaled sharply, only then realizing she had been holding her breath.

"Well, come in, both of you," she told them.

"Come in?" John asked. "That doesn't seem ..." His words

trailed off. In the entire year Wendy Darling had spent at Dover Castle, not one of the men had ever entered her private quarters, not even with a chaperone.

"We're on a *ship*," Michael reminded him. "Where else would you suggest we go?"

John paused for a long moment. "Right," he finally agreed, and he nodded a little, mostly to reassure himself. "You're right, of course."

Wendy ushered them in and secured the door behind them, sitting on the bunk with Nana while the men stood awkwardly near the door.

"Well?" she said finally. She felt a bit guilty about hiding her intentions, and she had to work hard not to look at the sea chest.

"Right," John said again. "We're here by Hook's orders. He knows you're planning to visit the island tonight, and he's sent us to accompany you. To ..." He glanced at Michael, who nodded his agreement. "To *help* you," John finished.

In fact, Hook had ordered them to protect her. He hadn't said anything about helping. *Has she ever rowed a boat in her life?* the captain had demanded. *She'll be swept out to sea! Or eaten by something the moment she lands! She's a woman, for God's sake. Impulsive. And unpredictable. If I don't let her go, she'll sneak off and do it anyway, and then I'll be forced to punish her. Just to maintain discipline on my own ship! I am trying, gentlemen, to avoid that situation.*

John and Michael had both seen the look in Hook's eye when he spoke of punishing Wendy, and they hadn't liked it one bit. On a ship, that usually meant flogging, but they had no intention of finding out.

Still, the moment they left the captain's quarters, they had both agreed that offering their help with whatever Wendy was planning would be far more effective than offering to protect her.

"But ..." Wendy said. "But how did he *know*?"

"I haven't the slightest idea," John told her, and Michael shrugged. That much, at least, was the complete truth.

"Well, I suppose I'm glad for it," Wendy admitted. "Even if I *am* surprised that he knew. Nana and I will both be grateful to have you with us."

"Not that it matters," Michael chimed in, "but to have us with you for *what*, exactly?"

"Hook didn't tell you?"

"No," both men replied in the exact same moment.

"Of course not," Wendy muttered. "Why would the great Captain Hook bother to tell anyone anything?"

If it occurred to John or Michael that *she* hadn't planned to tell them what *she* was doing either, they were smart enough to keep it to themselves.

"What we're doing ..." Wendy announced, but then she paused and stood up from her bunk. She opened the sea chest and retrieved her gear, lifted her pack onto her shoulder, and then stared both men in the eyes, one after the other.

"... is going to save Nicholas."

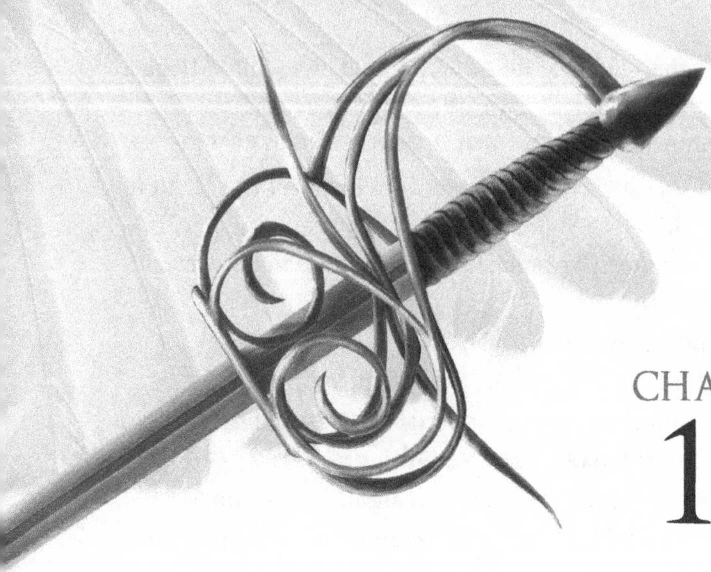

CHAPTER 13

Wendy sat in the back of the rowboat, watching the island inch closer, with Nana curled at her feet. John perched in the bow, looking out for rocks or other dangers that might lie ahead. The water was calm, and the moonlit waves made hardly any sound against the distant shore. In the still of the night, Michael was doing his best to row quietly.

He sat facing Wendy, moving in a slow rhythm. Dip the oars without a splash. Pull. Lift the oars, being careful not to rattle the oarlocks, and cycle them back to the beginning. This last part caused him to lean forward, and about every third or fourth cycle he caught Wendy's eye and grinned.

But Wendy just rolled her eyes, smiled ever so slightly (because they were friends), and turned her attention back to the island.

Now that they were on their way, Wendy wasn't at all sure that she and Nana could have made it this far on their own. The boat was heavy, and it had taken both men, working together, to lower it safely into the sea. Even if she had managed to accomplish that

much, she would not have been able to row and watch for dangers at the same time. So although she *might* have gotten this far without John and Michael, she found herself more grateful than ever to have them along.

But why had *Hook* sent them to help her?

The thought made her uneasy. No matter how hard she tried to lock it away, the question kept slipping through her grasp, scampering off to wander through the passageways of her mind, opening doors and peering here and there, searching for answers.

She *wanted* to believe he was just trying to help Nicholas. After all, Hook couldn't seek Pan out for himself. Even if he were willing to try (and Wendy doubted very much that he was), the two were enemies through and through. They would attempt to kill each other on sight, and there would be no help for Nicholas no matter what came of it.

And that, Wendy realized, was her answer. Hook would *hate* the fact that she was the only one on the ship who had a chance of saving Nicholas. He didn't tell John and Michael what they were doing because he never would have admitted the truth of it out loud. Not to anyone.

Feeling much better, Wendy grinned back at Michael the next time he winked at her. Her grin had nothing to do with the wink, of course, but it made them both happy nonetheless, albeit for entirely different reasons.

Calm waters meant gentle waves, and even the ones breaking against the shore posed no real threat to the boat. The company had no trouble riding the last ones in, with some well-timed help

from Michael, and soon enough the little hull surged forward one last time, scraping against the sand.

Michael yanked both oars into the boat, and then he and John leaped out into the light surf, each grabbing a side of the vessel and hauling it up the beach with Wendy still in it, John to port and Michael to starboard. (This was how Wendy still thought of the left and the right, even though the boat was very small.)

John held out his hand to her while Michael retrieved her pack, but Wendy was more than a bit annoyed. The two men had beached the boat without her and were now treating her more like a lady than a sailor, as though having sand beneath their feet had magically transformed her from the one into the other.

She ignored John's hand, vaulted over the side, and landed gracefully on the shore, proving by her actions that although port had just become left, decks had become floors, and passageways had become corridors, she herself was still the Wendy, and no amount of sand in the world was about to change that.

As for Nana, sand was not about to change her either. She caught a glimpse of a shell being carried along by the thin edge of the waves that licked the beach, and she threw herself merrily into the shallow water to try to fetch it.

"Nana, heel," Wendy ordered. Nana stopped where she was and looked up at her mistress, then looked back toward the small treasure, weighing her options.

"Heel," Wendy said again, even more firmly.

The dog abandoned the chase, shook herself off, and returned to sit at Wendy's side, filing the game away for later.

Wendy took her pack from Michael and then stood still. She listened to the night creatures calling to each other, rustling here and there throughout the vast canopy. She felt the sand beneath her boots—not quite as fine as she had expected, salted with larger grains of rock and shell. She watched for any flickering of

light, but the island was just as dark as it had appeared from the ship, with only the clear moonlight to guide them, painting the beach in soft hues of gray. And the jungle, darker still—shadows within shadows.

But mostly she breathed. Quietly and deeply. Now that she stood upon the shore, the scent of magic filled her senses. It came from everywhere and nowhere at once. *Neverland,* Wendy thought, despite the fact that it was not what she had expected. If Peter was here, the scent of the island itself was hiding him.

She reached into her pack and retrieved the compass he had given her. It glowed when she opened it, as it always did, but she could see now that it wasn't pointing toward the exact center of the island. Instead, it hovered a bit toward the right, indicating a rocky spire that loomed in the distance.

"We're heading for that peak," Wendy told the men.

"We can't hack our way through the jungle at night," John pronounced. "We'll have to wait until dawn."

"No, of course we can't," Wendy assured him, even though she didn't fully appreciate his tone. "But we could get closer by walking along the shore."

"I still don't like it. We should stay right here with the boat and wait for first light." John set his jaw stubbornly, and he made no move to go anywhere.

"Well, we can't light a fire and give ourselves away," Wendy pointed out. "So it's either sit here in the dark, exposed, knowing we can't see a thing in there ..." She swept one hand toward the jungle. "Or keep going, and try to find Peter before anyone *else* finds *us*."

John glanced at Michael. He wasn't thrilled with Wendy's plan to begin with. If they were going to face Pan again, even to ask for help, he would have preferred to do it in the daylight.

But Michael only shrugged. Now that Wendy was the ship's

navigator, he thought she might outrank him, and he wasn't about to take sides. Especially when he already suspected which of them was going to get her way.

"It's only about an hour until dawn," Wendy added gently. "By the time we've hidden the boat, we won't have terribly long before first light. We might as well keep moving."

John sighed. He stepped back into position next to the boat and nodded to Michael, who did the same. The two men dragged it up the beach, with Wendy pushing from behind, and all the while they scanned the jungle as best they could, trying to keep an eye out for trouble.

Which explains why none of them saw the second boat emerge from the edge of the fog behind them, or the silhouette of a man with a hook in the place of his right hand.

CHAPTER 14

They dragged the boat up the beach, shoved it into the undergrowth, covered it with fronds, and then swept away the trail they had made in the sand. It wasn't exactly invisible, but no one would notice it without looking closely. (And, hopefully, no one would have reason to look.)

They had landed on the northeastern shore of the island, and by the time the first hint of sunlight began to pale the sky behind them, they had trudged perhaps a mile or so along the northern beach toward the west. It was slow going, and they had been awake all night, but Wendy didn't feel tired. On the contrary, she thought she had never been so alert in all her life.

In fact, it reminded her very much of that night in Dover—the first night she had ever smelled the scent of magic.

She stopped in her tracks.

"What is it? What's wrong?" (John was always alert for trouble, even when they were *not* exploring magical enemy beaches.)

Wendy sniffed the air. It felt a bit like standing in a kitchen,

surrounded by the wonderful aroma of dinner on the way, when the cook suddenly opens the oven. Everything smells the same as before, but somehow *more*, too. Richer, and with the subtlest hint of *direction.*

Nana had noticed the same thing, and she growled low in the back of her throat, staring toward the jungle.

The men drew their pistols.

Wendy did not, but she thought later that she should have. There is a time for curiosity, and a time for caution. But whenever Wendy's curiosity was piqued, she forgot all about the latter.

Nana lowered her head and stalked toward the foliage, but she had taken only two steps before Wendy called her back.

"Nana," Wendy hissed. "Come. Let me go first."

"Absolutely *not.*" John kept his voice low, but his tone was exceedingly firm. "That is a direct order."

Wendy stared at him, and her eyebrow drew itself up to its full height, clearly indignant. But John's manner did not change in the slightest.

"*I* will go first," he insisted. "The two of you will stay behind me." John turned to Michael and continued. "If anything happens, her safety is your first priority. Get her back to *The Tiger* at any cost."

Michael nodded.

Wendy, on the other hand, thought she had never been so angry in all her life. For John to treat her this way, now, after all they had been through together, just because she was a woman—

But John saw it coming. With three long strides, he stood directly in front of her, and his next words interrupted the tirade she had been about to unleash.

"Before you even say it," he told her, "it's *not* because you're a woman. I need you to *stop* thinking that way and *trust* me. For once in your life. You're the ship's only diviner. And you're the

only one who can get close to Pan. You're too important to this mission to throw yourself into danger, and *as your superior officer,* I won't allow it."

Her protests died in her throat, and she stared up at him without a word, entirely dumbfounded. It had never occurred to her that he might be treating her differently out of respect, because she had earned it. Or because he thought she was important.

(It did occur to her that she was still only *attached* to the regiment—Hook had made that perfectly clear—which meant John was not *technically* her superior officer. But this didn't seem like the time to bring it up.)

John stared back at her for a long moment, the two of them perfectly still, but when she said nothing else, he finally turned away.

"Nana," he ordered. "To me."

Nana looked up at Wendy.

"Go on," Wendy told her softly. "It's all right."

Nana moved to John's side. When no one gave her any further orders, she returned to stalking the scent that waited in the jungle.

Nana's nose led them to a subtle break in the foliage, which turned out to be a narrow trail. It looked more like a natural thinning of the undergrowth, formed by animals perhaps, than any path made by the habitual trudging of men. (For that matter, Wendy didn't see why flying creatures would need any sort of trail at all.) Still, there could be no denying that the scent of magic was upon it, and that it headed off in the direction of the western peak.

In the end, they followed it.

John led the way, in case of traps, with Wendy some twenty paces behind him. Nana returned to Wendy's side, and Michael took up the rear of the procession, against the possibility of ambush.

The lush canopy overhead spanned several layers of foliage, but it wasn't so thick as to block out the sky entirely. Judging by the sun, Wendy knew they had been walking about two hours, moving slowly but steadily uphill.

Despite the fact that it wasn't even midmorning, it was already brutally hot. She was grateful she had chosen a linen blouse and jacket for the venture, but with underclothes beneath and the addition of a vest between—not so much for fashion as for propriety—she was beginning to feel lightheaded. And she had already gone through one of her two water bottles, which didn't bode well.

Her enthusiasm for the mission had devolved into the dull but persistent obstinacy of putting one foot in front of the other—which has more to do with all great undertakings than we might care to admit—when Nana's quiet snarl and a signal from John brought her to a halt.

And then, standing perfectly still, she heard it. A growly, gravelly baritone, somewhere off the trail to their left, singing quietly.

We'll catch as we can
A fine little man,
And fry-him-up-here-in-our-pan.
And we eats him!
And we eats him!

He'll squirm on the line;
He'll flash and he'll shine.
By-breakfast-he's-gonna-be-mine.
And we eats him!
And we eats him!

John turned around and placed a finger in front of his lips, as though he thought Wendy might decide to call out to it, whatever it was. Wendy rolled her eyes, then jerked her head toward the singing and raised her eyebrows.

John raised a silent hand, telling her to wait.

Wendy frowned but nodded.

She watched as he moved slowly along the trail, placing each foot cautiously so it wouldn't snap a twig or scuff against a stone. About thirty yards farther on, he stepped off the trail and disappeared.

Of course, Wendy couldn't resist.

She followed the trail to the point where she had last seen him, and Michael moved forward to join her. There, they discovered another trail, leading off to the left. John had obviously decided to investigate.

He was gone for what felt like an excruciatingly long time (but was probably only a minute or two), and Wendy was just about to go in after him when he reappeared around a bend up ahead. He saw them both, shot them a dirty look for not staying where he had left them, and then waved for them to follow nonetheless.

Wendy crept along the trail, relieved to be moving again, but when they reached the end of the little offshoot path, she stopped dead in her tracks and stared. Ahead of them lay a clearing, and in the middle of the clearing was a huge lake, nestled in a natural basin halfway up the mountain.

But even though Wendy was surprised to find a lake halfway up the mountain, and even though she was undeniably grateful for a place to refill her water bottles, neither of those thoughts captured her attention until later. Her *first* thought was for the strange creature squatting at the water's edge.

It was small and gray, with skin that looked like stone. It stood about the height of her knee, but it was dressed like a perfect,

tiny pirate, with a black linen shirt open all the way to its belly and dark blue leggings tucked into tall black boots. (Well, tall for a creature whose head was no more than eighteen inches off the ground.)

It held a fishing net in one hand and wore an eyepatch over one eye, but the patch seemed to be just for show because it was currently shoved up over the creature's left ear—a pointed ear that stuck straight up in the air, while the right one hung forward, folding in the middle.

But the thing that surprised Wendy the most, the thing that made her catch her breath softly and then clap her hand over her mouth, was a tiny red-haired innisfay, writhing and jerking desperately at the end of a delicate silver chain.

CHAPTER 15

Tinker Bell!

Hope soared in Wendy's chest. If Tinker Bell was here, Peter couldn't be far behind. But the little innisfay was clearly in trouble.

"We have to save her," Wendy whispered. "She can help us find Peter!"

"Stop that," the strange creature growled, but he was talking to Tinker Bell. He still had no idea he was being watched. "You love fishing."

The innisfay's hair turned an even angrier shade of red, and she pulled several times against her captor. The thin silver chain stretched to its limit each time, but the tiny silver cuff at the end was clamped firmly around her wrist, and the chain refused to break.

"That was good! Keep going!" The stone thing laughed—an ominous, gravelly sort of laugh that didn't seem possible from anything so small. "I'm sure you can get free if you try hard enough!"

How cruel, Wendy thought. Tinker Bell had not been kind to Wendy, to say the least, but Wendy still hated cruelty in any form.

The innisfay chimed indignantly at the end of the chain.

"That's fine by me," the stone pirate replied. "Don't do me any favors. Don't glow any brighter. It's not as though I'm hungry. Whatever you do, don't attract any fish. I hate catching fish. Miserable thing, breakfast. Nobody likes it."

The innisfay stopped trying to jerk against the chain and her hair shifted from an angry red into a sort of reluctant gold, glowing more brightly by the moment.

"You're a terrible fisherman," the pirate complained. "You'll never catch anything."

Tinker Bell flitted toward the water, but before she could even touch the surface, a fish leaped explosively out of the lake to snap at her. Its scales flashed in the sunlight, reflecting it straight into Wendy's eyes.

"No!" Wendy yelled. "Tinker Bell!" She leaped out of hiding and sprinted for the pirate, hoping she wasn't too late.

"What?" the pirate exclaimed. He turned to see a strange woman sprinting toward him—a woman several times his size—so he did the only natural thing under the circumstances.

He ran.

He had a decent head start over Wendy, and he darted straight for the trees, obviously hoping to lose her in the forest.

"No!" Wendy yelled again. But if he hadn't listened to her the first time, he was hardly about to listen to her now.

Even John and Michael, who were both much faster than Wendy in a full-on sprint, weren't sure they were going to catch up to him before he could duck into the underbrush and disappear. He was surprisingly quick for having such short legs.

Fortunately, Nana was faster still.

She raced past all of them and pounced on the pirate's back, knocking him face first onto the ground. Then she snatched the back of his waistband and a bit of his shirt in her jaws and picked him up, trotting proudly toward Wendy with her prize.

The pirate dangled from her mouth by his clothing, screaming incoherently. He tried as hard as he could to twist around and free himself, but hanging upside down was making things difficult. Besides, Nana had a firm grip. She wasn't about to let go.

All the while, the tiny innisfay trailed behind them in the air. She had not, thankfully, been eaten by the fish, but she hadn't been freed either. She was still attached to the delicate silver chain, which was secured at the other end to a loop at the top of the pirate's right boot.

"Oh, good girl!" Wendy exclaimed. "Good girl, Nana!"

Nana wagged her tail. Chasing pirates had turned out to be even more fun than chasing seashells.

But as Nana drew closer, Wendy finally noticed several things that she had failed to notice at a distance, innisfay being as small as they are.

First, the innisfay was flying by some kind of magic, because she was missing her wings.

Second, she wasn't a "she." This innisfay was distinctly male. His hair was flame red at the moment, and his chiseled jaw was set in an angry scowl.

Which meant that, third, he wasn't Tinker Bell at all.

"Why, who are you?" Wendy exclaimed.

She was clearly speaking to the innisfay, so he drew himself up to his full height and answered her with pride, his hair flashing into gold.

Unfortunately, Wendy couldn't understand a word of it. He spoke in the delicate jingle chimes of the innisfay language, pro-

nouncing his full name in the most beautiful set of runs and trills Wendy thought she had ever heard—and which she had no hope at all of repeating.

"Do you know Peter Pan?" she asked the tiny creature. But whatever he said in reply, she didn't understand that, either.

The knee-high pirate scowled and said nothing.

"At least you know who Peter is," Wendy surmised.

"No, I don't," the pirate barked.

"Then why would you frown when I said his name?"

"I didn't."

"You most certainly did."

"No, I didn't."

Wendy could see this was going nowhere, so she decided to try a different approach.

"And what sort of creature are you, then?"

"I'm a seagull," he said, crossing his arms in defiance, even though he was still dangling from Nana's mouth. "I'm an innisfay. I'm a rabbit. I'm a human, just like you."

"You're clearly not any of those things," Wendy said, frowning.

"I am," he insisted.

Wendy narrowed her eyes and began drumming the fingers of her right hand against her thigh. One-two-three-four. One-two-three-four. One-two-three-four.

"Come now, what are you, really?" she asked.

"I'm really all those things!"

"Are you a goblin?" she tried, and he nodded.

"Yes, that's it. That's the one. I'm a goblin. You guessed it!" He turned his head and smiled at her, but that only made Wendy suspicious.

"Are you an ogre?" she asked.

"Yes," he said, but he didn't sound nearly so happy now. "I'm an ogre. That's right."

Wendy narrowed her eyes even more. "Are you a dragon?" she demanded.

The pirate cast his eyes to the ground. "Yes, I'm a dragon. You guessed it again."

"Wendy?" John asked.

"He's lying, obviously," Wendy said, staring intently at the small creature.

"To say the least," Michael agreed. "I don't think he's said one honest word yet!" And he couldn't help but chuckle.

But that gave Wendy (who was a dedicated student of logic, remember) an interesting idea. She thought back on everything they had overheard him say to the innisfay, and her lips formed into a smile. She cocked her head to one side and addressed the pirate again.

"Is the sky green?"

"Of course the sky is green," he replied quickly. "It's always green."

"What about orange? Right now, I mean. Is the sky orange right now?"

"It is. Clearly orange. Anyone can see that for himself."

"And what color is the sky *not*?" she asked. She pronounced each word slowly, carefully, and the pirate scowled, even more deeply than before.

"It's not blue," he said, and he spat on the ground beneath him, hanging dejectedly from Nana's mouth, looking as miserable as any creature Wendy thought she had ever seen in all her days.

CHAPTER 16

"Oh, you poor thing," Wendy said, her heart going out to the creature at once. "Put him down, Nana."

"No!" John and Michael both exclaimed, but it was already done. Nana opened her mouth, and the creature dropped to the ground, scrambled to his feet, and took off running, with the innisfay trailing behind like a tiny, furious kite.

"Nana, fetch!" John ordered.

Nana didn't have to be asked twice. She tore after him and caught him before he had made it even ten yards. This time, she brought the creature back to John, and she dropped him immediately, which was the whole point of fetching. (Besides which, she had now discovered that letting him go might start the chase up again.)

But John saw it coming, dropped to one knee, and grabbed him before he could run off. He brought both of the creature's small wrists together behind his back, trapping them in one hand, and then grabbed the back of his neck with the other, careful to make sure his own hands were in no danger of being bitten.

"Sorry," Wendy said, sounding genuinely repentant. "He just looked so pathetic."

John looked up at her from the corner of his eye and said nothing. Nana flopped to the ground in a huff, laying her head on her paws, clearly disappointed that the game was already over.

"The sky is not blue," Michael prompted, with a merry twinkle in his eye.

"Right!" Wendy exclaimed. "I think he *only* lies! How peculiar!"

"That's not true!" the pirate protested. "I never lie! Never! Sometimes I even tell the truth!"

"Then tell the truth about this," Wendy suggested. "What kind of creature are you not?"

"I'm not an imp!" he shrieked. "I'm not! I swear it!"

"There! You see? He's an imp!" Wendy declared.

"I don't see how we can be certain of anything," John protested. "What if it only lies sometimes? Or even most of the time? That doesn't mean it lies *all* the time."

"You're right, of course," Wendy agreed. "Still, it's a good working hypothesis. Otherwise, why bother lying about the color of the sky? Something we can all see for ourselves? There's no purpose to it."

"You have a point," John admitted. He wanted to rub one hand under his chin, which was how he did his best thinking, but he had to satisfy himself with a nod and a small frown, since both of his hands were occupied.

"Is Pan on this island, yes or no?" Michael asked it.

"Oh, I'm sure Pan's here somewhere," the imp told them.

"Which could mean either that Pan isn't here, or just that the imp isn't sure whether he is or not," John pointed out.

"Right," Wendy agreed. She eyed the small creature with a thoughtful frown.

"Where is Pan *not*?" suggested Michael.

But the imp just glared back at him.

"I think he doesn't know where Pan is," Wendy mused.

"I do, too! I know exactly where he is!"

"Well, there. He definitely doesn't know, then," Wendy concluded. She was disappointed, to be sure. But Pan still might be somewhere on the island. She was trying to think how she might communicate with the innisfay when John stepped into the silence.

"Are you a member of Blackheart's crew?" John asked.

"What? No! Never!"

"That's a 'yes,'" Michael said. He lifted his left hand and bent his thumb inward, ready to tick various facts off on his fingers as they learned them.

"Is Blackheart here on the island?"

"Yes!" the imp shouted gleefully. "He'll eat you all for breakfast, he will!"

"That's a 'no,'" Michael declared. He bent his index finger as the imp glared up at him, snarling and baring his teeth.

"Well, he must be coming back," John deduced, "if part of his crew is still here. But I doubt he'd leave only one behind. Where are the others?"

"They're right here!" the imp announced, and then he laughed. "Don't you see them?"

"Where is the rest of the crew *not*?" Michael interjected.

"They're not in our hideout, I promise you!" the imp growled, looking more and more agitated.

Michael grinned and bent another finger.

The imp wiggled against John's grip with more desperation, but it didn't do him any good. "I'm not on watch," he blurted out. "I'm not fishing for breakfast, and I'm not supposed to be on duty! I would never disobey the captain's orders! Never!"

He gave up struggling and cast his eyes to the ground, adding quietly, "I didn't steal Jingles out of his cage either, in case anyone asks. Jingles doesn't mind. He loves fishing."

"His cage," Wendy said quietly, and she turned her gaze to the innisfay, but John was already speaking again.

"Where is your hideout *not*?" he demanded, finally getting the hang of it.

"It's not in the mountain," the imp replied glumly. "It doesn't open onto the sea."

John and Michael grinned at each other, and Michael stopped ticking facts off on his fingers. Instead, he asked the imp one more question.

"And what *isn't* the way to get there?"

They couldn't let the imp go, and they certainly didn't trust him to stay tied up. Who knew what strange feats an imp might be capable of? In the end, they gagged him with a stocking and bound his hands behind him with another, letting Nana carry him along. (John hated wet feet and had packed the extra pair of stockings, just in case. He wasn't happy about using them this way—particularly the bit about shoving one into the imp's mouth—but it seemed like the best option.)

As for the innisfay, they couldn't be sure whose side he was on. So they left him bound to the silver chain, deciding not to remove the tiny cuff that trapped his wrist. But they untied the other end from the imp's boot and tied it instead to one of the buckles on Wendy's pack. Then they stuffed him inside the pack to keep him quiet.

(Innisfay are very small, so the pack was large by comparison. He sat upon one of the leather-wrapped bottles, crossed his arms over his chest, and glared at Wendy like a tiny genie as she closed the top flap and secured it.)

He chimed in glorious protest for about a minute and a half, and then fell completely silent all at once. Wendy was concerned enough to open the pack, which only started up the symphony all over again. After that, she left him alone, determined to sort out his situation later.

They found the path to the hideout just where the imp had said it would be (or, rather, just where he had said it *wouldn't* be). It was another trail much like the last, and it wound through the undergrowth, leading slightly downward until it finally opened up onto a rocky ledge.

They were on the western end of the island now, with the ocean directly ahead of them and perhaps twenty yards below. To the right was the jungle. To the left was the base of the rocky spire they had been trying to reach all morning, with a very narrow cave entrance that stood twice as tall as a man—a natural fissure in the ancient stone.

When the imp saw it, he wriggled and writhed even harder, emitting muffled sounds of fresh distress. John ordered Michael, Wendy, and Nana to stay put, then disappeared into the narrow opening before anyone had time to argue. But he reappeared after only a few minutes with eyes the size of saucers, and he waved Wendy and Michael to follow.

Wendy set her pack on the ground, checking to make sure it was buckled down tight, and then turned to Nana, who still held the gagged, struggling imp in her mouth.

"Stay," Wendy ordered.

Then she twisted sideways and slipped through the crack.

The entrance opened out almost immediately, at least to the point where she could walk forward without having to twist. She hesitated a moment, waiting for her eyes to adjust to the dark. Once they did, she saw a scattering of stone rubble strewed along the ground.

She stepped carefully around the loose rock so as not to make any noise, following John farther into the cave, with Michael trailing behind her. Soon they could see a wider ledge with an opening up ahead, and John motioned to them both to wait. He got down on his hands and knees and began crawling, gesturing that they should do the same.

It was a slow and painful process, and Wendy had to stop several times to reposition after putting a hand or a knee down on a sharp stone. But, finally, after what seemed like ages, they all lay side by side, peeking over the lip of the ledge onto Blackheart's hidden lair below.

CHAPTER 17

It seemed to Wendy as though the entire contents of the mountain had exploded into the sea, leaving behind a dark, secret harbor nestled inside the peak. A wide, ragged mouth opened to the west, but the cavern was so deep that the rear wall would have been lost in shadow if it weren't for the lamps that hung along its length, illuminating a dock of rough wooden planks that had been lashed together.

But the thing that drew Wendy's eye immediately—the thing that kept her from noticing anything else at first—was the three-masted ship tied to the dock at the far end.

Her sails were furled and she flew no flags, but she was very much the same size and shape as the French ship that Blackheart had escorted away. Or perhaps, Wendy now suspected, the ship he had *stolen*, as there were no human sailors anywhere to be seen, French or otherwise.

Instead, at least a dozen everlost crewmen paced back and forth along the length and breadth of the deck. Their wings were

ragged and unkempt, and each held a tiny silver chain wrapped around his palm, attached at the other end to an innisfay. Every so often, one of the everlost would snap his wrist, jerking the little fairy and causing a puff of sparkling dust to burst into the air.

Several imps crawled on their hands and knees between the everlost. (They were all dressed like pirates, looking very much like the one Nana had captured, only without the eye patch.) Each had a sturdy glass jar sitting next to him and a small polishing cloth in his hands. Whenever a new innisfay cloud appeared, the closest imp would scramble to it, wet his cloth with liquid from the jar, and scrub at the deck, rubbing the dust carefully into the timbers where it fell.

Another everlost, who seemed to be the foreman, watched over these proceedings with a critical eye. He sat cross-legged on the ship's far railing, his ragged wings fanned out lightly behind him for balance. He had a lean face with a pinched nose and a cruel, angry mouth. His dark eyes observed the others from behind a shaggy veil of dirty-blond hair.

Without warning, his head snapped up and away from the ship. Wendy sucked in her breath, falling as still as the stone that surrounded her. The foreman's eyes scanned the dark recesses of the cavern, searching for something, then narrowed, settling on a spot along the back wall.

Wendy let her breath out slowly and followed his gaze.

The harbor's dock floated upon the water, allowing it to rise and fall with the tides. To keep it from drifting away, it was anchored by ropes to huge rings of iron, embedded low along the cavern's walls. Another line of rings had been set much higher, and from each of these hung a single lamp. It was one of these lamps that had captured the foreman's attention, only, upon closer inspection, Wendy realized that it wasn't a lamp at all.

It was a silver cage, containing a single glowing innisfay. As

Wendy watched, the poor creature collapsed, its light fading away.

"Oh, no, you don't!" the foreman shouted.

He leaped off the railing and flew across the cavern in the blink of an eye. Hovering in the air before the cage, he picked it up by the chain from which it hung and dangled it in front of his face, scowling at the innisfay within.

The poor creature's hair turned a sickly shade of yellowish gray, and it scrambled back to the far wall of the silver prison, huddling in fear.

"Glow!" the everlost shouted. "Now! Or I'll break your neck!" He shook the cage cruelly, slamming the innisfay against the bars.

It was all Wendy could do not to shout in protest.

The innisfay pushed itself up to its knees and then shivered all over, the glow slowly returning.

"That's better," the everlost growled. "No sleeping on the job!"

With one more shake, he released the cage. Then he flew back to the ship and landed behind the wheel, where he opened a small compartment that lay hidden behind the spokes. He pulled something from it that fit easily inside his fist.

Another thimble! Wendy thought.

The everlost flew to the railing, but instead of sitting down, he stood boldly upon it. He set his legs wide, cocked his elbows, planted his fists against his hips, and spread his wings out behind him.

"Let's try it again!" he shouted, and all the everlost cheered, launching themselves into the air with their tiny innisfay in tow.

"One!" the foreman yelled.

"One!" they all echoed.

"Two!"

"Two!" they cheered, and one near the stern placed his fingers to his lips, whistling loudly.

"Three!"

"Three!" they shouted.

Wendy watched as the ship lifted almost a yard out of the water and then suddenly dropped, sending a wave careening outward. It splashed against the cavern's walls, making the dock rock wildly up and down.

"Better!" the foreman called to his crew. "Keep at it, men! We'll have her aloft before the captain gets back!"

"Yo ho!" they all cried.

He laughed and arched his back, bellowing his reply.

"Yo ho!"

They cheered and answered in a chorus of voices, ranging from a high tenor to an impressively deep bass.

"Yo ho!"

"Oh, no," Wendy whispered under her breath.

They sang only one verse, but she knew the words before they even began.

Yo ho! Yo ho!
Where'er you dream to go,
Commanders of both sea and sky,
We'll break the bonds of earth and fly!
Yo ho!

It was the same song Peter and his crew had sung to her, the night she had flown their ship beneath the stars.

The everlost stomped their feet and burst into raucous cheers. Then they scattered across the deck and returned to their work, while Wendy's heart sank to the bottom of the sea.

These were Peter's men, after all.

She hadn't wanted to believe that Peter was behind their sea battle, crippling *The Dragon* and *The Cerberus*, but she still remembered what he had told her back on England's shores.

I have a whole fleet of flying ships!

Even if this wasn't his crew, they were still under his command. Under his orders. What they did, they did for him.

Wendy was furious. After everything she and Peter had been through together. She thought they were *friends*. And then he allowed his men to attack her ship, the very ship he had told her to bring!

(Admittedly, Peter had only told her to come find him. He hadn't told her to bring three British warships and Captain Hook along with her. But how else was she supposed to get to Neverland?)

Still, Wendy held her temper. They would report back to Hook, and they would formulate a plan. A crafty and brilliant plan. One that would put an end to Blackheart's marauding once and for all.

At least, that's what Wendy was *going* to do.

But then the little innisfay drooped in its cage again.

Its light flickered, and the foreman sped across the cavern. He grabbed the cage and shook it furiously.

"Get up!" he shouted. "Get up!"

He was going to kill the poor thing. Wendy's heart went out to the tiny creature, and in that moment she forgot all about her crafty and brilliant plan.

"We have to stop him," she whispered, speaking as much to herself as to anyone. She moved slowly, raising herself to her knees, watching the foreman all the while.

"Wait, what?" Michael whispered back.

"Stand down," John hissed.

But Wendy was already preparing to load a silver bullet into her musket when a hand clamped over her mouth, a rough arm wrapped around her from behind, and a low voice growled in her ear.

"Just what, exactly, do you think you're doing?"

CHAPTER 18

Wendy's eyes flew wide, then narrowed. She didn't have much hope of hurting an everlost without a silver weapon at the ready, but maybe if she could surprise him ...

His arm held her tightly, so she didn't have much room to maneuver, but she jabbed him sharply in the ribs with her left elbow.

"Stop *struggling*, Miss Darling," the voice murmured, "or you will place all our lives in danger, despite my intervention."

It was then that Wendy finally registered three important facts about her situation.

One. The voice had just called her "Miss Darling."

Two. Despite their horrified expressions, John and Michael weren't helping at all.

Three. Even murmuring quietly, the voice that chastised her sounded suspiciously like ...

Wendy clenched her jaw and tried to turn her head, straining her eyes to the left as far as she could. Hook's forget-me-not blue

eyes stared into hers, his eyebrows raised in a clear question: *Will you stop working against me or am I going to have to drag you out of here?*

He was kneeling behind her, using his good left hand to keep her silent and his right arm to hold her in place so she would not give their position away by flailing about in the alcove. He had not grabbed her with his right hand because, of course, he didn't have one, and because he did not want to skewer her on the hook by accident.

Her heart still hammering in her chest, Wendy nodded. (This wasn't easy with Hook's hand covering her mouth and holding her head in place, but it was enough to get the point across.) He released her and took a discreet shuffle backward, glaring at all three of them, then jerked his head back the way they had come, silently ordering them all to follow him out.

They reached the entrance to find Nana waiting for them, right where they had left her, the imp still bound and gagged and dangling from her mouth. A brief inspection of Wendy's bag proved that the innisfay was also still trapped within it, which was a new surprise for Hook, since he had only seen Nana and the imp on the way in.

"We—" Wendy started to explain, but Hook cut her off before she could say another word.

"Not here," he whispered furiously.

They followed the path back to the lake clearing, which gave Wendy more time to think than she might have liked.

What seems natural and right in the heat of anger does not always stand up to the scrutiny of calm reflection, and Wendy kept playing the scene out in her mind, whether she wanted to or not: everything that *would* have happened if she had fired on the foreman as she had intended.

First (and decidedly in the plus column), she probably would

have killed him. Wendy was an excellent shot, and she had the element of surprise on her side, so she felt confident she could have accomplished at least that much.

Second (this next bit required considerably more optimism), she *might* have had time to reload and shoot again. After all, she would have taken the everlost by surprise, and that *might* have given John and Michael time to fire as well.

But her mind could not make it beyond this point with any kind of enthusiasm. By the time Wendy had fired a second shot, the everlost would surely have understood what was happening. Wendy, John, and Michael would have been overwhelmed by sheer numbers, and the everlost would have made quick work of them.

In Wendy's initial fury, she had vaguely imagined the silver-chained innisfay joining the fight. But she realized now, as she trudged along the narrow path, that if the innisfay could perform any kind of magic with a silver cuff around their wrist, they would have freed themselves a long time ago. And, in any event, they were so very small ...

No, her anger had clouded her judgment. If Hook hadn't arrived when he had, she would have gotten them all killed.

She looked up from her thoughts to discover they had reached the lake. Hook led them around to the far side, well away from both the path to the beach and the path to the cove. They hid in the underbrush, and then Hook finally turned to Wendy with a look of dark and utter fury.

"What were you thinking?" he hissed. "You never should have gone into that cave in the first place! It wasn't just dangerous, it was stupid! Always assume the enemy is patrolling every entrance to a stronghold!"

By now, Wendy was as furious with herself as Hook sounded—she saw all too clearly the folly of her own mistakes. Which

meant she was in no mood for anyone *else* to point them out, let alone accuse her of any *other* mistakes she hadn't actually made.

"They did have a guard," Wendy hissed back. "We captured him, which made this the perfect time to investigate the enemy's position!" Her arm snapped out to point at the imp, who hung dejectedly beneath Nana's mouth.

"One guard! How could you possibly be certain there was only one guard on duty for the entire harbor? No, don't tell me. Let me guess. You *asked* him. By all the angels in heaven, the depths of your ignorance will be the death of us all!"

"We did not just *ask* him," Wendy shot back. "We *interrogated* him. It wasn't as though we just took his word for it."

John and Michael, who were crouched in the foliage behind Hook, shared a look that said, *We kind of did, though, since we took the opposite of everything he said at face value. In hindsight, that might have been rash.*

Wendy saw this exchange but chose to ignore it.

"You're *impossible*!" Hook's voice started to rise, but he brought it back under control before continuing, keenly aware of where they were. "You were about to get us all killed!"

This, of course, was the painful truth, but that didn't mean Wendy wanted to talk about it. Especially to Hook, and in front of John and Michael. Fortunately, when one is confronted by a direct and true accusation that one would prefer not to discuss, distraction is an excellent tactic if one happens to have a good one handy. Which, as it happened, Wendy did.

"I was *trying* to keep Pan from getting another flying ship!"

This gave Hook pause. He glared at her for a long moment, his jaw working back and forth, before he finally spoke again. "Explain," he said.

"They're getting that ship ready to fly," Wendy told him. "We all saw it. They haven't done it yet, but they're close."

Hook's eyes darted to John and Michael. Both men flinched at the sudden attention but then nodded in agreement.

"Aye, sir," John added. "They lifted her about a yard out of the water. And the foreman said he wanted it done before the captain returned."

"Did he say when that would be?" Hook asked.

"No, sir," John replied.

Hook turned back to Wendy. "All the more reason to return to the ship and report, Miss Darling. Had you fired on the everlost, there would have been no one left to warn the crew, and no chance of stopping them." His tone, however, was different than before. Firm, but calm.

"Aye, sir," Wendy replied.

He watched her for another long moment and finally nodded, just once. "And what, exactly," he asked her, "did you intend to do with your prisoners?"

"Well, Captain, Peter's blood saved poor Reginald," Wendy reminded him, "as I stated in my very first report, if you remember?"

"How could I forget," he said dryly.

"Unfortunately, we haven't been able to locate Peter himself, but I'm hoping we can use either the imp or the innisfay to save Nicholas by the same means."

"Fine. Bring them," Hook told her. "But we're returning to the ship at once. We'll need *The Tiger* if we are to have any chance of taking that stronghold."

CHAPTER 19

The trek down the mountain was much faster than the one up it, so it was still early in the afternoon when they reached the beach and the hidden boats, of which there were now two. Wendy was so on edge after the day's events that she almost screamed when she noticed something large moving in the trees, but it was only Gentleman Starkey, who had rowed Hook to shore and then stayed behind to guard the vessels.

"No sign of trouble," he reported. "In fact, I haven't seen a soul all day. But I'll still be glad to get back to *The Tiger*, I can tell you that much."

"Well done, Mr. Starkey," Hook replied. "It's just as well you weren't needed, but if you had been, I know you would have protected the boats with your life."

"Oh, aye, sir!" Starkey said with a proud grin.

Hook turned and stared pointedly at John, who had the good sense to look embarrassed. John had always done an excellent job at Dover Castle—training the men, keeping the platoon's accounts,

and making monthly reports to the Home Office—but he had a lot to learn about leading clandestine operations on magical islands.

Fortunately, the boats were safe and sound, so they dragged them to the water and returned as they had arrived, with Hook and Starkey in one vessel and the rest in the other. In no time at all, they were back aboard the ship, and Wendy headed straight for the infirmary, where she found Thomas leafing halfheartedly through a medical journal. He leaped to his feet as soon as he saw her.

"Any luck?" he asked. His eyes brimmed with hope, and he bounced lightly on the balls of his feet, running one hand absently through his hair.

Wendy tilted her head in surprise. "But ... how did you ..."

"You didn't come to the infirmary this morning, and I knew you would never abandon Nicholas. So you had to be working on a solution of some ... oh! What's this, then?"

Nana stepped through the door behind Wendy, the imp still dangling from her mouth, and Wendy shut the door firmly behind them.

"It's an imp," Wendy said. "Or, it seems to be. We need something to keep it in. A cage of some kind. It doesn't need to be silver. Or, at least, I don't think it does. Any cage should do. Nana hasn't had any trouble holding onto him."

"Silver?" Thomas asked. "Why would a cage need to be silver?"

"Sorry, never mind that for now. We need to secure him first. Then, I'll explain everything."

Thomas left the infirmary at a fast clip and returned with a brass cage that was just the right size. He lashed it to one of the many iron rings along the bulkhead, and then Wendy installed the imp within it, removing his gag and bindings and locking the cage door behind him.

"Well, that was just lovely, I can tell you," the imp complained. "A wonderful way to treat a new friend. You nearly killed me!"

"Meaning you were never in any real danger at all," Wendy commented.

"How extraordinary!" Thomas squatted down to peer at the imp through the bars of the cage.

"Oh, I *like* you," said the imp. "*Very* much."

"Goodness! Then I like you, too!" Thomas exclaimed, pivoting on the balls of his feet to look up at Wendy. "Are you sure he—"

"Has to be in the cage? Yes, I'm quite sure. He lies. And I don't mean he sometimes lies, or that he lies for convenience. I mean he *always* lies. I think he can't help it."

"Oh," said Thomas, looking disappointed. "So he doesn't—"

"No," Wendy assured him. "He doesn't."

"Ah," said Thomas. "But you think he can help?"

"I don't know yet," Wendy admitted.

"I'll help you! I'd *love* to help you! Just tell me what you need, and I'll gladly do it!"

"He certainly *sounds* helpful," Thomas said, staring at the small creature intently.

"Just assume the opposite of everything he says," Wendy told him.

"Right. That seems confusing." Thomas ran his hand through his hair again without standing up, bouncing a bit to maintain his balance.

"It can be."

"She's lying," the imp said, but Wendy just rolled her eyes.

"Can your blood heal human beings?" Wendy asked him.

"It can!" the imp exclaimed. "Definitely!"

"So it can't, then?" Thomas asked.

"No, it can't. It might even hurt him. We'd have to ask more questions to know for sure, but there's a better way." She looked the imp straight in the eye. "You see our friend in that bed there? What *won't* heal him?"

"The blood of the winged men," the imp replied, snarling.

"Everlost blood," Wendy snapped in frustration. "I already knew that."

"Good for you. Then you know everything I do," the imp said.

"That's unfortunate," Thomas commented, but Wendy was already holding up one hand.

"No, that means I *don't* know everything he does. What *else* won't heal him?"

The imp said nothing.

"What do you do if he won't answer?" Thomas asked.

"I think that means he doesn't *have* an answer," Wendy said slowly. "At least, that's been my hypothesis."

"I have plenty of answers," the imp objected.

"Not everlost blood," Wendy muttered under her breath. "There's something I still don't know, but he has no other answers."

"Actually, he never said 'everlost,'" Thomas pointed out.

"What?"

"He didn't say 'everlost blood.' He said, 'the blood of the winged men.' So whatever you don't know has to be part of that specific answer. Assuming your premise, I mean."

Wendy stared at him for a moment, saying nothing, but then her face lit up like the sun itself.

"Of course!" she exclaimed. "Winged men who aren't the everlost! Just as I was hoping!"

"What?" Thomas asked, but Wendy had already turned back to the imp.

"Will the blood of an *innisfay* heal him?"

"No," the imp said glumly, and he sat down with a sigh, looking positively sullen. "No, it won't."

CHAPTER 20

So the blood of an innisfay *would* heal Nicholas. Wendy was thrilled beyond measure until Thomas asked, innocently enough, "What's an innisfay?"

"Why, I'll show you!" she crowed. She leaped for her pack and opened it with a flourish, only to find herself staring down at the angriest creature she had ever seen.

"Oh, dear," she muttered.

"Is something wrong?" Thomas asked. He had turned toward her, waiting to see what an innisfay was, but he was still crouched in front of the imp and couldn't see into the pack.

Well, you can imagine how horrible Wendy felt when she realized her only hope of saving Nicholas had been chained at the wrist, stuffed in her pack, and carted off to a ship like the victim of a kidnapping—which was the same thing Blackheart's pirates had done to him, come to think of it—but that was nothing compared to the innisfay's feelings on the subject. Very few creatures

are inclined to help those who chain them up and stuff them into sacks, and the innisfay are no exception.

When Wendy opened her pack to discover the tiny, wingless innisfay with his arms crossed over his chest, a terrible scowl on his face, and the reddest hair Wendy thought she had ever seen, she realized immediately what she had done. Her heart crumbled into pieces and fell into her stomach, filling the hollow of her belly like a pile of rocks and making her want to throw up.

She wondered whether there was any hope at all of persuading him to help, and it occurred to her then, in that dark and terrible moment, that she might just grab him, prick him with a needle, save Nicholas, and sort the rest out later. But Wendy, as we already know, hated cruelty in any form. To do such a thing would have been expedient but heartless—just the sort of thing Hook would have done—and she was mortified that she had even thought of it.

No. She would set the possibility aside until she felt it was Nicholas' last and only hope, and even then she wasn't sure she would do it. She wasn't sure she *wanted* to know whether she would do it.

She had to find a better way.

All of this happened in the space of a few moments, so Wendy stepped away from the pack and left it open, silently inviting the innisfay to explore a little—at least as far as the silver chain would allow—while giving herself time to think of something, *anything* she might do that could possibly make things right.

The innisfay, surprised to be left alone, stood cautiously, and then, when nothing happened, he floated slowly to the top of the pack so he could peek over the edge.

"Why, they get smaller and smaller," Thomas commented in wonder. He rose to his feet for a better view, but he made no move toward the creature, content to watch, at least for now.

The innisfay shied away and ducked back into the bag, but when he saw he was still being left alone, he reemerged and floated up above the pack, looking around, the delicate chain trailing gracefully from his wrist.

"Extraordinary!" Thomas exclaimed again, and Wendy turned back from the infirmary cabinet to see the innisfay's hair changing color slowly (almost reluctantly) from flame red to a shimmering, pearlescent silver.

Wendy couldn't help but see this as progress, no matter how faint.

"Are you thirsty?" Wendy asked him. She spoke in a quiet, soothing tone, and she placed a cup she had retrieved from the cabinet on the desk next to her bag. "I'd like to reach into the bag, to get you some water, but I don't want to scare you. Is that all right? I promise not to hurt you."

The innisfay's hair turned bright red again, and he chimed at her angrily.

"I'm afraid I don't understand you," Wendy told him, "but I can see that you're angry. You have every right to be, of course, and I'm very sorry for mistreating you. We didn't know until we found Blackheart's cove that he was holding the innisfay as prisoners. We intend to save them, now that we know."

The innisfay crossed his arms over his chest in midair, and he stuck out his lower lip to blow a lock of hair away from his eyes. This simple action put a few strands of gold into his red hair, at least for a moment.

Like most innisfay, he was proud of his appearance—or he wanted to be. But this particular innisfay, having lost his wings, was the subject of frequent ridicule by the others. Remembering his loss all over again, his hair turned from red to blue. This made him angry, which only made his hair turn red all over again.

"Red, then gold, then red, then blue, then red," Wendy said out loud. "You must be very angry, to keep returning to it like that."

The innisfay eyed her coldly but made no attempt to chime at her.

"I know what it's like, you know. To feel angry all the time. That young man lying over there," and Wendy pointed toward Nicholas as she spoke, "was shot because of me. He jumped in front of me to save my life. I should have seen what was about to happen. I should have stopped him. But I didn't. And now he might die because of it. I've been angry at myself every moment of every day since, and I don't know any way to fix it except to save him."

Her voice broke as she said this last bit. She had to stop speaking to wipe away a tear—more than one, actually—and she found she couldn't speak at all for several moments. Thomas took a step toward her and placed a tentative hand on her shoulder, unsure what else to do.

Now, this innisfay, whose true name you wouldn't understand even if I could tell you what it was, had been stashed in Wendy's pack; that much is true. But he had been listening carefully to everything the humans had said ever since.

He knew Wendy considered Blackheart an enemy, and he knew she intended to attack his harbor. He hoped that meant she would free the rest of the innisfay, but he couldn't be sure she would.

He had also surmised that most of the men who knew her were somewhat enamored of her, but he didn't think that counted for much. She was the only woman on the entire ship, as far as he could tell. It was only natural that they would be interested in her. That didn't mean she was a good person. (It didn't mean she was

all that pretty either, he decided. He was *much* prettier than she was.)

And the captain didn't seem to like her at all.

On the other hand, she had cried out in distress when she thought he had been eaten by a fish, so she clearly had some sympathy for his kind. And it might be nice to live among these wingless people, at least for a while, where he would be the best looking one by far.

That is, assuming they could be trusted.

Narrowing his eyes, his hair still red, he held out his wrist—the one encircled by the silver cuff that bound him—and he shook it at her.

Wendy knew that if she released him he could turn into anything and slip away, and that they would risk losing him entirely if someone opened the door. If that happened, there would be no more chance of grabbing him and pricking him with a needle, and she hadn't realized until that very moment that she was still considering it, for Nicholas' sake.

It was no wonder the innisfay didn't trust her.

"All right," she said quietly. "Just a moment."

She found a tiny pair of shears in the cabinet, and she held out her other hand to him. He winced a little, but he let her take hold of the tiny silver cuff, and then she used the shears to snap it carefully away.

She thought she had never been more frightened in all her life.

The innisfay watched her for a long moment, hovering in mid-air, then darted away.

Wendy sucked in her breath, but he had only flown to Nicholas, alighting on his pillow. He nodded to her and gestured toward the boy.

"Oh!" Wendy cried. She ran back to the cabinet and brought

him a needle, which she placed carefully next to him so she wouldn't hurt him by accident.

The innisfay squatted down next to it, holding it steady with one hand while he carefully pricked his other palm. Then he flew up over Nicholas, whose mouth was half open in a feverish stupor, and the innisfay squeezed his hand, letting just two drops of blood fall into the boy's mouth.

He flitted away again, but that was all it took. In the mere shake of a lamb's tail, Nicholas' color returned to normal, his cracked and feverish lips took on a healthy glow, and the boy opened his eyes.

"What happened?" he asked, when he saw Wendy crying. Even Thomas was wiping his eyes with the heel of his hand.

"Oh, Nicholas! The most wonderful thing!" Wendy exclaimed. "A *miraculous* thing! By the most marvelous person anyone could ever hope to meet!"

The innisfay only smiled, but his hair shimmered all the way into gold.

CHAPTER 21

Hook frowned over the map spread out on his captain's table. The sketch was rough at best, depicting the basic outline of the island, with one mark for the spot on the northern shore where the trail led off into the jungle, and another for the cove to the west.

Charlie, as his first mate, stood dutifully by his side, awaiting his orders.

"We can't afford to wait another day," Hook growled. "We need to attack before Blackheart returns."

"Aye, sir," Charlie agreed. Neither of them said it out loud, but they had already seen the damage a flying ship could do against one that merely floated upon the sea. They had no chance of taking the cove if Blackheart's ship was hovering above it.

"But it would be best to attack at sunset, which doesn't give us much time."

"Aye," Charlie agreed again.

"And why will we attack at sunset?"

Hook turned his head to address the question toward Nicholas, who had insisted on returning to his duties immediately. The boy had stopped only long enough to thank the innisfay, to gawk momentarily at the imp, and to stuff his belly as quickly as possible because he had woken up ravenous.

"Because the cove's to the west, sir. The sun will be at our backs, shining into the cave so we can see it. And they'll have a hard time looking at us directly because the sun will be in their eyes."

"And why not just wait for cover of darkness?"

"Because we circled the whole island and saw no lights, which means they're smart enough to douse their lanterns at night. Even by moonlight, they'd still have the advantage."

"Very good," Hook told him. "We'll make a captain out of you yet."

"Aye, sir! Thank you, sir!"

Nicholas beamed with pride, and Hook went so far as to wink at him before turning back to Charlie, which showed Nicholas just how glad his captain was to have him back. Captain James Hook never winked at anyone. Ever.

"We'll stay in the edge of the fog for cover until *The Tiger* is in position," Hook continued, "but I want a diversion on land. Our lost platoon can take the trail to the back entrance. Blackheart's men will be missing their guard by now and will have posted another one. The platoon will sneak up on him, then signal us by lantern when they're in position. Hopefully by sunset.

"Their mission is to cause as much of a distraction as possible, to give us time to sail within range before we're spotted. But if they don't leave soon, they won't arrive in time. Especially with that march up the trail. Go give them their orders. Make sure they're armed with silver, both ammunition and blades. But tell

the quartermaster I want full records of all of it, down to the man. I want every blade back and every bullet accounted for."

"Aye, sir," Nicholas acknowledged. "Sorry, who am I telling, sir? Our lost platoon?"

"Miss Darling's platoon," Hook told him, his eyes still glued to the map.

"Aye, sir." But before the boy could race off, Charlie cleared his throat.

"What is it, Mr. Hawke?" Hook snapped. "Speak up. We're burning daylight."

"Did you mean for him to inform Miss Darling, sir? Or Mr. Abbot?"

Hook scowled, then turned to Nicholas. "Inform Mr. Abbot of his orders at once."

"Aye, sir," Nicholas repeated, and he left in a hurry, shutting the door behind him.

"As for *The Tiger*," Hook continued, "I don't want to fire her cannons if we can help it. I want that flying ship in one piece. We'll sail *The Tiger* close enough for muskets. But what I said for Mr. Abbot's platoon goes for everyone. I want a complete accounting down to the last bullet, collecting all the unspent ammunition when we're done. And I want as many of the spent ones back as we can get. There's only so much silver to go around."

"Aye, sir," Charlie said with a sharp nod. If Hook put a slight emphasis on Mr. Abbot's name—implying that it was John's platoon and not Wendy's—Charlie pretended not to notice. "But, sir, if the ship can't fly yet?"

"Pray that she can't, Mr. Hawke. We'll use the innisfay and the imp we've already captured to complete the job. But, now that you mention it, tell the platoon to capture as many more of them as they can. Imps and innisfay both. We'll use them to our advantage. Perhaps even *The Tiger* might earn her wings."

"Aye, sir. And if she's already flying, sir?"

"Then we have to keep her in that cove under a roof of rock at any cost. If she's flying and they try to bring her out into the open, we'll have no choice but to destroy her, or she'll sink us all."

"Aye, sir."

Charlie left to convey his captain's orders, and Hook stood staring down at the map, brooding.

By following Wendy, he had hoped to find Peter Pan. Killing Pan was the only way to be free of that menace once and for all. He didn't like it that Pan was still out there somewhere, and that they still had no idea where.

Was he with Blackheart? Or were Pan and Blackheart one and the same? He certainly wouldn't put it past Pan to pretend to be someone else.

For that matter, maybe Blackheart was his real name, and he was only pretending to be Pan.

Hook growled and slammed his hook into the table next to the map.

He had to get that flying ship.

It was the only thing that could even the odds against the everlost—and give humanity a fighting chance in this Godforsaken war.

CHAPTER 22

Before she knew it, Wendy was hiking up the jungle path for the second time that day. She had spent so much of her life wishing for adventures that a part of her was thrilled at the idea of it. She, Wendy Darling, was about to engage in a secret mission halfway around the world, to capture a flying ship from magical creatures!

It was more than she had ever dreamed possible. But still, there was a difference between the *dream* of the adventure and the adventure itself.

In the weeks since she had left England's shores, she had seen British ships riddled by cannon fire and almost sunk. She had seen good men die in battle. She had been shot at by Smee, and she had almost lost Nicholas because of it. And just this morning she had become so angry over the mistreatment of a single innisfay that she had almost died again, risking John and Michael's lives in the process.

There was only so much she could go through before questioning the wisdom of the entire enterprise.

As a matter of fact, she had a bad feeling about this particular mission—a very bad feeling indeed. If it had been up to her, she might have called the whole thing off. But, of course, it was not up to her. So she trudged dutifully amidst the men of her platoon, her head snapping toward the rustling leaves of the jungle and the small creatures that leaped and called through the trees, expecting every time to see the shining barrel of an everlost gun trained on her heart.

The sickening tingle in the pit of her stomach only worsened with every step, but she focused on her breath and forced her feet to move forward nonetheless—breathe in, breathe out, in, out—until her mind began to quiet. This was the life of adventure she had asked for, and the men needed her.

She would not let them down.

Her legs ached at the pace they were forced to keep, racing against the setting sun, but it seemed like almost no time at all before they were back at the lake. There was no sentry in sight, so they proceeded to the next path. Their feet moved quietly through the tall grass of the clearing, each man (and, of course, one woman) carrying a weapon at the ready.

When they reached the rear entrance of the cave, there was still no sign of a new guard having been posted. The platoon formed up, ready to slip through the crack single file on John's command, but Wendy couldn't help sharing her misgivings.

"We should wait and look for the guard," she whispered. "What if he comes in behind us?"

John frowned and jerked his chin behind him, where the sun hovered low over the sea's horizon. *The Tiger* waited somewhere in the fog to the west of the cove's entrance, watching for the platoon's signal.

"We're out of time," he told her. "Judging by this morning's encounter, their sentries don't take their duties seriously. It's a fortune in our favor. Don't question it."

John nodded to Michael, who raised a lantern high in the air and waved it slowly back and forth several times. He waited a long moment and then repeated the signal. Then John raised his arm and snapped it smartly toward the cave. Without a moment's hesitation, the first man crept through.

They had learned from the imp that a narrow path led down into the cove from the far side of the ledge, hidden from view behind a small outcropping of rock. (Or rather, they had learned from the imp that this was emphatically *not* how he had been sneaking in and out of the cove unseen.) Wendy didn't even realize she was holding her breath until she saw Michael disappear. When several seconds ticked by without any sign of trouble, she finally exhaled quietly.

The plan John had laid out involved splitting the platoon into two groups. One, led by Michael, would follow the hidden path down into the cove itself, ready to attack from below. The other, led by John, would crawl on their bellies to the edge of the upper ledge and prepare to fire on the everlost from above. They would not be able to see each other, so the signal was simple. Michael's team would fire a volley to begin the assault.

John moved into place first, and Wendy followed. She crawled as far as she could without being seen and then dropped to her belly, her legs and abdomen pressing uncomfortably against the uneven floor of the rock. Three men came in behind them, including poor Reginald, who settled himself to her left. Wendy wanted terribly to peek her head over the edge, but she didn't dare for fear she would give away their presence before Michael and the others were ready. Instead, she prepared her musket and held her position.

The waiting was terrible. It seemed to last forever, as though the entire world was holding its breath, and then everything happened at once. The crack of gunfire exploded from below, echoing painfully off the walls of the cove. The everlost shouted in alarm. And then something roared—a voice that started out so deep it reverberated through her chest, rising into an enraged wail like nothing she had ever heard before.

She thrust herself forward the last two feet until she could finally see over the lip of the rock ledge. Whatever that thing was, it definitely had not been there before. It stood some ten to twelve feet high, a massive beast shaped roughly like a man but with pale green skin, a bulging forehead, and no hair worth mentioning. Its chest was bare, as were its feet, and it wore only a rough leather kilt around its waist. For a long moment she could hardly move, staring at it in horror.

But then it started lumbering toward the sound of the gunfire below, and it looked extremely angry.

Wendy had no idea what it was, but she assumed its heart lay buried beneath its ribs, like every other creature she knew. She raised her musket, sighted down the barrel, and shot it in the chest with a silver bullet.

The beast screamed in agony and fell to its knees. At first she thought she had fired the luckiest shot in the world, but then she realized the truth. The terrible roar, combined with the basic shock of it, had drawn *all* their fire—every single shot. And now the everlost understood what was happening and knew where they were.

All of them.

She started to reload, but she could see in an instant that there wasn't time. The everlost crew spread their wings and launched themselves into the air, coming for them—both Michael's team below and John's above.

Heading the charge for the upper alcove was the foreman she had seen that morning, the one who had shaken the little innisfay in its cage. He locked eyes with her and registered a brief moment of surprise, but then he bared his teeth in a cruel grin.

Wendy barely had time to abandon her musket. She scrambled to her feet and drew her silver dagger from her belt, and then he landed on the ledge in front of her, flashing a calculating sneer beneath cold, dark eyes.

CHAPTER 23

John wasted no time. He plunged his own dagger into the foreman's side before the creature could fully draw his sword. The everlost laughed, but when he twisted toward John, the laughter became a hiss and a sudden grimace of pain. His eyes widened and he looked down at his side, where the wound was still bleeding.

Wendy had almost expected him to disappear, remembering the body of the everlost Hook had shot, but the foreman was only injured, not dead. He spread his wings and leaped backward, hovering away from the ledge, out of reach.

"Silver!" he roared, and the closest of his brethren took up the shout at once, echoing it throughout the cavern.

"Silver! Silver!"

Then he snarled, thrust his sword before him, and hurled himself at John. Wendy's heart leaped into her throat, but she couldn't afford to watch. She had her own problems.

Two more everlost had flown up from the ship behind the foreman, and now they drew their own swords. One landed to take on the two men from the platoon who were farthest to the left. The other came for Wendy and poor Reginald.

Wendy backed up, drawing the everlost farther into the alcove. She needed room to fight—room to take full advantage of the fact that she and Reginald could work as a team, two against one.

It was the only thing that could even the odds.

"Flank him," she said. Her eyes never left the everlost before her, but Reginald understood and circled toward his other side.

Wendy continued to back up, leading the everlost as far as she could from the others. She stepped to the right, giving Reginald the left. They held their silver blades out before them. The everlost—a bit shorter than the rest, thin and wiry—spat on the cavern floor.

"Since when did the Royal Navy start playing with dolls?"

Wendy said nothing, refusing to be distracted, but then a flash of intensity crossed Reginald's face. He was about to lunge.

Wendy flexed her knees and raised the tip of her blade, holding the everlost's attention. "What makes you think I'm playing?"

She feinted to the right, trying to draw his guard away from Reginald, but the creature was too fast. He realized the ruse just in time, spinning to knock Reginald's blade away. Before he could retaliate, Wendy attacked again. The everlost spun once more, and their blades caught at the hilt.

He snarled and tried to push her away, but Wendy held her ground. She flowed with his movement, dodging to the left and sliding her blade away. She plunged it toward him again, but he fell back howling before she could connect.

The everlost gripped his side where Reginald had wounded him. Enraged, he turned again, pulling his sword back and preparing to thrust it straight through Reginald's chest.

In the blink of an eye, Wendy stepped forward and swept his leg out from under him, knocking him off balance. Instead of skewering Reginald's chest, the everlost fell right in front of him.

Reginald raised his dagger and plunged it deep into the base of the creature's neck, just behind his collarbone, where his neck met his shoulder.

The creature's eyes flew wide. He dropped his sword and grabbed at his neck with a strange gurgling sound. Then he fell to his knees, toppled forward onto his face on the cold, hard stone, and slowly vanished. His body dissipated before their eyes into a thousand sparks of light that rose as a mass, hovered for a moment in the air, and then winked out, one by one—like smoldering ashes rising from a fire, only to extinguish themselves in the night.

Wendy looked up to find Reginald staring back at her in wonder, but there was no time for amazement. Shouts rang out throughout the cavern.

"Help the lieutenant," Wendy told Reginald. "The same as we did. Flank him. Work together."

Reginald nodded and ran back to the ledge. That left four men fighting two everlost in the alcove, but most of the crew had remained below, attacking Michael, where Wendy couldn't see what was happening.

She didn't like leaving John, but he had the help he needed now. And from what she could hear, things didn't sound good for Michael and his men. She glanced wistfully at her musket, which still lay at the forward edge of the rock, but the everlost fought to each side of it. Her pistols and her dagger would have to do.

She raced to the far boulder and peeked around it. Sure enough, there was the path Michael and the others had followed.

In truth, it was little more than a ledge—a cramped shelf of rock along the wall that descended steeply toward the floor. It was manageable, if only just. There were stone walls to either side, almost like a tunnel, so she pressed her hands against them for stability. Then she stepped onto the narrow path and began making her way down. The right-hand wall protected her from

view until she was close to the ground, when the entire cavern suddenly opened up.

Michael and the others were in trouble.

It seemed like forever since she had stood on the lawn at Dover Castle, watching Peter and his men fall upon them from the sky, but seeing them fighting again here brought it all back in a rush—their rough, swashbuckling style, and the way they used their wings to dart in and out from above. The ceiling of the alcove overhead had been an advantage in Wendy's favor. Here, the everlost were free to fly, and it was all Michael and the others could do to hold on.

He had organized them in a wide arc with their backs to the wall, protecting each other's flanks. It would have been a defensible position, despite the flying, if the men had been able to use their swords, but the silver daggers limited their reach. The everlost were only toying with them now, and the men were already tiring.

Wendy had just drawn her pistol when a shot rang out and a bullet slammed into the rock right next to her, missing her by mere inches. She snapped her head toward the ship to see an imp on deck holding a pistol of his own, with more of the small creatures emerging through the hatch behind him. They must have hidden at the first sign of trouble, Wendy realized, only to emerge when they thought it was safe to help.

She was loading her weapon when another shot echoed though the cavern, this one coming from the sea. The imp that had been standing on deck screamed and then fell out of view behind the ship's railing.

The Tiger had arrived.

With another resounding crack from the ship, and another after that, two of the everlost fell and disappeared, which evened the odds considerably. The imps scrambled back belowdeck, having

decided things weren't nearly as safe as they had believed, leaving only a handful of everlost to contend with.

Wendy felt an overwhelming surge of relief to see that the tide had turned in their favor, with all of her platoon still standing. But then the imp that had been shot staggered to its feet, sighting down the barrel of its pistol. *The Tiger* was only a few yards beyond the mouth of the cove, just to Wendy's right, giving her a clear view of the deck. But she had no way to stop the imp from firing.

She had no way to warn Hook, nor did she have any way to stop Nicholas, who saw the danger at the exact same time. And despite everything he had just been through, despite knowing exactly what it felt like to be shot, and exactly what it could cost him, Nicholas leaped in front of his captain just as the imp fired.

So she could do nothing to stop the look of pain that spread across his face, and she could do nothing to prevent him from toppling over the rail into the sea.

CHAPTER 24

Nicholas!" The scream tore unbidden from Wendy's throat, and she dove into the water without a thought, boots and all. She shoved her dagger into her belt so she could swim more easily, and then she stroked hard and sure, heading for the spot where she had seen him go in.

At the same time, Hook vaulted the ship's railing. He dove beneath the surface of the sea, but he came up moments later, empty-handed.

"Nicholas!" Wendy screamed again, but there was no sign of the boy. Hook sucked a huge breath into his lungs and dove once more.

Wendy stopped to tread water, but she wasn't waiting on Hook. She was watching the current. She seemed to be drifting to the right, which meant Nicholas was drifting in the same direction. She took three more strokes, making the best guess she could, and then she flipped head down and dove.

The boy's body would be weighed down by his clothing, his boots, and any ammunition he had been carrying. He would be sinking fast. So she swam down ... down ... as hard as she could, ignoring the fact that she was moving farther and farther from the surface. The water was relatively clear, but the sun was setting. The light was getting dim. And the cove was deep. She couldn't see anything. No coral, no fish. She had no idea how far the bottom was, but she already knew it was deeper than she could go.

Her lungs were starting to ache when she saw it. A hint of hair, flowing freely in the sea. Just as she had once imagined Peter's—just like the hair of the everlost Hook had killed, before his body disappeared. Wendy started to exhale, only the smallest bit at a time, trying to relieve the pain in her chest, and she kept swimming down.

Down.

Until she had him.

Her fingers snagged his hair first, then reached for his chin, his shoulder, his arm. She grabbed him and started pulling for the surface, but she had already come too far. She wouldn't make it. She knew she wouldn't make it. She saw the surface, and she had never wanted to reach anything so badly in all her life. But her lungs were screaming and tiny black spots were beginning to appear in the corners of her vision.

A part of her had started to accept it. She and Nicholas were both going to drown beneath the waves. Not every adventure has a happy ending, after all. But it wasn't in her nature to give up. So she swam for the surface anyway. She swam until her body finally betrayed her. And the last thing she saw in this life, besides the faint light at the surface of the sea, was a man diving toward her.

A man with forget-me-not blue eyes.

"Miss Darling!"

The words drifted toward her from someplace very far away. She tried to make sense of them. Who was calling her?

"Miss Darling! Wake up! That's an order!"

She wanted to answer, but there was a terrible pressure in her lungs. She tried to breathe in, then came half-awake into a panic when she couldn't, and finally coughed what felt like a bucketful of water out of her lungs.

"There. She's back. She'll be all right now, I think." A different voice.

She was going to pass out again. She tried to fight it, the panic returning, but then she finally understood where she was. She felt the deck of the ship beneath her, and never had anything so uncomfortable felt so welcome in all her days. She was right where she was supposed to be. It was her last thought before she slipped once again into the dark.

"Excellent! You're coming around. That's excellent."

Wendy groaned and opened her eyes to find Thomas smiling down at her. Her lungs burned, making her cough, and all at once her memories came slamming back, filling her heart with dread.

"Nicholas!" She tried to say the boy's name, but it came out as more of a croak and started a new round of coughing.

"Just breathe, Miss Darling. Don't try to talk yet."

But she sat up immediately nonetheless. She was in the infirmary, just as she had expected, and Nicholas was there on the other cot. She managed with considerable effort to stand up, pushing away Thomas' attempts to assist her, and she stumbled over to the boy.

It was much worse than she had realized. He was unconscious and barely breathing, his lungs rattling with every inhalation.

"Where's the innisfay?" Wendy managed to ask.

"Oh! Oh, of course! He's in the cabinet. There."

Thomas pointed toward a cabinet that Wendy now noticed was missing a door. In its place, a linen shirt hung across the opening on a small length of rope. Wendy rushed to it.

"Hello? Sir? Oh, please wake up! We need you! Please!"

She was so distressed that she was about to dispose of all decorum and just thrust the shirt-curtain aside when she saw the bottom corner move a little, and then the innisfay's tiny head peeked out around it.

"Thank you, sir. I'm so sorry to trouble you. But I'm afraid we need you desperately. Nicholas has been shot again."

At this, the innisfay raised both eyebrows, and then he frowned. But he flew out of the cabinet to take a look, his hair the pearlescent silver of curiosity.

Wendy watched as the innisfay approached the boy. He hovered above his chest, clearly listening to the sounds of his breathing, and then he motioned at the blanket that covered him.

"Of course!" Wendy said immediately, and she rushed to turn down the cover so the innisfay could see the wound.

He flew closer, and then closer still, until he hovered just above the bandaged wound itself. He frowned again, and then he lifted his nose and sniffed delicately at the air.

Instantly, his hair flamed red with anger, slowly shifting into

blue as he turned to Wendy, shaking his head in sorrow.

"What is it?" Wendy demanded, wringing her hands together. "What's wrong? You healed him before. I know you can do it!"

But the innisfay only shook his head again. He jingled at her, but of course Wendy still couldn't understand a word of the innisfay language. Realizing that he wasn't getting anywhere, the innisfay flew to the small desk and lifted the silver chain that Wendy had cut away only hours before.

"You're angry? I'm so sorry about that. I didn't—"

The innisfay only shook his head harder. He wasn't angry. It was something else. Turning an even deeper shade of blue, he flew with the chain over to Nicholas and held it over the boy, gesturing over and over. First to the chain, and then to Nicholas.

"What? Oh, what is it? I don't—"

The innisfay stopped her by holding up a tiny hand, and then he pantomimed a little scene. He held out an empty hand in the air, pointing it toward Nicholas. He cocked his thumb, an invisible weapon, and pretended to fire it at the boy. Then he held his own thumb between his fingers and rushed toward Nicholas, coming so close to the wound that he almost touched the bandage.

The innisfay flew to Wendy with the silver chain in his hand, pointing first to his thumb, then to the chain, and then to the boy.

"The bullet," Wendy guessed out loud. "Something to do with the bullet he was shot with."

The innisfay nodded dramatically. He held up the chain and rattled it back and forth.

"Silver," Wendy realized. "He was shot by a silver bullet, and you're saying you can't heal the wound—no more than you could heal a silver wound on your own person."

The innisfay nodded sadly.

"Would you try anyway?" Wendy whispered. "Please?"

The innisfay held her gaze for a long moment. Then he shrugged just the tiniest bit, and he nodded. But he was still a terribly sad shade of blue.

"Thank you," Wendy told him, but if there was any hope left in her eyes, you wouldn't have seen it. She moved to retrieve the needle, moving much more slowly now, and she placed it on Nicholas' pillow, opening the boy's mouth for the innisfay.

The tiny man pricked his palm, just as he had before, and he let two drops of blood fall into the boy's mouth.

Wendy and Thomas and the innisfay all watched as the seconds ticked by, but nothing changed. Nicholas did not wake up, and he still struggled for breath, his lungs wheezing and rattling.

Until, finally, they gave up altogether, and he exhaled for the last time. The soul that had been Nicholas departed his body, and Wendy was left with only her grief. And her memories.

CHAPTER 25

It is never easy to lose the people we care for in this world, but it is especially difficult to lose the ones for whom we feel responsible. Even though Nicholas was a full member of the crew, he was still young, and Wendy had always felt a sisterly kind of affection for him. Then he had risked his life for her, and she had saved his in return. To lose him now, after everything they had been through, felt like more than she could bear.

And so, for the first time in her life, all her defenses failed her.

She had spent years in the orphanage acting as though the taunts of the other children didn't bother her, and she had built that image up into a persona that she wrapped carefully around herself—always calm, always patient, always rational. She thought through every problem; she overcame every obstacle. But she could not overcome this.

Looking down at Nicholas, she wanted to scream. She wanted to pull glass vials from the infirmary cabinet and smash them

against the walls. She wanted to beat her own fists against the iron frame of the cot until they were black and blue and broken beyond repair. And if Thomas had not been there, she might have done all of those things.

But Thomas was there, and if she cried out in despair or lost her temper, all her hard work would come to nothing. She would just be an irrational woman, reinforcing everything Thomas had ever been taught about her gender. Still, Wendy had to do *something* or she thought she might lose her sanity altogether. So she lost her composure in the only way she could allow herself.

She ran.

She made sure, however, that it did not look like running to Thomas. To him, Wendy looked like a storm, gathering its strength above the sea. She said nothing, but her face darkened into a fury. Then, suddenly, she turned and strode in three quick strides to the door, hurling it open and bursting through it without bothering to close it behind her. Her boots stomped along the passageway, slamming against the boards in hard, determined strides.

Thomas, who became nervous in the face of any confrontation, did not run after her. But he was not the only one present. The little innisfay, whose magic was intricately attuned to emotion, understood immediately every nuance of the agony Wendy was feeling, and he was suddenly terrified she might find some way to harm herself, just to escape it.

(Not that he *cared* about her, mind you—this oversized human, who was so ugly and clumsy when compared to a beautiful innisfay such as himself. It was simply in his nature, as an innisfay, to be helpful.)

So whether he followed her because he did, in fact, care for her, no matter what he told himself, or because he was just a helpful sort of innisfay, we may never know. But he flew after her down the passageway, watching over her in silence, hovering just above

and behind her left shoulder like a tiny guardian angel, waiting to see what she might do and whether he might need to intervene.

As for Wendy, truth be told it flashed briefly through her mind to race to the upper deck and throw herself overboard into the sea, swimming down and down and down until she ran out of air. But the ship kept watch all night long, and someone would surely dive in after her. She would be hauled back to the surface, still very much alive, and she would be labeled hysterical for certain.

Or, at least, that was what she told herself to stop herself from doing it. She did not really want to die. She wanted to save Nicholas. She just had no way to do that, and the anguish of that simple fact was making her feel desperate.

What she really needed was to let go of this pretense of having everything together. She needed to fall very much apart, at least for a while, and there was only one safe place for her to do that.

Nana was waiting for Wendy in front of the door to their quarters, but her happy bark turned to a whimper when she saw the state of her mistress. She raced to Wendy's side, leaning supportively against her leg as Wendy strode the last few paces to her door and passed through it, taking Nana with her and allowing the innisfay to sneak inside as well by darting in through the top corner before she shut the door behind her.

And that, finally, was when she let go.

She threw herself onto her bunk, gathered a huge armful of blanket to her face to muffle her cries, and screamed into it at the top of her lungs until her scream turned into sobs. Then she wept until her body convulsed with it—until her stomach muscles hurt and the blanket in front of her face was soaked through with her tears.

And all the while, Nana lay squeezed onto the bunk beside her, her flank stretched as far as she could stretch it, her weight leaning heavily against Wendy's side, while she tried to lick the

tears away. Unfortunately, she couldn't reach Wendy's tears because the woman's entire face was buried in the blanket, so all Nana managed to do was lick the side of her head over and over, consisting mostly of her hair and her left ear.

"All right, Nana. All *right*," Wendy finally said, sniffling heavily, her voice still muffled by the blanket. "Thank you, but that's enough."

Nana wasn't convinced, so she gave Wendy's ear two more licks for good measure.

"I said that's *enough*."

Wendy sighed a little and pulled the blanket from her face. She rolled over and turned toward the dog, then opened her eyes. But to her surprise, Nana's face wasn't the only one she saw.

Instead, she saw *two* sets of eyes staring back at her in concern. Nana's huge brown ones framed most of her vision, but behind those, hovering in midair just behind the dog's head, was a tiny pair of pale green innisfay eyes—watching her sadly from beneath a gorgeous mane of blue-gray hair that seemed to Wendy to be the exact color of a stormy sky on one of those dreary winter days when the whole world seems to be crying with you.

"Oh," Wendy said, staring at him in wonder.

And then, "Oh!"

Wendy sat up and grabbed the blanket again, trying to use its course fibers to mop the remaining tears from her face. But the innisfay flew to her, slowly, and he reached a tentative hand out toward the blanket until she let it drop from her face. He wore a white, long-sleeved shirt that tied in the front, and he pulled one of those sleeves down over his hand, using it to dry the tears gently from her cheeks.

"Thank you," Wendy said quietly. It was the softest material she had ever known, and his touch felt like she imagined the wings of a tiny bird would feel if their tips were to brush lightly over her skin.

He nodded, and then he smiled. His hair remained blue, but it brightened a little—still the color of that cloudy winter sky, but now the sun peeked through here and there, heralding the quiet promise of spring somewhere down the road.

The innisfay began to flit about her head. At first Wendy pulled back in surprise, but then she realized he was fixing her hair, rearranging it where it had become scattered while she was crying. She closed her eyes and let him work, and the touch of his tiny, gentle hands soothed her.

"I'm sorry I can't pronounce your name," she said after a while. She opened her eyes, but he only shrugged and smiled, his hair now more like its usual gold, with just the slightest tinge of blue. "But I think we can do much better than Jingles, don't you?"

The innisfay nodded vigorously, and his hair flashed red for just a moment, proving what Wendy had suspected: that he had never liked the name the imp had given him.

"You're so handsome. And so kind. Every time I look at you, I think of Prince Charming, from the fairy tales. Do you like the name Charming?"

The innisfay grinned broadly, and his hair flashed bright gold.

"Well then, I shall call you Charming from now on."

Which is how Wendy found herself smiling, at least a little, when she heard a tentative knock on her door.

She looked toward the door in surprise, but then she stood, her hands reaching to smooth her dress out of lifelong habit, only to realize she was wearing the shirt, vest, breeches, and boots that had become her habit aboard ship.

Somehow, this simple fact brought a new strength along with it. She breathed deeply, and she stood straighter. She looked

around and realized how dark it had become in her quarters, now that the sun had set, and that Charming had been acting as a lamp for her, along with everything else.

"One moment," she called. She lit her lamp, and she hung it back on the hook overhead. Then she opened the door.

"Michael!"

"I'm sorry to bother you," Michael said, and then he stopped, searching her eyes.

"It's all right," she assured him. "Obviously, you've heard."

"About Nicholas. Yes," he confirmed. "I'm so sorry. I know ... I know you cared for him."

"Thank you," Wendy said, and she felt the tears threatening to return, but she inhaled a long, deep breath and exhaled slowly, until the worst of the feeling subsided. "It was kind of you to come look in on me, but I'll be all right."

"Oh, I ... I didn't," Michael stammered. "I mean, of course, I did. But it isn't just that. It's ... well ... I'm sorry, but we need your help."

"Oh! Of course. What can I do? What is it?"

"I think ..." Michael trailed off, and he tilted his head to one side, just now noticing the innisfay hovering in the air behind her. "I think you should come see for yourself. And I think you should bring your new friend."

CHAPTER 26

Wendy followed Michael through the passageways of the ship. He kept a steady pace, forcing her to lengthen her stride until she was almost trotting, while Charming floated casually behind her.

"The plan worked," Michael told her. "After you—" He fell silent and looked back over his shoulder, his eyes worried.

Wendy frowned and said nothing, steeling her emotions against the pain and returning his gaze in silence.

After she dove into the water. After Nicholas was shot.

She offered him the tiniest nod of her chin, and he lowered his eyes for a moment before continuing.

"The arrival of *The Tiger* turned the tide in our favor. The men and I were grateful, I can tell you that. Things weren't looking good for us."

Wendy's feet stuttered beneath her. Michael heard the change in her pace and looked back again, but she acted as though nothing had happened.

She had been on her way to help Michael and his men when she had seen Nicholas get shot. She had forgotten everything, diving in after the boy without a single thought for her own platoon. She realized now what could have happened—and how fortunate she was that her actions had not cost Michael and the others their lives.

If Michael understood what she was thinking, he was kind enough to move on without acknowledging the moment.

"The remaining everlost surrendered, and we took the ship. The *flying* ship," Michael clarified. "Only it doesn't fly. At least, not that we can manage. And we have no idea how to finish the job."

"The everlost won't say," Wendy guessed.

"The everlost *can't* say," Michael replied. "Hook executed every last one of them on the spot."

"What?" Wendy stopped in her tracks. "But they surrendered!"

Michael turned to face her, retracing his steps when he realized she was no longer following him, but he did not seem anywhere near as shocked as she felt over what Hook had done.

"We're at war," he reminded her. "He's the captain of a ship, and the sea is his domain. He's well within his rights to execute his judgment—and his enemies. For their crimes against England."

They stared at each other for a long moment, but Wendy did not reply.

"It does make things more difficult," Michael finally admitted quietly. "Whatever they knew died with them. About flying ships. About their fleet. About their plans. Now we have to get that ship in the air before Blackheart returns, and we have no idea how to do it."

Wendy frowned. "Then where are we going?"

"To the quartermaster," Michael told her. "You'll see."

They began to walk again, but it wasn't much farther before Wendy could hear a terrible ruckus up ahead. It was the strangest cacophony of deep gravelly voices and angry jingling chimes.

"Oh dear," Wendy whispered to herself. She looked over her shoulder to see Charming flying agitated loops in the air. "We'll take care of it," she assured him. "Whatever it is, we'll take care of it."

But when they finally arrived at the armory, Wendy could hardly think for all the noise. Several imps, all dressed in miniature pirate clothing, were growling low in their throats and throwing themselves against the silver bars of their cages, while a whole host of innisfay chimed angrily from their own cages along the walls.

Mr. Quinton, the quartermaster, scowled at the racket but was doing nothing to try to stop it, his habitually somber expression even more gloomy than usual.

"But ... how?" Wendy exclaimed.

"We had a few silver cages with us, Miss Darling," he told her, "what with the magical nature of the expedition. But nowhere near this many, I admit. Fortunately, the crew found plenty on *The Pegasus.* As for the innisfay, we transported them in the cages they were already in. I've made sure they have water, but I've no idea what to feed 'em."

"*The Pegasus?*" Wendy asked.

"It's what we're calling the flying ship, ma'am. Or, rather, the one we hope will fly for us. Assuming these here creatures can finish the job."

"But why are they in the armory?"

"Well, it was either this or put 'em down with the chickens. But they seemed more like weapons than food."

"Food? I'll show you who's food!" The closest of the imps snarled and gnashed his teeth at the quartermaster. "Come put your ear between these bars, you mangey human!"

"Interesting," Wendy mused. "I don't think he's lying."

"I don't think he is either," Mr. Quinton commented. "I wouldn't get near that one if I were you."

"No, I didn't ... never mind. I meant to ask why the innisfay are in cages at all. They are our allies, Mr. Quinton."

Charming's hair carved flaming trails through the air as he darted from one cage to the next.

"You'll have to take that up with the captain, Miss Darling. They arrived in cages, and I was ordered to keep them there."

"Yes, well. We'll see about that. Charming ... Charming!" She had to raise her voice considerably to get his attention, but the innisfay finally raced back to her, his own angry jingling only adding to the mayhem.

"I'll speak to the captain," Wendy assured him. "Stay here and see if you can calm them down. If they need anything, try to communicate it to Michael and he'll get it for you, all right?"

Charming trilled angrily in reply, and Wendy could only guess what he was saying—which, to be perfectly honest, was probably for the best.

Hook had posted Mr. Starkey as a guard outside his quarters with strict orders that he should not be disturbed. Unfortunately for the captain, Starkey was too much of a gentleman to lay a hand on a lady, no matter how she might be dressed, so Wendy barged past him despite his protests and pounded on the door.

"Truly, miss. He doesn't want to be bothered." Starkey wrung his hands in distress but made no move to stop her.

"Then he should not have left our allies in cages in the armory."

"Sorry, what?"

"Captain!"

"Go. Away." The reply from within was muffled, but the message was clear enough.

Starkey raised his eyebrows as though to say, "I told you so," but Wendy was in no mood to be cast aside. Especially not tonight. She raised her fist and pounded on the door again, even harder than before.

"Captain! It is imperative that I speak with you."

"Oh, for the love of heaven. Come in already, Miss Darling, before you break down the door."

Wendy practically threw the door open, without a hint of contrition in either her expression or her manner, but what she found on the other side of it stopped her cold. Hook sat as his desk with his head in his hands—or, rather, in his one good hand, his fingers buried in his hair, while the curved edge of his hook tapped a sad, slow rhythm against his forehead.

Of course, she realized. *He* had lost Nicholas, too.

She had never seen him look so vulnerable. Or so thoroughly, imperfectly human.

All the complaints she had been about to raise somehow melted away.

"I ... I'm sorry, Captain."

"Not your fault," he said. He stopped tapping his forehead with the hook and used it to wave her words away. "I know whose fault it was, and I killed him myself. Didn't do a damned bit of good for the boy, though."

"I couldn't do any good for him either," Wendy said quietly, and she had to work hard to keep her voice from breaking.

Their eyes met, and lingered, and then he nodded.

"You wanted to speak with me," Hook reminded her. "Something *imperative*, I believe."

"Oh! Oh, yes. I'm sorry for the timing, but it's about the innisfay. They'll be our allies in this if we give them the chance, Captain, but we have to let them go. If we hold them prisoner, they'll see no difference between us and the everlost who imprisoned them in the first place."

"I see," Hook said, watching her carefully. "And how can you be so sure?"

"Because I've befriended the first one we rescued."

"Of course you have," Hook commented, but he seemed to be speaking more to himself than to Wendy. "Well, it might surprise you, Miss Darling, but I was actually waiting to hear what you had to say before making a decision regarding any of our magical guests."

"I ... you were?" Wendy was so surprised, in fact, that she hardly knew what to say.

"I was. *The Pegasus* cannot yet fly, and we need her to. Desperately. A flying ship of our own is the only chance we have against a flying enemy. And so far, Miss Darling, you are the only one who has had any luck getting any of these creatures to do anything. We have to get that ship in the air *tonight*—before Blackheart can either steal it back or sink it."

"He's returning in the morning?" Wendy asked.

"I have no idea. But we can't afford to take the chance. We're risking *everything* on this mission. That ship is close to flying, and we can't be sure how much time we have left before Blackheart returns. We'll transfer to *The Pegasus* tonight—crew, cargo ... all of it. We're sending *The Tiger* back to England, so it won't fall into enemy hands. But if *The Pegasus* can't fly before Blackheart returns ..." Hook trailed off and raised a meaningful eyebrow.

"She'll be dead in the water," Wendy said.

"*We'll* be dead in the water. So, can we do it?"

"I don't know how long the process will take," Wendy admitted, "meaning the magic itself. But I'm sure the innisfay will help. And the quickest way to do that is to give them their freedom. Immediately. Not to make them bargain for it. They'll work much harder for us, and much faster, if they see us as allies."

Hook regarded her, lightly tapping the point of his hook against the desk, and then he finally made his decision.

"So be it," he said. "I hope you're right, Miss Darling. Our very lives may well depend on it."

CHAPTER 27

So Wendy returned to the quartermaster with a renewed sense of purpose. She explained the situation to the innisfay, who could all understand her perfectly even if *she* could not understand any of *them*. It also helped that Charming spoke to them on her behalf, assuring them he had been living on the ship of his own free will—and that they were all being freed, whether they chose to help or not.

But the innisfay were no friends to Blackheart, not after the way he and his crew had treated them, and they seemed more than willing to stay and help the enemy of their enemy.

The imps, on the other hand, were a different story. They were all members of Blackheart's crew, and while the loyalty of an imp to any master might well be questioned, they were clearly *not* loyal to Wendy.

"Let me out of here, and I'll bite your nose off!" one of the imps in the back shouted. He growled and spat through the bars.

"That's an awfully strange lie to tell," Wendy muttered.

"Who says he's lying?"

It was the closest imp who answered her, even though Wendy hadn't been speaking to anyone in particular—an imp wearing a light blue linen shirt tucked into wool breeches as black as his boots. His skin was a slightly more golden hue than the imp Wendy had already met, and his eyes were a deep amber to match.

"Why, no one," Wendy replied. "But I thought ..." She trailed off, but the imp raised one finger and tapped it knowingly against the tip of his nose.

"Oh, *I* see. Yes, *I* understand. *You've* met *Barnaby.* That explains where he was all day. But he's not here with *us*, now is he? I suppose you've killed him already." The imp scowled and gnashed his teeth, glaring at Wendy through the bars of his cage.

"Of course not!" Wendy protested. "He's in the doctor's quarters."

"So you didn't *kill* him, then. You just beat him up a bit, is that it? I'm supposed to feel better about that?"

"No! No one beat him. That's where he's staying, that's all. He's perfectly healthy, I assure you."

"Oh, you *assure* me. Yes, that makes me feel *much* better. The lady sailor who has me prisoner is *assuring* me that Barnaby is in perfect health. Well, forgive me if I don't take your word for it."

"Look," Wendy said, frowning, "I promise you there is an imp in the infirmary who is perfectly healthy. I can't promise you it's this Barnaby fellow. He never told me his name."

"Right, well he wouldn't, would he? He'd tell you every other name in the world, though. Jim, Lawrence, Clementine, Anastasia ... but never Barnaby. On account of he always lies, which is why I know it's him. He's the only one what always lies. We're not all the same, you know."

"I ... I didn't assume—"

"Bah! Course you did. Humans always assume. Meet one lying imp, expect us all to be liars. Bloody fools, humans."

Wendy narrowed her eyes. "And how many of *us* have *you* met?" she shot back. "Perhaps it's *you* who's assuming things about *us*. Maybe we don't *all* make those kinds of assumptions."

"*You* did, though. You practically said so yourself." The imp placed his hands on his narrow hips and scowled again, all but daring her to deny it. Which she could not. Because what he said was true.

"Yes, well," Wendy said quietly, "that doesn't mean we *all* do."

"Doesn't mean you *don't* either," the imp said, grunting at the end.

"Well, why does he always lie, then, if it isn't in his nature?"

"It *is* in his nature. It's just not in his nature as an imp. It's in his nature as *Barnaby*. Imps are all born with, well, let's call them *idiosyncrasies*. Barnaby's is lying. He can't help it. Just like Scrant threatens everyone with violence."

"Shut your mouth, Goldie, or I'll shut it for you! Permanently!" Scrant yelled from his cage in the back.

"See?" Goldie commented.

"Well, what's yours then?" Wendy asked.

"He's a thief!" Scrant yelled. "But he'll be a dead thief soon!"

Goldie just grinned and pulled a small coin from his pocket, flipping it into the air before catching it and stowing it away again.

"Mr. Quinton," Wendy said, getting the quartermaster's attention.

"Yes, Miss Darling?"

"I have orders for you, from the captain. We are transferring to *The Pegasus*. Everyone and everything. Tonight."

"Tonight?" Mr. Quinton repeated.

"By morning, with a little luck, she'll be flying!"

"Flying," he repeated.

"Flying, Mr. Quinton!" Wendy rocked back on her heels and grinned. "We must be ready!"

"Right! At least this will be a smaller job than the last. We'll be ready," Quinton agreed. And then he added, speaking only to himself, "Of all the things I never thought I'd see. A flying ship!"

He shook his head in wonder, but there was much to be done and very little time in which to do it. Even as Wendy left with her newfound flock of innisfay, the quartermaster was already barking out orders.

The rest of the night sped by in a whirlwind of activity. Wendy and Charming organized the innisfay into an energetic crew that flitted back and forth over the deck of *The Pegasus* with obvious enthusiasm, dropping innisfay dust anywhere and everywhere. They left bright, glittering trails in their wake, shimmering by lamplight as they darted between and around Hook's men, who carried barrels and crates and chests from *The Tiger* to *The Pegasus* (and sometimes from *The Pegasus* to *The Tiger*) in a flurry of organized chaos.

Because they could not rely on the imps, it fell to the human crew to oil the dust into the deck. Wendy had no idea whether the oil itself was magical, but they found plenty of it in the hold of *The Pegasus* itself, and Hook assigned Wendy's Fourteenth Platoon to the detail.

"Watch out!"

"Mind your head."

"Coming through!"

Men shouted warnings to each other as the platoon scrambled to keep up with the innisfay, rubbing dust into the deck with as much vigor as they could muster while trying to stay out of everyone's way. There was more than one instance in which warnings went unheeded and someone tripped over a scrubber, their crate crashing to the deck and skidding along the boards. This was always accompanied by loud hollering and explosive accusations in both directions, but in the end no one was seriously hurt, crates were repacked and stowed away, and the night progressed until Mr. Quinton proclaimed that, miracle of miracles, the last of the cargo had been transferred and the ship was ready to sail.

"But is she ready to *fly*?"

Hook stood at the helm, directing the inquiry to Wendy, who stood next to him, her eyes bright with excitement.

"There's only one way to find out," she said. She leaned toward him, and Hook took a quick step back in surprise. But she was just reaching through the spokes of the ship's wheel to find the hidden compartment.

Only, it was empty.

"What is it? What's wrong?" Hook asked. He could see from her expression that something unexpected had just happened, and day was already beginning to dawn. They could not afford any miscalculations.

"There's supposed to be a thimble," she said, feeling around in the compartment again, but it was just as empty as before. "We need it to fly the ship."

"A *thimble*?" Hook repeated, his voice incredulous.

"I know how it sounds, but yes. A thimble. It's tied magically to the ship. And the dust. And it makes the ship fly. By thinking."

"Miss Darling," Hook said, his eyes narrowing considerably, "you seem to possess a rather extensive knowledge of how all this

works. I don't suppose there was anything you might have left out of your reports?"

Wendy gave up fishing around in the compartment and knelt on the deck, searching the area beneath the wheel to see where the thimble might have fallen.

"I was already pushing the boundaries of your belief by claiming that the ship could fly, Captain. If I had mentioned a *thimble* being its primary source of movement, would that have made me seem more or less credible, do you think?"

She stopped searching the deck and stared up at him from where she was kneeling.

"I see your point," he admitted. "But where is it, then?"

"If I knew that, would I be down here looking for it?"

Hook sighed. "What does it look like?"

"Like a thimble," she replied, looking around again. "Like any other thimble. Although, I suppose it wouldn't *have* to be a thimble. It might be anything small, really. Metal, I expect. Something that could fit into your hand. A bullet, perhaps. Or ... oh!"

Wendy sprang to her feet.

"Mr. Quinton!" she shouted. "Where is the armory? I need to see the new armory at once!"

"Miss Darling," Hook growled, "are you about to tell me that we have to search out one particular bullet in the *armory*?"

"No, sir!" Wendy said, grinning. "Just one particular imp."

"That one!" Wendy declared, pointing toward the imp they called Goldie. "You! Give us that coin!"

"What coin?" Goldie asked. He raised his eyebrows and opened his empty hands as though to say, *I have no idea what you're talking about*. But, of course, he knew perfectly well what coin she meant.

"The coin you tossed in the air before," Wendy told him. "You thought I wouldn't know what it was. And I didn't. Not at first. But you're a thief by nature, and there's nothing more valuable on this ship than the token that flies it. Now, hand it over."

"Or what?" Goldie crossed his arms over his chest and stared at her smugly.

But Hook had had enough. He raised a pistol and aimed it squarely at the imp's chest. "This is not a negotiation. Hand it over, or I will take it from your dead body."

"Do it!" Scrant yelled from his cage, which had yet again been positioned near the back—for good reason. "Kill him! Stupid imp doesn't know how to keep a secret! I told you not to show 'em, you arrogant imbecile!"

Goldie scowled, but he fished the coin out of his pocket and handed it over. Wendy took it, and already it felt warm to the touch. She thought about moving, just an inch, and the coin twitched against her palm.

"This is it, Captain!" Wendy handed it over, placing it carefully in Hook's good left hand, and in that precise moment, they heard Smee's whistle from the upper deck.

Enemies spotted.

Blackheart had returned.

CHAPTER 28

They ran through the ship as shouts filled the air. Sailors rushed past them heading for the cannons even as Hook and Wendy raced for the deck.

"How does it work?" Hook shouted back over his shoulder.

"Just hold the coin, and think about moving—both speed and direction," she told him. "Don't think about moving the ship, though. Think about moving yourself. The coin binds you to the ship. So wherever you imagine yourself going, the ship will go instead."

"Simple enough."

"Well, yes and no. Make sure you hold the coin tightly. It ..." She wanted to say it would feel like the coin was fighting him, trying to jump out of his hand, but how would she know what it felt like? Hook had no idea she had navigated a flying ship before. "It's important," she said instead.

"Understood," Hook barked.

"And set the sails as though we were at sea. The wind helps, even in the air."

"Right. Anything else?"

There was, of course, one more thing. And since it was a matter of safety, she could hardly fail to mention it, no matter how much she might prefer not to. By now, they had reached the final ladder to the deck, and Hook began climbing it hand over hand. Or, rather, hand over hook.

At least she didn't have to look at him.

"When you first take off," she said, trying to speak casually, "do it quickly, so the keel doesn't catch in the water and tip her. But not so fast that you toss the men overboard."

Unfortunately, Hook was starting to know Wendy a bit too well for her own good. He emerged from the hatch and turned to watch her as she climbed onto the deck behind him.

"This is getting awfully specific, Miss Darling. I'm beginning to think you left more out of your reports than a thimble."

He had not technically asked her a question, so Wendy did not reply. But he held his hook out in the air in front of her to stop her from walking away, and he looked her straight in the eye.

"Miss Darling, have you flown an everlost vessel?"

There was no escaping it. He already knew the answer to his question, and Wendy knew that he knew it.

"Aye, Captain," she admitted. "The night Pan showed me his ship. He let me fly it to Dover."

"Then tell me what to do—specifically, step by step—before that ship gets close enough to realize what is happening and sink us right here in this cove." Hook gestured toward Blackheart's ship, flying above the distant horizon in the early morning light.

"Just hold the coin," Wendy told him. "Tightly. And think about moving forward through the water, without moving your feet, at about the speed we would normally sail. We have to get the ship out from under the rock before we can fly."

"Think about flying the ship without flying the ship?"

"Think about moving yourself along the water," Wendy told him. "The ship will move for you."

Hook stood and stared at her, doing nothing.

"Captain, we're running out of time. Do it. You have to trust me."

"I *am* doing it," he growled. "Nothing's happening. What am I doing wrong?"

"I have no idea," Wendy admitted. "You just *think* it, and it happens."

Hook glanced at Blackheart's ship. It was not flying especially fast—they clearly had no idea yet that *The Pegasus* had been captured by the enemy—but it was already significantly closer.

"Show me," he said. He turned back to Wendy, his eyes snapping to hers, and he handed her the coin.

The instant she took it, she felt its magic surge through her. She thought *forward*, and the ship moved forward, even with the sails still furled.

Hook stared at her for the briefest of moments, and then he made his decision, leaving all hesitation behind.

"Follow me," he barked, and he led her to the ship's wheel, where Charlie stood ready.

"Miss Darling has the helm," Hook muttered to Charlie.

"Aye, sir," Charlie replied, matching his captain's quiet tone. His face registered no surprise, but when Hook turned back toward Blackheart's ship, Charlie flashed Wendy a grin.

"You'll still need to steer for me, Charlie," she told him. She smiled back for just a moment, but there was no time for any more celebration than that. Wendy had the feel of the ship already, the coin tapping frenetically against the palm of her hand, and she began to accelerate, moving out of the cove as quickly as possible.

"Sails now?" Hook asked under his breath.

Wendy nodded, focused on the horizon.

"Set sail, Mr. Smee!" Hook hollered. The crew, which had been staring in wonder as their ship moved under no power they could discern, exploded into life.

The square sails unfurled from all three masts at once as the men in the rigging released them. Other men caught the ropes and lashed them into place, the sails snapping one by one as they caught the wind. And Wendy lifted the vessel into the air.

Immediately, Blackheart's ship picked up speed.

"They've seen us," Hook said. "Rise above them, Miss Darling. If they can fire downward upon us, we won't have a hope of returning fire. We'll be dead before we've even started."

"Aye, Captain," she replied.

A memory flashed before her eyes—of stopping too suddenly in Pan's ship, and of the everlost being tossed overboard in midair. She gritted her teeth and rose as quickly as she dared, careful to keep their motion smooth and steady.

But Blackheart saw their intention, even at a distance, and his ship rose, too, faster and faster. Wendy struggled to keep pace without losing control, as the wind raged around them, howling as though it wanted to hurl *The Pegasus* back into the sea.

They left the tropical morning below as the air got colder and colder, and eventually it became hard to breathe. Their height was dizzying now, the island so far beneath them that it seemed as small as a child's toy. But Blackheart was still gaining on them, almost in range to fire.

"Evasive maneuvers, Miss Darling! Now!" Hook shouted.

"Hang on!" she yelled, and then they dove. It was reckless, she knew, but it was better than cannon fire raining down on

them from above. Several of the men screamed in terror, clutching at masts and ropes and anything solid they could find, clinging desperately to the ship as it plummeted toward the sea. Wendy used their descent to her advantage, gaining speed and increasing the distance between the two ships, but it wasn't long before Blackheart followed.

No matter what Wendy did, the everlost ship matched her, slowly closing the distance, until the ships were almost within cannon range again.

"Prepare to fire!" Hook shouted, and Smee echoed the order by whistle. "Miss Darling, Mr. Hawke, on my mark, turn her broadside to the enemy as quickly as you can and then climb again."

"Aye, sir!" Wendy answered. "Hard to port. Ready."

"Ready," Charlie echoed.

"Three ... two ... now!"

Wendy spun the ship as quickly as she dared, the wood of the masts and even the deck creaking in protest with the strain of it, and then they rose hard and fast. Wendy felt her knees threaten to buckle beneath her, and more than one sailor lost his feet, slamming to the deck.

"Fire!" Hook roared.

Smee whistled the order, and the cannons exploded beneath their feet.

Without the weight of the sea against the ship's keel, the force of her own cannon fire knocked *The Pegasus* hard to the side. At first, Wendy fought to bring the vessel back under control. The feel of the ship slipping sideways went against every instinct in her bones—like a storm wave threatening to capsize her broadside.

But then the everlost fired back, and Wendy reacted on pure instinct. She moved into the slip instead of against it, edging sideways on purpose. The hull and the keel and the sails all resisted the

air, but Wendy ignored the bucking and the protest of the wood and *pushed,* desperately, broadside and up, as hard as she could.

With mere feet to spare, the everlost cannon fire fell short, dropping harmlessly into the sea.

"Well done, Miss Darling." Hook's voice was low and surprisingly calm, but it held a respect Wendy had never heard from him before. "Very well done."

"Thank you, Captain," Wendy replied. Her heart was pounding from the exertion, and her words stuttered out between heavy breaths, her lungs demanding air. "But I can't do this forever. We need to lose them. In the fog maybe, if we can reach it."

"The fog's too far," Hook countered. "They'd sink us before we got there."

"Not if we can put some distance between us first. Hang on!"

Between their rise to the heavens and their sudden, harrowing descent, they had ended up not far from where they had started. The mountain was close—Wendy only hoped it was close enough.

She pushed the ship in that direction, spinning her as she went, until they were sailing forward again.

"Full speed, Captain," Wendy muttered.

"Full speed ahead!" Hook shouted.

Smee whistled sharply, and the men scrambled to catch the wind. The ship bucked and surged forward. Soon the everlost were gaining on them again, but Wendy thought they had a big enough lead.

Or, at least, she hoped they did.

"Prepare the men for a sudden break to starboard, Captain," she told Hook. "And I do mean sudden. I don't want to lose anyone overboard."

"Hard to starboard, on my mark, Mr. Smee!" Hook shouted.

More whistles, and all eyes turned to the captain, who held his hook up high, waiting.

Wendy glanced over her shoulder, steering around the mountain and watching as the massive peak began to hide Blackheart's ship from view.

"Not yet," she said quietly. Blackheart's ship disappeared altogether behind the towering rock, but she needed more distance. So she waited. And waited.

"Five," she finally said, and Charlie's hands tensed upon the wheel. "Four ... three ... two ... now!"

Hook dropped his arm, and Wendy turned the ship as hard to starboard as the ship itself would allow—heading straight for the mountain. The hull creaked and groaned in protest, and the men hung on for dear life, doing their best to change the set of the sail without flying overboard.

It was a desperate ploy, but Wendy hoped that by changing direction and going straight over the mountain while they were out of sight, they might confuse the enemy just long enough to gain the lead they needed. And then they could make a run for the fog. If they could reach the fog before their enemies, they could turn and fire on the everlost from the relative safety of cover.

But that wasn't what happened at all.

Instead, they reached the very top of the mountain peak, and the entire island disappeared.

CHAPTER 29

For one terrifying moment, they were nowhere at all. But, of course, they must be *somewhere*, Wendy thought. Wherever they were, it was dark. And very, very cold. But that was all the time she had before everything changed and they were definitely somewhere again.

The air was warm. The sun was bright. And a new landscape spread out beneath them, stretching as far as the eye could see. There were green patchwork fields and meandering rivers. Mountains with cruel, snow-capped peaks scraped the heavens in the distance, with hints of jungle nestled below, glistening in the moonlight.

Wait. Moonlight?

Wendy turned to her right, where the sun shone brightly over the land, and then she turned back to the left, where the moon hung low over the mountains, the sky dark and full of stars. But how could it be day and night at the same time?

She spun around in wonder, only to discover that a vast desert

lay behind her. As she watched, a giant ripple shuddered through the sands—as though some tremendous beast was about to crest through the surface before changing its mind. The ripple sank and settled, leaving only a ridge of dunes behind.

Another hint of movement caught her eye, and she watched as a flock of birds rose from the mountainside. Only, they couldn't be birds, Wendy realized. She never could have seen anything as small as a bird from so far away. But they were white, like seagulls, and they soared through the air, lifting and turning as one, heading toward *The Pegasus.*

They moved in perfect unison, like a flock, Wendy thought. Or like a flotilla. Were those ... sails?

Wendy was about to raise a warning, but when she turned to Hook, he had already lifted his spyglass to his eye, watching them. He stood on the deck of his flying ship, his thick mane of hair tied loosely behind his neck, and he stared through the instrument without comment. When he finally lowered the glass, he turned to Wendy and locked eyes with her, saying nothing.

"Captain?" she asked.

By way of reply, he merely handed her the spyglass.

Confused, she raised it to her eye.

The sails were in clear view, but Wendy still could not make sense of them. Then they shifted again—and she realized with a sharp intake of breath that they were not sails at all. They were creatures. Tremendous creatures, easily as large as ships and yet elegantly simple in design. Wendy saw no heads or arms or feet. They seemed to be hardly more than thin, stretched membranes riding the wind, with long tendrils trailing beneath them.

But then the tendrils, which had appeared almost translucent, suddenly sparked into life.

Pulses of luminescence—first red, then blue, then green, then violet—raced along the length of every tendril in a coordinated

rhythm. Wendy wondered if they were trying to communicate with this distant flying creature that had appeared over their lands, echoing her own thoughts.

Who are you? What *are you?*

Without any warning, they changed the tilt of their sail-like bodies again, all of them at once, and they caught the wind to turn around, heading back toward the mountains.

Wendy lowered the spyglass and returned it to Hook, their eyes meeting in that special, shared intensity that says *I know what you're thinking.*

But Wendy said it first.

"Neverland," she breathed.

"Are you certain?" Hook asked. "Absolutely certain?" He spoke quietly, but his voice held an edge of excitement that she wasn't sure she liked.

There was not an ounce of doubt in her mind, but she didn't expect Hook to take her word for it. So she pulled out the compass, which she kept with her always, and she opened it. For the first time ever, the outline of the island within the compass had changed, and the needle spun around and around, refusing to land anywhere.

Because Pan's magic was all around them.

Where, before, she could smell the taste of it, or perhaps taste the feel of it, now she could feel the very life of it flowing through her veins. It pulsed in her chest. In her neck. In her wrists. In her fingertips. She felt it the way you might feel your own heartbeat after you have run as hard and as fast as you can—so hard that your heart pounds, and your lungs ache, and you can think of nothing else.

That was how Neverland felt, at first. But, already, she was learning to adjust to it. At least a little.

Not in the way that your heart slows down after running—

the feeling that washed over her would never lose its power, Wendy already knew that—but more in the way that one adjusts, eventually, to being in love. The feeling is still there, all the time, and you still count on it every single moment of your life. But you come to accept the miracle as something you can depend on, so that you can get on with the daily business of breathing and making sandwiches without feeling so much like your soul might burst into flames and fly away at any moment.

Which is how Wendy managed to show Hook the compass without any change in her expression, and with only the tiniest tremor of her hand to reveal the enormity of what she was feeling.

"But ... how?" he asked.

"I don't know. We were above that other island, and the moment we reached the top of the mountain, we were here." But then Wendy remembered the brief pause between the two. She remembered the dark, and feeling very, very cold. "No, wait. That isn't exactly true. There was a pause first. Did you feel it?"

But Hook was lost in his own thoughts. "And what are those ... I don't even know what to call them. Those giant flying jellyfish. Are they aggressive?"

"Why, how would *I* know, Captain? I only just arrived here, exactly when you did. I don't know anything about this place."

She said it almost breathlessly, as though it were the greatest sentence she had ever uttered. And, to Wendy, it was. This was her childhood dream wrapped up in a bow. Just being here, in this magnificent new land, was already a strange and surprising adventure, and they had not even begun to explore. She could hardly wait to see what grand mysteries and magnificent new creatures they might discover.

As it happened, Hook was having similar thoughts, but his were much darker and more foreboding than hers. Who knew what nightmares might lurk below? The everlost were enough of a threat on their own. Suddenly, Hook was imagining an army of everlost descending upon English shores with a host of mythical beasts. Like Hannibal with his elephants. Except they would be wyverns. Or dragons.

Or flying jellyfish.

Hook scowled. "What pause, Miss Darling?"

"I'm sorry?" She was staring down at the farmland, wondering what crops might be growing there. She hoped it was something more interesting than the usual grains and vegetables.

"You asked whether I felt a pause. What pause?"

"Oh! Yes. I felt a pause between the two places. It wasn't just now-you're-here and then-you're-there. There was a pause first. Someplace dark and cold. Like a tunnel perhaps."

"A tunnel," Hook echoed.

"Yes, a tunnel between the two places." Now she was staring at the desert again, hoping to see another sign of whatever was burrowing beneath the sands.

"If it was a tunnel, Miss Darling, then what is to prevent Blackheart's ship from using it to follow us?"

"Why, nothing, I suppose," she admitted.

Which is why they were both staring into the empty air behind them when Blackheart's ship suddenly burst into it, spun broadside, and fired.

CHAPTER 30

Wendy tried desperately to move *The Pegasus* out of range, but Blackheart's crew was well trained when it came to midair battle tactics. They burst into the sky over Neverland, spun, and fired, all in a matter of moments.

There just wasn't enough time.

A cannonball smashed through the ship somewhere below, sending a shuddering groan throughout the vessel and rocking the deck to starboard.

"Damage report, Mr. Smee! Full speed ahead!" Hook ordered, and Smee whistled the commands to the crew. "Give it everything you have, Miss Darling! We have to outrun them! Make it happen!"

Wendy knew he was right. They were outgunned, and they were in the middle of the open sky, with no hope of cover anywhere. She gritted her teeth and stared straight ahead, accelerating *The Pegasus* as fast as she could.

Her eyes were wide, and she had to use her free hand to grip

her own fist, just to keep it from trembling. They had barely managed to get away the first time. She was already exhausted, and now the ship had taken serious damage, making it harder to stay on course. *The Pegasus* felt as though it were fighting her even as the coin hissed and spat against the palm of her hand.

"I ... I don't know if I can do it, Captain," Wendy admitted softly.

Hook moved to stand directly in front of her, and his forget-me-not eyes locked onto hers with a quiet but firm intensity.

"You can, and you will," Hook told her.

"Aye, Captain," she mumbled.

"Navigator Darling, listen to me. You *can*, and you *will*. Now, outrun that ship!"

Wendy squared her shoulders. "Aye, Captain!" she said, and her voice held more of its usual confidence this time.

Knowing that Hook believed in her did seem to help, at least a little. A new surge of energy coursed through her, and her hands steadied. The men rigged the ship for as much speed as they could muster, and Wendy *pushed* it even faster until they were hurtling through the sky at a breakneck pace.

But it wasn't long before Blackheart's ship was gaining on them again.

A sailor emerged from the hatch and raced toward them.

"Mr. Starkey," Hook snapped, "report!"

"The hull's intact, sir. They must have hit the rudder. I won't know how bad it is until we can get underneath her."

"Mr. Hawke?" Hook asked, turning to Charlie, who still held the wheel.

"Aye, sir. I can feel it. I'm not sure how much good I'm even doing anymore. Miss Darling's doing most of the steering now. But I'll keep doing what I can."

"Good man. Miss Darling, report."

"We're losing ground, Captain. I don't ..." Wendy tried to swallow the lump in her throat. "I don't know what else to do. I can't go any faster."

"What if we were lighter?" Hook asked. "Would that make a difference?"

"I don't know, Captain. But we have to try something. I'm barely managing to keep us out of range."

"Mr. Starkey, see to it," Hook ordered. "We're over land. Toss anything we can restock."

"Aye, Captain." Starkey turned to leave, but Hook stopped him.

"Wait. Keep half the water and half the hard rations. At least for now. There's no telling what effect the local fare might have on the crew."

"Aye, sir," Starkey agreed. "But if it comes to it?"

"Get some men working on it and come back to wait for my orders. If it comes to it, we'll take our chances. But not until we have to."

"Aye, sir."

Soon enough, a line of men emerged from the hatch passing crates and barrels and chests from one to the next. They emptied a few over the side but tossed most of them overboard entirely. At first, Wendy could hardly notice the difference, but eventually the gallons upon gallons of water and ale and rations being dumped overboard began to add up. The ship lightened, and it became easier to maneuver.

But, still, she couldn't help but think they were only delaying the inevitable. She felt more exhausted by the minute, so the ship getting lighter was only helping her keep pace, buying them a little more time, at best. And for what?

She kept scanning the land ahead, looking for anything she could use for cover, at least long enough to set up for a good shot.

But there was only farmland ahead, as far as the eye could see, and Blackheart had made his grand appearance in between *The Pegasus* and the mountain range. There was no way to make it back to the night side of Neverland without being cut off by the enemy.

She was so tired. And her head was starting to throb. But worst of all, she was furious with herself. She should have thought about the possibility of a magical gateway. She should have headed for the mountains as soon as they had found themselves here—should have looked for a safe harbor instead of gawking at Neverland like a fool. Now they were going to be shot out of the sky. All of them. John and Michael and Charlie and poor Reginald and even Hook.

And it was all her fault.

She felt the weight of that thought on her heart, so heavy she hardly knew how to carry it. But she fought on anyway—fighting the coin, fighting the ship, fighting her own sense of guilt, fighting for more time. Time for something miraculous to happen.

And then something *did* happen. But it did not seem like a miracle. It seemed like the exact opposite of a miracle. Another ship lifted off from the ground up ahead, rising into the sky, unfurling her sails, and heading straight for them.

The admiral himself. The great Peter Pan.

Wendy recognized the ship the moment she saw it. She had flown it herself, that night beneath the stars. And now, apparently, it would be the death of her. And that was her fault, too, she suddenly thought. All of it. Befriending the enemy, taking the compass, following it blindly to Neverland. Every stupid moment of it. Trusting him.

That last thought brought her up short, and she paused in the middle of her silent tirade. She *had* trusted him. And she could still feel that trust, even now, no matter how stupid it seemed.

Even though Peter *might* have used the compass to trick her, even though he *might* have brought them all to Neverland just to

blow Hook out of the sky, and even though Peter's ship was already turning broadside and preparing to fire, Wendy didn't think any of it was true. She didn't *feel* like it was true. So she did the one thing she knew how to do—the one thing she had always done when faced with overwhelming odds—she trusted her own heart.

And she ran *The Pegasus* straight toward Hook's greatest enemy.

Needless to say, Hook did not like this plan.

"Miss Darling, what are you doing?" he demanded.

"I have a feeling, Captain."

"You have a feeling? You have a *feeling*? Are you mad, woman? They're within firing range!"

"And yet they're not firing," Wendy pointed out.

Which was true. Pan's ship had not fired. Hook stared at the ship, incredulous, and then he smiled—a slow, wicked smile. "Then at least we'll go down fighting. Mr. Smee! Prepare the cannons!"

Smee whistled the order.

But there was no time left. Or, rather, Wendy made sure there was no time left. She sped toward Pan's ship as fast as she could.

"Turn us broadside, Mr. Hawke!" Hook ordered.

"I can't, Captain," Charlie told him, and he spun the wheel to prove it. "The ship's rudder isn't responding anymore."

"Miss Darling! Turn us broadside!"

"I ... I can't, Captain," Wendy told him, refusing to meet his gaze.

And by then, they were too close anyway. Several men screamed as they bore down on Pan's ship, threatening to ram straight into it. But at the last possible moment, Wendy pulled up, just high enough to clear Peter's sails, and flew over the enemy.

Only then, with *The Pegasus* safely out of the way, did Pan open fire. And that, as they say, was the end of that. The moment

Pan fired on the other everlost ship, Blackheart turned tail and ran.

Wendy brought her own ship to a halt. It seemed safe enough. If Pan had wanted to kill them, he could have done it easily. She wanted to sink to the deck and sleep for a week, but she was still the only thing keeping them in the air. At least coming to a standstill relieved some of the pressure in her pounding head.

She expected Peter to follow Blackheart, caught up in the battle, but, instead, he let the other ship go. He raised a flag of truce, and then a small boarding party lifted off from the everlost deck and headed their way: a brown-haired, blue-eyed everlost man, followed reluctantly by a tiny red dragon.

CHAPTER 31

Peter.

Relief flooded through Wendy as she watched him fly between the two ships, executing three spiraling loops along the way.

She had found him. *Finally*. And he was not her enemy after all.

(Or, rather, he *was*, she supposed. Because he was still England's enemy. But he was not *her* enemy in particular.) He had not tried to sink *The Dragon*. He had not tried to shoot *The Pegasus* out of the sky. On the contrary. He had run Blackheart off and saved them all. That simple fact made her feel a lot better than she would have liked to admit.

Especially to Hook, who did not share her sense of relief.

The captain stood ramrod straight. His eyes narrowed, and his jaw clenched rhythmically as he glared at the flying man. Then his good left hand twitched above his holstered pistol, and Wendy found herself terrified all over again. She thought of the winged

men Hook had executed after the raid on Blackheart's cave, and then another everlost flashed through her memory: the one Hook had shot and killed on this very deck.

Peter was close now. So very close. She was about to step forward and shout a warning when her stomach suddenly rose into her throat and the deck dropped out from under her feet.

She was falling. They were *all* falling.

Wendy looked down in a panic and realized instantly what had happened. She had become so afraid for Peter that she had forgotten all about keeping the ship in the air, and now there was nothing holding it up. Fortunately, they only fell about a yard before Wendy recovered her wits and thought about flying again. Despite a few frightened shouts across the span of the deck, no one appeared to be injured.

"Miss Darling?" Hook inquired. His voice sounded surprisingly calm, as though he were asking whether she would like a scone with her tea rather than why they had fallen several feet toward their death for no apparent reason.

"I apologize, Captain," she began. "I—" But then she noticed that Hook's good left hand was no longer twitching above his pistol, and that gave her an idea. She had been about to say that she had everything under control, but instead she said this: "I'm getting tired. Flying takes a lot of concentration, and I don't know how much more I can take."

The implication, of course, was that it would be best not to give her a fright. And although she had no intention of letting them all plummet to their deaths, not even if Peter were to be shot right before her eyes, what she said was still true enough. She was tired all the way down to her bones. She needed a safe place to set the ship down, and then she needed to sleep for a very long time.

She expected to be met by a flash of annoyance, that habitual condescension that flitted across Hook's eyes whenever he felt burdened by her "feminine limitations." But, instead, his expression softened, and he said, very quietly, so that only she could hear him, "You saved all our lives, Miss Darling, and, thanks to you, England now has a flying ship—and a fighting chance. Can you keep her in the air a bit longer? We'll find somewhere safe to set her down."

"Aye, Captain," she told him, and she cocked her head slightly to the left, staring at him in surprise. For one brief moment she thought that his forget-me-not eyes had never looked quite so blue as they did here, set against the sky of Neverland. But then he nodded and turned away.

"Hold your fire!" he shouted. "Hold your fire!"

Smee whistled the command, and a dozen muskets that had been aimed at Peter's chest were reluctantly lowered as the everlost touched down right in front of Wendy. He ignored Hook altogether and beamed at her with his usual smile—the wide, innocent smile that always took her breath away—and then he bowed deeply, his hawk-like wings fanning out behind him.

If Wendy had been anyone else, and if Peter had been anyone else, she might have expected him to welcome her to Neverland or to ask politely how she had been after all this time. But Wendy was Wendy, and Peter was Peter, so what he said to her in greeting did not surprise her in the least.

"Hello, the Wendy. Did you see how I saved you at the last possible moment? You must admit, it was very clever."

Wendy's eyes danced, and it was all she could do not to laugh out loud and throw her arms around him, wings and all. He *was* clever, but he was not *cunning*. He was not *devious*. He never had been. And seeing him here, standing in front of her once again, she could hardly imagine that she had ever doubted him.

Nonetheless, she maintained her composure and managed to answer with just the smallest of smiles, and with all the solemnity in her tone that the moment clearly deserved.

"Why, yes, I did," she said. "Thank you, Peter. I thought you were very clever indeed."

"Ha!" Peter exclaimed, dancing a little on the balls of his feet. "I knew you would! Tink said you wouldn't. But I told her she was wrong about you." The little red dragon that had landed on his shoulder turned an even deeper shade of red and jingled loudly in his ear. "That's enough," he scolded the tiny thing. "You must apologize at once!"

Tinker Bell jingled again, but with significantly less enthusiasm.

Peter cocked his head back and turned it as far as he could so he could address the dragon sitting on his shoulder. "That was a terrible apology," he told her. "You didn't mean it at all. Look at you. You're just as red as before."

"I'm sorry," Wendy interrupted, "but what is she apologizing for, exactly?"

Peter answered without looking away from Tinker Bell. "She was following you. She was *supposed* to tell me when you reached the island with the portal. Then I was going to come get you and fly you through it. It was a very clever plan, but Tinker Bell didn't tell me when you got there." He said this last in a firm sort of tone that left no question how he felt about the matter, and Tinker Bell finally shimmered into a desultory shade of blue.

Only then did Peter turn to face Wendy. "At least you found your own way, which was very clever of you, too. I've always known you were clever. Perhaps even as clever as *I* am. How did you do it?"

Wendy smiled. He always *had* known she was clever. From their very first sword fight, the moment he realized she had tricked

him. She hadn't had to prove it over and over again. Not like she had with John and Michael and even Hook, who was only just now beginning to acknowledge her capabilities. Peter had seen it and accepted it from the very beginning.

She was about to reply when Hook stepped forward and scowled (whether because of Peter himself or because of the way Wendy was suddenly smiling at him is anyone's guess.)

"You signaled for a truce. Did you come aboard to discuss anything of importance, or merely to tell us how clever you are?" Hook demanded.

"It's only the truth," Peter replied, very matter-of-factly. "I *am* clever. Not that *you've* ever bothered to notice." He frowned at Hook in profound disappointment, but then the moment passed and he turned back to Wendy, smiling broadly. "But, as it happens, there *is* something else. The Wendy, I came to ask you something."

He paused and frowned again, but just a little—the sort of frown that said he was trying to work something out—and then he started to mumble. "This isn't how it's done, is it? When a man asks a woman something important. I've seen it done before. How does it go? Oh, right! Yes, I have it now."

He lowered himself to one knee, and then he stared up into Wendy's eyes. "The Wendy," he said, "would you please do me the honor of being my navigator?"

CHAPTER 32

"What?" For one brief moment, Wendy had thought Peter was about to ask her something else entirely, and the mere thought of it had filled her with—well, perhaps with just the tiniest hint of a thrill at first, followed by a profound wave of terror. Then she had realized her mistake—that *that* was *not* what he was asking, and she had felt a tremendous surge of relief, trimmed with perhaps just the smallest hint of disappointment, which led in turn to a wave of embarrassment that left her blushing for all the wrong reasons.

The whole experience had lasted barely a moment, but it left her feeling thoroughly befuddled. "What?" was all she could come up with to say.

As it happened, Hook said the exact same thing in the exact same moment, although in a very different tone and for very different reasons. His "what" sounded more like this: "*WHAT?*"

Wendy and Peter both turned to stare at him.

"She cannot," Hook declared. His voice was much quieter now, but he sounded decidedly firm on the subject.

Although he couldn't help but recognize the irony.

If anyone had told him, back when he first met her, that this woman would soon be serving on his ship in even the lowest, most limited capacity, he would have laughed them right out of London. Now, she was the only member of the crew who he knew for certain could keep his flying ship in the air. He had to keep her, at any cost.

"Why not?" Peter asked. He remained poised in front of Wendy on one knee, showing no sign of rising. "She's an excellent navigator. She's proven it. She found her way here, after all, which isn't easy. Not even with a kiss, although she did a very good job in procuring it."

Hook's eyes widened, then narrowed, then snapped to Wendy, demanding an explanation.

"It isn't what you think," she blurted out. "Or, rather, it isn't what *he* thinks. I ... argh!" She expelled her breath in a mild burst of exasperation. She held up her fist but couldn't open it for fear that the coin within might leap away. "The trinket that's tied to the dust. The one that flies his ship. He calls it a kiss."

"Because that's what it is," Peter insisted.

Wendy sighed and closed her eyes for a moment, then opened them and met Hook's gaze, wiggling her fist subtly back and forth in the air.

"Yes ... well ... be that as it may," Hook replied slowly, "Miss Darling's competence is not in question. In fact, far from it. She cannot serve as your navigator because she is already serving England as the navigator of *The Pegasus*."

Charlie, who was still at the helm, raised both eyebrows and glanced at Hook out of the corner of his eye. In fact, every crewman

who had been close enough to hear the sudden pronouncement did the exact same thing, each of them glancing at Hook while trying studiously *not* to look as though they were looking.

Hook did his best not to sigh. This was exactly what he had been trying to avoid. Everyone knew she had been acting as the ship's navigator, but he had never given her the official rank and title. Now, he had acknowledged the woman's position in front of his crew, and any special accommodations he made for her from this moment forward would be seen as a weakness. A crack in the discipline of his ship. An invitation to the kind of grumbling that could eventually lead to mutiny.

Well, he wasn't about to let anyone think she would be getting special treatment. Not from him.

"Besides which," he added, addressing Pan but knowing full well that Wendy could hear every word, "you are an enemy of the crown. If she were to join your crew, it would be an act of treason."

Wendy's left eyebrow, which had remained eerily quiet throughout the entire journey from England—through everlost attacks and mystical fogs and mountain treks and clandestine raids—now stretched, awakening from its long slumber, and arched itself to its full height. When one small corner flicked upward in the barest hint of triumph, Hook felt such a sinking in the pit of his stomach that his eyes glanced to the horizon, checking to see whether *The Pegasus* had begun to fall again.

"Well," Wendy said lightly, "that *might* be true, I suppose, if I were an *actual* member of the Royal Navy. That is to say, if I were not merely *attached* to the regiment, but were a true naval officer. A true, *commissioned* naval officer."

Wendy's right eyebrow, which only just now had come to understand what was happening, raised itself in full unity with the left, and together they offered up a silent challenge—a challenge that left Hook no choice.

He set his lips in a tight line, but then he nodded, subtly, and Wendy smiled. But only for a moment. Then she turned to Peter with a look of sincere regret—a look *so* sincere that Hook understood how sorely tempted she had been by the offer, and how close he had come to losing her.

"I'm truly sorry, Peter," she said softly, "but I must honor my commission, and my position as the navigator of *The Pegasus*, until such time as I am at liberty to leave the king's service. But perhaps we might assist each other in some other way. Tell me, why did your men attack us? And why did they run from you?"

"Oh, those aren't my men. That was Blackheart. He doesn't understand the game."

"The game?" Wendy asked.

"The raiding game. Gathering flour and sugar and stories for the things they miss. Blackheart doesn't play with us anymore."

"What do you mean? That he doesn't play anymore?"

"He doesn't like games," Peter said. "He only likes fighting if it's real." His expression fell, so briefly that neither Hook nor Wendy could be sure they had seen it change at all, and then his smile returned, as bright as ever. "The Wendy," he said, "you *must* be my navigator. How can I convince you?"

If there was any moment during the entire exchange in which Hook was most tempted to shoot the everlost and be done with it, this was that moment. But as badly as he wanted to kill Peter Pan, they were flying through enemy territory, and he needed information even more. If Pan was willing to tell Wendy what they needed to know, then he was too valuable alive, at least for now.

Besides which, Hook could see the subtle signs of fatigue wearing on his navigator, no matter how hard she struggled not to let them show. Her eyelids were starting to droop, her shoulders had lost their usual square defiance, and she kept pressing one hand to her head, massaging her right temple.

They needed a safe place to land—a refuge where she could rest. Even if he had to procure it from the man he hated most in all the world.

"Before you convince *her*, you must convince *me*," Hook replied coldly. "*I* am her captain. If you can prove to me that she is of more use to the king's service aboard your own vessel, as an emissary to the crown, then, perhaps, I might permit it. But first—"

"Yes!" Peter blurted out, and he leaped to his feet. "An emissary and a navigator and a storyteller and a Wendy. She could be all four things to us at once! That's a brilliant idea!"

"But *first*," Hook repeated, even more firmly, "we need information. And a safe haven, from which to plan our ... our joint operation."

It hurt him to say the words, even as a ruse, but he managed to spit them out nonetheless.

"It is a fair request," Peter agreed. "I know a place where you will be safe. And I will take you to someone who can answer your questions. You'll like her. She blames me for everything." A tiny smile played across Wendy's lips, but it disappeared before either Hook or Peter could catch it. "Follow our ship, and I'll show you where you can hide. But follow us *exactly*. You don't want to attract Snaggleclaw's attention. He might be old, but he could still rip you to shreds."

"Snaggleclaw?" Wendy asked.

"You'll be all right," Peter assured her. "What you did, flying straight at us and then up and over just in time? Why, I don't think anyone but me could have done better!" And then he added, his tone exceedingly gentle, "Even then, only just a *little* better. And I've been flying a very long time."

With that he spread his wings and lifted off into the sky. The action dislodged Tinker Bell, who had remained on his shoulder looking blue ever since he had forced her to apologize. She hovered in midair, waiting until she was sure Peter wasn't looking, and then she glanced back at Wendy, her hair flashing from blue into red into a calculating bronze before she took off after him.

CHAPTER 33

A commission!

Wendy could hardly believe it. She was an officer in the Royal Navy. A real officer, just like the ones at Bartholomew Fair—the ones who had laughed at her all those years ago. And not *any* officer, but the *navigator* of England's only *flying* ship! The gentle wind caressed her hair as she looked out across the unexplored mysteries of Neverland. The living green scent of magic filled her senses—even better, she thought, than the rich tang of the sea.

It didn't seem possible.

Wait, it *wasn't* possible.

The thought brought her up short. Hook might be willing to pay the price of her commission, but that didn't mean it would be permitted. Women weren't even allowed to be *sailors* in the Royal Navy, let alone officers.

But the captain wouldn't lie to her, would he?

No, she refused to believe it. He was a man of his word. A man

of honor. He might not fully appreciate her. He might not even like her. But he would not make her a solemn promise without the intention of carrying it through. He would find a way to accomplish it, one way or another, once they returned to England.

Still, she resolved to requisition a blue officer's coat from the quartermaster just as soon as they were able to land the ship. *If* they ever landed.

Neverland was not the sort of small, deserted island one reads about in stories of shipwrecked sailors. Wendy understood that now. It was an island in the same way that Britain was an island—a vast and diverse landscape that spread out beneath her as far as the eye could see.

In fact, she only knew it was an island because Peter had said that it was.

They had been flying toward the mountains for what felt like forever. The fields that had started out as a patchwork quilt in varying shades of green had given way to more exotic colors. What sort of vegetable could possibly reflect the sun in this silver sheen? Or that sparkling amethyst? Was it some exotic blood vine glistening scarlet in the field below? Or were they merely poppies in full, eternal bloom, stretching unbroken from one perfect corner to the other?

This, of course, made Wendy think of Poppy, her companion dog at Hook's estate, which reminded her of her young friend, Colin, and how much he would have loved it here. But that, in turn, made her think of Nicholas. He had died, she suddenly realized, only yesterday. She had worked through the night to prepare *The Pegasus*—they all had—and then Blackheart had appeared, forcing them to leave Nicholas with *The Tiger*. There had been no time for a funeral. Her skeleton crew would bury him at sea on the way back home.

For all Wendy knew, they were doing that very thing right

this instant, his body slipping forever beneath the waves instead of standing here beside her where he belonged, gasping and pointing, while she smiled and wondered about poppies.

The full force of Wendy's grief slammed into her chest, stealing her breath away, and it was all she could do to remain standing, let alone keep the ship in the air.

She had never lost anyone before, and although she had read many books and understood death as *an idea,* she hadn't expected grief to feel like a living thing. Like a tiger that lies in wait, stalking you, so that one moment you're smiling, thinking about poppies, and in the very next moment, without any warning, you're reliving that terrible loss, fresh and raw, as it shreds your heart all over again.

Her eyes brimmed with tears, and she closed them tightly against the memory. She wished they had taken him aboard *The Pegasus,* so they could have laid his body and soul to rest here in this magical earth instead of relinquishing him to the deep.

But then she thought, *No, he would not be safe here. None of us is safe here.*

She shivered. Where had the thought come from? And what did it mean? She didn't know, but she felt the truth of it, as sure as she felt the grief in her chest and the throb in her temples.

She took a deep breath and steadied herself. She was the navigator now. She was responsible for her crew, and she would not let another man die on this journey. Not if she could help it. She straightened her back, squared her shoulders, wiped the tears from her cheeks, and turned her eyes toward the mountains.

All the while, Hook stood behind Wendy near the helm, silently watching her. The tears in her eyes. The determined set of her shoulders. He understood it all too well. Hook had lost his share of men to England's enemies, and every one of them was a burden on his heart.

Nicholas was not the first, nor would he be the last. Hook accepted that. His entire crew accepted that. They understood the price of war. But the first casualty was always the hardest for any new member of the crew. The way they responded was as good as any barometer—the tool that revealed the weather of their character.

Some showed no emotion whatsoever, barely even blinking over the loss of a human soul. These, in Hook's opinion, had been born without that natural affection that binds one man (or woman) to another. They had no place amidst the camaraderie of a ship's crew, and he set these ashore at the first opportunity.

Others retreated into rage. They drank and they fought and they railed against the brutality of the enemy. Against the cruelty of fate. These, he suffered gladly, despite the storm. He gave them their drink, or men to fight, or a night in irons when that was what they needed. But he kept them. Because he knew they loved the crew. And they loved England. And they would do whatever was necessary to protect them both.

But the ones who shed their tears and allowed the clouds to pass—the ones who accepted the winds and tides of war, understanding them to be as impersonal as the sea itself—those he groomed and promoted. Those were the men who knew how to walk in the eye of the storm.

And Wendy was one of them.

He saw it in the set of her jaw. In her unflagging focus on the horizon. And he recognized the moment when she set her grief

aside to move forward. For the mission. For the men. It was unfortunate that her career would be so limited. If they both survived this cursed island, he would buy her a commission, as he had promised (under an assumed name, of course), and she would retire immediately. She would have an income in return for her service here. He would see to it.

She would certainly deserve it.

Every time they sent a ship back home, he lost more of his best men—the ones he knew he could count on to deliver those ships to London. *The Dragon, The Cerberus,* and now *The Tiger.* Charlie was the only man left whom he trusted to that extent. If Wendy were a man ... but there was no point in dwelling on it. He found himself in an impossible situation, and like his own heroes of the past, he would adapt. For the mission. And for England.

He would elevate her status as much as he could, but no further. And only because he needed her.

He looked up from his reverie to realize they were finally nearing the mountains. As the ship approached the closest of the peaks, the light suddenly dimmed, as though they had passed all at once from daylight into dusk. Hook glanced uneasily along the ridge line, looking for the flock of jellyfish-sails, but there was no sign of them now. Instead, a small family of monstrous four-legged beasts covered in long, shaggy white hair trudged across the exposed slope. They looked, he thought, like sheepdogs crossed with elephants, and it made him wonder what other strange creatures might be waiting for them on the full night side of the mountains, which seemed to be where they were headed.

The ship passed between two peaks, and now they sailed beneath the light of a full moon, so bright that he could hardly see the stars. As they made their way silently into the valley on the other side, the rock of the left-hand peak began to give way—the start of an avalanche. Hook was about to tell Wendy to lift higher

into the air, to make sure they were well clear of the snowy slopes below, when he realized suddenly that it was not an avalanche at all.

It was a dragon.

Hook stared in shock as the tremendous creature—easily twice as long as *The Pegasus* from head to tail—raised its spiked snout and swiveled its head toward the incoming ships. It wasn't any color Hook might have expected of a dragon (not that he would have had any colors in mind for a dragon if you had asked him even five minutes ago.) It was a mottled white and brown, splashed in jagged patches all across its hide, blending perfectly into the rock and ice of the peak upon which it lay. Even its face was white on the top right and dark on the bottom left, split along a rough diagonal line.

The men of *The Pegasus* were in such a state of shock that not one of them cried out. But the dragon made no move to attack. It lay facing them along the ridge line, and it turned its dark left eye toward Pan's ship, tilting its chin just a bit and then snorting a puff of smoke into the night air before laying its head back down, apparently satisfied.

A watch-dragon. How had a dim-witted fool like Peter Pan managed to train a watch-dragon?

Hook hated him. He hated him with the burning fire of a thousand circles of hell. But that didn't mean Pan was the most dangerous enemy they would face here. The more Hook saw of that confounded everlost idiot, the more it made sense that he was just a pawn in a larger game—that someone else was behind the violence that had been perpetrated against England. Absentmindedly, he rubbed the stump of his right wrist with his good left hand, massaging it a bit where it met the steel of his hook. He owed Pan for the loss of his hand, no matter what else came of their time in Neverland.

Hook would use him for now. He would set the ship down in the valley and let his crew get some rest. Then he would meet with this local informant and get as much information as he could. He would formulate a plan to defeat Blackheart. But Pan's assistance today did not make up for what he had stolen before.

Once Hook didn't need him, Peter Pan would die.

CHAPTER 34

When they finally brought the ship in to land, Wendy thought she had never felt so relieved in all her life. She had been concerned at first about how she would manage to set the ship down without doing any more damage than had already been done during the battle, but they had arrived in the shelter of the night valley to discover not one but two giant wooden frameworks, each standing ready to cradle a ship safely off the ground.

Wendy watched as Pan guided his own ship into the first of the two air docks, and then she guided *The Pegasus* carefully into the second, moving the ship mere inches at a time despite her aching head. The human crew reluctantly threw their mooring lines to the everlost, who came to help as soon as their own ship had landed. The flying men hovered in the air around *The Pegasus*, gently maneuvering her into position, until finally, with hardly so much as a bump, the ship came to rest and the coin fell still in the palm of Wendy's hand.

Hook had disappeared early on during this procedure, threatening bodily harm to anyone and everyone if he found even one scratch on England's only flying ship and muttering something about not being able to watch. He reemerged just in time to see the ship docked safely. The captain nodded to Wendy in silent approval, set the watch command, and then escorted her to her new quarters.

Much to her surprise, it was a significant step up from anywhere she had ever before slept in her life. True to his word, Hook had assigned her a stateroom that befit her new station.

There was a much larger bed to the left and a much larger desk to the right than she had enjoyed in either of her earlier rooms. A table stood in the center, bolted to the floor, with a chair that could be secured to the wall as needed. A small bank of windows was set into the bulkhead, and Wendy realized that they looked out toward the rear of the ship, just like the captain's own windows did. There was also a small cabinet set into the near wall, and her sea chest was secured next to it.

But she hardly had the energy to appreciate any of it. She had eyes only for Nana, who bounded to Wendy the moment she opened the door, wriggling back and forth in a vain effort to wag her entire body. Wendy chuckled and greeted her, then stumbled to the bed and collapsed onto it without even removing her boots, let alone bothering to notice when Hook left, shutting the door softly behind him.

She had no idea how long she slept because she opened her eyes to the exact same moonlit night, despite the fact that her arms and legs ached as though they had been lying motionless for hours. She turned her head before she had fully awoken, sensing that she was in unfamiliar surroundings, but everything was just as she remembered, right down to the windows that currently looked out onto the dark sky of Neverland.

Neverland!

It all came back in a rush. Blackheart. The chase. The portal. Neverland. The giant jellyfish-sails. The cannon fire. Peter. The mountains. The dragon.

The dragon!

Wendy rushed to the windows. She could see well enough to make out the mountains they had passed through, the moonlight reflecting off the snow-capped peaks. But the ridge line was eerily dim against the dark sky, slumbering in twilight and shadow. If the dragon was there, she could no longer distinguish him from the rock and snow upon which he rested.

Mildly disappointed, she turned her attention to the ground below. There was no mistaking the sounds of men working—shouts and grunts and chopping and hammering, punctuated by an occasional explosive curse, usually followed by a round of laughter. The men were hidden from sight, working almost directly below her, but she had to assume they were repairing the damage to the ship.

Then Nana growled low in her throat, and Wendy spun toward the center of the room. The huge Newfoundland was staring intently at the cabinet, and more precisely at the tiny innisfay who had poked his head out from behind a hanging linen shirt and was now jingling back at Nana in a scolding sort of way.

"Charming!" She turned her attention back to Nana. "No, Nana. Hush now," she told the dog gently, and Nana stopped growling.

Nana sat down (because she knew Wendy would tell her to if she didn't), but she did not take her eyes off the tiny innisfay. Surrounded by a vast landscape of magic, Nana had spent her first hour or so in Neverland barking at everything and nothing in particular. When the scent showed no sign of changing—and no one responded to her insistent and constant alarm—she had finally given up. But she still didn't trust the little flying man who

smelled just as suspicious as the big ones, even if everything else now smelled the same way.

"Good morning, Charming," Wendy said, and then she added, mostly to herself, "if one can call it morning, that is, even if the sky never seems to change. Now, where did you get such a fine shirt-curtain for your quarters?" The linen shirt looked very much like the one that had previously been hanging in the infirmary of *The Tiger*, and she made a mental note to thank Thomas for his kindness.

Charming jingled a merry greeting.

"Oh!" Wendy exclaimed suddenly. "Why, I suppose you're home, aren't you! Does this mean you'll be leaving us?" She was a bit sad at the idea of losing his company, especially so soon after gaining it in the first place, but Charming shook his head. He accompanied the motion with a long, melodious explanation that Wendy couldn't understand at all, but at least he didn't seem to be going anywhere.

Just then, a hesitant knock sounded at her door, so she wandered over and opened it.

Gentleman Starkey stood on the other side, hunching his shoulders a bit and wringing his hands in his shirttail.

"Why, hello, Mr. Starkey," Wendy said.

"Miss Darling," he replied. "I hope I didn't disturb you. The captain said very specifically that you were *not* to be disturbed. But he also told me to ask you to go see him as soon as you woke up. So I've been waiting, you see, trying to hear when you might be awake, but without actually listening in, of course ..." His voice trailed off, and he cast his eyes toward the floor.

"Of course, Mr. Starkey. I only just woke, and I was not disturbed in the least. If you'll show me the way?"

"Yes, miss!" he said, looking considerably relieved. "Right away, miss. The captain's quarters are just one level up."

Wendy didn't want Charming to be trapped in her room, so she let him out and then followed Mr. Starkey up to Hook's own quarters. She let Nana come with her as far as the captain's door, asking Mr. Starkey if he would be so kind as to take the dog for a bit of a walk outside.

(Mr. Starkey seemed much more eager for this arrangement than Nana did, but she followed him down the passageway nonetheless when it seemed to be what her mistress wanted.)

Wendy took a deep breath and knocked on the door.

"Enter!"

She opened it to find both Hook and Charlie in the captain's quarters. They stood side by side, staring in puzzlement at some kind of parchment that had been unrolled and placed on the table.

"Miss Darling," Hook commented. "Good. Come tell me if you can make anything of this nonsense."

"Sir?" Wendy asked, but Hook just waved his good left hand at the sheet in front of him in a vague gesture of dismissal.

"It's a map," Charlie added. "I think." He frowned a little, and the corner of his mouth twisted to one side in uncertainty.

Wendy approached the table, and Charlie carefully turned the parchment around so she could look at it right side up. Not that it made any difference.

In the bottom right-hand corner was a cartoonish representation of the two ships in their cradles. Beneath these, in a surprisingly elegant hand, was a single word: "Here." In the top left corner was an elaborate "X." This was marked with the word "Tiger." Between the two was a line that curved sporadically along the page, climbing upward and then swooping downward with no apparent rhyme or reason. The turns were not marked in any way. Instead, sparse drawings populated the outer portion of the page.

One at the top was a surprisingly accurate depiction of penguins with an arrow pointing upward, indicating that the penguins were not actually on the map at all but rather somewhere beyond its boundaries. This was labeled, rather unhelpfully, "Penguins." Another near the bottom caught Wendy's eye: a drawing of three mermaids sunning themselves on a large rock. This was labeled, "Lagoon."

Wendy looked up at Charlie and then at Hook, and then she ducked her head, smiling just a little. It was the smallest smile she could manage under the circumstances. Hook's grimace was downright dour, and she did not want to antagonize him. But she could hardly help herself.

"Peter," she guessed.

"I sent Lieutenant Abbot to request a map to this woman we're supposed to meet with," Hook growled, "and Pan gave him this ... this ..."

"Cartographical mockery?" Charlie supplied.

"This cartographical mockery!" Hook echoed.

"I see," said Wendy.

She said nothing else, and Charlie said nothing else—because neither one wanted to say what all three of them were now thinking. More importantly, they didn't want it to seem later that it might have been their idea in the first place and then be blamed for it when things went, inevitably, horribly wrong.

So they all remained silent for an uncomfortably long time, until Hook, as the captain, finally shouldered the responsibility and *said* the thing, with the exact expression one makes when one has just eaten an entire lemon slice after mistaking it for an orange, and the thing was this.

"We're going to have to bring him with us."

CHAPTER 35

They left at ... well ... at night. Because it always seemed to be night in this part of Neverland. At least the moon was still full—that had not changed either—but they packed several torches, just in case. Peter remained on the deck of *The Pegasus* while they were getting ready. "For consultations," he said. But these did not turn out to be very helpful.

"How long will we be traveling?" Wendy asked him.

"I have no idea," Peter said. "Neverland is unpredictable. We might be killed before we've gone even a hundred yards." He said this in a very matter-of-fact sort of way, but then he shrugged, as though the possibility did not concern him.

"Yes, but assuming we *don't* die before we get there," Wendy tried, "how many days will it take?"

"There are no days in Neverland," Peter told her.

Inquiries regarding the terrain they would be hiking through, the weather they might encounter, and the dangers they might face were equally unproductive.

"Every kind of terrain. It only depends which way you want to go," Peter said.

"The weather could change at any moment," he told her. "It hasn't yet, since you've been here, but it might. It would be fun if there were a storm, wouldn't it? That would be a grand adventure!"

"Listing the number of dangers between here and there would take a very long time. It would be much easier just to see what happens along the way," he suggested.

This sort of talk made Wendy uneasy, and she asked if perhaps they should use innisfay dust instead and teach the men who were going how to fly.

"Could Hook fly the ship?" Peter asked, sounding surprised.

"Well, no," she admitted.

"Then he can't fly himself either. But we could always go without him. You and I could meet Tigerlilja together, just the two of us. It would be far less trouble."

Wendy knew what Hook would think of *that* idea, so she nipped it in the bud and went below to report that, in summary, she had no idea how long they would be traveling and they should try to be prepared for anything.

At last, they gathered on deck. There were ten of them besides Peter: Hook, Wendy, John, Michael, Thomas, Gentleman Starkey, and four other men whom Wendy did not know very well. They could bring only ten, and no more. Peter had been very specific. But Nana was allowed to come along, by special permission, without counting against them.

Charlie would be in charge while they were gone, so he had to stay behind. Thankfully, Mr. Smee was overseeing the repairs to the rudder, which had been blown apart by Blackheart's cannons, so he would be staying too.

They climbed down long rope ladders to reach the ground, and Charming decided to follow them, simply because it was more interesting than staying in Wendy's quarters by himself.

"You can't come," Peter told the innisfay. "We already have ten."

Charming hovered just behind Wendy's right shoulder, jingled melodiously, and pointed at Tinker Bell, who was seated on Peter's left shoulder in her natural form. Tink's hair flashed instantly to red, and she jangled back at him with a furious expression.

"She doesn't count," Peter proclaimed, to which Tinker Bell replied by turning into a tiny red dragon and biting Peter on the ear.

"I didn't mean it like that," Peter protested. "You count as a *person*. You just don't count as part of the ten. We can only bring ten *new* people. You've been there before, and so have I."

Tinker Bell's scales slowly shifted back into gold, but she remained a dragon, just in case.

"Have you ever been to see Tigerlilja before?" Peter asked, turning his attention back to Charming.

Charming's hair turned blue, but then it flashed in an instant to gold and he jingled merrily at Peter. When he was finished, he crossed his arms over his chest with a triumphant expression and landed on Wendy's shoulder.

"Well, yes," Peter agreed, "I suppose you could have flown there on your own. Since you don't need me to show you the way, you can come. But if Tigerlilja asks, you're only *following* us. I'm not *taking* you."

✦

The gently sloping valley in which the ships had landed was covered in an array of short grasses and night-blooming wildflowers. It was chilly, but not cold enough for snow—the perfect temperature for hiking at a brisk clip with a heavy pack. But the moment they reached the jungle trail at the base of the mountain, everything changed.

To Wendy, it felt like passing through an invisible curtain. On one side was a chilly alpine valley, and on the other was a tropical forest. It was night in both places, and the same silvery moon bathed them in its quiet glow. But everything else was thoroughly different—the temperature, the humidity, the scent of the air. Wendy took one step backward, and she was in the valley again. One step forward, and she was in the jungle. Backward, forward, backward, forward.

"How extraordinary!" she exclaimed.

She wondered for a moment if there was another portal right here on the ground, but that couldn't be it. She could see the jungle perfectly well from the valley, and she could see the valley perfectly well from the jungle.

"What is?" Peter asked. "You mean the plants? I thought you would like that." He smiled at her fondly.

"Plants? Why, no," Wendy said. "I meant this sharp line between the valley and the jungle. How it's one thing on one side and something different on the other. You can feel it change!"

Thomas, who had been walking behind Wendy, came upon the same phenomenon, and now it was his turn to take one step forward and one step back, over and over again. He pulled a leather-bound journal from his pack and began to scrawl earnest notes across the pages with what looked like a metal quill.

"Why, what is that?" Wendy asked. She took a step closer, trying to get a better look.

"What?" Thomas replied, distracted by his writing. "Oh, this?

It's a barrel pen. Made of steel. Present from a friend of mine. Well, more of an acquaintance than a friend, if anyone asks."

She was about to ask if she could hold it when Peter interrupted her.

"So you haven't even seen the plants yet?"

Wendy looked around at the varied plant life that flourished in the warm, humid air, their leaves jockeying with each other for space and encroaching upon the narrow trail. A strange, glowing insect suddenly lifted off into the air nearby, its delicate wings whirling in circles while its body hung limply below.

Peter saw that the movement had caught Wendy's attention. "No, the *plants.* Look," he insisted. "Tinker Bell, if you please."

Tink was still in dragon form. She harrumphed without moving from his shoulder, and her golden scales took on a slightly reddish hue.

"Tinker Bell," he said, "we talked about this, and we agreed it would be such a good surprise. Especially the way you said you would do it. I could show her myself, but no one else would do it nearly as well as you."

The dragon's tiny scales glowed more brightly, gaining in intensity until she was almost painful to look at. Suddenly, she launched herself from his shoulder and flew in a long sweep over the closest leaves, leaving a glowing trail of innisfay dust falling slowly in her wake.

Wendy gasped. The moon cast only a hushed, secret sort of light as it filtered through the foliage, painting the world in grays and shadows. But when Tinker Bell flew over it, she revealed the true colors of the jungle, and they weren't the green that Wendy had assumed. Instead, the leaves were a thousand gleaming hues of sapphire and turquoise, cobalt and opal. A *blue* jungle that reminded Wendy of the sea, with flowers like coral, in twisting stalks of yellow and pink and scarlet.

"Oh!" she exclaimed.

"Extraordinary!" Thomas agreed. He set to sketching in his journal, trying to capture what he could as the light of the innisfay dust slowly faded away in Tinker Bell's wake.

"Do you like it?" Peter asked.

"It's wonderful!" Wendy told him.

But then Hook's voice cut through the magic—quiet and furious.

"Put. That. Light. Out."

Peter and Wendy turned to look at him while Thomas continued muttering to himself and scribbling in his journal.

"Do you want to attract every living creature within three miles?" Hook demanded. "I said put it out!"

"I wouldn't worry about the light," Peter told him. "Most of those creatures can smell a lot farther than they can see. And you don't smell like Neverland at all."

Hook's expression never changed, but Wendy saw John and Michael share a distinctly nervous glance just before Tinker Bell's glow winked out.

CHAPTER 36

They walked in silence, strung out in single file, surrounded by the dim hush of the night, but as their own voices fell still, the forest came alive. Something that sounded very much like a cricket chirped somewhere to their left. A frog croaked to their right. And within a few short moments, an entire chorus of peeps and chirrups took hold, serenading them along their journey.

Birds called to each other, and a small creature raced through the treetops, chittering in annoyance. An entire troop of unseen somethings started to hoot in deep, haunting voices. Wendy found herself wondering whether they might be dark blue owls or light blue monkeys or perhaps something else altogether when a terrible roar ripped through the jungle, followed immediately by profound silence.

Wendy stopped in her tracks, as did Michael in front of her and Thomas behind. Nana growled, low and quiet in the back of her throat, but Wendy hushed her immediately. The men raised their muskets, licking their lips. Their wide eyes darted back and

forth, hunting for openings in the foliage, trying to see anything beyond the thick underbrush that grew right up to the edge of the trail.

Suddenly, the sound of a desperate chase broke out somewhere off to their right. Cries of distress moved deeper into the jungle, and something large crashed through the undergrowth in pursuit. Then there was a scream, and everything fell deathly still. Moments later, the night chorus returned, trilling and squawking and warbling and hooting as though nothing had happened.

"What was that?" Wendy whispered to Charming, who was sitting on her shoulder, but of course he had no way to answer her that she could understand.

Peter, who had been walking in front, flew back to land in front of her.

"You don't have a name for it," he said, looking very proud of himself. "They don't exist anymore. Except here, I mean. I have the very last one."

"Only one?" Wendy asked.

"Only one," Peter confirmed.

"How sad," she said quietly. "The last of its kind left in all the world. Without even a mate, or any chance of there ever being any more." She still had no idea what it was, but the thought of it being the last seemed very sad indeed.

Peter cast his eyes to the ground, and his shoulders slumped for just a moment, but then he grinned and met her gaze.

"You wouldn't want another one," he told her. "This one causes all kinds of trouble. Why, Tigerlilja and her people had to rebuild two entire houses not so long ago. And it ate one of her brother's wolves. I doubt I'll ever hear the end of it."

"It ate a wolf?" Wendy exclaimed. She glanced down at Nana, who was still staring into the darkness.

"It did," Peter said lightly, "but at least it didn't eat Tigerlilja."

✦

They continued along the jungle trail for what felt like hours, flinching and spinning to point their muskets at every glow-bug along the way. Wendy heard more new calls and whistles over the course of those few miles than she had ever heard before, from the almost familiar chirps and pops of unseen tiny things to long, eerie wails that rose and fell in the twilight.

Then, about an hour after the wolf-eater, they heard something entirely different: the distinct sound of a human infant crying in distress.

"Halt!" Hook called out, and they all stopped to listen, trying to hear where the sound was coming from.

"Is that the village?" Wendy asked Peter, who had flown back to her side.

"No," he assured her. "We're still a long way yet. Why? What do you hear?"

"A baby," Wendy told him. "Don't you hear it? She's crying."

"She sounds like she's over there," Michael said, and he stepped off the trail, trying to move toward the sound. "I don't think she's far."

"Wait!" Wendy called out, and she ran to stop him, grabbing his arm before he could disappear into the dense foliage.

"Why?" Michael asked, turning to her in surprise. "Don't you want to help her?"

"Look at me," Wendy told him. "Michael. Look at me." His eyes kept drifting back toward the sound of the infant's wails. They were growing louder and more insistent the longer they waited. "Michael!" she finally shouted, and he turned his attention to her fully, his eyes regaining their focus. "Captain!" she shouted, still holding his gaze. "Gather the men! Please!"

"All hands to me!" Hook shouted at once. "To me!" He strode back to her position with a pistol at the ready. "We'll organize a rescue party."

"Aye, Captain," Starkey barked.

"No, wait," Wendy insisted. She placed a hand on Hook's arm, just above the stump of his right wrist, startling him. "Something's wrong. It isn't a child. Or, at least, I don't think it is. It's ... it's *pulling* us somehow."

"What do you mean?" Hook demanded.

Peter was watching her carefully, but he said nothing, waiting for her to reply.

When they had first arrived in Neverland, the pervasive magic of everything at once had overwhelmed her senses. Nothing smelled more magical than anything else. Nothing had a *direction.* But as they had been trudging through the jungle, Wendy had felt her senses begin to sharpen, becoming different somehow, until she was *feeling* the magic more than smelling it.

She could still sense *The Pegasus,* despite the fact that it was now miles away, and she felt completely certain that if it moved, she would know it. She didn't know how she *could* be certain, which bothered her a bit, but that didn't change what she knew. Just as she could now feel Peter standing before her, and as she could feel the wrongness of the baby crying in the dark.

But she knew Hook didn't put much credence in feelings, so instead she turned to Michael and said this: "How do you know it's a girl?"

"What?" Michael asked, looking confused.

"You said, 'Don't you want to help her?' Her. You called the baby a girl. How could you possibly know that?"

"I ... I don't know," Michael admitted. He turned back toward the jungle, but this time he wore an expression of confusion rather than the intensity he had shown before.

"You can't," Wendy pointed out. "I don't think it's an infant at all. I think it's something magical, trying to lure us to it."

"It's a siren!" Peter blurted out. "I knew it was a siren, but I didn't expect you to be able to tell!"

"A siren," the men muttered, all clustered around them. More than one now stared nervously toward the sound of the child, but not one of them looked like he wanted to go find it. They were sailors, after all. They knew about sirens.

"But sirens lure men with songs," Starkey protested. "That's no song."

"That's a myth," Peter told him. "Sirens don't use songs. They use the sound of whatever you would feel most compelled to protect."

"You're absolutely certain it isn't an infant?" Hook directed the question to Wendy. The fingers of his good left hand still clutched the grip of his pistol, but his eyes focused only on her, refusing to dart back to the crying that still emanated insistently from the jungle.

"Yes, Captain. I'm certain."

Hook nodded and lifted his voice to the crew. "No man is to leave this path except upon my orders. Not for any reason, no matter what you hear or see. Is that clear?"

"Aye, Captain," they all replied, including Wendy.

"Fall into formation. We're moving on."

They did as they were told. John and Michael followed Hook forward while Thomas and the others drifted back, forming a line again.

Peter lingered a moment longer. "That was very well done, the Wendy," he said, and he smiled at her fondly.

"I hesitated, though, at least at first," she protested. "It almost fooled me! You were never affected by it at all."

"Of course I was," he admitted. "I just knew it wasn't real."

"But how? How could you know right away?" The sound of the baby's wails still carried over the noises of the jungle, and it left her feeling unsettled.

"Because I never heard an infant," he told her, his eyes holding her gaze. "I heard *you.* And I knew exactly where you really were."

CHAPTER 37

After another hour or so, things changed again, and when they changed, they changed completely, as they seemed to do in Neverland. One moment Wendy was in the warm, humid jungle, surrounded by eternal twilight, and with one more step she was in the full glory of day. She still stood in a forest, but this was a much more open forest, with very little underbrush. It reminded her of the woods near Hook's estate, except there were far more evergreens.

She could see now that the path rested upon on a kind of plateau, with a steep, wooded drop-off to the left and a river valley far below, the soothing vista peeking here and there through the trees. Wendy took a step back, into the blue twilight jungle, and she realized the drop had been there the whole time, just a few yards beyond the edge of the path. She simply hadn't recognized it because of the height of the trees and the thickness of the foliage.

She stepped forward again, and there was the pine-scented

forest. The air was cooler (and not nearly as humid), and she could smell the subtle fragrance of woodsmoke carried on the gentle breeze, laced with roasting fish. She exchanged a smile with John and Michael, who had emerged from the jungle ahead of her.

"The village!" she said. They couldn't see it yet, but the scent on the wind told them it was close.

"Remain vigilant!" Hook ordered from up ahead, his voice pitched deep and loud to carry down the line. "These are still unknown lands, and we don't know what might be waiting for us."

Just then, something hit the ground at Wendy's feet. She flinched and leaped backward, ready to draw her sword, then saw in the same instant that it was only a pinecone. She grinned at herself and glanced up to find Peter crouching on a tree limb above her with a second pinecone in his hand.

"Remain vigilant, the Wendy," Peter echoed. He laughed and leaped off the branch to fly straight up into the air. He performed several loops and spins against the bright blue sky, dropping the pinecone and swooping down to catch it over and over, whooping and hollering all the while. He sped off ahead only to return almost immediately, repeating this process several times. "Come on!" he yelled. "We're almost there!"

"Hold your formation!" Hook shouted to them all. "Remain *vigilant!*"

Wendy ducked her head, casting her eyes to the ground and doing her best not to giggle as Peter burst into song overhead.

Ohhhhhhhhhhhhhh,
If I could choose a lazy life,
I just might be a bear.
I'd sleep right through the winter
and never comb my hair.

But still I think an everlost
a better thing to be.
To sail beneath the starry skies,
my heart forever free.

Over land and over sea,
a flying ship for me!

Wendy whispered the words again, repeating them as was only proper for any seafaring shanty, "Over land and over sea, a flying ship for me." She waited for the next verse, but Peter had flown ahead again, his words lost to the sky.

They proceeded in this way for at least another mile, or possibly two. (Or, Wendy admitted to herself, it might have been as many as three. Normally, she was very good at keeping track of that sort of thing, but Peter's antics were highly distracting.)

They had left the forest behind and entered an open field of short grasses, white rock, and wildflowers. The trail had been sloping downward ever since they left the jungle, and the steep drop-off was nothing more than a gentle hill now, but the mountains still rose up to their right, their slopes inhabited by animals that looked for all the world like perfectly normal goats and sheep. Up ahead, the river took a slow turn in their direction and then a sharp bend away again, with a stand of tall trees that blocked their view beyond it.

Overhead, Peter darted back and forth from the trail to the

river bend and back to the trail again, laughing and whistling and telling them to walk faster while he dove or spun or sometimes merely lay on his side in midair, propping his head up with one hand and sighing in a long-suffering sort of way.

At least they could all see each other now, but Wendy wasn't sure whether that was a blessing or a curse under the circumstances. Hook led the way, followed by Starkey, then John, then Michael, then Wendy, then Thomas and the rest. So everyone could see the resigned set of Hook's shoulders as he trudged steadily forward, setting the pace and refusing to acknowledge Peter's presence despite the slight twitch in his neck whenever the everlost started shouting again.

When Peter began practicing his trick of slamming into the ground hard enough to leave knee prints, Hook's shoulders rose dangerously. He turned to look behind him, catching Wendy's eye with a very particular look that said, *Do something about him or I will take care of it myself, once and for all.*

"Peter," Wendy called out, when his next landing came close to her, "come walk with me."

The everlost flew to her at once, landing gently to walk alongside her as though he had not only moments ago been crashing over and over into the ground.

"Look!" he told her. "You can see it now!"

As the trail bent farther toward the right, they could finally see past the trees that grew on the spit of the left bank. There, along the near shore, was a simple but sturdy wooden dock, and moored to the dock were two small ships that looked exactly like the illustrations of Viking ships Wendy had seen in her history books. They had seats for rowing down each side, but they also had masts for sails, and their carved wooden prows reached proudly toward the water.

"Are those ... oh!" Just then, the village itself came into view.

There was a large building in the center—a longhouse, Wendy thought—with several homes around it, each with a timber foundation and a thatched roof. There were smoking racks drying fish, and cooking fires roasting fish, and dozens of villagers of all ages sitting around the fires, licking their fingers, having just finished eating fish, watching uphill toward the trail for Peter's arrival.

The men, women, and children wore a mix of wool and leather clothing, and Wendy could see a field of crops extending behind the farthest houses. The goats and sheep on the mountain must be theirs, she thought. She looked up again, thinking of the flocks, and she caught a hint of movement at the very top of the peak.

Snaggleclaw.

She felt him before she saw him—suddenly, she realized she had *always* felt him, this entire time, without knowing what she was sensing. But he did not seem to be moving from his perch, just shifting in his sleep. She could barely make out the vague outline of his massive head against the camouflage backdrop of snow and rock. She waited a moment to make sure he wasn't waking up, but Peter didn't seem to be concerned in the slightest. (Not that he ever was.) So she turned her attention back to the village.

It looked for all the world like a Viking village, frozen in time, with one small exception. What Wendy had thought at first to be sparks from the cooking fires now moved with the villagers as they stood. The embers zipped and whirled around them, but, as Wendy drew closer, she realized they weren't sparks at all.

They were tiny fairies, even smaller than the innisfay, with hair of fire and lightning.

The villagers swarmed out to meet them, surrounding Peter with smiles and big bear hugs, and the fairies swarmed his body, standing upon his shoulders, his wings, and his hair, and even clinging to his leather clothing. They all seemed tremendously glad to see him.

All, that is, except one.

A young woman stood apart from the others, not much older than Wendy was herself, and she glowered at Peter with a stern look of disapproval.

"Hello, Tiger!" Peter said cheerfully.

"Peter," the woman replied. "What have I told you about bringing new people here?"

"You said not to bring so many," Peter told her. "But last time I brought eleven, and this time I brought only ten. I was very careful. Nana is a dog, and you never said anything about dogs. Charming only followed us here. I didn't bring him." Peter pointed straight at Charming when he said this last bit, and the innisfay darted behind Wendy's head, peeking cautiously out from behind her neck to see what might happen next. "The Wendy, I present to you Tigerlilja. Tiger, this is the Wendy."

"I'm very pleased to meet you," Wendy said, and she gave Tigerlilja a small curtsy, just to be on the safe side of politeness, which is usually the better side, especially when one is first meeting people.

Tigerlilja eyed Wendy up and down but otherwise ignored the introduction.

"Why. Are. They. Here?" Tigerlilja asked, sounding very much like Hook, Wendy thought.

"They're from England," Peter told her. "They want Blackheart off of Neverland, just like you."

Hook stepped forward at this, but he had not yet been introduced, so Tigerlilja turned to Wendy to reply.

"If you're from England," she said, "you don't just want Blackheart off the island. You want him dead. He intends to destroy your homeland, and he's building a fleet and an army to do it."

CHAPTER 38

Tigerlilja invited them to join her in the longhouse. When they entered, they discovered a huge table set for thirteen and piled high with food. Even Tigerlilja hesitated when she first walked through the door.

"Interesting," Wendy heard her mutter, but the woman recovered quickly. She was dressed in simple leather leggings and a wool knit sweater with a knife at her belt—the only other woman Wendy had ever seen dressed like a man. Nothing about her clothing indicated her position as the head of the Norse clan, but Wendy had no doubt she was in charge and was not surprised at all when she strode forward and took the seat at the end of the table.

One of the other Norsemen—a tall man with broad shoulders and long braids in his hair—entered with them and sat to her left.

"My brother, Vegard," Tigerlilja announced, and then she looked expectantly at Wendy.

Apparently, this was all the introduction they were going to get.

Wendy bit back the long list of formalities she had been preparing in the proper British etiquette and instead said only, "Our captain, James Hook." She turned and nodded at Hook, who strode to the table and sat to Tigerlilja's right, across from Vegard.

Wendy wished she could have sat next to Tigerlilja herself. She was mesmerized by the woman—tall and strong, more fierce than beautiful (at least by English standards), and so clearly the leader of her people. Wendy blushed in embarrassment. Her own place in her ship's company was so uncertain that she didn't even know where she was supposed to sit. Fortunately, Gentleman Starkey came to her rescue.

"Navigator Darling," he said, taking her gently by the elbow. "If you please, ma'am." He led her to the seat next to the captain —the seat designated by her new rank rather than her gender— and Wendy smiled at him gratefully. The rest of the men filed in, sitting along the table more or less according to their station, and it was only then that Wendy noticed a fourteenth plate at the far end of the table.

A very tiny plate, just right for an innisfay.

Wendy couldn't see what was on it, but Charming's face lit up as he sat cross-legged in front of it and dove right in with his hands, bringing fistfuls of the stuff to his face and stuffing his cheeks with obvious relish.

"Please," Tigerlilja told them all once they were seated. "Eat. Drink. I will tell you what I can."

Wendy discovered what looked and smelled like roast pheasant with gravy on the dish before her, and she smiled in delight. Roast pheasant was her favorite. There was a goblet etched with a single raindrop set above her plate and another etched with a small cluster of grapes, holding water and wine respectively.

Hook, to her left, had what seemed to be duck with orange sauce. John, across from her, had a bowl of meat stew. Michael, to her right, had a plate piled high with pork ribs. Thomas, across from him, had a plate of mashed potatoes. Nothing but mashed potatoes. He looked as happy as she had ever seen him.

As Wendy glanced down the table, she realized that everyone had something different—even Nana had bowls of food and water near the door—and most of the men had pints of ale. Both Tigerlilja and Vegard had roasted fish, but Tigerlilja's plate also held a small piece of toasted bread smothered in butter and honey, which somehow made her seem at least a little less intimidating.

Peter, down at the far end next to Charming, was devouring a stack of pancakes.

"To understand the true danger of Blackheart," Tigerlilja began, "we must begin at the beginning. And everything in Neverland begins with Peter."

Hook scowled at this and skewered a piece of duck on his hook. Peter looked up and grinned, his mouth full of pancakes. Tigerlilja rolled her eyes.

"The land itself is tied to Peter," she continued, "and he to it. It is his sanctuary. Quite literally. And because of the nature of his heart, the land has expanded to become a safe haven for those who need it. We, meaning our clan, were among the first he brought here. Since then, there have been others. Many others. People. Creatures. Both magical and mundane. Peter finds those who are lost or forgotten—those who are out of place—and he brings them here. When he discovered the orphanages of England, well, you can imagine the treasure trove of lost souls *that* opened up."

Some of us don't have to imagine it, Wendy thought.

But her childhood in the orphanage had not been without hope. She had had Charlie and Mr. Equiano for company. And Mrs. Healey had treated them as kindly as she could, given how many children there were. Wendy had often been cold and hungry, but she knew there were many orphans in England who suffered far

worse. She cast her eyes down to her plate, suddenly feeling guilty over the meal she was enjoying, and Tigerlilja seemed to read her thoughts.

"Peter tries to save the ones who have it the hardest. The ones treated with the most cruelty. Beaten. Starving. The ones with the loneliest hearts. And those too weak to survive. He offers them a place, and of course they come.

"The moment they set foot in Neverland, they leave the past behind. That's the true magic of Neverland. The magic of *home.* The land itself creates a place for every creature that comes to its shores."

"That's why everything's so different!" Wendy blurted out. She didn't mean to interrupt, but she was too excited not to. "The desert and the mountains and the jungle and the fields, all right next to each other! And the night and day at once!"

"Yes," Tigerlilja acknowledged. "If Peter brings a lion, the island creates a veldt. With all the grasses and sounds and heat of its native land. Even its prey. The lion still hunts and eats to survive. Neverland can be a very dangerous place. But the magic here creates a home for everything that needs one. And for most of Peter's orphans, it might as well be a paradise. A home is all they ever wanted. But then Blackheart came."

Tigerlilja cast her eyes down to her plate. She picked up the bread idly but did not eat it. She seemed more to be considering it, lost in her own thoughts. She put the bread down without taking a bite and began speaking again.

"At first, he seemed like any other lost boy. He loved Neverland as much as anyone. Maybe more. He took to Peter's games with more enthusiasm than anyone Peter had ever brought to the island, and soon they were inseparable. Peter taught him to use a sword and fire a gun and made him his first mate. Then Blackheart convinced him to capture another ship and make it fly, so they

could have two ships and battle each other. The best game they had ever played."

When Peter heard his name, he looked up, but as Tigerlilja spoke, Wendy saw his eyes lose their focus, and he returned to his meal.

"For a while," Tigerlilja continued, "they were happy together. Blackheart was the captain to Peter's admiral, and they brought both ships on their English raids, which were partly to find more orphans and partly just for fun. A child's idea of adventure. *Playing* at war, not waging it. Or so I always thought. But then Blackheart became more violent. He started killing the orphans' caretakers. He stopped following Peter's orders. And, finally, he stole the ship for himself, using it to capture others, to build his own fleet.

"By the time I realized the truth, it was far too late. Blackheart had never wanted a home to live in. He wanted a home to *rule*, and that desire took root, feeding on the magic of Neverland.

"Some of the orphans who had left their anger and resentment in the past found that it had reawakened in their hearts, and they chose to follow him, becoming his crew. Eventually, things began to appear here that shouldn't exist anywhere. Just as Neverland creates antelopes for the lions, it created wicked things for Blackheart—creatures formed of cruelty and hatred, ready to serve his will. An army that he intends to take to England, to destroy it forever."

"What kind of creatures?" Hook demanded. "How many? And how big is his fleet?"

At this, Peter finally spoke up. "It doesn't matter how many ships he has! I can battle a thousand ships and win!"

Tigerlilja and Hook both ignored him, refusing to acknowledge that he had spoken at all.

"He has at least five ships and one hundred times that many

creatures," Tigerlilja replied. "Vile things of all kinds. And his numbers continue to grow. As for us, we have only Pan's ship and his crew, who still think of everything as a game. We've been trying to work out a strategy, but we have yet to come up with anything that has even a hope of working."

She shared a glance with her brother.

"We'll think of something," he told her, but his expression was grim.

"We have another ship," Pan said cheerfully.

Tigerlilja, Vegard, and Hook all turned to stare at him.

"What?" Tigerlilja asked.

"The Wendy has a ship now," he clarified, pointing at her with a butter knife.

"*I* have a ship," Hook snapped. "Blackheart had stolen another ship and was about to make it fly. We stole it from him and finished the job."

"So we have two ships!" Tigerlilja exclaimed. It was the first time Wendy had seen her look even remotely hopeful since they had arrived.

"I have a ship," Hook said slowly. "And Pan has a ship. *We* do not have anything."

"But the enemy of our enemy ..." Tigerlilja said.

She left the adage hanging in the air for Hook to finish for himself. At last, he nodded. He didn't look happy about it, but he nodded.

"Still, two against five," Vegard commented.

"Three," said Tigerlilja.

"What? No. Absolutely not." Vegard flashed her a dark look.

"With three we'd have a chance!" Tigerlilja stared her brother down.

"Sorry?" Wendy asked.

"There's another ship Blackheart lost," Tigerlilja explained.

"And we know where it is."

"He didn't *lose* it," Vegard protested. "He *abandoned* it. Big difference. We agreed not to go after it."

"We agreed when we would have had two against five. Now it could be *three* against five. We might never have better odds."

Vegard scowled but fell silent. Apparently, the matter had been decided. Tigerlilja turned to Hook and spoke again.

"One of the creatures that Neverland created for Blackheart was too strong-willed for him to control. It looks like a giant crocodile, but it's far more than that. It's some kind of demon-spawn, with powerful magic in its own right. It broke free in the hold of one of his ships. The crew grounded the vessel and abandoned it before they could be eaten alive.

"Blackheart sent a few men back to try to retrieve it, but none of them escaped. The croc never forgets a man once he has his scent. A dark, foggy swamp formed around the entire ship, and the croc lives there now, feeding on anything unfortunate enough to wander into its territory."

"How long ago was this?" Hook asked, his eyes narrow.

"I know what you're thinking," Tigerlilja told him, "but the ship still seems to be in good shape, as far as we can tell. The croc hasn't destroyed it. And Neverland has a way of preserving things. You'd never believe how old *I* am." She smiled grimly when she said this last bit, but she forged ahead without waiting for a reply. "The ship is still salvageable. If we can retrieve it and use it to fight Blackheart before he gets any stronger, we might actually have a chance. I would gladly pledge my warriors to the cause."

Vegard nodded in silent agreement.

"Why?" Hook demanded, watching both with suspicion. "Why would your men risk their lives for England?"

"We wouldn't," Tigerlilja said simply. "But we would fight to the death for Neverland."

CHAPTER 39

An alliance. With Pan. And a Viking woman.

How had his life come to this?

Hook stood next to Vegard in the bow of a clan longboat, silently bemoaning his fate. The river, they had been told, was a faster way to return, so they had split up the party between the two boats and were now rowing toward the valley. Hook had refused to be in the same vessel with Pan, but in the end it hadn't mattered. The flying man was executing loop-the-loops in the clear blue sky.

"Stop that right now! Are you trying to get us all killed?" Tigerlilja turned her face toward the heavens, yelling at Peter—and several of the tiny fairies that zipped around the Vikings stopped in midair to shake angry, sparking fists in his direction—but Peter paid them no heed.

"Killed?" Hook was standing next to the clanswoman, and he asked the question calmly. Casually. As though nothing could possibly make the situation any worse, so they might as well add the immediate threat of death to the list.

"Blackheart watches the skies," she told him. "I'd rather not attract his attention."

"Is he likely to have a ship nearby?" Hook scanned the sky for any sign of Blackheart's fleet, but he saw only Pan, who was now executing such a large loop through the air that the bottom of it took him all the way down to the river. He sliced through the surface and sped along underwater on his back, surfacing near the other longboat to smile up at Wendy.

"No. Neverland is vast, and he tends to stay clear of the village. We might not fly, but we can still hold our own in a fight."

Although she wore the same casual clothing as she had in the longhouse, she carried a bow with her on the longboat and had a quiver of arrows strapped to her back. In the blink of an eye, she knocked an arrow to the bow and whistled two quick notes. The closest of the tiny fairies darted in to grab the arrow just before Tigerlilja let it fly. The missile thudded into the trunk of a tree near the shoreline, and a small fireball exploded around it, presumably thanks to the fairy.

It was one of the fastest, most efficient shots Hook had ever seen. He barely had time to react before the rest of Tigerlilja's clansmen in both boats had stowed their oars and risen to their feet, bows in hand and arrows at the ready, scanning for danger. Tigerlilja gestured twice with her fingers splayed wide, palm flat to the ground, and they all turned and sat in the same moment, picking up their oars again.

"Impressive," Hook said, which was high praise indeed.

"It's enough to keep Blackheart from attacking us directly. After all, we're not really in his way. Or, at least, we haven't been. But it's no defense against cannons," she replied gravely.

"Still," Hook told her, "I've seen British platoons that weren't as well trained. If Blackheart's ships leave you alone, where's the threat?"

"The fairies," she said simply. "They're a proud people, and their favorite thing to do in all the world is brag to each other. So all the goings-on of Neverland spread from one to the next like wildfire. Our tiny elementals tend to stay with us, and Tinker Bell is fiercely loyal to Peter, but the innisfay are everywhere. If they see Peter in the sky, they'll investigate. And then Blackheart will hear about it. He'll know you're here. And that you've met with us."

"Putting your village in danger," Hook realized.

"Yes."

Hook watched in silence as Peter took off into the sky again. The everlost was out of control. Even if Hook put their past aside—which he could only just barely do, even for the sake of his own hypothetical musings—Pan could still destroy the alliance before it had even begun. And if they survived long enough to salvage this croc ship and put some kind of war plan in place, how in all the heavens were they supposed to count on that idiot in the heat of battle? He'd be throwing verbal taunts against cannon fire.

For a moment, Hook indulged himself in the fond image of Pan hurling an insult at Blackheart's warship only to have that smirk wiped off his face by a cannonball to the gut.

A small smile played across Hook's lips, and his hair danced joyfully in the light breeze, but then his expression fell, his hopes dashed to the proverbial rocks by reality. He needed Pan. *Needed* him. For his ship and his crew. But not like this. Not this impish, undisciplined boy who couldn't focus on anything serious to save his life.

Or, at least, anything except Wendy.

Hook watched as Peter flew back toward the woman, circling her and laughing before flying high into the sky.

Wendy. Of course. She could control him. He didn't like to admit it, not even to himself, but of all his crew that remained, she stood second only to Charlie—not just in rank, but in his trust. She had proven her competence and dedication under fire. She had saved the ship in the heat of battle. She was clever. Resourceful. And Pan listened to her. No, more than that, Pan lived to please her. Even a fool could see that. She was everything Hook could ask for in a British presence on Pan's ship. She could bring Pan under control and make sure the ship carried out its mission.

But she was also the only one who could fly *The Pegasus.*

By solving one problem, he would only create a new one. Unless ... unless she could teach someone else?

He thought of himself, but only for a moment. He couldn't spend all his concentration on flying the ship. He needed to orchestrate the battle. Command the men. Besides which, he couldn't allow his crew to see him struggling under the tutelage of a woman. It would undermine his authority, and he had not risen through the ranks by allowing the seeds of mutiny to be sown among his crew.

No, it had to be someone else. And the first answer was obvious.

Charlie.

He was her childhood friend and one of the few men on the ship who would take her instruction. The young man had been the ship's navigator before Wendy arrived. Mr. Hawke would merely be returning to his post, a fact that might even help with the men, some of whom were already grumbling about a woman navigator and what the Royal Navy was coming to.

Ideally, Hook mused, they would needed at least one more—a

man to fly the croc ship. Perhaps the lieutenant or sergeant of Wendy's own platoon might show some affinity for flying. They were the only other men on board who would listen to her and held enough rank to be trusted with an entire ship. If they couldn't do it, he would leave the croc vessel to the Vikings and pray for the best.

He already had a feeling that their fleet was going to consist of himself; Peter Pan (his mortal enemy, held in check by a woman); and a female Viking commander. Together, they would save England, or by God he would die trying.

Because if he failed, he didn't want to live to hear what they would say about him in London.

CHAPTER 40

Remember," Wendy said to John, "don't think about moving the ship. Just think about moving yourself. The ship will move with you. Up, but only a little, and not very quickly. That part's important."

"Is it? Because the bit about not letting us plummet to our collective death seems like the important thing to me," John grumbled.

Wendy only smiled. "You can do it," she told him. "I believe in you."

They stood together at the helm of *The Pegasus*, the repairs to the keel having been completed in record time. Hook stood on deck next to Michael, several yards away—partly to watch the proceedings, partly as a silent show of faith, and partly to make sure the rest of the crew didn't get out of line.

Most of the men stood safely on the ground, well away from the ship's berth, crowded around the ale kegs that Smee had

"protected" by having them hauled out of the galley and off the ship altogether.

"Let's see it then!" Smee shouted up at them. "Fly, little pigeon!"

The men around him erupted into a chorus of cooing noises, and then a tiny golden pigeon burst out of the trees nearby, heading straight for the ship. The men pointed and cooed even more loudly.

"Knows its own kind, it does!" Smee shouted, and the men laughed in approval.

The pigeon—who was Tinker Bell, of course—circled John's head twice, mocking him in dulcet tones, until Charming turned into a little red hawk and chased her off.

Hook glared at the men severely, and they quieted—at least for the most part. But the moonlight made it hard to tell one man among the crew from another, and this made them braver than they might have been otherwise. Every so often, a barely audible warble floated up through the night, followed by a new round of muted chuckles.

John pretended not to hear them. He frowned a little, holding the coin tightly in the palm of his hand, and everyone on the deck fell still. "I think ..." he said quietly, and then, "almost ..." at which Wendy held her breath, her eyes flashing with excitement, and then, finally ...

"No. No, I can't do it," John pronounced. He dropped his hand down to his side, puffed out his cheeks, and expelled a huge breath in frustration.

"Perhaps," Hook commented dryly, "you don't have the proper motivation. Take us up, Miss Darling."

"Captain?" she asked. "But—"

"Take us up," he snapped. In truth, his motivation had nothing to do with her lessons. He just wanted to get the ship off the

ground—both to prevent the rest of the men from watching and to remind them of Wendy's skill.

John handed her the coin, and as soon as she closed her hand around it, the familiar hum of magic surged against her palm, ready to respond to her command.

Up, she thought, and up they went, moving about as fast as the average crew member could run.

"That's enough," Hook finally told her, once they were well out of range of the jeers below. They were quite high now, in fact, having risen about halfway up the mountainside. The wind was stronger here, but Wendy barely felt the pull of it—the sails remained furled for the purpose of their experiments, with no men in the rigging. "Now, let's try it again. Miss Darling, if you please."

Wendy's eyes opened wide, and her eyebrows rose to their fullest height in protest. "But, Captain, the coin becomes quite animated during flight," she tried to explain. "If I open my hand, we'll risk it jumping out altogether. Not to mention that we're very high up."

Michael, who was standing close to the railing, leaned closer to glance over the edge and then slowly leaned away again. Charming perched nearby, still in the form of a hawk, his talons gripping the polished and oiled wood, and the two of them shared a look that said, quite clearly, "This seems like a very bad idea."

"Miss Darling," Hook said (whether he failed to notice their opinion or simply ignored it is impossible to say), "how does a baby bird learn to fly?"

"It leaps from the nest," Wendy admitted, but then she added, rather hastily, "when it knows it's ready."

"And how can it know until it tries?" Hook asked. "I would posit that it *becomes* ready in the moment it comes face to face with its own mortality. With this as our working hypothesis, Miss Darling, hand the coin to the lieutenant."

She hesitated a moment longer, but Hook's gaze held steady, and she knew he would not reconsider. She squared her shoulders, trying to look confident, and turned to John.

"You can do it," she said gently. "The coin will try to get away from you, but it isn't strong, just insistent. Hold on tight and you'll be fine. Put your hand over mine, and get ready to close your fist around it."

John gulped and nodded mutely. Wendy held out her fist, palm up, and John covered it with his hand.

"Are you ready?" Wendy asked.

John gulped again and closed his eyes. He took a deep breath, exhaled it, opened his eyes, and said, "Ready."

The moment Wendy opened her hand, the coin jumped away from her, just as she had expected, but John's hand was waiting for it. He closed his fist around it, and then the ship fell out from under them.

Fortunately, gravity seemed to work the same way in Neverland that it does everywhere else, so they remained with the ship, but they were not so much standing on it as they were falling with it, which is not at all the same thing. When one is standing *on* something, that something is pushing back against the soles of the feet—a sturdy platform upon which one can faithfully rely. When one is falling *with* something, one is still very much falling, despite the illusion of stability beneath, and any wrong sort of bump or shove will end that illusion immediately.

This is exactly what happened to John.

In his surprise, he stumbled, so instead of falling in a dignified manner like the others, with his feet beneath him, he ended up tumbling through the air, and before he knew it he was completely upside down, his hands now where his feet had been. If John had started out this entire business in a panic, his new circumstances

only made things worse, and he scrabbled uselessly at the deck, trying to grab hold of it.

Which, sadly, meant that he let go of the coin.

So there they were—the ship, Captain Hook, John, Michael, Wendy, and the coin—all falling together and yet each of them now falling alone, without the simple benefit of the earth that had always connected them to each other. Realizing his mistake, John tried to reach for the coin, but in his panicked state he only knocked it farther away, so that none of them had any chance to reach it.

None of them, that is, except Charming.

The innisfay, still in the shape of a hawk, was not falling. He was clinging to the rail with his sharp hawk talons and taking in the entire situation with his sharp hawk eyes. So when John knocked the coin out of reach, Charming leaped off the railing and sped toward it, grabbed it in his claws, and delivered it to Wendy in the nick of time.

She had just enough time to slow their descent safely without smashing into the valley below, and she settled the ship into its cradle as though she did this sort of thing every day, although her legs were shaking so badly she had to sit down for a moment once they had landed.

"With your permission, Captain," she said, "I think I've had enough flying for today."

Hook merely nodded his agreement. If he chose to avoid his quarters for the next several hours, napping instead in a hammock strung tightly between two trees, no one said a word.

CHAPTER 41

Flying lessons proceeded more cautiously after that, beginning always from the safety of the ground, but the men no longer laughed. The sight of their beloved ship falling toward them like a stone had been sobering. Now they watched from farther away, standing beneath the pines in small, silent clusters.

The tension seemed far worse to Wendy than their ridicule, and she could tell Michael felt it, too. She had been so sure he would be able to do it—to lift the ship into the heavens and fly beneath the stars—but throughout several long hours, the vessel showed no sign of moving at all.

"Enough," Hook finally muttered. "Everyone rest. Eat something. Not that you can tell when it's time to do either in this Godforsaken darkness."

Wendy had never been one for brooding, but in her heart of hearts, she was beginning to agree. It was exhausting never to see the sun. Unsettling. She wished she could hold these flying

lessons in the light of day, where the men would be at their best. She hadn't spent this much time beneath the night sky since ...

Since she and Charlie had studied the stars.

"Permission to try it with Mr. Hawke, sir?" Wendy asked.

"If you wish to continue, Miss Darling, you're welcome to do so. I'll be in my quarters. Try not to get us all killed."

"What should I do?"

Charlie and Wendy stood next to each other on deck, beneath the stars. John and Michael were there, too, but far enough away so as not to be able to hear them. Wendy had insisted.

"Don't do anything yet," Wendy said. "Just look up at the stars."

He did, standing next to her as they had when they were children, marveling at the wonders of the universe.

"They never move here," he said. "I don't understand why they don't move."

"I don't either," Wendy agreed. "It must be part of the magic of this place. The day and night never changing."

"It's strange," he told her, "to work so hard to learn about something, only to find that everything you thought you knew has changed in a single moment."

"You haven't changed," Wendy said.

"That's not true." Charlie looked down at her and smiled. "I'm much taller now."

Wendy laughed. Charlie had always been able to make her laugh, even in the middle of their most difficult lessons. Even when she felt trapped by her station in life, running out of hope, he had always made things seem ... less impossible.

"Wendy, I've been meaning to tell you ..."

"Yes?" He looked so serious all of a sudden. "Is something wrong?"

"No!" he said quickly. "No, that's just it. Everything's wonderful. And I've been meaning to thank you. I just haven't known how."

"Thank me? What for?"

"For this!" he exclaimed. He waved his arm through the air, taking in the whole world at once. "For *The Pegasus.* For Neverland. For my commission. If it weren't for you, I'd be a house servant, slopping out piss buckets in London. Instead, I'm first mate on a ship in the Royal Navy—an officer, Wendy, serving under one of the most respected captains in the fleet. You changed my life."

"Oh, Charlie, I didn't do those things," Wendy protested quietly. "You did. You studied as hard as I did. You learned everything Mr. Equiano taught us. You earned this all on your own."

"Not on my own," he said, his voice rough with emotion. "Never on my own. You found Mr. Equiano, and you shared him with me. You didn't have to do that. You believed in me, Wendy. And that made me believe in myself. You gave me so much more than the stars."

"Charlie, I—" She hardly knew what to say, but whatever it might have been, he interrupted her with a whisper.

"It's warm. And ... and it's moving."

"What?" She looked into his eyes, then followed his gaze to his hand. "Oh!" she said softly. "Oh, I knew it would! Think *up,*" she told him. "Slowly."

Charlie gazed into her eyes, and then he smiled. And the ship moved.

After that, Wendy and Charlie were inseparable for days—or what would have been days, had there been such a thing in Neverland. Technically, they were inseparable for one very long night, which was even worse as far as John and Michael were concerned. But the night was about flying, and the flying was for England, so they held their peace on the matter.

Between their sessions, Wendy tried to show the other men how to fly. Hook was thrilled with Charlie's success and still hoped to find another capable pilot among the crew, but the effort proved fruitless. (If Wendy was secretly pleased that Smee, in particular, couldn't do it, one can hardly blame her. She knew it was petty, but she didn't want to share the skies with Mr. Smee. Not even for England.)

In any event, they had what they needed to rescue the croc ship from its swamp. Charlie would fly *The Pegasus*, and Wendy would lift the new ship out of the mire.

Assuming they could find the ship's trinket, that is, Wendy thought wryly. And assuming the ship wasn't too badly damaged. And assuming the croc didn't eat them alive. On that note, Tigerlilja, having stayed to watch the preparations, had sent for reinforcements.

As busy as Wendy was, she was fascinated by the clanswoman who led the Norsemen. Fascinated, and a little intimidated. Tigerlilja was both self-assured and self-contained. Wendy had not seen her speak to anyone but her brother ever since they had returned to *The Pegasus*, and she had refused a berth in the ship, sleeping instead beneath the night sky. Wendy knew almost nothing about her, but one thing was certain: She held the profound respect of her people.

What would it have been like, Wendy wondered, to be raised in a place where women were respected as leaders and warriors? It reminded her again of Mr. Equiano, and Wendy thought how much he would have liked Tigerlilja—how she might even have reminded him of his own mother. But it wasn't until she was out taking Nana for a walk, during one of her rare moments of solitude, that she found the opportunity to speak with her.

Or, rather, the opportunity found her.

Tigerlilja approached them as Nana was sniffing through the grasses and wildflowers of the night meadow. Wendy looked around, surprised, but there was no one else the woman might have been coming to meet. Suddenly nervous, Wendy moved to smooth her dress, remembered that she didn't wear dresses anymore, and tugged lightly at the bottom of her vest instead.

"Hello," Wendy said. "It's a lovely evening, isn't it?" She felt foolish immediately. Habitual English greetings didn't apply in Neverland, where an evening seemed always to be an evening, but Tigerlilja didn't laugh.

"It is," the woman agreed. She didn't smile, but she didn't frown either. She simply was. Like an element of nature. A tree, perhaps. Or the sky. Or the calm before a storm.

She moved to stand next to Wendy, so that they were shoulder to shoulder, watching Nana together, and she was quiet for quite some time, gathering her thoughts. Finally, she said this: "How long have you known Peter?"

The question surprised Wendy, and then the answer surprised her too. She had first seen him in Dover only a few short months ago. So much had happened since—it felt like years. Sometimes it felt like a lifetime.

"Not long, I suppose," was all she said in reply. She glanced at the other woman, but Tigerlilja gave no indication of her thoughts, her expression as unchanging as the night.

"He brings them here to save them," she said.

"The orphans?" Wendy asked.

"All of them," Tigerlilja clarified. "The ones who have no safe place to call home. Or who don't quite fit. Or the last of their kind. The orphans. The lost creatures. Perhaps even you."

Her? Peter hadn't brought her here. Had he? No, she had brought herself here. She had followed the compass.

The compass, she suddenly realized, that he had given her.

Before Wendy could respond, Tigerlilja continued. "My clan was the first. We few were all that remained of my people. But we were only the first of many. He brings them because they remind him of himself, I think. In his own way, he is trying to save himself from a fate he does not deserve."

"Save himself?" Wendy asked. "What do you mean?"

"Peter lives under a curse," Tigerlilja said, her eyes never leaving Nana. "A gift from his mother. An intentional act with unintended consequences."

"His mother? He acts as though he never had a mother."

"All creatures have mothers," Tigerlilja told her. "Or, at least, all that I know of. But Peter's mother is dead, as is his father. There are others like him, or so I've been told, but in a very real way, he is the last of his kind."

Hook is my enemy! He is death to all my kind! Peter's words echoed through her mind—the only time she had ever seen Peter angry. The sudden implication left her reeling.

"Did Hook ..." She could hardly bring herself to ask the question. "Did Hook kill his parents?"

"What? No. His parents died long before you were born. Centuries ago. What would make you ask that?"

"Nothing," Wendy said. "Just ... something Peter said once."

Tigerlilja waited in silence, but when Wendy chose not to elaborate, she finally continued.

"Peter gets confused about things. It's part of the curse. His parents were killed by one of the Old Ones. The oldest, in fact. A ..." She paused, obviously searching for the right words. "An Old One named Buri. He was spurned by Peter's mother and jealous of what he couldn't have for himself. But she was a powerful dryad, and on her deathbed, she gave Peter what she thought was a gift—from that moment on, he could remember nothing that brought him grief."

With those words, a dozen memories flashed through Wendy's mind. Seeing Peter after their argument at Hook's estate, and how he had already forgiven her. How he refused to believe she had stolen the thimble from his ship, even though she clearly had. How he treated prison like a game.

It made perfect sense, but more than that, it *felt* true. She found herself nodding without even realizing she was doing it.

"So, you believe me," Tigerlilja said. It was not a question.

"Yes."

"I thought you would. I didn't want to tell the others. They stand at the very precipice of what they can believe, just being in this place. But Blackheart is only a gateway to a greater evil. Buri has found some way to use him. To reach his icy tendrils into Neverland. I don't know how, but I'm certain of it."

"But if Buri already killed Peter's parents, why would he care about Peter? Is he really that jealous of a woman who died so long ago?"

"He was never as jealous of her love as he was of her power. And she has thwarted him, even in death. Buri controls the ice and all that lives within its domain. But as long as Peter carries his mother's dryad magic, Buri cannot expand his realm. And with her dying breath, she tied Peter to Neverland. As long as there is a single blade of green upon its shores, Peter remains almost invincible. He cannot age, and those he brings here do not grow old.

My people and I have been charged with protecting this place, but Buri has finally found his way in. And now we are all in danger."

"Not just Neverland," Wendy realized.

"No," Tigerlilja agreed. "If Neverland falls, Peter will lose its protection. Buri will kill him, and he will spread his ice across the world."

CHAPTER 42

It was a lot to take in. Old Ones and dryads and curses and ice that could swallow a planet. But, mostly, Wendy's thoughts kept returning to Peter himself. It seemed sad that he couldn't remember his own parents. Not that Wendy could remember *her* parents, but if she had known who they were, she would have wanted to remember them.

Or would she?

What if they had been cruel? What if they hadn't wanted her? Would she want to remember that?

But then she thought of Nicholas. His loss haunted her. It probably always would. And yet, if someone had offered to erase his memory from her mind, she would have fought tooth and nail against it. Even if, afterward, she would not have known what she had lost.

That, she thought, was the saddest part about Peter. The not knowing. The people whose lives had touched his—their tender moments burned away along with the sad ones. How much love had he forgotten across the centuries?

She had wondered aloud to Tigerlilja, before they had parted ways, whether anything might be done to cure him. The Norsewoman thought not. She had been searching, she said, all this time, but to no avail. Still, she had not been unkind to Wendy's hopes. She would like to believe it was still possible, she had said.

It would certainly make her life easier.

The biggest problem with the curse, Tigerlilja had pointed out, was that it prevented Peter from learning from his mistakes. Everything was a game to him, which was tremendous fun for Peter, but far less so for the clan that had sworn to protect him. By definition, the only missteps he remembered were the ones he didn't mind repeating.

It also made it difficult to include him in working against Blackheart. The very *idea* that Buri might prevail—that his ice might cover the world and everything in it—was so miserable and depressing that Peter always forgot it immediately. He had no idea why they were doing anything, so he could not be relied upon to take his part seriously.

Which was why Wendy volunteered to brief Peter on his role in salvaging the crocodile ship, to Hook's obvious relief.

She found the everlost on his own vessel after calling up to the watch for assistance in coming aboard. (It wasn't as though an everlost ship needed ladders, and the ship's cradle raised the deck quite high in the air.) It was Curly who heard her call, but he relayed the request to Peter, who flew down to her at once.

"Hello, the Wendy," he said.

"Hello," she said in return. "Permission to come aboard, Captain?"

"Permission granted!" he exclaimed. He seemed very pleased by the way she had formed the request.

He picked her up in his arms, just like the night he had flown her from Hook's estate to his ship off the coast of Dover, and she

realized suddenly that even here on Neverland, when he was very close, she could still smell the forest-and-pickle green scent of him—a fact that made her happier than she would have cared to admit. But she hardly had time to appreciate it. They reached the deck in mere moments, and before they even touched down, the crew was shouting out to her in excited greetings.

"The Wendy! Oh, good form! The Wendy is here!"

"They missed you," Peter said, smiling at her fondly. He set her feet gently upon the deck, where she was mobbed immediately.

They laughed and grinned and touched her arms respectfully, even timidly, like old friends who hoped they would be considered close enough for a hug but weren't entirely sure. Curly was there, of course, as well as the twins—and the tall one who had shed a single tear off the coast of Dover when Peter had mentioned mothers. She didn't know most of their names, but their faces were familiar. She found herself suddenly hoping she would get to know them all.

"Where's Tootles?" Peter asked Curly. "He was just here a minute ago."

"He went to find berries for dinner. Cook wants to make fresh tarts."

"Of course he did," Peter said, and then he laughed. "Tootles always misses everything."

They invited Wendy to stay for dinner, so, of course, she did. The tarts, it turned out, were not for dessert but were dinner themselves. They were filled with a mixture of thick-set custard and the most delicious berries Wendy had ever tasted—tiny orbs of brilliant, powder blue that burst between her teeth, filling her mouth with the taste of roses and lavender and honey all at once.

As incredible as the dinner was, the company was even better. The crew begged her for stories, so between great mouthfuls of honey custard she told as many as she could remember. Stories of princes and dragons. Fairy tales—both romantic and cautionary. And, of course, the story of how *The Pegasus* had escaped from Blackheart's grasp, complete with the part in which Peter and his crew had arrived in the nick of time to scare him off.

And although they all cheered and clapped each other on the back at the end, congratulating each other on their wonderful cleverness and bravery, Peter was as attentive as the rest through it all. He did not try to interrupt her with his own stories or claim to be any more clever than the rest, and Wendy found herself enjoying the evening more than any she could remember in a very long time.

She realized, then, that at least part of it was due to the fact that not one of the everlost ever spoke down to her. They never suggested she had gotten a part of the story wrong. Or interrupted her to comment that wasn't it "just like a woman" when the witch or queen or princess was cruel or livid or foolish.

They simply listened, happily yielding the floor, which made her realize, by contrast, just how hard she had been working to fit in with Hook's crew. And how much she wished for quiet, simple evenings like this one, with people who made her feel welcome.

Dinner had gone so well that recruiting the everlost for the mission of the crocodile ship was as simple as telling them what she needed them to do. Because they were the fastest, and because they could fly without a ship, it would be their job to distract the beast while the rest of them freed the crocodile's ship from the swamp. They all agreed immediately, and because only Peter was affected by the curse directly, Wendy had no doubt they would see

their part through no matter what sort of game Peter might decide to play.

She was about to take her leave of them, albeit reluctantly, when Peter said, quite suddenly, "Did I ever tell you the story of how Hook lost his hand?"

His crew erupted into cheers. "Story!" they shouted. "One more! Tell us, Peter!"

But he hadn't been asking them. He had been asking Wendy. Her eyes met his across the table, and she said quietly, "Why, no, Peter, you haven't. But I would very much like to hear it."

"Well then," he began, "it goes like this. Once upon a time, there was a boy. He was born with two hands, as are most boys, but this particular boy was unusual in that he was born into a very important family, of the surname Hook, and having two hands was something of an embarrassment. His father had a hook, you see, instead of his right hand. As did his father's father. And his father's father's father, and so on. That's how they had gotten their name. From one of those fathers very far back. I don't know how far back, but very far, and at any rate it isn't important to the story."

If Wendy already suspected that Peter's version of the story was not going to be entirely accurate, she kept that thought to herself.

"Now, young Hook begged his father time and again to take his hand and give him a hook instead, like his father's own. It was a beautiful steel hook, polished and cruel, and far more imposing than a mere hand could ever be. It commanded respect. But the father refused.

"'No,' he told the boy. 'You were born with a hand instead of a hook, and that is who you are meant to be. Be proud of who you are, and stop asking me to cut off your hand.'

"But the boy was determined to follow in his father's footsteps, and so he looked everywhere for a way to be rid of his boring flesh-and-blood hand. He considered cutting it off himself but decided against it. It's a very painful thing to do, after all, and generally ill-advised.

"He asked the butcher, who had a magnificent cleaver and could have taken it off for him in a single blow, but the butcher refused. 'Don't be daft,' the butcher said. 'Nothing wrong with having two hands. I have two hands, and I do just fine.'

"The boy asked a woodsman, who was chopping wood for his fire one winter morning. But the woodsman didn't recognize the boy and confused him for an addled beggar. He gave the boy a hunk of bread and a hunk of cheese and sent him on his way.

"Finally, the boy joined the Royal Navy. It was a dangerous life, and he thought surely he would find a way to lose his hand in service to the king. Then they would give him a fine, shining hook, just like his father's. Which is how I met him.

"My crew and I had arrived in England to free a poor orphan boy from brutal, daily lashings, but on our way to the orphanage, we had the misfortune of running across Hook and his men. A great battle ensued, with excellent form on both sides."

"Good form! Good form!" the everlost cheered, interrupting for a moment, but Peter only nodded.

"He tried to run me through, but I grabbed him by the wrist just in time."

"Unhand me, vile creature!" he shouted, so, of course, I obliged him, lopping off his hand with my sword in a single blow. Now, I had no idea how badly he had wanted to be rid of his hand, so I tried to put it back on for him. The entire battle had meant to be in good fun, without any serious injury on either side. But he refused.

"'Stay away from me,' he shouted. I tried a second time, extending his hand toward his wrist, which was bleeding fiercely, but he screamed and ran from me, escaping into the city before I could return the limb to its rightful place.

"Now, I am a collector of stories, as I'm sure you know, so I understand that these things must always happen in threes. I stored the hand in Neverland, to preserve it in case he might want it back, and I searched for him for several months until I finally discovered a tavern where he often dined. I fetched the hand from Neverland, approaching him a third and final time, but again he refused my assistance, trying instead to run me through for my trouble.

"That's how, in the end, I came to understand that he didn't want me to put it back. I tried three times, and I was refused three times. He got his hook, and I was glad to be the one to finally help him after all those years."

"Good form!" the everlost all cheered, pounding their mugs on the long table. "Good form!"

Wendy sat in silence for what seemed like a very long time, until she finally asked, "What did you do with it?"

"With what?" Peter asked.

"With the hand," Wendy clarified.

"Oh, that." Peter waved his own hand in the air dismissively. "Well, we were in England for a while after that before returning home, so I'm afraid it had begun to stink. In the end, I threw it overboard. It's just one more way in which a hook is much better than a hand, if you stop to think about it."

CHAPTER 43

At last, it was time, and those who would carry out the plan assembled on the deck of *The Pegasus*.

"We fly together!" Hook's strong baritone carried easily through the night air. If he failed to look any of the everlost in the eye as he said these words, no one blamed him—least of all Peter, who would have forgotten the slight right away even if he had noticed it.

Which he didn't.

"Mr. Hawke will fly *The Pegasus* to the crocodile's swamp, where the everlost will debark to distract the beast, luring it away from the vessel below. Once that has been accomplished, they will continue to engage the creature while we drop a second crew to free the abandoned ship, commandeer its flying trinket, and sail her to safety.

"Once I reach the deck of the abandoned vessel, Mr. Hawke will take command of *The Pegasus*, raising her to the safety of the skies. When we free the new ship and raise her into the air, the

everlost will know that the mission has been successful and shall then disengage, either rejoining *The Pegasus* or sailing with us on our new vessel, whichever is most expedient.

"It is a simple plan and a good one, and I fully expect it to be successful. If, however, I should not return, Mr. Hawke will become your captain, and you are to follow his command in carrying out the interests of England and the Kingdom of Britain."

Tigerlilja, Vegard, and several of their clansmen were also on board, both as local guides and as additional hands, given how depleted Hook's forces had become in sending so many ships back to England. It was understood, however, that no Englishman would ever be *their* captain, so they raised no objection to the matter.

And so *The Pegasus* took off, rising into the sky in Charlie's capable hands, and soon enough they had left the night behind them, much to everyone's relief. They followed the river back to the Norsemen's village and then continued on, until the forested hills gave way to a vast open grassland that reminded Wendy very much of the plains of Africa, or at least what she had read about them and seen in occasional illustrations.

She thought of Tigerlilja's example of lions in Neverland, and as though the very idea had conjured them, a tremendous herd of antelope that had been grazing among the tall grasses, all but hidden from view, suddenly burst into motion, fleeing from the shadow of the ship overhead.

"Oh!" Wendy exclaimed. "They're beautiful! Charlie, come see!"

But Charlie didn't answer, and his eyes never left the sky. As hard as Wendy had to focus when she was flying a ship, the process was even harder for Charlie. She found herself watching him a little sadly, glad he had learned to fly but sorry he was missing all the sights below.

Thomas interrupted her thoughts, joining her at the railing

and leaning over the edge, much farther than was probably wise. "Extraordinary!" he exclaimed. "*Hippotragus leucophaeus!*"

"I'm not familiar with that one, I'm afraid," Wendy told him. She could have identified most of the larger species of African animals by their scientific names, but she certainly didn't know every variety of antelope.

"Bluebucks, as they're more commonly known. From the Cape Colony. Rumors would suggest their numbers have been dwindling, but these don't seem to be suffering in the least."

They watched together as the herd flowed along the plains, running and leaping through the tall grass, until it finally veered away toward the right and diminished into the distance.

The grasslands extended on for miles until finally they began to change. Unlike the hard line between the night valley and the blue jungle, this distinction was more subtle, the swamp-like nature of the land emerging gradually. But the closer they got to the croc's lair, the swampier things became.

The isolated trees that dotted the plains gave way to tall, moss-laden trunks that grew straight out of the muck. Each one grew shoulder to shoulder with the next, eerily smooth, with warped branches that twined around each other—whether reaching out for comfort or trying to choke the life out of its neighbors, Wendy couldn't say.

Small, unseen creatures plunked into the water or slithered through the hanging foliage, but the thing Wendy noticed above everything else was the ungodly stench of the place. It reeked like death, and the closer they came to the center, the worse it got, as though anything that died here was never quite finished decaying—hanging on to the gruesome tatters of zombified flesh, clinging to the memory of life far longer than anything had a right to.

It gave Wendy the chills, and goose bumps raced up her arms. Everyone else just covered their noses and tried not to retch.

“Captain?” Charlie asked. He had brought the ship closer to the ground as they approached their destination, but now he wondered if he should raise it again, seeking fresh air while they waited to spot the croc.

“Hold steady, Mr. Hawke,” Hook responded immediately. “We’ll never find the beast from up high.”

“We might not find it anyway,” Wendy commented. “We can’t take the ship beneath the canopy. She’ll never fit through. But we can’t see a thing from here.”

It was true. The boughs from which the moss hung were twisted so tightly together that the crew would be lucky to make it through themselves, let alone an entire ship.

“The grounded vessel is below us, more or less,” Tigerlilja told them. “We’re very close. The croc will be nearby.”

Hook grunted. “Then we shall adapt,” he told her. “Pan! Get down there with your men. Find the beast. Send one of your little bell people to tell us when you have him.”

Charming frowned in disapproval, and Tinker Bell, who had been riding on Peter’s shoulder, launched herself toward Hook in a fury. She proceeded to lecture him soundly on the rudeness of speaking down to people—*especially* people who had been protecting his kind for centuries and practicing the most intricate and complicated of magics while his own ancestors were still building homes out of foraged sticks and mud.

But, of course, all Hook heard was a tirade of jumbled, discordant jingling.

“She’ll do,” he said.

“Now, Tink,” Peter interjected quickly, “don’t be angry. It isn’t an insult to be called a little bell person. Being small has a lot of advantages! You can explore all sorts of places that I can never go. It makes me quite envious, to tell you the truth. And your language is lovely. I wish I could speak it myself, but I don’t have the

means. No one can imitate an innisfay. Your people are unique in all the world."

At this, Tinker Bell seemed mollified. She turned her nose up at Hook and returned to Peter, her hair morphing from red into its habitual golden hue.

"Would you please go find the croc for me and tell me where he is?" Peter asked her. "Don't get too close, though. I couldn't bear it if anything happened to you. But I would appreciate it very much if you would find him. It would be a great service to me."

Peter delivered this request in the most solemn tones, and with every passing word Tinker Bell's hair glowed more brightly until it hurt Wendy's eyes even to look at her. With a tiny, proud trill, Tinker Bell darted to the railing and dove through the foliage. For a brief moment, Wendy followed her light through the leaves, but then even it too was swallowed up by the reek and the darkness, until there was no sign that the tiny innisfay had ever been there at all.

CHAPTER 44

They waited for what felt like ages—Wendy, Charming, Peter, Thomas, Hook, John, Michael, Tigerlilja, Vegard, and the rest—all lined up at the ship's railing. They stared into the unfathomable depths below, straining their eyes and ears for any sign of what might be happening. But there was nothing to see. Just trees and moss and more trees in a vast blanket of green and shadow. And all was quiet. Rancid, unfortunately, but quiet.

Until it wasn't.

The scream was unlike anything Wendy had ever heard. Halfway between a roar and a cry of anguish, it started as a rumbling growl she could feel down to her bones, then rose into a gravelly sort of screech that set her teeth on edge and made her clap her hands over her ears.

"What is that?" she shouted, hardly able to hear her own voice over the cacophony.

"Tinker Bell," Peter shouted back.

"Tinker Bell? That's *Tinker Bell* making that awful racket?"

"No, that's the demon croc," Peter yelled with a grin. "But only Tinker Bell could have made it that angry. Time to go!"

He circled one hand over his head to signal the rest of the ever-lost, and with a grand whoop, he leaped to the railing, jumped off, and spun, so that he ended up facing Wendy. He watched as the rest of his crew did the same, until all seven of them hovered in midair. Then Peter crossed his arms in front of him with his palms pressed flat to his chest, winked, and dropped through the foliage like a stone.

Wendy leaned over the railing and watched, her hands pressed tightly to her ears, as the swamp swallowed him whole. Suddenly, the screaming stopped, followed by a loud crash. The treetop beneath them listed wildly before snapping straight again. One after another, more trees did the same. The swaying proceeded in a line from one tree to the next—a wave through the canopy that moved away from their position much faster than Wendy would have predicted.

"Come and get me, you yellow-bellied excuse for a lizard!" they heard Pan shout. "You'll never catch me!"

Wendy wanted to chuckle as the sounds faded into the distance, but she turned at that exact moment to find Hook glowering at her.

"Let's go," Hook said. They had prepared long ropes for this part of the plan, and now the crew slung them over the side of the flying ship, dropping them through the trees.

As it happened, Wendy had never climbed down a rope over the edge of a flying ship before, but she discovered very early on in the process that she did not care for it. She did not care for it at all. The line was rough and scraped her hands, so she did her best to support most of her weight with her legs, which she wrapped around the rope tightly, clinging on for dear life.

To make matters worse, the rank air of the swamp was hot and humid, making her palms sweat terribly. She had to pause every

few moments to wipe her hands on her vest, carefully, one at a time, before she could descend another few feet, only to stop and wipe them off all over again.

At least she could see the ground once she broke through the upper canopy. The ship lay directly below her—a beauty, in Wendy's opinion. (But, then again, she was partial to ships, so her opinion might have been somewhat biased.) In any event, it was about the same size as *The Pegasus* and did not seem to be damaged, at least not as far as Wendy could tell. She hoped the same would be true once they could see the hull beneath.

The descent proceeded uneventfully, and it was not until Wendy had almost reached the bottom of the rope that everything started to go horribly, terrifyingly wrong.

Hook, you see, reached the deck of the ship just before Wendy, and the moment his feet touched the deck, a chill raced through Wendy's entire body. Suddenly, she was freezing cold, despite the heat of the swamp, and something made her turn toward the right, peering into the depths of the swamp, even though nothing at all seemed to be out of the ordinary.

"It's coming," she whispered.

"What's that?" Hook asked, entirely unconcerned.

"It's coming!" she shouted. "It knows we're here!" She let go of the rope and dropped the last few feet to the deck. "Charming, find me the ship's trinket! Hurry!"

"Miss Darling," Hook said, looking confused, "it can't possibly know that. You can't possibly know that."

But even while he was speaking, John and Michael had already exchanged a look that said, "When have we ever known Wendy to be wrong about magic? And even if she *could* be wrong, wouldn't it be smarter to act now and discover later that there was no need for it, rather than the other way around?"

"Find the anchor!" John shouted. "Free the ship! Guards, to arms!"

The men all looked to Hook, surprised that anyone else was barking orders at them in such a commanding way. Hook, in turn, stared in surprise at John, who looked right back at him with such an intense look of pleading in his eyes that Hook eventually nodded. The orders were strictly according to plan, after all, and hurrying seemed like a good idea, even if Wendy was just responding to her feminine sensitivities.

Which, in a way, she was. But not in the way Hook believed.

In fact, Hook had a terrible habit of forgetting why they had brought Wendy along in the first place—why she had been employed by the Home Office, why she had been such an important part of the goings-on in both Dover and Hertfordshire, and why she had ultimately earned a position on Hook's crew.

Wendy was highly sensitive to magic.

And the croc, as Tigerlilja had told them, was a creature of an intensely magical nature—a hideously dark magic, to be sure, but magic nonetheless. So Wendy could feel it. She knew exactly where it was, and the moment Hook's feet had touched the deck, she had felt it turn back toward them. Even now, it was crashing through the swamplands at an alarming rate. They couldn't hear it yet, but by the time they could, it would be too late. Wendy knew all this, and, fortunately for everyone involved, John and Michael trusted her.

So John mustered the designated guards, making sure their muskets were at the ready, loaded with silver bullets and gunpowder, while Michael led a team in hauling up the abandoned lines and preparing for flight. And all the while, Hook stood on deck looking suitably commanding, even though he was doing nothing in particular to move the job along.

Not, that is, until Peter appeared by the side of the ship.

"Pan!" Hook shouted. "What are you doing here? You're supposed to be distracting that croc!"

"I was," Pan said, shrugging in midair, "but it doesn't want to play anymore."

"What?"

"That's what I came back to tell you," Peter said. "It won't follow us anymore. It's heading straight back here. If I didn't know better, I'd swear one of you has been here before. It's acting like it has your scent."

Wendy stared at Peter. "No," she said.

"What?" Peter asked.

"Peter," she said slowly. "I need you to think for a moment, all right? This is very important. Where ...?" Her voice trailed off. She stared at Hook. And then she stared at Peter. She knew exactly what had happened. Peter had thrown Hook's hand away in this swamp. The croc's swamp. And now it was coming back for Hook. But she also realized that, under the circumstances, it was probably best not to let Hook know that.

"Never mind," she said, to which Peter just shrugged. "Charming," she called out. "Charming! I need that trinket! Now!"

The innisfay darted out of the bowels of the ship, carrying what looked to Wendy like the knucklebone of a sheep. It surprised her, since it was the first trinket she had seen that was not made of metal, but as soon as she took it in her hand, it warmed to her touch.

"Oh, well done, Charming! This is it! Michael!" She raised her voice toward the crew that was now working at the end of a heavy chain some distance from the ship. "Michael, are we ready?"

"Still working on it," he hollered back. "The anchor's embedded in the trunk. We'll have to chop it out. It's going to take a while."

"Hurry!" she yelled. Then she turned back to Hook. "Captain, may I suggest we man the cannons, just in case?"

Hook stared at her as though she had gone daft.

"Please, Captain," she entreated him, bouncing nervously from one foot to the other. Which was when they finally heard the croc crashing and splashing through the swamp, heading straight for them.

"Man the cannons!" Hook shouted. "Man the cannons!"

"Prepare to fire," John added, addressing his own men, who stood shoulder to shoulder with him, their muskets raised toward the sound of the great beast.

Vegard dropped the line he had just finished hauling in and raced to the deck cannon that faced the croc's general direction.

"There aren't any cannonballs," he shouted to them. "But there's a whole keg of powder here."

"Load it!" Hook ordered. "Load the cannon with anything you can find!" He was starting to sound genuinely concerned. They still couldn't see the croc, but they could see entire trees in the distance bending beneath the weight of it as it rampaged toward them.

"It's too big, Captain. The cannon might not kill it," Wendy said in a rush. "Fire at the anchor chain instead. Free the ship! It's our best chance!"

She held his gaze for a long moment.

"Do it!" he finally ordered, and he turned his attention toward the crew. "Stuff that cannon with anything you can find! Target the chain! All hands on deck!"

Michael and his small crew abandoned their efforts and slogged their way back toward the ship as fast as they could. Meanwhile,

the rest of the men scrambled to shove anything they could find into the cannon. A line of men formed a kind of bucket brigade, handing things from one man to the next out of a cache someone had found inside the ship. Jewelry, coins, trinkets.

The beast came into view, and, for a moment, Wendy couldn't move. It was a crocodile in the same sense that a land cannon was a gun. It was *massive*, with red, glowing eyes, green dragon scales for its hide, and teeth the size of Wendy's entire forearm.

She gathered her wits and tried to raise the ship, but the anchor line groaned and held.

"Hurry!" Hook yelled.

Peter flew back to the croc, trying to stab its tail with his sword to distract it, but the effort was obviously useless. The croc's attention was focused on Hook and Hook alone.

"Fire!" John shouted to his men. Every one of them fired his musket at the speeding demon, but the creature didn't even slow down. Hook was standing directly behind the cannon now, and the croc was heading straight for Hook.

"Fire!" Hook ordered.

The cannon fired, and the world disappeared in an explosion of gray smoke.

CHAPTER 45

For the briefest of moments, Wendy wondered if they had somehow been transported through another portal. But, unfortunately, the world hadn't *really* disappeared. The smoke was just obscuring her view. The croc had been thrown from the ship by the blast, but she could still hear it, not far away, thrashing in the swamp. And as the smoke dissipated, she could see it shaking its massive head. It did not appear to be damaged in the slightest.

Wendy tried desperately to raise the ship, but nothing happened. It still held fast, trapped by the anchor's chain.

The croc's nose found Hook and its eyes refocused, snapping toward the captain with single-minded purpose.

"Miss Darling?"

It was all he said, but Wendy knew what he was asking. *Will you be raising the ship anytime soon, Miss Darling? Or am I about to meet my demise, eaten alive by a demon crocodile in this Godforsaken sulfurous swamp?*

“I’m doing my best, Captain,” she told him through gritted teeth. The chain groaned under the strain, but it did not break.

“Trying your best is not what I need, Miss Darling. I need you to make it happen. Now.”

His eyes never left the crocodile, which had gathered its wits and was clearly about to charge again. There would be no time for a second shot. Wendy thought *up* as hard as she could, with the intention to move much more quickly than was probably safe. The chain was attached to the ship by a heavy iron ring that was, in turn, bolted to the deck, and the surrounding wood creaked against the pressure, but it did not give way.

The croc charged.

“Now, Miss Darling!”

The beast sped toward the ship. Wendy pulled against the chain with the full force of her determination. The croc’s nose breached the cannon. Hook stood his ground in silent defiance and fired one final shot at the monster, knowing full well it would do him no good.

The croc opened its jaws, and then Wendy felt it—the opportunity she needed. The anchor chain, weakened by the blast, screamed one last, defiant protest and snapped in two.

The moment the ship was free, it catapulted into the sky. Several of the crew were thrown to the deck, but Wendy was careful to slow the ship gradually, making sure none of them were tossed overboard.

Hook inhaled, his breath sharp and deep, and he exhaled slowly. He rolled his shoulders. Then, as calm as you please, the right corner of his mouth curled into a small, satisfied smile.

“Return us to the valley, Miss Darling.”

He did not raise his voice to issue the order, but Pan heard him nonetheless. The everlost was hovering just off the side of the ship (having followed it mostly to be sure Wendy wasn’t hurled

into midair by the speed of her own escape), and he hollered out a long, joyful whoop. Vegard picked it up and their voices blended into something greater—a cry of victory that lit a fire in the chests of the crew.

Soon they were all shouting at once, and even Cecco, the handsome Italian (who was dark and brooding by nature), removed the kerchief from his neck and waved it through the air.

"A celebration is in order," Hook added, raising his voice to address the men. "England's fleet of flying ships has just doubled in size!"

That started the cheering all over again, and one or two of the nearest crew members might even have considered clapping Wendy on the back, forgetting in their enthusiasm to treat her like a lady. They *might* have, that is, if she had not been an officer. Not a single man among Hook's crew would *ever* clap an officer physically on the back—no more than they would have dared to touch the captain himself.

But for one shining moment, it was her status rather than her gender that prevented it, which was a small victory in its own right, even if Wendy had no idea what she had accomplished.

Hook, on the other hand, saw the whole thing. He noticed everything about his crew. He saw that they were becoming more comfortable, if not with her exactly, then at least with the idea of her. It helped, he supposed, that her platoon respected her. And it helped even more that no one could fly a ship better than she could.

She seemed so natural at the helm. When Charlie flew *The*

Pegasus, it clearly took everything he had just to keep the hull off the ground and moving in the right direction. But Wendy flew as though the ship were an extension of herself. First *The Pegasus* and now this new vessel, salvaged from the swamp, likely full of holes and still reeking from the fumes that had infused the wood with their stench. Despite everything, Wendy flew as easily as if she had known the ship all her life. She flew it like she loved it.

Which was the moment when Hook first realized something about himself—something so surprising that even his glorious hair took issue with it, whipping him about his face with the force of a stiff wind and an even more righteous indignation.

He actually wished he could give her the new ship.

He frowned. And then he narrowed his eyes. But the feeling remained. In some ways, it even made *sense*. The ship would need both a pilot and a captain. As first mate, Charlie was next in line for a ship of his own, but there was no way he could pilot a ship and command it at the same time. Flying took too much of his focus. He just wasn't capable of keeping the ship in the air while maintaining the crew's discipline, let alone directing a battle.

But Wendy could. Hook was sure of it. That is, if she had a crew that would take orders from her.

Unfortunately, his crew would not. He was sure of that, too. It was one thing for them to accept her presence. It was another thing altogether for them to accept her leadership. Most of them would start planning a mutiny the moment they set foot on any ship under her command, and, by definition, Hook wouldn't be there to stop it. Her own platoon wasn't big enough to sail a ship on its own, and, even if it were, there wasn't a single trained sailor within the entire useless lot of them.

Which, of course, made Hook think of Peter. At the moment, the everlost was hovering in the air in front of Wendy, lying down

on nothing at all. His face was no more than a foot away from her own, and he spun slowly, like a pig on a spit, so that first he was lying on his back, and then his stomach, and then his back again, watching her all the while.

That was the other reason Hook couldn't give Wendy the ship.

Pan.

Wendy might be capable of serving as both captain and pilot at once, but Hook couldn't afford for her to do either. He needed her on Pan's ship to keep the everlost on target and under control. Which meant Charlie would have to fly *The Pegasus*, Wendy would fly with Pan, and Hook was back to his original problem: what to do with the new vessel.

He wasn't about to turn it over to the everlost. He'd rather rot in hell. But perhaps one of the Viking men. At least long enough to defeat Blackheart. Vegard, maybe. He had kept his head well during the battle with the croc and obviously had some knowledge of the ship's cannons.

"Captain! Look!"

Wendy's voice interrupted his musings. The ship was passing between the mountains into their safe "harbor," such as it was, and Wendy was leaning around Peter to point straight ahead. Hook turned to follow her gaze and was shocked to discover a brand new ship's cradle waiting for them, just the perfect size for their new vessel.

"But ... how?" was all he could think to say.

"How what?" Peter wanted to know. He sat up in midair to see what everyone was looking at.

"We've only been gone a few hours!" Hook exclaimed. It staggered the mind, but there it was. There could be no denying its existence as Wendy brought the ship in to dock, settling her down gently onto the timbers that stretched beneath.

"This is its home," Peter said, and then he added, "obviously." As though the fact that the ship fit perfectly into the new cradle explained anything at all.

With considerable effort, Hook managed not to respond. Instead, he raised his voice to project it over the deck.

"Mr. Starkey!" he shouted. "Would you be so kind as to tell us the name of the newest ship in the British fleet?"

The crew cheered anew, and Starkey called back a jaunty, "Aye, Captain!"

He slung a line over the stern and disappeared over the edge, letting himself down hand over hand while the crew rushed to watch. They fell silent, waiting, and then Starkey looked up toward the deck, saying nothing.

"Well?" Hook leaned over the edge. He couldn't imagine what was making Starkey so reluctant. "What does it say?"

"Uh ... begging your pardon, Captain. But it says, 'Death to the King.'"

"Does it?" Hook let the tension build for a moment, just for, well, *fun,* if you can imagine that, and then he broke into an easy grin. "Right. I don't think we'll be keeping that one."

The crew roared with laughter and then immediately started calling out suggestions.

"The Penelope!"

"The Sarah!"

"The Margaret!"

Smee growled back, "We're not naming her after any wives!"

"Wait a moment, Captain," Starkey called up again. "This is a new board on the top, but there's something else under here."

"All right. Let's hear it, Starkey. What's her real name then?"

Cecco dropped a pry bar down to Starkey, and the crew fell still while he worked at the board. Finally, the new one fell away, exposing the original name plate beneath.

"Not sure it's much better, Captain," he hollered up. "Might not be worthy of her, if you know what I mean."

"It certainly can't be any worse," Hook called back, which elicited a new round of chuckles. "What is it then?"

"Her name's *Jolly Roger*, sir. She's the *Jolly Roger*."

CHAPTER 46

"*Jolly Roger*?" Smee sneered in disgust. "What kind of name is that?"

"It's a terrible name!" Cecco declared. "We should call it the Da Vinci!"

"We're not naming it after some stupid Italian any more than we're naming it after some stupid wife!"

Smee was considerably shorter than Cecco, but he walked straight up to him and stared him down nonetheless. (Or, technically, stared him up, crossing his arms over his barrel chest and glaring at the larger man in a distinctly challenging way.)

"Da Vinci was a genius, you ignorant heathen!" Cecco placed his hands on his hips and leaned forward, towering over Smee.

"Whose wife are you calling stupid?" This was uttered by Jukes, one of the men who had confronted Wendy when she had first come on board. (But he had also been one of the first to stop glaring at her.) He moved to stand next to Cecco, clenching his jaw and flexing his tattooed arms, making the ink ripple along his

skin. A giant squid waved its tentacles with the movement, and a ship floated up and down, riding its tattooed waves.

"We're not naming it after an Italian," Smee growled again, ignoring Jukes.

"She needs a name of power," Vegard chimed in. "To protect her in the skies. I'd call her Odin's Eye."

"We're not naming any British ship after your false gods!" Poor Reginald had always been a pious man. Vegard, with his muscled physique, easily outweighed the lean redhead by at least fifty pounds, but Reginald shook his head to clear his hair from his eyes and glared at the Viking in obvious contempt.

"We're keeping the name!" Hook roared. "If it's going to cause this much trouble, she'll remain the *Jolly Roger.* Stop arguing and be glad we have her. All of you. Stand down."

Cecco stood up straight, Smee uncrossed his arms, Jukes let his hands drop to his sides, and Vegard shrugged. (After all, Vegard had never threatened anyone. He had only made a suggestion.) Reginald gave Vegard a final suspicious glance, then shook the hair out of his eyes again and retreated through the crowd that had gathered, parting the larger men with a sharp wave of his hands, like Moses parting the Red Sea.

"We have a lot of work ahead of us," Hook declared. "Today was a victory, but we have a long way to go before she's battle ready. We have to get our *Jolly Roger* back in top shape, worthy of the British fleet, and we only have days to do it. Even now, Blackheart is preparing to fly against England. Are we going to let him do it?"

"No!" the crew shouted at once.

"Are we going to let him reach England's shores with his army of abominations?"

"No!" they shouted, even more loudly.

"Then let's get to work! Smee, I need a damage report on the

hull. Cecco, we have one mast missing. Take a team and go find me a tree worthy of the king's service."

"Aye, Captain!" Cecco shouted.

"Starkey! Starkey, are you back aboard?"

"Aye, Captain," Starkey acknowledged. He stood next to the stern, having just climbed over the railing.

"The sail from that mast has been lying on the deck in that rotting swamp for who knows how long. See if you can save it. If not, talk to Vegard. I'm sure his people can help."

"Aye, Captain," Starkey said again, and Vegard nodded.

"The rest of you, start cleaning her up. I want this deck gleaming, is that understood?"

"Aye, Captain," the crew replied, this time with varying degrees of enthusiasm.

Hook turned to head below, opened the hatch, immediately scrunched up his face in disgust, and spun back toward the deck. "Lieutenant Abbot," he said, addressing John, "take your platoon below and assess the ship's condition. Make a note of any holes or rotted planks. And, while you're at it, try to get rid of that God-awful stench."

"*I* found it. That makes it *my* ship. And I'm making Curly the captain."

They were standing in Hook's quarters, clustered around his map table: Hook, Charlie, and Wendy; Pan and Curly; Tigerlilja and Vegard. Pan had just made this pronouncement with a triumphant grin, as though finders-keepers were the be-all and end-all of arguments.

"Thanks, Peter!" Curly exclaimed.

"That's ridiculous," Hook growled. "The *Jolly Roger* was salvaged in the name of England. She is the king's ship and part of the British fleet."

"Why is it ridiculous?" Peter demanded. "It was on *my* land. If you want my ship, you'll have to duel me for it. That's the law."

"It most certainly is not the law," Hook informed him. "And your argument presupposes that the ship is yours to begin with, which it is not."

"It is."

"It is not."

"It is."

"It is *not*!"

Negotiations, as they say in matters of foreign affairs, were rapidly breaking down. Fortunately, Wendy knew Peter much better than Hook did, so she saw the solution at once.

"Peter," she said, interrupting, "the ship was not found on your land."

"Explain," Peter demanded. He lifted his chin and narrowed his eyes at her in obvious suspicion, but at least he was listening.

"The ship was in the swamp, which was clearly the domain of the crocodile," Wendy began.

"Ha! But the swamp is on my land!" Peter argued.

"I'm afraid it isn't," Wendy told him, trying her best to look disappointed. "The crocodile was Blackheart's creation, and Blackheart is at war with you. Therefore, he must be treated as a foreign entity. When a foreign entity establishes a presence elsewhere, it creates a sort of island within the new realm, surrounding itself, and that island is the official territory of the foreign entity no matter where it lies. Like a ship at sea, with the emissary as its captain."

Hook flashed Wendy a look that said, *You can't be serious*, but she pretended not to see it.

Peter tapped his fingers on the table. "The crocodile is Blackheart's emissary," Peter mused.

"Precisely," Wendy agreed. "Which means the ship was stolen directly from Blackheart's territory. A *remarkable* feat, wouldn't you agree?"

"I do!" Peter exclaimed. "I am always *quite* remarkable."

"Therefore," Wendy finished, "the ship belongs to those who appropriated it from the enemy."

"But *you* stole it," Peter pointed out, "so now it's *your* ship." He turned to stare at Hook, daring him to disagree.

"The mission was achieved under Captain Hook's direction," Wendy said quickly, "and he has rightfully claimed it for the Kingdom of Britain. The *Jolly Roger* is his to assign as he wishes."

If she happened to agree that it *should* be her ship, and certainly *wanted* it to be her ship, she was careful not to say so. The captain outranked her. It was for him to decide.

"The *Jolly Roger* belongs to England," Hook declared, "but for the time being, Vegard will be her captain, if he is willing to accept the responsibility."

Vegard raised his eyebrows and darted a glance at Tigerlilja, who frowned at first, then subtly nodded.

"Agreed," Vegard said, but Peter wasn't finished.

"The Wendy stole the ship," he insisted. "It belongs to the Wendy!"

"Miss Darling cannot be the captain," Hook told Peter evenly, "because she will be flying with you."

"Oh, good form!" Peter exclaimed. He turned to grin at Wendy, who was now doing her best *not* to look disappointed.

"Can any of your people fly it?" Hook turned to Tigerlilja with the question. After all, the ship still needed a pilot, but the Norsewoman answered him with a look of steel in her eyes.

"We prefer to fight on the ground. Flying ships are best left to flying men. We will make an exception in this case only because these are dire circumstances." She might have agreed to the arrangement, but she clearly wasn't pleased by it.

"*All* flying is best left to flying men," Peter crowed. "We are the best fighters. We'll shoot *all* of Blackheart's ships out of the sky before the battle even begins. All this talk and planning and idling about! It's so very *British*." He leaned toward Hook in a meaningful sort of way. "Boring and unnecessary."

Hook's face darkened as he fought to maintain his composure. His eyes narrowed, and the muscles of his jaw began to twitch.

"Peter," Wendy said quickly, "I'm sure you're right. You don't need to be part of all this dull planning. They can tell us later what we need to do. Instead, perhaps you'd be kind enough to show me ..."

She drew out the final words, stalling for time, and her eyes fell on the map that still lay open on the table before them: Peter's unhelpful depiction of Tigerlilja's camp. But, in fact, there was something on it that had caught her attention from the beginning. Something she would very much like to see.

Triumphantly, she jabbed her finger down on the map and blurted it out before anyone could stop her.

"The mermaids!"

CHAPTER 47

It should be no surprise to anyone that Peter agreed to Wendy's suggestion. He hated standing around and talking when there were no stories involved, and going to see the mermaids sounded like a lot more fun. He flew off to find Tinker Bell, but by the time Wendy came out onto the deck of *The Pegasus* with a pack containing rations and two bottles of fresh water, he had already returned.

"You won't need that," Peter declared. "We're going to fly. Tinker Bell will help."

Charming had followed Wendy back from her quarters, and now he jingled ominously, eyeing Tinker Bell with suspicion. But Wendy had her own concerns. Hook still didn't know she could use innisfay dust to fly, and she wasn't ready to admit to leaving anything else out of her reports. The thimble had been bad enough. Besides which, she wasn't keen on any of the crew watching Peter carry her off into the countryside.

"I'd rather walk for a bit," she told him. "If that's all right with you. Neverland is very beautiful. I'd like to savor it."

"It's more beautiful from the air if you ask me," Peter told her, "but suit yourself."

He watched impatiently as she picked up the pack, slung it across her back, and then clambered over the stern, letting herself down to the ground hand over hand, a few painstaking inches at a time.

"Are you sure you don't want me to help you?" he asked when she was about halfway down. He stood in midair with his feet spread apart and his arms crossed over his chest, descending slowly so as to remain at eye level with her.

"I'm sure, yes," she told him, although she wished the subterfuge weren't necessary. It would have been much easier to fly. The pack was heavy, and the drop below was farther than she would have liked. But at least the chilly night air was keeping her hands from sweating.

"All right, then," he said, shrugging a little.

Charming hovered on her other side, jingling occasionally in small, worried fits until she finally made it safely to the ground.

"There we are!" Wendy said cheerfully. "All right, then. Which way are we going?"

"This way," Peter said, and he landed lightly on the ground to walk beside her.

They headed off in a different direction than they had taken to visit Tigerlilja's village, so Wendy had never seen this side of the clearing before. But, in truth, it looked very much like the rest of the valley. The twilight grasses and wildflowers spread out before her without any particular path to define the way, but Peter seemed to know where he was going.

At long last, they entered the edge of the forest, well out of sight of the ships. Wendy sighed and dropped her pack in relief. "We can fly now," she announced. She turned to Tinker Bell, but the tiny innisfay crossed her arms, jingled angrily, and flew away.

"Why ... what did I say?" Wendy asked.

"You said, 'We can fly now,'" Peter told her.

"Yes, thank you, Peter," Wendy replied with just the smallest hint of a smile. "That *is* what I said. But what I meant was: What did I do to make Tinker Bell angry?"

"Oh. She thinks you're rude."

"Rude?" Wendy asked, astonished.

"That's what she said before she flew off. She said you're rude and always tell people what to do. First, we can't fly. Then, we can. All on your say-so." He leaned toward her with an uncharacteristically serious look on his face. "Is what *she* said," he reminded her. "I don't mind it at all."

"Oh," Wendy said, feeling embarrassed. She supposed she *did* sound that way, or at the very least *could* sound that way, now that she thought about it. "I'm sorry," she told him.

"Don't be," he said quietly. "Like I said, I don't mind. I like it that you know what you want."

But, in that moment, with Peter leaning toward her in such a gentle and earnest way, Wendy didn't know what she wanted at all. He was so handsome, but at the same time so strange. And, in any event, it would be highly improper to kiss him out here in the forest, with only Charming as a chaperone.

What on earth was she thinking? It would be improper to kiss him *anywhere.*

Wendy blushed, but then Charming interrupted her thoughts by jingling in her ear, saving her from any further embarrassment.

"What did he say?" Wendy asked.

"He said he'd be happy to provide the innisfay dust, if you'd still like to fly."

"Oh!" she exclaimed. "Oh, yes, please! Thank you, Charming!"

Charming bowed in midair, smiled, and then flew up over her head in a tiny, rising spiral, leaving a trail of shimmering innisfay dust behind to settle onto her head and shoulders.

"Excellent," Peter told him. "That should be enough." He gazed down into Wendy's eyes. "Did it work?" he asked her.

For the first time since Hertfordshire, Wendy lifted herself an inch off the ground, smiled broadly, and then soared into the sky.

They flew over the same fields they had seen when they first arrived in Neverland, and Wendy dove with a laugh, racing low across the squares of silver and amethyst and crimson, delighted to see them up close. The sparkling silver field turned out to be filled with flowers—flowers that looked exactly like tiny metal bells growing on vines along the ground.

She wanted to pick them, but she didn't know anything about them and was afraid she might hurt the vine. Instead, she hovered for a moment to brush one with her fingertip, surprised to discover it wasn't metallic at all. It didn't ring, and it felt like any other flower, if perhaps a bit smoother than most.

"Why, they're only flowers!" she exclaimed.

"What did you think they were?" Peter asked her.

"Bells," she admitted.

"That's what they're called," he told her. "Bell flowers." He picked several and clustered them together into a bouquet, then handed them to her with a bow.

"Oh! Thank you!" she exclaimed. "How lovely!" Even up close, they still sparkled with a silver sheen.

They flew onward, although Wendy had no idea in which direction, since the sun in Neverland was no help at all. Rather than heading toward the center of what Wendy now thought of as "farm country," they skirted the edge, passing a wide vista of red rock spires and plateaus that eventually gave way to a thick jungle canopy woven through with a fine white mist.

Here, they turned, passing over the trees to the lively sounds of birds and frogs and monkeys calling out to their own kind in an oddly melodious chorus, and then a rainbow appeared in the sky overhead.

"A rainbow!" Wendy cried. "I've never seen one before!"

"Then how did you know what it was?" Peter asked. Wendy had stopped in wonder when she saw it, and he came back to hover beside her.

"I've read about them," she said, her voice sounding almost breathless. "There's no mistaking it, is there? Once you've seen one, I mean."

Peter didn't answer her, and eventually her eyes broke away from the view to find him. He was watching her so closely, so adoringly, that she thought he might kiss her after all. She should have turned away, she supposed, but she didn't want to. There are some moments that are completed by a kiss—moments that a single kiss can make into a star, shining so brightly in your memory that you can find it there like the North Star in the sky for all the rest of your life.

As it turned out, this was not one of those moments. But it was *something*—or at least the *beginning* of something—because she saw something in his face change. Something she had never seen before.

"Wendy," he said, "be careful around the mermaids. They can be dangerous, and I couldn't stand the thought of losing you. We have so many adventures left ahead of us. I want you to be there for all of them."

Then he smiled and darted away, the same Peter she had always known, laughing and flying loop-the-loops in the sky as though nothing had happened.

And, for a moment, Wendy started to doubt whether anything *had* happened. Perhaps she had only *imagined* that they had shared a moment, as one does sometimes when one would like very much to kiss a person but that person, sadly, doesn't want to kiss one back. Then again, he had called her by her name. Not *the* Wendy. Just Wendy. He never did that. Surely, it meant something. Didn't it?

Just then, a tiny flash caught the corner of Wendy's eye, and she turned toward it to discover Tinker Bell, who had returned just in time to witness the whole thing. She had transformed into a dragon again, and her tiny scales were glowing such a fierce and terrible red that Wendy almost expected them to catch fire and set the entire innisfay ablaze.

So Wendy knew for certain that something important had happened. She just didn't know what it was.

CHAPTER 48

They flew for what felt like hours, over plains and forests and great spires of rock, each new place feeling slightly different than the last, and yet all of it filled with the rich, green scent of Neverland. Early on, they saw a herd of winged horses grazing in a clearing. Wendy wanted to see them up close, but when she dove toward them, they startled and lifted into the air like a flock of birds, darting away.

Later, Peter stopped to play a game of chase among the trees with a pack of small foxlike creatures. They had jet-black fur, with long, tufted ears and huge bushy tails, and they raced merrily after Peter with tiny yips of excitement until he laughed and flopped onto the ground. Then they piled on top him with a chorus of happy chirps and warbles and immediately fell fast asleep.

Wendy couldn't help herself. She reached down and gently picked up one of the smallest. It opened its eyes at the movement but seemed satisfied with its new situation, nestling into Wendy's arms and closing its eyes again.

"It's precious!" Wendy said quietly. "And so soft!"

"Mmmm may mmm maym mammem," Peter said. Or, at least, he said something that sounded very much like this from beneath a snoring pile of fur.

Wendy laughed. "I can't understand you at all," she told him.

Peter sat up, making several of the creatures roll off him. They woke, stretched, then scolded him in clicking chatters, already trying to climb back on.

"I said, 'They make a great blanket,'" he told her, and Wendy laughed again.

She wished they had time to stay and explore every new place they found, but she was already getting concerned about how far they had flown.

"Is it very much farther to the mermaids?" she asked Peter as they rose back up into the sky.

"No," he told her, and then he pointed. "Look."

Ahead, some few miles in the distance, she realized she could see the ocean. It had been hidden from view as they were flying low through the trees, but now it spread out before her, an eternal promise of possibility.

They flew to it at once, heading for a long line of towering cliffs that held back the sea. Peter led her toward a spot where two huge rocky arms jutted out into the water, circling wide and almost closing at the farthest point to form a protected cove. Even though the sun had been high above them throughout most of their journey, it was only just rising here, cresting the distant horizon in a breathtaking display.

Wendy could already see the mermaids. Several were swimming through the water, and others were sunning themselves on large rocks that jutted above the calm surface. She could hardly wait to see them up close, but Peter landed on the high cliff instead, waving her down to join him next to a gigantic pile of boulders that

she now saw formed a rough statue of a man sitting in a pose of quiet contemplation, staring forever out to sea.

"Why, how marvelous!" Wendy exclaimed, distracted for a moment by this latest discovery. She flew around to get in front of it, where she could see it better, and then she swore it moved.

At first she could hardly tell. The change was so subtle that she thought it might be a trick of the light. But a few moments later, the statue's lips did seem to be smiling a bit more. She continued to watch, mesmerized, and within a minute or so it seemed to be laughing, its head now tilted back just a bit and its mouth open in a wide grin.

"How is it doing that?" Wendy asked Peter.

"Doing what?" he wanted to know.

"Smiling!" she exclaimed, pointing to the statue.

"The same way you do," he said. He flew around the statue, studying it, and then landed on the cliff again and sat down, adopting the same pose. "Like this." He grinned, matching the statue's expression exactly.

"But ... it's alive?" she asked, incredulous.

"Of course," Peter told her, standing up again to address her. "They all are."

Wendy glanced along the cliff line and realized that what she had first overlooked as natural irregularities in the rock were, in fact, more statues. Only she was beginning to understand they were not statues at all. Some were sitting, and some were lying on the rocks, apparently napping. One, about thirty yards away, seemed to be in the agonizingly slow process of raising its hand to wave at them in greeting.

"My goodness! Can they speak?" She reached out a hand to touch the nearest one, then thought better of it, as she wasn't sure how to ask its permission to do so.

"They can, but it takes an entire afternoon just to get through

the opening pleasantries," Peter said. "You'll have to set aside at least a month if you're going to ask them anything they need to think about."

Wendy had no idea what she would ask them, but she resolved then and there to ponder it in case she ever had the opportunity.

"Did you still want to see the mermaids?" Peter asked her.

"Oh, yes!" she exclaimed, turning her attention back to him at once. "Very much!"

"All right, then," he agreed. "But, first, I have to tell you something. Something very important." His face fell into an expression so uncharacteristically grave that Wendy couldn't help but feel a little nervous.

"I'm listening," she promised.

"You must never go into the water with any of the mermaids. Never ever. No matter what they say or do. They'll try very hard to persuade you, so you have to be strong. Stay on the rocks. Only the rocks are safe."

"All right," Wendy said. A slight motion caught her eye, and she turned to discover that the giant statue was now staring in her general direction, its mouth set in a grim line. "I promise," she added.

"Good," Peter said solemnly. "Then, let's go!" Immediately, any sign of concern vanished from his face, and he leaped off the cliff, falling into a swan dive but then arcing out of it at the last moment to skim just above the water's surface, racing toward the middle of the lagoon.

Wendy raised her eyebrows and shook her head, following at a much safer height.

They landed on a large, flat rock that jutted out of the center of the lagoon, just large enough for perhaps three or four people to lie down next to each other. Almost immediately, several mermaid women swam up to it, resting their arms on the edge to smile up

at Peter while their tails wove slowly back and forth through the water below. Every one of them was stunningly beautiful, with hair that dried the moment it left the water, bouncing in long, perfect ringlets.

"Hello," Peter said to them all.

"Hello, Peter!" they all replied, and they laughed together in voices so melodious that their laughter almost sounded like a song.

"Come swim with us," the closest said, and she reached toward him gracefully with an elegant, sensuous hand.

"No, thank you," Peter said easily. If the mermaid was trying to charm him, he did not seem affected by it at all. "I only came to introduce you to the Wendy."

Two of them refused even to look at Wendy, despite the introduction. The third, the closest, who had just spoken, turned to Wendy and hissed at her, baring her teeth. The moment she did, the others followed suit, and a ripple ran over their bodies from their heads to their hips.

Their skin, which had reflected the same hue as Peter's, turned varying shades of blue, from the blonde woman, whose skin was now the turquoise of the Caribbean, to the brunette, who was now the steel gray of a storm-heavy sea. Their hair changed into long, green braids, and their teeth revealed fangs. The sudden transformation made their hissing all the more frightening, and Wendy took a cautious step back.

"Stop that at once," Peter scolded them. In a flash, another ripple ran through them, and they looked just as they had before.

"We're sorry, Peter," the merwoman in front of him said with a sultry smile.

"Yes, we're sorry," the other two echoed, batting their eyes at him shyly.

Peter ignored them, rising into the air and glancing about as though searching for something. The three merwomen all glared

at Wendy with narrowed eyes and delicate, pouting lips, then slipped back into the water and swam away. As Wendy looked around at the cove, she noticed two mermen drawing closer. Although the women had been wearing some sort of delicate netting, the men wore nothing at all. Their bare, perfect chests glowed in the light of the rising sun, and even though Wendy knew their appearance was only an illusion, she found herself feeling drawn to them nonetheless.

"Hello, the Wendy," one of them said, and his voice sounded like sweet honey dripping fresh from the comb.

"Why, hello," she replied, but the words were hardly out of her mouth before Peter had landed again, brandishing one of the two swords he always carried.

"Get back, fish!" Peter yelled. "The Wendy is not yours to take!"

The merman snarled, but he swam away, followed by the other.

"Gwendolyn!" Peter called out. "Gwendolyn!"

This, apparently, was the merwoman he had been looking for. She made no attempt to disguise herself, swimming toward them wearing blue skin and dark green braids. As she crossed her arms on the rock to rest, looking up at Peter, Wendy could see a delicate arc of light spots that crossed the bridge of her nose and continued onto her cheekbones. Wendy didn't know whether they were freckles or tattoos of some significance, but she thought they were very beautiful.

"Gwendolyn," Peter said, "this is the Wendy. She is my friend, and my navigator, and she wanted to meet you."

"The Wendy," Gwendolyn said, turning toward her. "Ah. Peter has told us stories about you. You're very brave to come here."

"Why ... thank you," Wendy said in reply. "It's very nice to meet you." She wasn't sure whether Gwendolyn had meant she was brave to come to Neverland or brave to come to the cove of

the merpeople, but the comment made her feel more nervous than she had before.

"A brave woman like you," Gwendolyn told her, "could be friends with a merwoman, I think. Would you like to be friends?"

"I ..." Wendy trailed off and looked for Peter, but he had already flown off over the water, playing some game that involved tossing shells back and forth through the air with the merpeople. "Is it dangerous to be friends with merpeople?" Wendy asked.

The merwoman laughed. "Sometimes," she admitted. "But some people do it. Perhaps even our parents were friends. Perhaps it's our destiny." She tilted her head, staring at Wendy thoughtfully.

"Oh, I doubt that very much," Wendy told her. "I don't even know who my parents are."

"Well, if you don't know who they are," Gwendolyn replied, "then it's even more possible, isn't it? Not knowing makes almost anything possible."

Wendy was so surprised by this idea that she said nothing at all. Gwendolyn watched her for a moment, then shrugged her shoulders and swam away. A subtle splash drew Wendy's attention behind her, and she realized with a start that the merman who had spoken to her had snuck up behind her while she was talking to Gwendolyn. He reached out his hand, and Wendy tried to step away from him, but something was pressing against her back, trying to push her toward the edge.

"What? No!" Wendy cried out, and then an explosion of jingling bells broke out just behind her. The pressure disappeared and she backed away in a panic. She saw Charming chasing Tinker Bell off toward the shore, but in her haste to retreat from the merman she tripped on the slick rock. She twisted as she fell, and she managed to catch herself on her hands, only to end up face to face with the other merman on the other side of the rock.

He grinned and reached for her, but Wendy scrambled back to the center of the stone.

"Fly," she heard Peter shout.

"What?" She leaped to her feet and drew her own sword, pointing it first toward the one and then toward the other.

The first merman began to raise himself up onto the rock. She thrust her sword at him, but he dodged to the side, faster than she would have thought possible.

"Fly!" Peter yelled again.

"Oh!" Wendy exclaimed. In her panic, she had reacted on instinct and had forgotten all about the innisfay dust. The merman's hand darted toward her ankle, but it closed around empty air, just missing her as she leaped into the sky.

CHAPTER 49

Wendy flew back to the cliff, landed next to the sitting rock man (which somehow made her feel safer, although she couldn't have said why), and exhaled a huge breath, letting it puff out her cheeks in relief. Peter followed and landed beside her.

"Oh, good form!" he told her. "That was a *brilliant* escape! Out of his clutches at the last possible moment! I couldn't have done it better myself!"

"But I wasn't *trying* to escape so narrowly," Wendy protested. "That's just how it happened." In fact, now that she was safe, it was embarrassing how close she had come to being caught. She had forgotten she could fly!

"Wendy," he told her gently, "there's no need to be modest. There's nothing wrong with knowing what you're good at."

He was being sincere again and looking at her with such an air of fondness and admiration mixed together—over something she didn't deserve any admiration for at all—that Wendy didn't know

what to say. She took a small step away from him, trying to gather her thoughts.

"Yes, well, we should be getting back," she told him.

"There's no hurry," he said, smiling at her. "They still have to fix the *Jolly Roger.*"

"With everyone working together, it will be done before we know it. We've been gone long enough."

Peter looked sorry to have to go, but, of course, only for a moment. Then he burst into a wide grin and waved his sword through the air. "And then we'll have our battle!" he crowed. "We'll defeat the nefarious Blackheart once and for all! What is it, Wendy? What's wrong?" As quickly as that, he was tender again, watching her with an air of quiet concern.

She was frightened, was the truth of it. The last time they had fought in a real battle, Nicholas had died. She had abandoned Michael to try to save Nicholas, and Michael was lucky to be alive. The wonders of Neverland had distracted her, at least for a little while, but just now, when she forgot she could fly and had almost been caught by the merman, it brought all her fears and doubts churning to the surface again.

What if someone else got shot and she couldn't save them? What if she made a mistake and someone died? Michael or John or Charlie or Thomas or even Hook?

Or Peter.

She couldn't think about that. She just couldn't.

"Show me the dragon!" she blurted out.

"Snaggleclaw?" he asked her.

"Yes, Snaggleclaw. I'd like to meet him." It was the first thing that came to her. The dragon was very near the ships, so she wouldn't feel guilty about staying away any longer. But, at the same time, going to see the dragon wasn't the same thing as going back, so she could put off thinking about everything that lay ahead just a bit longer.

"Why, that's a fantastic idea!" Peter exclaimed, grinning again. "I'd like very much for you to meet him. And I think he'd like to meet you, too."

But it was a long flight back to the mountains.

Wendy tried to lose herself in the wondrous views, and sometimes she did. But returning from an adventure always feels different than embarking upon it, and Wendy was not just returning to the comfort of her own bed and her books and her friends and Nana. Instead, she was returning to something she had come to dread, and there was a trembling sickness in her gut that she couldn't quite shake, no matter how hard she tried.

When they reached the farmland, the tears she had been fighting threatened to spill over. She reached up with one hand to wipe them away before they could fall, and suddenly Peter was there by her side, taking her other hand in his and smiling at her tenderly.

She gripped his hand tightly, feeling the warmth and the strength of it in her own, and the sickness that had lodged itself in her gut finally fell away. She closed her eyes and breathed in and out, and although she still didn't know what would happen, her heart eased, remembering she was not alone.

They found Snaggleclaw draped across the same ridge he had been lying on when they left. The air as they approached him was cold but not as bitter as Wendy had expected, given the thin layer of snow on the ground.

"Does he ever move?" Wendy asked, but then she remembered who she was asking. "I mean, I know he *moves*, obviously. But does he ever ... well, does he ever fly?"

"From time to time," Peter told her. "He's very old, even for a dragon. He sleeps a lot. But he's an excellent watch-dragon. He always knows when people come and go."

As though to prove it, Snaggleclaw opened one eye and focused intently on Peter, then slowly shut it again.

"See?" Peter said, laughing. "Hey, wake up, old man. I want you to meet someone."

The dragon opened its eye again, focused this time on Wendy, and snorted. A small puff of smoke trailed in thin wisps up into the sky. Peter laughed.

"She's a friend," he said. "You'll like her."

The dragon's eye rolled first toward Peter, then back to Wendy. A ripple of small, shifting movements ran through its body, and it lifted its head, tilting it to the side and exposing its chin.

"He wants you to scratch him," Peter said. "He likes you."

"Truly?" Wendy asked. She was used to animals liking her. They always had. But somehow a dragon seemed like a different thing altogether, especially since it could clearly eat her in one bite.

"Truly," Peter said with a laugh. He landed next to the dragon's head and began scratching it roughly along the jaw line with both hands. The dragon groaned and snorted in obvious contentment, making Wendy chuckle. She lowered herself to the ridge and stood beside Peter, watching as his fingers disappeared beneath the saucer-sized scales that lined the dragon's jaw.

"Scratch him underneath?" she asked.

"He can't feel it on top of his scales," Peter told her. "But the skin beneath itches sometimes. Especially when he's shedding."

"He *sheds*?" Wendy asked, incredulous.

"Just a few scales at a time," Peter explained. "Old ones fall off and new ones come in underneath."

The dragon kept inching its head forward, trying to get Peter to scratch farther back, so Wendy reached her hands between two scales about a foot behind the ones Peter was working on. The skin beneath was surprisingly warm. And ... soft?

"He has fur underneath!" Wendy exclaimed.

"Just a little," Peter agreed. "It helps him stay warm up here."

"Why, that's amazing!" She scratched between the next two, and then the next, moving backward systematically. And then, between the sixth and seventh scales, the bottom one came away in her hands.

"Oh, no!" she cried. "I'm sorry!"

But the dragon didn't look angry. Far from it. He sighed in relief and laid his head back down on the rock.

"Don't be sorry," Peter said, laughing. "That's what he wanted. You must have found the one that was bothering him. I told you, he sheds."

Wendy looked down at the dragon scale in her hands. It felt lighter than she would have expected, but it looked like stone—mostly gray with hints of white along one edge.

"I ... may I keep it?" she asked shyly.

Peter laughed again. "Well, he doesn't want it back. He's glad to be rid of it! Look."

Already, the dragon had fallen asleep and appeared to be snoring.

"Thank you," Wendy said.

"No need to thank me," Peter said. "It wasn't ever mine, and he didn't want it anyway."

"No, I mean, thank you for this. For today. For bringing me to meet him. I ... I've never seen a dragon before." It seemed rather obvious that she had never seen a dragon before, but she couldn't think of any other way to express how special it felt to meet one.

"Well, there aren't many left to see," Peter admitted. "But at

least he's not the last. I try to find them *before* they're the very last one. So they won't get lonely."

"And so they won't be gone forever," Wendy realized.

A glaze washed over Peter's face, like a cloud scudding across the moon, but then he grinned. "I'm glad *you're* here, the Wendy," he told her.

"Thank you, Peter," she said with a smile. "I'm glad I am, too."

CHAPTER 50

They retrieved Wendy's pack before returning to the ship, but she was almost sorry they did. Climbing the rope to *The Pegasus* was not easy now that the innisfay dust had worn off, and the pack only made things worse. Had Wendy thought of it, she might have asked Peter to drop the bag off for her, even if she climbed up herself. Unfortunately, she had not thought of it, so she struggled her way up bit by bit, using the system of knots to stand on, one after another, until she finally arrived at the top.

By the time she reached her quarters, she would have been more than happy to drop her pack next to her sea trunk and fall right to sleep, but she did not have that luxury. Gentleman Starkey was waiting for her.

"The captain would like to see you, Miss Darling," he told her politely.

"Of course, he would," she replied, speaking mostly to herself.

"I'm sorry, miss?"

"Nothing, Mr. Starkey. Nothing at all. Let me set down my bag, and I shall report to him at once."

She opened the door to do just that, only to be greeted by an obviously anxious Nana.

"Oh, Nana," Wendy said as she scratched the dog behind her ears, "I'm so sorry. I left you here for hours, didn't I?" She turned to Starkey, who was waiting patiently in the passageway. "Mr. Starkey, would you be so kind as to take Nana out for a walk? I'll report to the captain immediately."

"Aye, miss," Starkey said at once. "I'd be glad to."

Had Starkey known what was going on in the captain's quarters at that very moment, he would have been more than glad to do it. In fact, he would have been downright grateful.

Wendy arrived to the muffled sounds of shouting. She knocked on the door twice and finally opened it herself, only to see Hook and Tigerlilja squared off across the map table, each of them trying to out-glare the other.

"It's about *trust*," Tigerlilja shouted at Hook. "If you intend to insert your precious 'English presence' on my ship, then Vegard will serve as a Norse presence within your ground forces."

"She isn't your ship!" Hook reminded her loudly. "She's the king's ship, which is why one of the king's men needs to be aboard. And Vegard can't be on the ground because he is her captain. At least temporarily."

"Lest we forget," Tigerlilja said, grunting in disgust.

"What's this?" Wendy asked, looking from one to the other.

"She doesn't want Mr. Abbot on the *Jolly Roger*," Hook informed Wendy, "even though it's a perfectly reasonable request." He said the last bit while staring pointedly at Tigerlilja, but she did not look intimidated in the slightest.

"And I said I was happy to have Mr. Abbot aboard as long

as Vegard is included in the group that will be capturing Blackheart," she responded.

"Or killing him," Hook muttered.

"At last, we agree on *something*," Tigerlilja exclaimed.

"I thought it was decided that Vegard would captain the *Jolly Roger*," Wendy said, careful not to point out who had done the deciding.

"It *was* decided," Hook agreed.

"No, *you* decided," Tigerlilja shot back. "*I* had the decency to wait until we were not in front of your men to discuss the matter. There's no reason why I can't captain my own ship. Excuse me," she said, holding up a hand before Hook could reply, "*your* ship crewed by *my* people."

"There is a reason," Hook growled.

"Then explain it to me," Tigerlilja said, crossing her arms. "Explain to me why I am incompetent in your eyes."

Hook ran his good left hand through his hair and sighed. "It isn't you," he said finally, in a very different tone of voice. "And it isn't about what I think. It's about my men. They won't have faith in the plan if a woman is in charge of any of our ships. They simply won't."

Tigerlilja stared him down, but Hook simply stared back at her—no longer angry, but clearly resolute. Finally, she grunted again.

"English," Tigerlilja said grimly. "How such a backward people have spread so far across the world is beyond me."

"Perhaps," Wendy suggested quickly, "there is someone else who could serve as a figurehead? You could take over as soon as you were in the air. John—I mean, Mr. Abbot—would have no problem with it. And then Vegard could come with us. We'd be glad for his help."

They both turned to look at Wendy. Hook raised his eyebrows

and then looked back at Tigerlilja, obviously waiting for her reply. She cocked her head to one side, then sighed.

"I suppose it works," she admitted. "Argus would do it. Although I find the necessity of the ruse ... distasteful."

"Who is Argus?" Hook asked her.

"He's the man you will accept as your puppet captain unless you want to start this argument all over again," Tigerlilja snapped.

"Fine," Hook said. "Pan's everlost will still pilot the *Jolly Roger.*"

"Curly," Tigerlilja informed him. "His name is Curly."

"Miss Darling will fly with Pan himself," Hook continued, ignoring the interruption, "to keep him on task, as will Vegard and the rest of the Fourteenth."

You mean the useless Fourteenth, Wendy thought. How many times had he called them that? Just because they weren't sailors. Now, at long last, their skill as trained soldiers was needed. She didn't expect an apology, but she thought a little appreciation would have been nice.

"Blackheart has confined himself to his base," Hook continued. That drew Wendy's full attention. If they had good intelligence regarding where Blackheart would be, the attack was imminent. "Apparently, he's been working on creating new everlost of his own. We can't let that happen. But he's ordered his crew not to disturb him, which makes this the perfect opportunity."

"We're certain?" Wendy asked, and Tigerlilja nodded in reply.

"The innisfay have been watching him," she said. "This might be our only chance to catch him alone, or nearly."

"*The Pegasus* and the *Jolly Roger* will attack his base to draw his fleet away," Hook explained. "They won't be looking for Pan's ship because they won't expect him to be in league with us. You'll slip in behind us after we've drawn them off: you, Vegard, Starkey, Mr. Bennet and the Fourteenth, Pan and his crew."

Wendy couldn't help but wonder if Starkey was meant as a

strong *Hook* presence in the ground party. The man was fiercely loyal to his captain.

"Even leaving most of the crew with the ship, you should have enough to handle any guards who remain in the base and eliminate the threat," Hook finished.

"You'll have your hands full with Pan," Tigerlilja warned her. "Whatever you find in Blackheart's lair, I wouldn't count on Pan for much help."

Wendy only nodded, acknowledging the comment, but Wendy had always found Peter to be reliable when it really mattered. He had saved poor Reginald's life. He had saved her own life more than once. Wendy couldn't help but believe in him, no matter what Tigerlilja said.

"You have your orders," Hook said. "The Norsemen brought some spare pieces of leather armor. You'll find them with the quartermaster." He looked down at the map table as though there were something profoundly interesting on it, even though there clearly wasn't.

Wendy raised her eyebrows and turned to Tigerlilja.

"What he doesn't want to say," she explained, "is that we train our women to fight from childhood. *All* our women. And, of course, we make armor for them, the same as the men. I made sure they brought pieces that will fit you."

"Thank you," Wendy said shyly. She averted her gaze from Hook just as carefully as he had from her until she had left his quarters.

At the armory, Tigerlilja proved to be true to her word, not that Wendy was surprised. She tried on several things, but the vests felt too stiff, and the leg bracers interfered with her holsters.

In the end, she took only two pairs of leather leggings that seemed to have been tailored for a woman about her size (instead

of the boys' leggings she had been belting down at the waist) and a pair of bracers. They were very stiff, molded roughly to the shape of her wrist, with leather laces to tie them down. Despite their obvious function, they had been painted blue on their outer face, and Wendy thought they were as lovely as they were practical.

She returned to her small quarters to pack, and, of course, to say goodbye to Nana, who had already returned from her walk with Mr. Starkey. Wendy had decided to send the dog with John. None of them were likely to be safe in the battle to come, but Wendy wasn't sure how good Nana would have been at sneaking into a magical fortress.

"It isn't personal," Wendy was telling her. "You know you have a mind of your own when it comes to magical creatures. It's one of the things I love about you. But I think you'll be safer with John."

Nana, for her part, always felt safer with Wendy than with anyone else in the world. She was trying to point that out by whining softly when they were interrupted by a knock at the door.

Wendy opened it to find John and Charlie standing there together.

"We just wanted," John said, but then he gulped and fell silent.

Wendy, of course, understood him perfectly. He wanted to say goodbye, but at the same time he *didn't* want to say goodbye because he didn't want to admit, not even to himself, that they might be saying it forever.

"I'll be fine," she assured him. "We'll all be fine. You'll see." She had no way of knowing that, but it seemed like the right thing to say. John nodded and gulped again. "Take Nana with you. Take care of her for me, until we all get back?"

John nodded again. "I will," he said roughly.

"Charlie," she said, turning to her lifelong friend, "whatever happens, remember that this is what I always wanted. There's nothing you could have done to turn me away from it. Nothing. Understand? *Whatever* happens."

It was Charlie's turn to gulp and nod. "Or me, either," he told her. "This is more of a life than I ever thought possible. No matter what."

A tear formed in Wendy's eye, but she wiped it away furiously.

"All right, now. Both of you, go on," she told them. "We're all being silly. We'll see each other as soon as it's over." She tried to sound sure of it, but she hugged them both, just the same.

When she shut the door behind them, only Charming remained.

"I'm glad you're coming with me, at least," she told him, but then there was another knock at the door.

"Honestly," she said as she was opening the door, "we're all going to be fine." But it was not John and Charlie, as she had assumed. It was Hook.

"Miss Darling," he told her, "I don't know whether to believe you are eerily prescient or simply have a woman's instinct for fashion. Either way, you never cease to astound me."

"Sorry?" she asked.

He pointed to her blue bracers with his good left hand, and then he lifted his right arm to show her the blue officer's jacket that was draped across it, just behind his hook. He picked it up, exposing a perfect column of polished gold buttons, and he handed her the garment without further ceremony.

"I believe," he said simply, "this is somewhat overdue."

CHAPTER 51

Her blue coat. Wendy kept running her hands over it. A Royal Navy officer's jacket, with polished gold buttons. It was just like the ones the men had been wearing at Bartholomew Fair all those years ago. The men who had laughed at her for wanting to be in the navy at all. And, now, here she was. An officer. A *commissioned* officer. With a fine blue jacket of her own.

It was just a tiny bit large for her, but she liked it that way. She could move in it. She could *fight* in it. It felt heavy on her shoulders, and she liked that, too. It felt solid. Dependable. Reassuring.

It made her feel like she could do anything.

She checked her pistols one more time, making sure she could reach them easily in the leg holsters strapped to her thighs. She checked the musket slung across her back. She checked her ammunition pouches. She checked the silver dagger in her belt and the silver blade at her hip—a full sword from the quartermaster, reserved only for officers. It must have been worth a small fortune.

She bent her knees deeply and leaped to her feet several times.

The new leggings fit her perfectly, and her gear remained secure. She was ready.

"Come along, Charming. It's time to go."

Charming jingled and emerged from behind his curtain.

Together, they made their way up to the deck, where, of course, it was still dark. It was always dark here. She wished they could have used the cover of darkness to their advantage, but just because it was nighttime here in the valley didn't mean it would be nighttime where they were going. She had no idea where Blackheart's base was, and she hadn't thought to ask what time of day it was there.

Well, she would find out soon enough.

Starkey was waiting for her when she arrived on deck.

"The Fourteenth is already on Pan's ship, miss," he told her. "Vegard and I are the last to transfer. Everyone's accounted for."

"Excellent, Mr. Starkey. Thank you."

She moved toward the stern, intending to climb down as she always did, but Starkey stopped her.

"No need for that, miss," he told her. "They put a bridge up for us."

"A bridge?" she asked, incredulous.

Starkey led her to the side railing, where she saw that a kind of rope bridge had been slung between the two ships. Vegard was already in the center of it, so they watched as he moved his hands along the top ropes at either side, placing his feet carefully on the thin boards at his feet.

"It's a bit shaky, miss, but it'll hold," Starkey assured her.

Vegard finished crossing, Starkey went next, and then Wendy followed. She had to admit, it was far easier than climbing down and back up again. She didn't even mind the swaying. In what seemed like no time at all, she was standing on Pan's ship, where a new surprise awaited her.

"Starkey? What's this?"

"Your men, sir. They are presenting themselves for your inspection."

The entire platoon stood at attention, lined up in proper military formation. Michael stepped forward from the end and shouted, "Officer on deck!" In perfect unison, they turned their heads toward her and saluted.

Slowly, Wendy saluted back, feeling all the while as though she had stepped into a dream. At the end of her salute, the men dropped their hands smartly.

"Sir," Michael shouted, "do the troops meet with your approval, sir?"

"I ... oh, yes," Wendy said, her eyes filled with wonder. "Very much so!"

The men all grinned to one degree or another, but it was the only break in their military bearing.

"Men," Michael barked. He was about to issue a new order when a flurry of activity cut him short. From all across the deck, everlost flew to join in the fun, jostling each other as they lined up behind the platoon and adopted the same pose. Peter landed next to Michael, studied him carefully, and then imitated his posture and expression so perfectly that Wendy had to stifle a laugh. Peter broke his pose just long enough to nudge Michael, who grinned from ear to ear.

"Sir," Michael shouted again, "do *all* the troops meet with your approval, sir?"

"They do," Wendy said, imbuing her pronouncement with all the gravity the occasion deserved.

"Men," Michael barked, "to your stations!"

They grinned and broke ranks, spreading out to take up lookout positions all along the ship's rail, both port and starboard.

"Michael, you scoundrel," Wendy said, laughing.

"It wasn't even my idea," he protested. "Reginald put us all up to it. With John on the *Jolly Roger,* you're our ranking officer now."

She hadn't thought about it until that moment, but what Michael said was true. She was the ranking officer. And Hook knew that when he gave her the jacket. He might not have given her a ship, but without bringing it to anyone's attention, he had handed her the command of the most important part of this entire mission.

Wendy squared her shoulders and turned to Michael with a new look of determination. "Whatever waits for us in Blackheart's stronghold," she told him, "we're ending this. Today."

They flew over the same route Wendy and Peter had traveled on their way to see the mermaids: the farmlands, the rocky vistas, the mist-laced jungle canopy. Finally, near the very end of their journey, they veered off toward a different part of the coastline, and the landscape changed again.

To Wendy's amazement, it reminded her of England.

No, she decided, it did more than just remind her. The resemblance was uncanny. These fields and forests could have been on Hook's own estate in Hertfordshire, assuming Hertfordshire had been transported to the eastern coast. Even the birds and insects sounded the same, giving Wendy the impression of a cool spring morning. And, like so many mornings in England, there was a thick fog rolling in below.

Here, at the outer edge of the fog, only its long, soft fingers wove through the trees, but it thickened up ahead, covering the land like a quilt. Only a few lonely hills broke through the gray

here and there, and Peter turned toward the nearest before handing off the ship's thimble to an everlost with a prominent nose, an easy smile, and (somewhat improbably) a full-length black cape with a red silk lining draped across his shoulders.

The dapper crewman cupped both hands around Peter's fist, then suddenly snapped them shut around the thimble as Peter removed his own hand from between them.

"Are we close?" Wendy asked Peter.

"Very," he told her. "It's just ahead. We'll be able to see it through the spyglass from the top of that hill." He pulled a spyglass from a compartment behind the wheel—right next to the one that would have housed the thimble if he hadn't been using it.

"Then they'll be able to see us, too," Wendy said, thinking out loud. "Is there a safe place near that hill where we can settle under the cover of the fog and wait?"

"There's an open field this side of it," Peter told her.

"Good. Take us down, then."

Peter nodded. "As the navigator says, Nibs."

"Aye, Captain," Nibs replied cheerfully.

As the ship descended, the air grew colder and the mist curled around them, happy to swallow them whole. Wendy shivered. She could hardly see the bow, let alone the surrounding countryside.

"Michael, Vegard, Starkey," Wendy said, "and you, too, Peter. Come with me."

They used the lines to drop down to the ground and then climbed halfway up the nearby hill. Wendy breathed deeply, trying to imagine what lay ahead. What did the base look like? How large was it? How many guards would be left behind? Was their intelligence even accurate? Wendy snuck a glance at Tinker Bell, who was sitting on Peter's shoulder, her hair gold and bright.

Charming, who was sitting on her own shoulder, jingled in her ear.

"Charming!" Wendy exclaimed. "Can you fly just high enough to see when *The Pegasus* and the *Jolly Roger* have reached the base? So we'll know when their attention is turned away from us?"

Charming lifted off and hovered in front of Wendy, saluting smartly in midair. Then he zipped away, flying up through the fog cover until she couldn't see him anymore. She could not have asked for a better scout, and then she smiled a little, remembering a time when Tinker Bell used to spy on her from among the flowers of Hertfordshire.

All was quiet for a few moments longer, but then they heard an explosion of shouts and alarm bells off in the distance. The ships had been seen. She heard a volley of cannon fire. Was that *The Pegasus*? Or were they the ones being fired upon? A golden dart fell from the sky, landing on Wendy's shoulder. Charming. With a small, chiming trill, he pointed toward the top of the hill.

"Come on!" Wendy shouted.

They raced up the hill and burst out under the open sky, thin tendrils of fog clinging for a moment to their hair and shoulders, reluctant to let them go. Wendy squinted against the low morning sun, trying to make out the stronghold, and then she gasped.

Blackheart had a castle. Not a *pretend* castle. An honest-to-goodness stone castle. With towers. And battlements. It sprawled gravely at the edge of the cliffs, overlooking a proper naval base in a protected harbor, with ships floating on the sea. Peter handed Wendy the spyglass so she could count them. Five. Six. Seven. Her heart sank into the pit of her stomach. And an eighth, sitting up in a dry dock cradle. The largest warship Wendy had ever seen.

Eight ships.

And ... wait ... was that ... ?

"Heaven preserve us. He has dragons," Wendy whispered. Two smoke-gray dragons twined around the tallest tower, their

heads screaming in rage at *The Pegasus* and the *Jolly Roger*, which hovered over the harbor.

"Those are wyverns," Peter said.

"Wyverns?" she asked.

But it was Vegard who answered. He stood a bit ahead of her and to her left, his arms folded serenely across his chest, a longbow slung across his back. His long hair with its intermittent braids was tied behind his neck with a leather thong, the ends swaying gently as he turned his head toward her.

"Cousins to dragons, but not dragons. Smaller, and with only two legs. Their back end is just a long tail, like a snake."

Wendy did her best not to look horrified.

"They're formidable," he continued. "Very hard to control. I'm amazed he's managed to tame even one, let alone a pair of them. But they're easier to kill than dragons." He said the last bit with a wicked grin, which made Wendy feel at least a little better, if not much.

"I killed three just yesterday!" Peter declared.

"Oh, you did not, you winged idiot," Vegard told him, but his gruff tone was more brotherly than antagonistic.

Men swarmed out of the castle like angry hornets. Some were clearly everlost, flying to the ships in moments and unfurling the sails. Others had no wings, racing instead to a line of rowboats, desperate to reach their posts. A second round of cannon fire emerged from the ships in the sky, and Wendy heard its roar a moment later. The largest vessel in the harbor took heavy damage, and one of its masts toppled over.

"Why aren't they shooting at the one in dry dock?" Wendy wondered aloud. The ship was massive—clearly more of a threat than any of the others.

"I don't think it's sky-worthy," Vegard commented.

Only then did Wendy notice that the dry dock was covered in

scaffolding. It did, in fact, look as though Blackheart's crew had been working on it.

By this time, the last of the rowboats had reached their destinations and Blackheart's crew had begun to scale the ropes that hung from the sides of the fleet. Humans, imps, and several other kinds of creatures that Wendy couldn't quite make out all rushed hand over hand toward the decks. Were those ... lizard people? Wendy tried to look at one more closely, through the spyglass, but the pirate fell from the rope and splashed into the water below. She lowered the glass in time to see an everlost fly down and scoop him up, depositing him on the deck of a ship that was already rising into the air.

One, two, three ... Wendy counted the ships as *The Pegasus* and the *Jolly Roger* picked up speed, ready to draw them away. Four ... five ... six. Even the ship that had lost its mast took to the air, limping valiantly behind the others. The wyverns unwrapped themselves from the tower and took off after the fleet when they saw it leaving to pursue their attackers. A few scattered flying beasts lifted off from the ramparts to chase the wyverns, and then everything seemed to quiet.

No one appeared to be left on the battlements, and only two ships remained behind: the warship in dry dock and Blackheart's own vessel, floating serenely in the water. Wendy recognized it as the one that had chased them into Neverland, but there was no one on it now. Or, at least, not anyone she could see.

Wendy drew in a deep breath and let it out slowly, watching all the while. Nothing moved. This was their chance. She said a quick, silent prayer for *The Pegasus* and the *Jolly Roger*, and then she turned to her crew.

"It's time."

CHAPTER 52

They were able to fly Pan's ship almost to the castle without losing the cover of the fog. Or, at least, without losing it entirely. Wendy ordered the sails furled, and Nibs stayed low within the light gray mist, rising only high enough to follow Charming, who flew above them in the form of a tiny golden bird.

Finally, just a few dozen yards from the outer wall, the fog broke, and there was nowhere left to hide. Wendy stepped forward, speaking quickly but quietly.

"Peter, Michael, Reginald, Vegard, Starkey. You're with me. And, Peter, choose three more everlost who can be especially cunning. We need to sneak through the castle without alerting any guards who might be left behind."

"The twins," Peter said immediately. "And Slightly."

"Obviously."

Wendy had to assume the everlost who said this was Slightly himself. He stepped forward with a grin and shook the blond hair out of his eyes with an exaggerated snap of his head.

"Nibs," Wendy said, "bring us right up to the ramparts. But move fast. As soon as we're away, retreat into the fog. Assign a lookout to the crow's nest. Stay hidden until you see us on the ramparts again. The Fourteenth will provide cover fire, but only if necessary. If worse comes to worst and the fleet returns, fire the cannons and try to draw them away again. Buy us whatever time you can."

"Aye, aye, sir," Nibs said with a gallant bow.

The extra flourish did not exactly fill Wendy with confidence, but it would have to do. There was no time left. The ship burst from the fog and raced the last few yards to the ramparts, fully exposed. The next thing Wendy knew, she was dropping hand over hand down a rope as fast as she could, and then she was standing on the high ramparts of Blackheart's castle.

The courtyard below was empty and deathly still. A handful of guards stood on the far battlements, but they were still looking out over the water, shading their eyes against the morning sun, trying to watch the fleet.

"Stay low," Wendy whispered. She ducked down far enough that the protective wall at the edge of the rampart would hide her from view if any of the guards decided to turn around, and the rest of her team followed suit. "We're going to have to search for Blackheart's inner sanctuary—probably a laboratory of some kind. Remember, stay quiet. We'll fight if we have to, but we'd rather not bring the whole castle down on our heads if we can help it."

"Tinker Bell knows where it is," Peter said. "She spies on the castle all the time." He answered Wendy in a perfectly normal speaking voice despite everything she had just said.

"Shhhhhhhhh!" Wendy hissed. Vegard rolled his eyes and shook his head. They all fell silent and waited, but after several breaths, there was still no sign they had been discovered.

"Tinker Bell knows where Blackheart has been working?" Wendy finally asked in a whisper.

Tinker Bell crossed her arms over her chest and hovered proudly in midair. She caught Wendy's eye and nodded emphatically, answering for herself. Wendy snuck a glance back at the ship, which was already disappearing into the fog.

"All right," Wendy told her. "Lead the way."

An archway at the next corner opened onto an enclosed stairwell. They descended into a long corridor with heavy wooden doors to either side, but they scurried only a few yards along it before Tinker Bell ducked through another archway. These stairs were clearly less used than the others, but Wendy still cringed at the way every small scuff echoed against the stone.

There were no torches to light their way, so they crept along to a golden glow provided by Tinker Bell and Charming until this new stairwell opened into a system of corridors that twisted and turned like a labyrinth. Tinker Bell turned left, then right, then right, then left again, changing course so often that Wendy soon felt hopelessly lost. She would have accused Tinker Bell of leading them in circles, but every so often they came to another stairwell and descended to new depths, only to begin the process all over again.

"This isn't much of an adventure," Peter finally complained.

By Wendy's reckoning, they were two levels below ground. They hadn't heard anyone else since the level above them, and even that had sounded distant, barely echoing through the tunnels. But they had no idea who might be down here working in some hidden corner or even shirking their duty by hiding away in a forgotten dungeon.

"Shhhhhhhhh!" Wendy hissed again.

"Well, it isn't!" he said, speaking even more loudly than before. "I thought we would have fought *someone* by now. But nothing's

happening at all. We're just walking around and around and around. I could have done that without ever leaving the valley!"

The men all glared at him—especially Reginald, who had just been thinking the exact same thing but had had the common sense not to blurt it out during a clandestine operation.

"Peter," Wendy whispered, "it *is* a great adventure. Think about it. I'm certain Blackheart and his men have fought to defend this castle many times." (In point of fact, she wasn't certain of it at all. But it seemed like a reasonable premise.) "But how many teams do you think have ever snuck into Blackheart's castle right under his nose?"

Peter looked thoughtful, obviously considering her argument.

"Only a true *master* of stealth could *sneak* all the way to Blackheart's private lair and surprise him, giving him no chance to escape," she told him. "*That* would be worthy of a *great* story."

"I suppose that's true," Peter agreed, finally whispering. "But do you think there might at least be *some* fighting?"

"Oh, come on," Wendy told him, and they fell silent again.

The truth, though, was that Wendy *did* think there would be fighting. She just didn't want to admit it out loud. The deeper they pushed into the very bowels of Blackheart's realm—which was how Wendy had begun to think of this entire expedition—the more she could sense a great evil lurking somewhere below.

Waiting for them.

The thought made her shudder, but she pressed on, nonetheless. She would not shirk her duty to England, no matter what it might cost her. And she would not abandon Neverland.

Finally, just as Wendy had begun to think they might wander the corridors and tunnels of Blackheart's stronghold forever, they came out into a large space that almost made Wendy gasp in surprise. Several different tunnels converged here into an ornate entrance hall. Pillars of stark-white stone rose along each side with

elaborately carved arches between them. Raised carvings stood out up and down the pillars, like some long-forgotten language Wendy had never seen before. Each letter—or were they words?—was as tall as her fist and covered in gold leaf. Torches flared between the pillars, glinting along the metal and bathing the entire area in dancing light.

"What is this place?" Wendy whispered.

"Some kind of temple," Vegard replied. He wasn't exactly whispering, but his voice was pitched so low she could barely hear him. "These symbols were carved by Norsemen."

"Norsemen?" Wendy asked in surprise. "What do they say?"

"I don't know," he said simply. "I recognize them, but they're older than I. Far older. Tigerlilja studied the old ways, long ago. She might know them, but I do not."

Wendy shivered. She wanted to know what it meant, but there was nothing she could do about it. They certainly couldn't stand here waiting for someone else to emerge from the tunnels.

"Michael," she whispered.

"Aye." He had not spoken a word in all this time, but he had moved to her side protectively the moment they had first entered the chamber.

"I need you to stay here with Starkey, Reginald, and the twins to cover the rear flank. Pan, Vegard, Slightly, and I are going in to investigate."

Michael flexed his jaw and glanced at Peter. "I don't like it," he told her, and then he added, even more quietly, "I have orders to protect you. Orders from John *and* from Hook."

But Wendy knew that wasn't his real objection. Michael didn't want to leave her side with or without those orders. "I'll call for you if we get into trouble," she promised. "Right now, I need to know nothing else is coming through that door behind us. That's how I need you to protect me. Can you do that?"

Michael stared at her a moment longer, and then he sighed a little. "Aye, sir."

Returning to silence, Michael used hand signals to set his team up behind the pillars. Wendy didn't like leaving them any more than Michael liked staying behind, but at least it was a highly defensible position. With a final glance at Michael, she turned and made her way toward the other end of the entry hall, followed by Pan, Vegard, and Slightly.

As for Tinker Bell and Charming, they hadn't been given any orders at all. They were so small that even Wendy tended to overlook them, which was just one of the many reasons why Tinker Bell didn't like her. But the innisfay are almost as curious as they are proud, so they both followed Wendy into Blackheart's inner sanctum, even if Tinker Bell did give her a dirty look behind Peter's back.

Peering out of the entry hall, Wendy's immediate thought was that they were back outside again—the space was huge and as bright as day—but, of course, that was impossible. They couldn't be outside. They were several stories underground. Still, it *felt* like being outdoors.

Rows and rows of giant columns stood before her, wrapping in a huge oval around a large open space in the center, almost like an arena. In fact, it was *very* much like an arena. The columns were all lit by torches, and, on top of the arched columns, empty rows of tiered stone seating curved around the room, raised high above the sand-filled floor. The only difference Wendy could see from a typical arena design was that there was nothing to stop her from walking among the columns beneath the seating platforms.

That, and the roof of the giant underground cavern. It loomed far overhead, supported at least in part by an outer ring of massive columns that reached all the way to the ceiling, with equally impressive arches between them.

It would have been a magnificent arena, but it wasn't an arena at all. Vegard had been right. It was a temple. Wendy knew this because a huge statue stood in the center of the open space, depicting a giant gate—with an equally giant Norseman pushing the upper half of his body roughly halfway through. The statue was so large, in fact, that it took Wendy several moments before she noticed three *other* things about it that she had not realized at first.

One, it was the source of evil Wendy had been feeling all this time. She was certain of it.

Two, there was nothing at all supporting the Norseman statue's torso. It simply hung in midair, thrusting forward through the gate.

Third, the statue moved.

It didn't move much, and it didn't move often, but it moved. Every few seconds, the entire figure would *ripple* with energy. It only lasted for a fraction of a second each time, but during that instant, the statue looked real, made of flesh and bone like any other man, but with eyes as dull and black as coal.

The first time it happened, Wendy ducked behind one of the nearby pillars, but the giant didn't react to her presence, if he had even seen her at all. He was turned slightly away from them, and as fast as it had appeared, the ripple vanished, leaving behind a white marble statue, just as before. Wendy turned to look for the others, only to discover that Vegard, Peter, and Slightly had all crowded in right behind her. She flinched, grabbing halfway for her sword before she managed to stop herself, her heart galloping in her chest.

She glared at Peter and pushed him away because he was closest, but he hardly seemed to notice. Slightly grinned. Vegard only shrugged as though to say, *What was I supposed to do? Stay out in the open with the giant living statue?* He narrowed his eyes at Peter but said nothing.

Huge sets of stone steps on either side of the temple's entrance led up to the seating above. Wendy waited until the next ripple had passed through the statue and then she dashed for them across the sand, followed by the rest. She wanted a higher vantage point. Blackheart had to be here somewhere. He *had* to be.

They reached the bottom level of seating only to realize there was almost no cover here. Nothing separated them from the statue except a low retaining wall at the front edge of the curving balcony. Wendy crawled forward from the relative safety of the stairwell, motioning to the others to follow. When Peter looked like he was going to ignore her and simply walk forward, she reached up and grabbed his shirt, tugging him down below the wall. Peter opened his mouth but before he could say a word, Wendy gave him such a withering look that the protest died on his lips.

They crawled along behind the wall, moving closer to the statue, but as they crawled, they heard someone speaking. Wendy risked a quick glance over the edge and realized there was a man standing next to the gate, which had hidden him from their view before. She ducked again, holding up a warning hand to Peter and the others.

"There has to be a way," he was saying. "I need more forces. The beasts are too hard to control."

There was a long pause, and then Wendy heard the answer in her own mind, as clearly as if someone had whispered it into her ear.

Chaos.

Wendy was so shocked that she almost missed what the man said next. She was too busy exchanging a wide-eyed stare with Vegard, who had clearly heard the whisper, too, and she had to play the man's words over in her mind to make sense of them.

"Yes, of course, my lord. They will wreak havoc when they are unleashed. But that will not be enough to bring the Kingdom

of Britain to its knees. I need men. Stronger, faster, better men. *Flying* men."

And a few moments later, the answer came.

Everlost.

"Yes! That's what I've been saying. I need more. I've taken all I can. The rest are loyal to Peter."

There was a much longer break this time, until Wendy wasn't sure the man was going to get an answer. It was Blackheart speaking. It had to be. Slowly, carefully, Wendy eased the musket from her back and loaded it. But then the answer came, along with a chill that settled like ice in her heart.

Evil.

Comes.

To Neverland.

"When, Lord Buri?" The man's voice rose in agitation. "When will you come through?"

Soon.

Buri. Wendy had already suspected that this was Buri. The Norse god Tigerlilja had warned her about. The one who had killed Peter's parents. But Peter hadn't known it. Thanks to the curse, Peter had forgotten all about Buri.

Until now.

Wendy turned to Peter just in time to see a look of confusion cross his face. But then he stared straight into Wendy's eyes. The confusion fell away, only to be replaced by the most terrible combination of grief and rage Wendy had ever seen.

"BURI!" Peter screamed.

No. In one fluid motion, Wendy rose and trained her weapon squarely on Blackheart's chest. And then, with her finger already applying pressure to the trigger, she made the worst mistake of her life.

She looked Blackheart in the eyes just as she was about to fire.

If women ever sail the sea,
They'll scrub the decks for men like me!
They'll marry none but Davy Jones,
And for their children, only bones!

Blackheart.
Black. Heart.
Blackheart was Mortimer Black.

CHAPTER 53

Wendy finished pulling the trigger, but that single moment of hesitation was all it took. As fast as any everlost, Blackheart moved, and Wendy's shot flew wide.

It was a miracle she had managed to fire at all. The world seemed to slow around her. Everything was happening at half speed, and yet she still had no time to react to any of it—like in the kind of dream where you want so badly to run but your legs just won't listen.

She saw Mortimer dodge her bullet. Then she saw an arrow slice through his shirt. An arrow? That seemed strange, but then she remembered Vegard had a bow. Mortimer hissed, but the arrow continued on, its silver tip crashing into the pillar behind him. The projectile had only nicked his side.

Ragged wings sprang from his back, and he soared into the air.

Peter reached the statue, but it had already turned back to stone. The everlost hacked and slashed at it furiously with a sword in each hand, but the strikes were futile. It did not turn to flesh again.

A dozen or so of Mortimer's men rushed onto the sands from somewhere beneath them. Where had they even come from? Michael, Starkey, and Reginald ran in from the entry hall and fired at Mortimer's crew, killing three of them immediately. Their bodies shimmered, broke into a million flying embers, and disappeared. Wendy's mind tracked the numbers by habit. Three down. The odds were even now. The twins whooped and flew into the air, engaging two of Mortimer's everlost in a sword fight even as Mortimer flew away.

Blackheart was flying away.

England. Neverland. The mission.

Peter.

Wendy blinked, and her body moved again.

"Peter!" she shouted. "Mortimer's getting away!"

But she had called him by his given name.

Peter tore himself away from the statue and looked toward Wendy, but Wendy was looking at Blackheart.

And Blackheart was staring right back at her.

He hadn't recognized her at first. She had her hair pulled back behind her head, which was the same way most of Peter's everlost wore it. And she was wearing a slightly oversized blue officer's coat. To be sure, the British uniform had surprised him for a moment, but he hadn't thought much of it. Peter and his everlost stole things from England all the time. It wouldn't have been the first royal item to serve in Peter's ridiculous games.

So Mortimer had not seen Wendy Darling at all. He had only seen one of Peter's foolish boys playing dress-up with a real man's clothes.

Until she had yelled his name.

That had stopped him. All the everlost called him Blackheart now. He hadn't even been sure they remembered the other name. But here it was, being yelled by—and then he realized that, too.

Being yelled by a woman. In a voice, come to think of it, that seemed strangely familiar.

So he looked again. Really looked.

And then he saw her. Wendy Darling. Of all the people in the world, Wendy Darling was staring back at him across the sands of his underground temple ... in his stronghold ... in *his* Neverland. Wearing the coat of an officer in the Royal Navy.

In the space of that single moment, Mortimer Black understood everything.

"Kill her!" he screamed. "Kill the woman!"

Blackheart's men, below on the sands, turned to look up, following the line of their leader's trembling hand, which pointed straight at Wendy. They spread their wings to leap toward her, and Peter Pan fell upon them in a fury.

Two of them died before they could even blink, each skewered through the heart by one of his blades. Their bodies disappeared, and the rest of Blackheart's men backed away, suddenly uncertain. Even the twins stopped fighting with the two everlost in the air, and they all stopped to watch what would happen.

It did not seem like a game anymore.

They all knew Peter. Even Blackheart's crew had once been Peter's men. They were deeply familiar with the exaggerated boasting and the wild stories. The Peter who rescued orphans and played catch with mermaids.

But *this* Peter—the Peter whose face wore the anger of the gods—he was unknown to them, and they saw immediately the danger they were in.

Two more flew away without a word.

Of the three remaining on the sand, only one faced Peter directly. He let his hand fall timidly to his side, lowering his sword. "Peter?" he asked. His voice shook, and his eyes were wide with fear.

Peter took a step toward him, and the everlost stumbled backward.

"No, Peter."

But it was not the everlost who spoke. It was Wendy, calling him back to himself. Back to the Peter she knew and trusted.

Calling him home.

"It's over now," she told him gently.

Peter blinked. "No one harms the Wendy," he growled, but it was a warning, not a threat. "No one."

The other two remaining everlost glanced at each other, and then they all flew away—even the ones who had been fighting the twins—each heading in a different direction. As Wendy watched them go, she realized the upper tier of the arena's seating was practically littered with the open mouths of various tunnels, all leading out of the arena in different directions.

"What? No!" Wendy cried. "Blackheart! Which way did he take?"

But no one had an answer. By this time, Michael and the rest had gathered around her, and Peter flew up to join them.

"Blackheart? Was he here?" Peter asked.

Vegard sighed and rolled his eyes. "Welcome back," he muttered.

"We have to find him!" Wendy looked from one tunnel to the next, but there was no hint as to where Blackheart had gone. "Charming?" she asked desperately.

But the innisfay shook his head sadly.

"Next time," Michael told her. "Wherever he went, it won't be long before he sends reinforcements. If we want to live to fight another day, we need to leave. Now."

Even as he said it, they could already hear pounding footsteps and the distant sounds of men shouting.

Wendy uttered a strangled groan of frustration, but then she turned her attention to Tinker Bell.

"You know this place better than anyone," she said to the innisfay. "Is there a way to get out of here that will avoid Blackheart's guards?"

Tinker Bell didn't think that was a very polite way to ask. *Especially* after she had done her part to get them all down here, only to see them botch the entire operation and let Blackheart get away. But then Peter looked at her in that special way he always did, like she was the most important person in the world, and Tinker Bell forgot all about Wendy Darling.

"Please, Tinker Bell," Peter said. "We need you."

With a blush and a grin, Tink darted toward one of the exits, above them and to the left, and everyone followed her, running as fast as they could (even Wendy) proving yet again that Tinker Bell was the most important one, after all.

It didn't seem possible, but Wendy was convinced that the route back up to the ramparts was even more roundabout than the trip down had been. It was also harder, since there were so many stairs—going both up *and* down this time, which Wendy secretly thought Tinker Bell might have been doing just to be the leader a little bit longer.

The journey also felt more harrowing, since they were accosted by the distant, echoing shouts of Blackheart's men at every turn. *Mortimer's* men, Wendy corrected herself. She could still hardly believe it, but she didn't have the energy to think about it. By the

time they reached the ramparts, Wendy thought her heart might burst out of her chest.

And then things got even worse.

She was waving toward the fog, hoping the lookout could see them, when a shot went off somewhere behind her.

"There they are!" It came from the battlements on the harbor side of the castle. The fleet wasn't back yet, so at least the guards weren't in full force. But already men were running in their direction. And firing.

"That isn't good," Vegard commented.

Michael and Reginald each aimed a pistol toward the nearest of the guards, sending them diving for cover, but then a shot from the far battlements screamed past Wendy's ear and slammed into the stone behind her.

"Everyone down!" she ordered. They all ducked behind the retaining wall, Michael and Reginald already reloading their weapons.

"We can't stay here," Michael commented. "Not that I intend to stand up any time soon."

Wendy did a quick head count. Peter, the twins, Slightly. That was four everlost. Vegard, Michael, Starkey, Reginald, and Wendy. Five humans. But Wendy didn't count for what she had in mind.

"Michael's right. We can't wait for the ship to get here," she said. "Peter, take Vegard. Slightly, take Reginald. Twins, take Starkey and Michael. Fly them to the ship. That's an order, do you understand?" She looked pointedly at Peter. "Promise me."

"Absolutely not," Vegard protested.

Peter narrowed his eyes and stared at her.

"Promise me!" she insisted, staring right back.

"Fine," Peter finally said. "I promise."

A guard rounded the corner. Wendy raised her pistol and fired, forcing the guard back around the battlement. But he wouldn't stay there for long.

"I'm not leaving you," Michael told her.

"You won't have to," Wendy assured him, but she didn't look at him when she said it. She couldn't. She was afraid she'd lose her nerve. Another guard rounded the corner. And another. There was no time left.

"Charming!" she shouted. "Let's go!"

She stood up and took off running along the rampart, drawing their fire.

A bullet hit the battlement in front of her. And another just behind her.

"Wendy!" Michael shouted. He tried to run after her, but one of the twins picked him up and lifted him off the ramparts, carrying him toward the ship that was just now emerging from the fog.

"At least turn me around, you idiot," she heard Vegard growl, and then an arrow flew past her, and another, providing cover fire.

"Dust!" she yelled to Charming, but he already understood. He had been trying to shower her in innisfay dust ever since she had taken off running, but he couldn't get the timing right. Either he shook too soon, so it dissipated by the time she got there, or too late, and she ran by underneath it. The light breeze off the water wasn't making things any easier.

"Over the wall!" she shouted, and she pointed dead ahead, where the end of the rampart was coming up fast. "I'll jump into it!"

Charming's eyes widened but he darted ahead, diving over the edge until she couldn't see him anymore.

"Three!" she yelled. Ignoring the sounds of gunfire, she focused on the wall ahead, sprinting with all her might. "Two!" A bullet hit the corner of the battlement just by her side, sending chips of stone flying. "One! Now!"

Wendy vaulted onto the retaining wall and leaped off, executing a perfect swan dive into the cloud of innisfay dust that waited for her a few feet below. She thought *up*, and she soared into the sky.

In only moments she was out of range, but Wendy Darling wasn't done yet. She might have lost Blackheart, but there was still something she could do to make a difference. And she wasn't about to leave empty-handed.

She looked around for Peter and found him flying backward, not far away, with Vegard perched on his shoulders. She caught up to them in no time.

"Peter," she said breathlessly, "there's something we need to do. Can you take Vegard back to the ship and then follow me? I'll get the others."

"Excellent!" Peter replied immediately, even though he had no idea what she had in mind.

"Vegard, take the ship back to the valley. Keep her safe. We'll meet you there."

"And where will you be going?" the Norseman asked. He tucked his bow behind his shoulder and crossed his arms over his chest, as though riding on the shoulders of a winged man was the most natural thing in the world.

"Me?" Wendy grinned. "One does not keep one's commission by standing around in a London office staring at maps on the wall."

"Wait. What?" Vegard asked, but Wendy had already flown away.

CHAPTER 54

Wendy and the others flew into the fog for cover and then circled wide over the ocean. She wanted to come at the stronghold from the east—or, at least, what *felt* like the east, since the sun was rising behind them over the water. In any event, she wanted the guards to have to shoot into the sun, to throw off their aim.

Not that she *wanted* anyone to shoot at them.

Maybe this wasn't such a good idea.

"This is a *terrible* idea," Michael grumbled. One of the twins cradled him safely in his arms as he flew, which Michael did not seem to appreciate.

"Don't be such a mud lump," Peter told him. "Stealing Blackheart's ship? It's a *grand* adventure! One of the greatest adventures ever! Besides," he added, apparently as an afterthought, "some of the very best stories are born from the absolute *worst* ideas."

"You're not making me feel better."

In point of fact, he wasn't making Wendy feel better either.

But Blackheart's ship was sitting there in the harbor, as unguarded as it was ever likely to be, and the rest of the fleet was off chasing Hook and Tigerlilja. It was now or never. They had to at least *try.*

"We don't have much time," Wendy told them. "We'll fly low over the water, straight to the ship. Slightly and the twins will take care of the anchor. Michael, Reginald, and Starkey will provide cover fire as necessary. Charming and I will get the ship's trinket, and then we fly away. Simple, but effective." *Hopefully,* she thought, but she didn't say that part out loud.

"What about Blackheart's everlost?" Michael pointed out. "They can fly, too, you know."

"Yes, I'm aware they can fly, Michael. That's what the cover fire is for. I didn't say it would be easy. But Blackheart has escaped, and he'll be on high alert after this. He has eight ships, including the leviathan, which looks like it's almost finished. As of this moment, we have three. The future of England is at stake, and we are severely outnumbered. I'd much prefer the odds to be seven ships to four. Which we can accomplish. Here. Today. But only if we hurry. The fleet could return at any moment, and then we'll be out of time."

"What should I do?" Peter asked.

"Sorry?"

"You said what everyone else should do. What should *I* do?"

Tinker Bell's hair turned red, and she chimed into Peter's ear.

"That's not true," Peter told her. "The Wendy would never forget us. She's saving the most important job for last."

It wasn't that Wendy had forgotten him. Not exactly. He just seemed too unpredictable to depend on. She stared at him for a long moment, trying to decide what to say. He was as erratic as ever, if not more so. After what she had seen in Buri's temple ...

Chaos.

The word echoed in her mind. She shivered, remembering where she had heard it, but it still gave her an idea.

"Your job is to distract the guards," she told him. "*Both* of you. Cause them as much trouble as you can. But do *not* get shot. When you see us leaving, come aboard. That's an order."

Peter grinned and did a backflip in midair. "Ha!" he crowed. "I'm *excellent* at causing trouble!"

"You really are," Slightly agreed.

Wendy was already starting to regret her decision.

As they flew toward the harbor, Wendy could see there were easily twice as many men on the ramparts as there had been before. They stood just a few feet apart, taking cover behind the battlements and aiming through the crenellations. They were still a good distance away when the first alarm cry sounded.

"They've seen us," Wendy shouted. "Remember, stay low over the water until the last possible moment. They can't stare directly into the sun. Peter, try to keep them busy. But be careful!"

She had no idea whether he heard the part about being careful because he was already whooping at the top of his lungs and racing for the stronghold. Wendy's heart fell into her stomach, but there was nothing she could do about it now. At least Tinker Bell was with him. The little innisfay seemed like a force to be reckoned with.

When they reached the harbor, the guards began firing. Three shots. Four. And then they were behind the ship itself, where the hull could protect them.

"Anyone hit?" Wendy looked worriedly from one man to another, each carried by an everlost, but they all shook their heads.

"All right, this is it," Wendy told them. "With any luck, I won't be long. Take cover behind the masts. Return fire while they're reloading. Make every bullet count."

"Aye, sir," Starkey barked.

"Ready?"

Everyone nodded.

Wendy took a deep breath and soared into the air.

Everything seemed to happen at once. Bullets flew from the battlements. The everlost deposited their charges on deck and flew off to find the anchor. Michael, Starkey, and Reginald returned fire, forcing the guards to seek cover while they reloaded. Wendy searched the sky for Peter and soon found him. He was holding an unarmed guard upside down over the water by one ankle.

"Don't shoot at the Wendy," Peter scolded him, and then let him go. Even as the man fell, Peter was already flying back toward the stronghold.

A glint of sunlight on steel flashed between the crenellations.

"Peter! Watch out!" Wendy shouted.

A shot rang out, but Peter seemed unharmed. A tiny dragon zipped up over the battlements just where the man had fired. A hand reached up to grab her, but it closed on thin air.

Wendy breathed a sigh of relief and turned her attention back to Blackheart's ship. She wanted to reach the captain's wheel, but there was nothing there to hide behind. She decided to settle for the closest mast instead.

"Charming," she asked, pressing her side tightly against the mast as another round of bullets rained down from the battlements, "can you bring me the ship's trinket?"

Charming zipped away, but he returned in mere moments, empty-handed and jingling in a highly agitated way.

"What is it?" she asked, but of course she couldn't understand his answer. Instead, he grabbed her sleeve and tugged on it, then pointed toward the wheel.

"I need to go there myself?" she asked.

He nodded emphatically.

"Michael!" she called out. "I have to get to the wheel! I need cover fire!"

"Give us a minute!" he hollered back. "I'll tell you when!"

Wendy tried to visualize it in her mind. Flying to the wheel. Finding the trinket. Lifting the ship into the air. She had to be ready to move fast.

A round of shots rang out from the stronghold.

"Now!" Michael shouted.

Wendy darted out from behind the mast. Michael, Reginald, and Starkey opened fire behind her. She reached the wheel, went to open the compartment, and discovered the problem. A silver padlock secured the latch. That was why Charming had seemed so agitated.

Obviously, she didn't have a key, but there was more than one way to open a lock. Moving as quickly as she could, Wendy snatched one of her pistols from its holster, loaded it, aimed it at the latch, and fired. An explosion of wood chips burst from the post where the latch had been, and the entire locking assembly fell to the deck.

"Wendy!" Michael shouted.

Without thinking, Wendy dove to the deck. More shots rang out from the battlements, and a bullet whizzed over her head. Michael and the others shot back. A man on the battlements screamed. Wendy looked up to see him being carried away upside down. She scrambled to her feet again.

She reached into the compartment, and found nothing.

"No. No!" Wendy blurted out. She reached her hand into the empty compartment again. There had to be something. A coin, or a thimble, or a knuckle bone, or ... or a piece of paper? Wendy felt a small, folded sheet pressed against the back of the cubbyhole.

Maybe it was a clue? Or a map? Whatever it was, she couldn't stay here. Wendy grabbed it and ran for the relative safety of the

mast. She ducked behind the thick, solid wood, pressing her side against it just in time as another round fired from the stronghold.

With trembling hands, she opened the paper, and read this:

"Mortimer Black."

It was penned in a woman's delicate hand, and, suddenly, Wendy knew exactly what it was. It was the note that had been left with him at the orphanage. The note from his mother. The most precious thing Mortimer Black had ever owned.

But ... was it also ... ?

Wendy closed the note carefully and pressed it into her palm. She concentrated on it, and the paper warmed and fluttered in her hand.

"I have it!" she shouted. "Peter! Come back! I have it!"

Wendy lifted the ship into the air as quickly as she dared.

"Sir?" Starkey shouted from the bow.

"It's all right, Starkey," Wendy assured him. "We're clear!"

"Beg to differ, sir," Starkey shouted back. "But we're not, sir."

Wendy peeked around the mast and drew in a sharp breath. Dozens of everlost streamed from the castle's ramparts. The light of the eternal sunrise gleamed across their leather-armored bodies and ragged wings, painting them in a blood-red glow. If Peter's everlost had always looked to her like hawk-men, these looked like demons straight from hell.

Wendy lifted the ship higher and tried to speed up, but she could already tell she would not be able to outrun the hordes. The sails were still furled, and they didn't have the manpower they needed to set them.

"Take down as many as you can!" Wendy shouted. "Try to buy us some time!"

Time to do what, she had no idea, but her men fired loyally

into the ranks of the flying everlost, and two fell from the sky. Only two out of dozens.

They weren't going to make it.

"Good form, the Wendy," Peter said. Suddenly he was there, landing on the deck next to her, and even though they were all about to die, it felt at least a little better not to be alone.

"I've really done it this time, haven't I?" she said.

"I'll say!" he replied cheerfully. "Using the same trick against Blackheart again. Now he'll feel twice as foolish!" Peter laughed, and then Wendy finally saw what he meant.

A shadow, just ahead. In the fog. And then a ship rose out of the light gray mist, thin tendrils clinging to its sides and reluctantly falling away.

"Vegard!" Wendy shouted.

She hadn't been alone, after all. She never had been.

CHAPTER 55

Pan's ship was already turning broadside, preparing to fire, so Wendy sped right for it, and then over it, just as she had when she first arrived in Neverland. The cannons exploded beneath them, and then the men of the Fourteenth, lined up at the railing, fired into the hordes. Six more fell, disintegrating in mid-air, and just like that, the enemy scattered.

A dozen or so of Peter's everlost streamed from the ship. With raucous shouts, they gave chase to the enemy for a hundred yards or so, but it was just a game to them. They came back laughing and jostling each other's shoulders in the air, but they didn't return to their own ship. Instead, they landed in the rigging of the new vessel—*England's* new vessel, Wendy thought proudly—and unfurled the sails with practiced ease.

They had hours ahead of them for the flight back, so Wendy turned the paper trinket over to Pan to let him fly the ship for a while. After all, Wendy thought, it had been his before it was England's, since he had created it for Mortimer as a gift. (And then

she realized it might also have been England's before it was his because who knew where Peter had gotten it. French ships, crocodile ships, twice-stolen ships ... England's new flying fleet had a questionable pedigree, to say the least.)

But Wendy wasn't too tired to fly. She just wanted an excuse to slip away and talk to Michael, Starkey, and Reginald before they returned, to ask them not to tell Hook that Peter had yelled Buri's name and alerted Blackheart to their presence.

"I take full responsibility for my own actions," Wendy told them. "I hesitated, and, as a result, the enemy was able to escape. *That* is why the mission failed. I ask only that you not mention Peter's shout. Our alliance with the everlost is fragile, at best, and his outburst would have had no effect on the outcome if I had performed my duties as ... as a commissioned officer."

And that, of course, was the hardest thing about all of it, at least for Wendy. She had worked so hard to become an officer, and now that she finally had her chance, she had let England's greatest enemy get away.

"I didn't hear anything," Michael said immediately.

"I *never* hear anything," Starkey agreed. "Or see anything. Or remember anything. It's a matter of personal policy."

"I didn't see any *hesitation* either," Reginald added. "I saw the *Viking* arrow miss. That's all I saw."

Wendy was touched by their loyalty and thanked them all, but she would include the hesitation in her own report nonetheless. As well as Blackheart's true identity. She was done leaving things out of reports. Hook would believe her now. Let *him* worry about what to say to his superiors once they returned.

Assuming he had survived.

Wendy shivered. She had had so much to worry about in trying to execute her own mission that she hadn't given any thought to the others. Now, worries poured in, one on top of another. John

and Nana were on those ships. And Charlie. And Tigerlilja, who was already becoming a friend. And Hook. She might not have called Hook a *friend* exactly, but she had come to see the value of his experience. And his leadership—the leadership of his *men*, at least, if not actually of *her*.

Would she return to the valley, only to find it empty?

No, she refused to think that way. They would be there. John and Nana and Charlie would be there waiting for her. The fleet was intact. It had to be.

She hated just sitting and waiting, so she took the trinket back from Pan to fly the rest of the way. Having something to do helped keep her mind off her worries, but when they finally passed old Snaggleclaw and entered the valley to find *The Pegasus* and the *Jolly Roger* sitting neatly in their cradles, looking relatively unscathed, she breathed a huge sigh of relief nonetheless.

Pan's ship, flying ahead of them, settled in its usual dry dock, but then Wendy noticed something else. There was no cradle waiting for their new flying ship. They had nowhere to land.

Wendy blinked. And then she blinked again. She looked all across the night valley, but despite the thin light of the moon, she was still absolutely certain there was no dock for them anywhere. She had assumed there would be, and it had seemed like a reasonable assumption. Yes, she had been counting on a fully formed dry dock cradle just appearing for them magically out of thin air, but in Wendy's defense it had happened twice before. There had been a dock for *The Pegasus*. There had been a dock for the *Jolly Roger* as soon as they had procured it. But there was no dock for her new ship.

What did that mean? Did it not belong here? Did the magic of Neverland still think the ship belonged to Blackheart?

And, more importantly, where were they going to *land*?

In the end, she settled the vessel down very slowly and gently

in the long grass of the open field. The keel was shallow enough that the ship didn't topple over, although it did list significantly to starboard once it had come to rest.

Wendy didn't feel right about placing the folded paper trinket back into its compartment, now that the latch had been blown away and the little door no longer shut properly, so she placed the paper in her pocket for safekeeping. She would find a good spot for it later. Right now, she needed to report to Hook. The process of landing had taken long enough that Vegard would have reported in already. Which meant Hook knew *everything.*

She didn't look forward to facing her failure yet again and seeing it reflected in Hook's eyes, but Wendy had never been one to put off uncomfortable tasks. Better to get it over with.

The innisfay dust had not worn off yet, but flying in front of Michael and Reginald and even Starkey was one thing. Flying in front of Hook's men would be something else altogether. So she pretended to climb down one rope and up another, secretly using the magic of the dust to think *down* and then *up,* which made the entire process much easier. It also gave her less time to worry about things like whether the alliance was still intact, whether Hook would shoot Peter when he found out what had happened, and whether the captain had already renounced her commission.

She hoped he had not, but suspected he probably had, which is why she was entirely unprepared for the scene that awaited her when she walked through the captain's door.

Pan was already present, and he wasn't at all dead. That, at least, was something. He must have flown across while she was preoccupied. Vegard and Tigerlilja were there as well, along with Charlie, which wasn't any surprise. But Hook was—Wendy frowned in puzzlement—was Hook ... smiling?

He was. He was smiling. At *her.*

He had been leaning his good left hand casually on the map

table when she walked in, but he straightened as soon as he saw her, smiled, and said, "Miss Darling! Congratulations. Vegard told me what you did—capturing Blackheart's flagship and salvaging the mission."

"Salvaging ..." Wendy said, confused, but Vegard interrupted her.

"I told him," Vegard said, "how Blackheart's guards remained behind and warned him of our arrival. I took the liberty of providing my report while we waited."

"Oh. I see," Wendy said. "Of course." Apparently, Vegard had had the same concern about the alliance. When Wendy didn't contradict Vegard's version of events, both he and Tigerlilja seemed to relax. Fortunately, Hook wasn't watching them. He was watching Wendy.

"As we all know, Blackheart's forces are much larger than anticipated," he said. "Against such odds, both teams were incredibly fortunate to make it out alive. And to steal a ship out from under their noses! Again, my congratulations, Miss Darling. My faith in you is proving to be well founded."

"I ... thank you, Captain," Wendy said. But she couldn't accept his congratulations. It wasn't right. Not after what she had done. "But ..." Her voice trailed off, and she looked down at her feet—at her strong sailor's boots that she loved so much. "I admit that stealing the ship was my idea, sir. But I had a chance to kill Blackheart, and I missed the shot." She stood up straight, squared her shoulders, and met his gaze directly. "I hesitated, sir. I hesitated, and it cost us everything."

Hook stared back at her for a long moment. When he finally spoke, his voice was quiet. Almost gentle. "I assume, Miss Darling, that you have never taken a human life?"

"I have not, sir," she admitted.

"It is extremely common to hesitate the first time one is called upon to do so in the line of duty. The fact that you took the shot at all is commendable."

But that wasn't why she had hesitated. Or, maybe it *would* have been, if it hadn't been for the other thing. She had already promised herself she wasn't leaving things out of her reports anymore, and yet here she was, keeping Pan's shout from him. For good reason, yes—to protect the alliance and Neverland and England and all the world, if what Tigerlilja had said was true—but she couldn't hide this, too. It was too important.

"I knew him," she blurted out.

"You ... knew him?" Hook asked.

"Yes," she said. She tugged unconsciously at her vest and then smoothed it with her hands. "I knew him from the almshouse where I spent my childhood. His name is Mortimer Black."

"What?!" Charlie exclaimed.

Suddenly remembering the ship's trinket, Wendy fished it from her pocket and handed it to Charlie, who opened it and then stared at it in wonder.

"What is that?" Hook demanded.

"The ship's trinket," Wendy told him.

"He used to brag that he had a mother," Charlie explained, showing Hook the note. "She had left a note at the almshouse in his basket, with his name. It seems a strange thing to brag about, I suppose. But most of us were given names by the orphanage. Having a real mother and a real name ..." Charlie shrugged. "But we were all just children. I don't think we know anything that can help us. He was apprenticed to a shipwright. We never heard from him again."

Charlie handed the note back to Wendy. She folded it neatly and put it in her pocket.

"Still," Hook said, thinking aloud, "it's more information than we had before. Good work, Miss Darling."

Wendy didn't see how recognizing someone from her childhood was especially commendable, but she didn't reply one way or the other. She was just relieved Hook hadn't renounced her commission the moment she told him the truth about missing the shot.

"Thanks to your daring escape," he continued, "not only do we have a new ship, but we also have a veritable treasure of new information. We know Blackheart's identity. We know the size of his fleet. We also know he is a pawn in a greater game, and that this giant called Buri is England's true enemy."

Wendy glanced worriedly at Peter, but he showed no sign of recognizing the name. Vegard must have told Hook about Buri. Perhaps not *all* of it, but at least what they had heard in the temple. Still, Hook had come a long way from the man who would not even believe a ship could fly. Imps and innisfay and dragons and wyverns and Neverland itself had a way of doing that to a person, she supposed.

"We must return to England at once," Hook declared. "Now that we know exactly where we're going and what we're facing, we can bring back far more ships than Blackheart can possibly steal in the same amount of time. We'll make them fly, and we'll hit him with overwhelming forces, crushing his insurrection before it leaves these shores."

"You can't," Tigerlilja told him.

"What?" Hook barked. "Why can't I?"

"Because time works differently here. It isn't just that the sun doesn't move. People don't age beyond adulthood. *Animals* don't age beyond adulthood. Copper doesn't green. Iron doesn't rust. At least ... not usually. There are places where you can jump backward and return to the same time you left. My point is, by the

time you got back, even with fifty ships, Blackheart could have one hundred times that number. He could have figured out how to turn the rest of his men into everlost."

She paused to share a worried glance with Vegard.

"By the time you got back," she finished, "Neverland could already have fallen. And Odin help England if it does. If you want to defend your kingdom, you must defend Neverland. Here. Now. While there's still time."

Hook stared at her for a long time, engaged in a battle with himself. He had accepted flying men. And then flying ships. He had seen them with his own eyes. He had accepted imps, and tiny little flying creatures that liked to chime at him angrily. He was even willing to believe in a giant ancient Norseman that could turn an orphan into England's greatest enemy. But time behaving differently in different places?

And yet, the proof was right here. Where in England had anyone seen a dragon in the modern world? Nonetheless, there was a dragon lying on a mountain that he could see from his window. A living creature thought to be long dead. Not to mention Vegard and Tigerlilja themselves. Any Vikings that had come to England's shores had become a part of England itself hundreds of years ago.

If Hook had ever once in his career been tempted to lose his composure, it was now. Here, in this moment. He wanted to yell at the top of his lungs, cursing at men for flying and at time for being malleable and at Neverland and all its magic for even *existing* to threaten his every last belief about the universe, not to mention threatening his beloved England.

Nor was it lost on him that Wendy Darling was somehow a part of all of it.

Nonetheless, he did not give in to temptation. He took a long breath in through his nose and expelled it through his mouth, and then he nodded without saying a word.

"We have taken one of Blackheart's ships and evened the odds," Tigerlilja said then, "but he will not be so easy to surprise again. Furthermore, we have only seen a hint of the forces he controls. He will soon complete his warship, and there are rumors of other bases we have yet to discover."

Hook ran his good left hand through his hair, which he had left loose after their return. "Then what do you propose?"

"We must raise our own army," Tigerlilja replied. "We must rally the peoples of Neverland and prepare for war. Our clan will help you, but we're done fighting in the air. We'll lead the ground troops. I won't have my people falling out of the sky before they can even draw a weapon. If we die, we die fighting, knowing Valhalla awaits. There are plenty of everlost to man your ships, and they are not the only flying peoples of Neverland."

"*Are* there plenty?" Hook demanded. "Ground troops aren't enough. We'll need far more of a fleet than we have now if we want to stand any chance, and those ships need captains. Even if we can cobble together enough sailors to crew them, who will lead them? We need *competent* captains—"

But Tigerlilja interrupted him. "Then stop being so stubborn and use what you have! This woman standing before you just salvaged a mission by stealing a ship and flying it to safety. She has proven herself more than competent!"

"She's almost as good a captain as I am," Peter chimed in. It was the first he'd spoken throughout the entire meeting, a wonder in itself, and all eyes turned to him. "She's better than *you*," he added, speaking directly to Hook.

Hook rolled his eyes, but then he turned back to Wendy, standing there in her blue officer's jacket, earnestly waiting for his reply.

"It just isn't done," he told them. "It's not permitted in the Royal Navy." But even as he said it, he could feel his conviction

crumbling. She *had* just stolen a ship, in the kind of bold move that had earned him his own promotions within the ranks of the Royal Navy. And the Fourteenth Platoon followed her without hesitation.

"You're not in England anymore," Tigerlilja said gently, "and she is one of the bravest among you. I know Neverland would be proud to have her. Surely England would be just as proud of its own subjects."

"Sir," Charlie added, "it has been the greatest honor of my life to serve under your command. I have always followed your orders, and I appreciate everything you have done for me. I trust your judgment in this, as I do in all things. I only ask that you take a moment and consider what is truly best for England."

Hook took another deep breath.

"It *is* a time of direst need," he finally said.

A whirlwind of butterflies fluttered in Wendy's stomach.

"It will be a wartime commission that stands only here, in Neverland," Hook told her, "and only for the duration of the battle that lies ahead. I can't do more than that. The admirals would never allow it."

But then his voice softened.

"Still," he continued, "you are, in fact, the best choice. And so, Miss Darling, if you will accept the promotion, will you solemnly swear your allegiance to the crown, to serve the interests of the Kingdom of Britain honorably and faithfully, as the captain of the *Jolly Roger*?"

CHAPTER 56

The captain's quarters of the *Jolly Roger* were not really much larger than the room Wendy had slept in at Dover Castle, but they felt opulent by comparison. Where her repurposed servant's room had been stark and unfurnished, her new accommodations included a captain's desk and table; a bed with several layers of quilts and blankets (that could be added or removed, of course, according to the weather); an actual dresser (complete with latching drawers so they wouldn't come open in heavy seas); and a hutch above the desk, with cabinets for books and tiny latching compartments to hold whatever knickknacks she might desire.

But the very best thing about it was the window.

The captain's quarters were located at the stern of the ship and at the very top level of the living quarters, just below the main deck, which allowed for an entire bank of windows to span the outer bulkhead, with a long, padded bench just below and more cabinets beneath. It was the most perfect window seat Wendy

could have imagined, and she was sitting there now, taking a moment to enjoy the view, on her very first day as its new owner.

(Or was it her very first night? Time truly was confusing in Neverland.)

She had taken the liberty of removing one of the cabinet doors above the desk and installing a curtain in its place so that Charming would be comfortable in his new quarters. When she had begun to pack her trunk, Charming had realized her intention, jingling in concern until she had told him where she was going and had assured him that he could come with her. Apparently, he now lived wherever she did, as did Nana, of course, who was currently occupying about two-thirds of the window seat.

"Who do you think they'll assign to us, Nana?" Wendy said, musing aloud while stroking the dog's head. "Most of the Fourteenth, I expect, since they already know me. They might have to give John his own ship, though. He doesn't know much about sailing, but we're short on officers. At least we should have Michael with us. And Reginald."

(Without consciously realizing it, Wendy had finally stopped thinking of Reginald as *poor* Reginald now that he had survived an entire everlost mission without dying even once.)

"We'll need more of a crew than that, though. The Fourteenth just isn't large enough. Tigerlilja mentioned the peoples of Neverland, as though there are other sorts we haven't met yet. I wonder what they'll be like?"

Nana thought they would be exactly the same as all the others because everything in Neverland smelled like green, and every dog knows that scent is the only useful way to distinguish anyone from anybody else.

"All I know for sure is that I'll be glad to have anyone and everyone who wants to help. I was even thinking of trying to talk to the imps," Wendy continued. "Mortimer was using them as his crew, so clearly they're able. But they might still be loyal to him. And I'm not sure how I feel about the one who threatens everyone all the time."

Wendy paused for a moment.

"Come to think of it, the stealing could be a real problem, too. What do you think?"

Nana had no opinion on the subject, but it didn't matter because there was a knock on the door in that exact moment.

"Oh!" Wendy said excitedly. "A visitor!"

She extracted herself from Nana's head, which had been resting on her leg, and she scrambled off the bench. She opened the door to discover an everlost she did not remember ever seeing before. He had a sort of gentle melancholy about him, and a sweet but humble smile. Wendy liked him immediately.

"Hello," she said. "May I help you?"

"Aye, Captain," he said. Wendy smiled. She liked the sound of that very much. "My name is Tootles. I'm to be assigned to you."

"Tootles! Wonderful! I believe you might be the first official crewman Hook's sent me. Has he finished the rosters, then?"

"Oh, no, sir. Or rather, I don't know about the rosters. It wasn't Hook that sent me. It was Peter."

"Peter?" That surprised her. She hadn't known Peter intended to send her anyone from his own crew.

"Aye, sir," Tootles confirmed. "Peter said I needed to serve on the *Jolly Roger*, sir. With you as my captain, from here on out. Assuming you'll have me."

"Well, that's wonderful, Tootles! I'm glad to have you aboard. Do you have a specialty I should be aware of?"

"Aye, sir. In a manner of speaking, I do. I think Peter sent me here because of it. To keep you safe, sir. But you might not like it."

Tootles rubbed his shirt nervously between his fingertips, and Wendy couldn't help but smile again.

"And why is that?" she asked him.

"Because nothing ever happens when I'm around. I've been in fewer adventures than any of them, because the big things constantly happen just when I've stepped round the corner, so to speak. Everything will be quiet, I'll take the opportunity of going off to gather a few sticks for firewood or some such, and when I get back, the others are already sweeping up the blood. It happens to me all the time. I'm not the least brave of the crew, sir, but I'm the most unfortunate by far, at least when it comes to adventures."

Wendy couldn't help but chuckle. "Let me get this straight," she said. "Peter sent you because you always miss their adventures, and he thinks that as long as you're close by, nothing dangerous will happen."

"Aye, sir," Tootles said sadly. "Which is why I told him I didn't think you'd want me, even though I promised I'd ask."

"Well, you're wrong about that, you know. I'm *extremely* glad to have you. Welcome aboard!"

"Oh, do you mean it, sir? Thank you, sir! Peter's crew, they sent me away a lot, on account of they wanted things to happen. I'm telling you, sir, nothing ever happens when I'm around."

"You know, I wouldn't worry about that if I were you," Wendy told him.

"Aye, sir?" he asked, starting to sound a bit hopeful.

"Aye, I wouldn't. Tootles, I have a feeling your luck is about to change."

ACKNOWLEDGMENTS

If you read the acknowledgments in *The Wendy*, you'll know this whole series began as a Patreon experiment. To the patrons who have been with us from the beginning, you made this entire series happen. Literally. And to our newest patrons, welcome aboard.

We can't thank you all enough for your support and encouragement over the last three years.

To Dwayne "@ThatDwayne" Melancon, we can't wait to write your character into the story, whoever—or whatever—it may be. Thank you for your extreme generosity and faith in us.

To Rae McManus and Steff Pasciuti, your perseverence is inspiring. Thank you for your unflagging patronage and for providing kind words, guidance, and suggestions whenever we need them.

To Kelly Peterson at INscribe Digital. Thank you for jumping in and believing in us right from the get-go. You are galaxies beyond what we ever expected.

To our families, for putting up with the late nights, tight schedules, and occasionally frayed nerves of the craft, we love you all.

To the book bloggers who have gathered readers and shouted our books to the rooftops, you are profoundly dedicated souls and deserve all the swag in the world.

To Stephanie Plotkin, author of *TeacherofYA's Book Blog*, we will never forget you. Thank you for continuing to watch over our journey.

As the Tales of the Wendy series moves deeper into the fantasy realm, you might think the intense historical research would finally fall away. *We* certainly thought it might, but we were wrong.

Is "burning daylight" a phrase Hook might have used in 1790? (It is.) Had germ theory made it into medicine? (It had not.) How would Thomas, as a Royal Society Fellow, have treated a gunshot wound? (With a mixture of egg yolks, rose oil, and turpentine.)

We offer our thanks once again to the dedicated historians, curators, and librarians who work tirelessly to preserve the past, helping us immerse ourselves so thoroughly in Wendy's world.

Finally, to Donna Alvis and all the librarians who have believed in our books and helped us to spread the word by stocking and sharing them with the reading public, we are eternally grateful for your support.

ABOUT THE AUTHORS

As a child, Erin fell in love with llamas and with the books of Anne McCaffrey, whose Dragonriders of Pern series inspired her to become a writer. When she finally met Anne McCaffrey at a fantasy convention some two decades later, she wept uncontrollably throughout the entire affair. She does significantly better with llamas.

Steven spent his childhood reading anything he could get his hands on, sharing his favorite stories with his younger brothers and then acting them out, especially if this required sword fighting on horseback. When they ran out of books, he wrote his own, including his brothers as the main characters by sketching original illustrations on magazine clippings.

Together, they are the team known as Dragon Authors, writing science fiction and fantasy for teens and adults. Their first novel, *The Intuitives,* was published in July of 2017.

You can find them online at DragonAuthors.com.